Short Stories

1887

Anton Chekhov

First Edition, 2013

ISBN: 978-1492726364

The author has asserted their moral right under the Copyright, Designs and Patents Act, 1988, to be identified as the author of this work.

All Rights reserved. No part of this publication may be reproduced, copied, stored in a retrieval system, or transmitted, in any form or by any means, without the prior written consent of the copyright holder, nor be otherwise circulated in any form of binding or cover other than that in which it is published and without a similar condition being imposed on the subsequent purchaser. This is a work of fiction: any resemblance to persons living or dead is purely coincidental.

CONTENTS

Champagne	7
Frost	13
The Beggar	20
Enemies	26
Darkness	40
Polinka	45
Drunk	51
An Inadvertence	58
Verotchka	63
Shrove Tuesday	77
A Defenceless Creature	83
A Bad Business	89
Home	96
The Lottery Ticket	106
Too Early!	112
Typhus	118
In Passion Week	126
A Mystery	131
The Cossack	137
The Letter	143
An Adventure	156
The Examining Magistrate	163

Aborigines	169
Volodya	176
Happiness	191
Bad Weather	202
A Play	208
A Transgression	214
From the Diary of a Violent-Tempered Man	219
Uprooted	230
A Father	246
A Happy Ending	254
In the Coach-House	259
Zinotchka	266
The Doctor	273
The Pipe	279
An Avenger	288
The Post	293
The Runaway	300
A Problem	309
The Old House	317
The Cattle Dealers	323
Expensive Lessons	341
The Lion and the Sun	349
In Trouble	353

The Kiss	361
Boys	381
Kashtanka	389
A Lady's Story	410

CHAMPAGNE

A WAYFARER'S STORY

In the year in which my story begins I had a job at a little station on one of our southwestern railways. Whether I had a gay or a dull life at the station you can judge from the fact that for fifteen miles round there was not one human habitation, not one woman, not one decent tavern; and in those days I was young, strong, hot-headed, giddy, and foolish. The only distraction I could possibly find was in the windows of the passenger trains, and in the vile vodka which the Jews drugged with thorn-apple. Sometimes there would be a glimpse of a woman's head at a carriage window, and one would stand like a statue without breathing and stare at it until the train turned into an almost invisible speck; or one would drink all one could of the loathsome vodka till one was stupefied and did not feel the passing of the long hours and days. Upon me, a native of the north, the steppe produced the effect of a deserted Tatar cemetery. In the summer the steppe with its solemn calm, the monotonous chur of the grasshoppers, the transparent moonlight from which one could not hide, reduced me to listless melancholy; and in the winter the irreproachable whiteness of the steppe, its cold distance, long nights, and howling wolves oppressed me like a heavy nightmare. There were several people living at the station: my wife and I, a deaf and scrofulous telegraph clerk, and three watchmen. My assistant, a young man who was in consumption, used to go for treatment to the town, where he stayed for months at a time, leaving his duties to me together with the right of pocketing his salary. I had no children, no cake would have tempted visitors to come and see me, and I could only visit other officials on the line, and that no oftener than once a month.

I remember my wife and I saw the New Year in. We sat at table, chewed lazily, and heard the deaf telegraph clerk monotonously tapping on his apparatus in the next room. I had already drunk five glasses of drugged vodka, and, propping my heavy head on my fist, thought of my overpowering boredom from which there was no escape, while my wife sat beside me and did not take her eyes off me. She looked at me as no one can look but a woman who has nothing in this world but a handsome husband. She loved me madly, slavishly, and not merely my good looks, or my soul, but my sins, my ill-humor and boredom, and even my cruelty when, in drunken fury, not knowing how to vent my ill-humor, I tormented her with reproaches.

In spite of the boredom which was consuming me, we were preparing to see the New Year in with exceptional festiveness, and were awaiting midnight with some impatience. The fact is, we had in reserve two bottles of champagne, the real thing, with the label of Veuve Clicquot; this treasure I had won the previous autumn in a bet with the station-master of D. when I was drinking with him at a christening. It sometimes happens during a lesson in mathematics, when the very air is still with boredom, a butterfly flutters into the class-room; the boys toss their heads and begin watching its flight with interest, as though they saw before them not a butterfly but something new and strange; in the same way ordinary champagne, chancing to come into our dreary station, roused us. We sat in silence looking alternately at the clock and at the bottles.

When the hands pointed to five minutes to twelve I slowly began uncorking a bottle. I don't know whether I was affected by the vodka, or whether the bottle was wet, but all I remember is that when the cork flew up to the ceiling with a bang, my bottle slipped out of my hands and fell on the floor. Not more than a glass of the wine was spilt, as I managed to catch the bottle and put my thumb over the foaming neck.

"Well, may the New Year bring you happiness!" I said, filling two glasses. "Drink!"

My wife took her glass and fixed her frightened eyes on me. Her face was pale and wore a look of horror.

"Did you drop the bottle?" she asked.

"Yes. But what of that?"

"It's unlucky," she said, putting down her glass and turning paler still. "It's a bad omen. It means that some misfortune will happen to us this year."

"What a silly thing you are," I sighed. "You are a clever woman, and yet you talk as much nonsense as an old nurse. Drink."

"God grant it is nonsense, but . . . something is sure to happen! You'll see."

She did not even sip her glass, she moved away and sank into thought. I uttered a few stale commonplaces about superstition, drank half a bottle, paced up and down, and then went out of the room.

Outside there was the still frosty night in all its cold, inhospitable beauty. The moon and two white fluffy clouds beside it hung just over the station, motionless as though glued to the spot, and looked as though waiting for something. A faint transparent light came from them and touched the white earth softly, as though afraid of wounding her modesty, and lighted up everything -- the snowdrifts, the embankment. . . . It was still.

I walked along the railway embankment.

"Silly woman," I thought, looking at the sky spangled with brilliant stars. "Even if one admits that omens sometimes tell the truth, what evil can happen to us? The misfortunes we have endured already, and which are facing us now, are so great that it is difficult to imagine anything worse. What further harm can you do a fish which has been caught and fried and served up with sauce?"

A poplar covered with hoar frost looked in the bluish darkness like a giant wrapt in a shroud. It looked at me sullenly and dejectedly, as though like me it realized its loneliness. I stood a long while looking at it.

"My youth is thrown away for nothing, like a useless cigarette end," I went on musing. "My parents died when I was a little child; I was expelled from the high school, I was born of a noble family, but I have received neither education nor breeding, and I have no more knowledge than the humblest mechanic. I have no refuge, no relations, no friends, no work I like. I am not fitted for anything, and in the prime of my powers I am good for nothing but to be stuffed into this little station; I have known nothing but trouble and failure all my life. What can happen worse?"

Red lights came into sight in the distance. A train was moving towards me. The slumbering steppe listened to the sound of it. My thoughts were so bitter that it seemed to me that I was thinking aloud and that the moan of the telegraph wire and the rumble of the train were expressing my thoughts.

"What can happen worse? The loss of my wife?" I wondered. "Even that is not terrible. It's no good hiding it from my conscience: I don't love my wife. I married her when I was only a wretched boy; now I am young and vigorous, and she has gone off and grown older and sillier, stuffed from her head to her heels with conventional ideas. What charm is there in her maudlin love, in her hollow chest, in her lusterless eyes? I put up with her, but I don't love her. What can happen? My youth is being wasted, as the saying is, for a pinch of snuff. Women flit before my eyes only in the carriage windows, like falling stars. Love I never had and have not. My manhood, my courage, my power of feeling are going to ruin. . . . Everything is being thrown away like dirt, and all my wealth here in the steppe is not worth a farthing."

The train rushed past me with a roar and indifferently cast the glow of its red lights upon me. I saw it stop by the green lights of the station, stop for a minute and rumble off again. After walking a mile and a half I went back. Melancholy thoughts haunted me still. Painful as it was to me, yet I remember I tried as it were to make my thoughts still gloomier and more melancholy. You know people who are vain and not very clever have moments when the consciousness that they are miserable affords them positive satisfaction, and they even coquet with their misery for their own entertainment. There was a great deal of truth in what I thought, but there was also a great deal that was absurd and conceited, and there was something boyishly defiant in my question: "What could happen worse?"

"And what is there to happen?" I asked myself. "I think I have endured everything. I've been ill, I've lost money, I get reprimanded by my superiors every day, and I go hungry, and a mad wolf has run into the station yard. What more is there? I have been insulted, humiliated, . . . and I have insulted others in my time. I have not been a criminal, it is true, but I don't think I am capable of crime -- I am not afraid of being hauled up for it."

The two little clouds had moved away from the moon and stood at a little distance, looking as though they were whispering about something which the moon must not know. A light breeze was racing across the steppe, bringing the faint rumble of the retreating train.

My wife met me at the doorway. Her eyes were laughing gaily and her whole face was beaming with good-humor.

"There is news for you!" she whispered. "Make haste, go to your room and put on your new coat; we have a visitor."

"What visitor?"

"Aunt Natalya Petrovna has just come by the train."

"What Natalya Petrovna?"

"The wife of my uncle Semyon Fyodoritch. You don't know her. She is a very nice, good woman."

Probably I frowned, for my wife looked grave and whispered rapidly:

"Of course it is queer her having come, but don't be cross, Nikolay, and don't be hard on her. She is unhappy, you know; Uncle Semyon Fyodoritch really is ill-natured and tyrannical, it is difficult to live with him. She says she will only stay three days with us, only till she gets a letter from her brother."

My wife whispered a great deal more nonsense to me about her despotic uncle; about the weakness of mankind in general and of young wives in particular; about its being our duty to give shelter to all, even great sinners, and so on. Unable to make head or tail of it, I put on my new coat and went to make acquaintance with my "aunt."

A little woman with large black eyes was sitting at the table. My table, the gray walls, my roughly-made sofa, everything to the tiniest grain of dust seemed to have grown younger and more cheerful in the presence of this new, young, beautiful, and dissolute creature, who had a most subtle perfume about her. And that our visitor was a lady of easy virtue I could see from her smile, from her scent, from the peculiar way in which she glanced and made play with her eyelashes, from the tone in which she talked with my wife -- a respectable woman. There was no need to tell me she had run away from her husband, that her husband was old and despotic, that she was good-natured and lively; I took it all in at the first glance. Indeed, it is doubtful whether there is a man in all Europe who cannot spot at the first glance a woman of a certain temperament.

"I did not know I had such a big nephew!" said my aunt, holding out her hand to me and smiling.

"And I did not know I had such a pretty aunt," I answered.

Supper began over again. The cork flew with a bang out of the second bottle, and my aunt swallowed half a glassful at a gulp, and when my wife went out of the room for a moment my aunt did not scruple to drain a full glass. I was drunk both with the wine and with the presence of a woman. Do you remember the song?

> "Eyes black as pitch, eyes full of passion,
> Eyes burning bright and beautiful,
> How I love you,
> How I fear you!"

I don't remember what happened next. Anyone who wants to know how love begins may read novels and long stories; I will put it shortly and in the words of the same silly song:

> "It was an evil hour
> When first I met you."

Everything went head over heels to the devil. I remember a fearful, frantic whirlwind which sent me flying round like a feather. It lasted a long while, and swept from the face of the earth my wife and my aunt herself and my strength. From the little station in the steppe it has flung me, as you see, into this dark street.

Now tell me what further evil can happen to me?

FROST

A "popular" fête with a philanthropic object had been arranged on the Feast of Epiphany in the provincial town of N----. They had selected a broad part of the river between the market and the bishop's palace, fenced it round with a rope, with fir-trees and with flags, and provided everything necessary for skating, sledging, and tobogganing. The festivity was organized on the grandest scale possible. The notices that were distributed were of huge size and promised a number of delights: skating, a military band, a lottery with no blank tickets, an electric sun, and so on. But the whole scheme almost came to nothing owing to the hard frost. From the eve of Epiphany there were twenty-eight degrees of frost with a strong wind; it was proposed to put off the fête, and this was not done only because the public, which for a long while had been looking forward to the fête impatiently, would not consent to any postponement.

"Only think, what do you expect in winter but a frost!" said the ladies persuading the governor, who tried to insist that the fête should be postponed. "If anyone is cold he can go and warm himself."

The trees, the horses, the men's beards were white with frost; it even seemed that the air itself crackled, as though unable to endure the cold; but in spite of that the frozen public were skating. Immediately after the blessing of the waters and precisely at one o'clock the military band began playing.

Between three and four o'clock in the afternoon, when the festivity was at its height, the select society of the place gathered together to warm themselves in the governor's pavilion, which had been put up on the river-bank. The old governor and his wife, the bishop, the president of the local court, the head master of the high school, and many others, were there. The ladies were sitting in armchairs, while the men crowded round the wide glass door, looking at the skating.

"Holy Saints!" said the bishop in surprise; "what flourishes they execute with their legs! Upon my soul, many a singer couldn't do a twirl with his voice as those cut-throats do with their legs. Aie! he'll kill himself!"

"That's Smirnov. . . . That's Gruzdev . . ." said the head master, mentioning the names of the schoolboys who flew by the pavilion.

"Bah! he's all alive-oh!" laughed the governor. "Look, gentlemen, our mayor is coming. . . . He is coming this way. . . . That's a nuisance, he will talk our heads off now."

A little thin old man, wearing a big cap and a fur-lined coat hanging open, came from the opposite bank towards the pavilion, avoiding the skaters. This was the mayor of the town, a merchant, Eremeyev by name, a millionaire and an old inhabitant of N----. Flinging wide his arms and shrugging at the cold, he skipped along, knocking one golosh against the other, evidently in haste to get out of the wind. Half-way he suddenly bent down, stole up to some lady, and plucked at her sleeve from behind. When she looked round he skipped away, and probably delighted at having succeeded in frightening her, went off into a loud, aged laugh.

"Lively old fellow," said the governor. "It's a wonder he's not skating."

As he got near the pavilion the mayor fell into a little tripping trot, waved his hands, and, taking a run, slid along the ice in his huge golosh boots up to the very door.

"Yegor Ivanitch, you ought to get yourself some skates!" the governor greeted him.

"That's just what I am thinking," he answered in a squeaky, somewhat nasal tenor, taking off his cap. "I wish you good health, your Excellency! Your Holiness! Long life to all the other gentlemen and ladies! Here's a frost! Yes, it is a frost, bother it! It's deadly!"

Winking with his red, frozen eyes, Yegor Ivanitch stamped on the floor with his golosh boots and swung his arms together like a frozen cabman.

"Such a damnable frost, worse than any dog!" he went on talking, smiling all over his face. "It's a real affliction!"

"It's healthy," said the governor; "frost strengthens a man and makes him vigorous. . . ."

"Though it may be healthy, it would be better without it at all," said the mayor, wiping his wedge-shaped beard with a red handkerchief. "It would be a good riddance! To my thinking, your Excellency, the Lord sends it us as a punishment -- the frost, I mean. We sin in the summer and are punished in the winter. . . . Yes!"

Yegor Ivanitch looked round him quickly and flung up his hands.

"Why, where's the needful . . . to warm us up?" he asked, looking in alarm first at the governor and then at the bishop. "Your Excellency! Your Holiness! I'll be bound, the ladies are frozen too! We must have something, this won't do!"

Everyone began gesticulating and declaring that they had not come to the skating to warm themselves, but the mayor, heeding no one, opened the door and beckoned to someone with his crooked finger. A workman and a fireman ran up to him.

"Here, run off to Savatin," he muttered, "and tell him to make haste and send here . . . what do you call it? . . . What's it to be? Tell him to send a dozen glasses . . . a dozen glasses of mulled wine, the very hottest, or punch, perhaps. . . ."

There was laughter in the pavilion.

"A nice thing to treat us to!"

"Never mind, we will drink it," muttered the mayor; "a dozen glasses, then . . . and some Benedictine, perhaps . . . and tell them to warm two bottles of red wine. . . . Oh, and what for the ladies? Well, you tell them to bring cakes, nuts . . . sweets of some sort, perhaps. . . . There, run along, look sharp!"

The mayor was silent for a minute and then began again abusing the frost, banging his arms across his chest and thumping with his golosh boots.

"No, Yegor Ivanitch," said the governor persuasively, "don't be unfair, the Russian frost has its charms. I was reading lately that many of the good qualities of the Russian people are due to the vast expanse of their land and to the climate, the cruel struggle for existence . . . that's perfectly true!"

"It may be true, your Excellency, but it would be better without it. The frost did drive out the French, of course, and one can freeze all sorts of dishes, and the children can go skating -- that's all true! For the man who is well fed and well clothed the frost is only a pleasure, but for the working man, the beggar, the pilgrim, the crazy wanderer, it's the greatest evil and misfortune. It's misery, your Holiness! In a frost like this poverty is twice as hard, and the thief is more cunning and evildoers more violent. There's no gainsaying it! I am turned seventy, I've a fur coat now, and at home I have a stove and rums and punches of all sorts. The frost means nothing to me now; I take no notice of it, I don't care to know of it, but how it used to be in old days, Holy Mother! It's dreadful to recall it! My memory is failing me with years and I have forgotten everything; my enemies, and my sins and troubles of all sorts -- I forget them all, but the frost -- ough! How I remember it! When my mother died I was left a little devil -- this high -- a homeless orphan . . . no kith nor kin, wretched, ragged, little clothes, hungry, nowhere to sleep -- in fact, 'we have here no abiding city, but seek the one to come.' In those days I used to lead an old blind woman about the town for five kopecks a day . . . the frosts were cruel, wicked. One would go out with the old woman and begin suffering torments. My Creator! First of all you would be shivering as in a fever, shrugging and dancing about. Then your ears, your fingers, your feet, would begin aching. They would ache as though someone were squeezing them with pincers. But all that would have been nothing, a trivial matter, of no great consequence. The trouble was when your whole body was chilled. One would walk for three blessed hours in the frost, your Holiness, and lose all human semblance. Your legs are drawn up, there is a weight on your chest, your stomach is pinched; above all, there is a pain in your heart that is worse than anything. Your heart aches beyond all endurance, and there is a wretchedness all over your body as though you were leading Death by the hand instead of an old woman. You are numb all over, turned to stone like a statue; you go on and feel as though it were not you walking, but someone else moving your legs instead of you. When your soul is frozen you don't know what you are doing: you are ready to leave the old woman with no one to guide her, or to pull a hot roll from off a hawker's tray, or to fight with someone. And when you come to your night's lodging into the warmth after the frost, there is not much joy in that either! You lie awake till midnight, crying, and don't know yourself what you are crying for. . . ."

"We must walk about the skating-ground before it gets dark," said the governor's wife, who was bored with listening. "Who's coming with me?"

The governor's wife went out and the whole company trooped out of the pavilion after her. Only the governor, the bishop, and the mayor remained.

"Queen of Heaven! and what I went through when I was a shopboy in a fish-shop!" Yegor Ivanitch went on, flinging up his arms so that his fox-lined coat fell open. "One would go out to the shop almost before it was light . . . by eight o'clock I was completely frozen, my face was blue, my fingers were stiff so that I could not fasten my buttons nor count the money. One would stand in the cold, turn numb, and think, 'Lord, I shall have to stand like this right on till evening!' By dinner-time my stomach was pinched and my heart was aching. . . . Yes! And I was not much better afterwards when I had a shop of my own. The frost was intense and the shop was like a mouse-trap with draughts blowing in all directions; the coat I had on was, pardon me, mangy, as thin as paper, threadbare. . . . One would be chilled through and through, half dazed, and turn as cruel as the frost oneself: I would pull one by the ear so that I nearly pulled the ear off; I would smack another on the back of the head; I'd glare at a customer like a ruffian, a wild beast, and be ready to fleece him; and when I got home in the evening and ought to have gone to bed, I'd be ill-humoured and set upon my family, throwing it in their teeth that they were living upon me; I would make a row and carry on so that half a dozen policemen couldn't have managed me. The frost makes one spiteful and drives one to drink."

Yegor Ivanitch clasped his hands and went on:

"And when we were taking fish to Moscow in the winter, Holy Mother!" And spluttering as he talked, he began describing the horrors he endured with his shopmen when he was taking fish to Moscow. . . .

"Yes," sighed the governor, "it is wonderful what a man can endure! You used to take wagon-loads of fish to Moscow, Yegor Ivanitch, while I in my time was at the war. I remember one extraordinary instance. . . ."

And the governor described how, during the last Russo-Turkish War, one frosty night the division in which he was had stood in the snow without moving for thirteen hours in a piercing wind; from fear of being observed the division did not light a fire, nor make a sound or a movement; they were forbidden to smoke. . . .

Reminiscences followed. The governor and the mayor grew lively and good-humoured, and, interrupting each other, began recalling their experiences. And the bishop told them how, when he was serving in Siberia, he had travelled in a sledge drawn by dogs; how one day, being drowsy, in a time of sharp frost he had fallen out of the sledge and been nearly frozen; when the Tunguses turned back and found him he was barely alive. Then, as by common agreement, the old men suddenly sank into silence, sat side by side, and mused.

"Ech!" whispered the mayor; "you'd think it would be time to forget, but when you look at the water-carriers, at the schoolboys, at the convicts in their wretched gowns, it brings it all back! Why, only take those musicians who are playing now. I'll be bound, there is a pain in their hearts; a pinch at their stomachs, and their trumpets are freezing to their lips. . . . They play and think: 'Holy Mother! we have another three hours to sit here in the cold.' "

The old men sank into thought. They thought of that in man which is higher than good birth, higher than rank and wealth and learning, of that which brings the lowest beggar near to God: of the helplessness of man, of his sufferings and his patience. . . .

Meanwhile the air was turning blue . . . the door opened and two waiters from Savatin's walked in, carrying trays and a big muffled teapot. When the glasses had been filled and there was a strong smell of cinnamon and clove in the air, the door opened again, and there came into the pavilion a beardless young policeman whose nose was crimson, and who was covered all over with frost; he went up to the governor, and, saluting, said: "Her Excellency told me to inform you that she has gone home."

Looking at the way the policeman put his stiff, frozen fingers to his cap, looking at his nose, his lustreless eyes, and his hood covered with white frost near the mouth, they all for some reason felt that this policeman's heart must be aching, that his stomach must feel pinched, and his soul numb. . . .

"I say," said the governor hesitatingly, "have a drink of mulled wine!"

"It's all right . . . it's all right! Drink it up!" the mayor urged him, gesticulating; "don't be shy!"

The policeman took the glass in both hands, moved aside, and, trying to drink without making any sound, began discreetly sipping from the glass. He drank and was overwhelmed with embarrassment while the old men looked at him in silence, and they all fancied that the pain was leaving the young policeman's heart, and that his soul was thawing. The governor heaved a sigh.

"It's time we were at home," he said, getting up. "Good-bye! I say," he added, addressing the policeman, "tell the musicians there to . . . leave off playing, and ask Pavel Semyonovitch from me to see they are given . . . beer or vodka."

The governor and the bishop said good-bye to the mayor and went out of the pavilion.

Yegor Ivanitch attacked the mulled wine, and before the policeman had finished his glass succeeded in telling him a great many interesting things. He could not be silent.

THE BEGGAR

"Kinf sir, be so good as to notice a poor, hungry man. I have not tasted food for three days. I have not a five-kopeck piece for a night's lodging. I swear by God! For five years I was a village schoolmaster and lost my post through the intrigues of the Zemstvo. I was the victim of false witness. I have been out of a place for a year now."

Skvortsov, a Petersburg lawyer, looked at the speaker's tattered dark blue overcoat, at his muddy, drunken eyes, at the red patches on his cheeks, and it seemed to him that he had seen the man before.

"And now I am offered a post in the Kaluga province," the beggar continued, "but I have not the means for the journey there. Graciously help me! I am ashamed to ask, but . . . I am compelled by circumstances."

Skvortsov looked at his goloshes, of which one was shallow like a shoe, while the other came high up the leg like a boot, and suddenly remembered.

"Listen, the day before yesterday I met you in Sadovoy Street," he said, "and then you told me, not that you were a village schoolmaster, but that you were a student who had been expelled. Do you remember?"

"N-o. No, that cannot be so!" the beggar muttered in confusion. "I am a village schoolmaster, and if you wish it I can show you documents to prove it."

"That's enough lies! You called yourself a student, and even told me what you were expelled for. Do you remember?"

Skvortsov flushed, and with a look of disgust on his face turned away from the ragged figure.

"It's contemptible, sir!" he cried angrily. "It's a swindle! I'll hand you over to the police, damn you! You are poor and hungry, but that does not give you the right to lie so shamelessly!"

The ragged figure took hold of the door-handle and, like a bird in a snare, looked round the hall desperately.

"I . . . I am not lying," he muttered. "I can show documents."

"Who can believe you?" Skvortsov went on, still indignant. "To exploit the sympathy of the public for village schoolmasters and students -- it's so low, so mean, so dirty! It's revolting!"

Skvortsov flew into a rage and gave the beggar a merciless scolding. The ragged fellow's insolent lying aroused his disgust and aversion, was an offence against what he, Skvortsov, loved and prized in himself: kindliness, a feeling heart, sympathy for the unhappy. By his lying, by his treacherous assault upon compassion, the individual had, as it were, defiled the charity which he liked to give to the poor with no misgivings in his heart. The beggar at first defended himself, protested with oaths, then he sank into silence and hung his head, overcome with shame.

"Sir!" he said, laying his hand on his heart, "I really was . . . lying! I am not a student and not a village schoolmaster. All that's mere invention! I used to be in the Russian choir, and I was turned out of it for drunkenness. But what can I do? Believe me, in God's name, I can't get on without lying -- when I tell the truth no one will give me anything. With the truth one may die of hunger and freeze without a night's lodging! What you say is true, I understand that, but . . . what am I to do?"

"What are you to do? You ask what are you to do?" cried Skvortsov, going close up to him. "Work -- that's what you must do! You must work!"

"Work. . . . I know that myself, but where can I get work?"

"Nonsense. You are young, strong, and healthy, and could always find work if you wanted to. But you know you are lazy, pampered, drunken! You reek of vodka like a pothouse! You have become false and corrupt to the marrow of your bones and fit for nothing but begging and lying! If you do graciously condescend to take work, you must have a job in an office, in the Russian choir, or as a billiard-marker, where you will have a salary and have nothing to do! But how would you like to undertake manual labour? I'll be bound, you wouldn't be a house porter or a factory hand! You are too genteel for that!"

"What things you say, really . . ." said the beggar, and he gave a bitter smile. "How can I get manual work? It's rather late for me to be a shopman, for in trade one has to begin from a boy; no one would take me as a house porter, because I am not of that class. . . . And I could not get work in a factory; one must know a trade, and I know nothing."

"Nonsense! You always find some justification! Wouldn't you like to chop wood?"

"I would not refuse to, but the regular woodchoppers are out of work now."

"Oh, all idlers argue like that! As soon as you are offered anything you refuse it. Would you care to chop wood for me?"

"Certainly I will. . ."

"Very good, we shall see. . . . Excellent. We'll see!" Skvortsov, in nervous haste; and not without malignant pleasure, rubbing his hands, summoned his cook from the kitchen.

"Here, Olga," he said to her, "take this gentleman to the shed and let him chop some wood."

The beggar shrugged his shoulders as though puzzled, and irresolutely followed the cook. It was evident from his demeanour that he had consented to go and chop wood, not because he was hungry and wanted to earn money, but simply from shame and *amour propre*, because he had been taken at his word. It was clear, too, that he was suffering from the effects of vodka, that he was unwell, and felt not the faintest inclination to work.

Skvortsov hurried into the dining-room. There from the window which looked out into the yard he could see the woodshed and everything that happened in the yard. Standing at the window, Skvortsov saw the cook and the beggar come by the back way into the yard and go through the muddy snow to the woodshed. Olga scrutinized her companion angrily, and jerking her elbow unlocked the woodshed and angrily banged the door open.

"Most likely we interrupted the woman drinking her coffee," thought Skvortsov. "What a cross creature she is!"

Then he saw the pseudo-schoolmaster and pseudo-student seat himself on a block of wood, and, leaning his red cheeks upon his fists, sink into thought. The cook flung an axe at his feet, spat angrily on the ground, and, judging by the expression of her lips, began abusing him. The beggar drew a log of wood towards him irresolutely, set it up between his feet, and diffidently drew the axe across it. The log toppled and fell over. The beggar drew it towards him, breathed on his frozen hands, and again drew the axe along it as cautiously as though he were afraid of its hitting his golosh or chopping off his fingers. The log fell over again.

Skvortsov's wrath had passed off by now, he felt sore and ashamed at the thought that he had forced a pampered, drunken, and perhaps sick man to do hard, rough work in the cold.

"Never mind, let him go on . . ." he thought, going from the dining-room into his study. "I am doing it for his good!"

An hour later Olga appeared and announced that the wood had been chopped up.

"Here, give him half a rouble," said Skvortsov. "If he likes, let him come and chop wood on the first of every month. . . . There will always be work for him."

On the first of the month the beggar turned up and again earned half a rouble, though he could hardly stand. From that time forward he took to turning up frequently, and work was always found for him: sometimes he would sweep the snow into heaps, or clear up the shed, at another he used to beat the rugs and the mattresses. He always received thirty to forty kopecks for his work, and on one occasion an old pair of trousers was sent out to him.

When he moved, Skvortsov engaged him to assist in packing and moving the furniture. On this occasion the beggar was sober, gloomy, and silent; he scarcely touched the furniture, walked with hanging head behind the furniture vans, and did not even try to appear busy; he merely shivered with the cold, and was overcome with confusion when the men with the vans laughed at his idleness, feebleness, and ragged coat that had once been a gentleman's. After the removal Skvortsov sent for him.

"Well, I see my words have had an effect upon you," he said, giving him a rouble. "This is for your work. I see that you are sober and not disinclined to work. What is your name?"

"Lushkov."

"I can offer you better work, not so rough, Lushkov. Can you write?"

"Yes, sir."

"Then go with this note to-morrow to my colleague and he will give you some copying to do. Work, don't drink, and don't forget what I said to you. Good-bye."

Skvortsov, pleased that he had put a man in the path of rectitude, patted Lushkov genially on the shoulder, and even shook hands with him at parting.

Lushkov took the letter, departed, and from that time forward did not come to the back-yard for work.

Two years passed. One day as Skvortsov was standing at the ticket-office of a theatre, paying for his ticket, he saw beside him a little man with a lambskin collar and a shabby cat's-skin cap. The man timidly asked the clerk for a gallery ticket and paid for it with kopecks.

"Lushkov, is it you?" asked Skvortsov, recognizing in the little man his former woodchopper. "Well, what are you doing? Are you getting on all right?"

"Pretty well. . . . I am in a notary's office now. I earn thirty-five roubles."

"Well, thank God, that's capital. I rejoice for you. I am very, very glad, Lushkov. You know, in a way, you are my godson. It was I who shoved you into the right way. Do you remember what a scolding I gave you, eh? You almost sank through the floor that time. Well, thank you, my dear fellow, for remembering my words."

"Thank you too," said Lushkov. "If I had not come to you that day, maybe I should be calling myself a schoolmaster or a student still. Yes, in your house I was saved, and climbed out of the pit."

"I am very, very glad."

"Thank you for your kind words and deeds. What you said that day was excellent. I am grateful to you and to your cook, God bless that kind, noble-hearted woman. What you said that day was excellent; I am indebted to you as long as I live, of course, but it was your cook, Olga, who really saved me."

"How was that?"

"Why, it was like this. I used to come to you to chop wood and she would begin: 'Ah, you drunkard! You God-forsaken man! And yet death does not take you!' and then she would sit opposite me, lamenting, looking into my face and wailing: 'You unlucky fellow! You have no gladness in this world, and in the next you will burn in hell, poor drunkard! You poor sorrowful creature!' and she always went on in that style, you know. How often she upset herself, and how many tears she shed over me I can't tell you. But what affected me most -- she chopped the wood for me! Do you know, sir, I never chopped a single log for you -- she did it all! How it was she saved me, how it was I changed, looking at her, and gave up drinking, I can't explain. I only know that what she said and the noble way she behaved brought about a change in my soul, and I shall never forget it. It's time to go up, though, they are just going to ring the bell."

Lushkov bowed and went off to the gallery.

ENEMIES

Between nine and ten on a dark September evening the only son of the district doctor, Kirilov, a child of six, called Andrey, died of diphtheria. Just as the doctor's wife sank on her knees by the dead child's bedside and was overwhelmed by the first rush of despair there came a sharp ring at the bell in the entry.

All the servants had been sent out of the house that morning on account of the diphtheria. Kirilov went to open the door just as he was, without his coat on, with his waistcoat unbuttoned, without wiping his wet face or his hands which were scalded with carbolic. It was dark in the entry and nothing could be distinguished in the man who came in but medium height, a white scarf, and a large, extremely pale face, so pale that its entrance seemed to make the passage lighter.

"Is the doctor at home?" the newcomer asked quickly.

"I am at home," answered Kirilov. "What do you want?"

"Oh, it's you? I am very glad," said the stranger in a tone of relief, and he began feeling in the dark for the doctor's hand, found it and squeezed it tightly in his own. "I am very . . . very glad! We are acquainted. My name is Abogin, and I had the honour of meeting you in the summer at Gnutchev's. I am very glad I have found you at home. For God's sake don't refuse to come back with me at once. . . . My wife has been taken dangerously ill. . . . And the carriage is waiting. . . ."

From the voice and gestures of the speaker it could be seen that he was in a state of great excitement. Like a man terrified by a house on fire or a mad dog, he could hardly restrain his rapid breathing and spoke quickly in a shaking voice, and there was a note of unaffected sincerity and childish alarm in his voice. As people always do who are frightened and overwhelmed, he spoke in brief, jerky sentences and uttered a great many unnecessary, irrelevant words.

"I was afraid I might not find you in," he went on. "I was in a perfect agony as I drove here. Put on your things and let us go, for God's sake. . . . This is how it happened. Alexandr Semyonovitch Paptchinsky, whom you know, came to see me. . . . We talked a little and then we sat down to tea; suddenly my wife cried out, clutched at her heart, and fell back on her chair. We carried her to bed and . . . and I rubbed her forehead with ammonia and sprinkled her with water . . . she lay as though she were dead. . . . I am afraid it is aneurism . . . . Come along . . . her father died of aneurism."

Kirilov listened and said nothing, as though he did not understand Russian.

When Abogin mentioned again Paptchinsky and his wife's father and once more began feeling in the dark for his hand the doctor shook his head and said apathetically, dragging out each word:

"Excuse me, I cannot come . . . my son died . . . five minutes ago!"

"Is it possible!" whispered Abogin, stepping back a pace. "My God, at what an unlucky moment I have come! A wonderfully unhappy day . . . wonderfully. What a coincidence. . . . It's as though it were on purpose!"

Abogin took hold of the door-handle and bowed his head. He was evidently hesitating and did not know what to do -- whether to go away or to continue entreating the doctor.

"Listen," he said fervently, catching hold of Kirilov's sleeve. "I well understand your position! God is my witness that I am ashamed of attempting at such a moment to intrude on your attention, but what am I to do? Only think, to whom can I go? There is no other doctor here, you know. For God's sake come! I am not asking you for myself. . . . I am not the patient!"

A silence followed. Kirilov turned his back on Abogin, stood still a moment, and slowly walked into the drawing-room. Judging from his unsteady, mechanical step, from the attention with which he set straight the fluffy shade on the unlighted lamp in the drawing-room and glanced into a thick book lying on the table, at that instant he had no intention, no desire, was thinking of nothing and most likely did not remember that there was a stranger in the entry. The twilight and stillness of the drawing-room seemed to increase his numbness. Going out of the drawing-room into his study he raised his right foot higher than was necessary, and felt for the doorposts with his hands, and as he did so there was an air of perplexity about his whole figure as though he were in somebody else's house, or were drunk for the first time in his life and were now abandoning himself with surprise to the new sensation. A broad streak of light stretched across the bookcase on one wall of the study; this light came together with the close, heavy smell of carbolic and ether from the door into the bedroom, which stood a little way open. . . . The doctor sank into a low chair in front of the table; for a minute he stared drowsily at his books, which lay with the light on them, then got up and went into the bedroom.

Here in the bedroom reigned a dead silence. Everything to the smallest detail was eloquent of the storm that had been passed through, of exhaustion, and everything was at rest. A candle standing among a crowd of bottles, boxes, and pots on a stool and a big lamp on the chest of drawers threw a brilliant light over all the room. On the bed under the window lay a boy with open eyes and a look of wonder on his face. He did not move, but his open eyes seemed every moment growing darker and sinking further into his head. The mother was kneeling by the bed with her arms on his body and her head hidden in the bedclothes. Like the child, she did not stir; but what throbbing life was suggested in the curves of her body and in her arms! She leaned against the bed with all her being, pressing against it greedily with all her might, as though she were afraid of disturbing the peaceful and comfortable attitude she had found at last for her exhausted body. The bedclothes, the rags and bowls, the splashes of water on the floor, the little paint-brushes and spoons thrown down here and there, the white bottle of lime water, the very air, heavy and stifling -- were all hushed and seemed plunged in repose.

The doctor stopped close to his wife, thrust his hands in his trouser pockets, and slanting his head on one side fixed his eyes on his son. His face bore an expression of indifference, and only from the drops that glittered on his beard it could be seen that he had just been crying.

That repellent horror which is thought of when we speak of death was absent from the room. In the numbness of everything, in the mother's attitude, in the indifference on the doctor's face there was something that attracted and touched the heart, that subtle, almost elusive beauty of human sorrow which men will not for a long time learn to understand and describe, and which it seems only music can convey. There was a feeling of beauty, too, in the austere stillness. Kirilov and his wife were silent and not weeping, as though besides the bitterness of their loss they were conscious, too, of all the tragedy of their position; just as once their youth had passed away, so now together with this boy their right to have children had gone for ever to all eternity! The doctor was forty-four, his hair was grey and he looked like an old man; his faded and invalid wife was thirty-five. Andrey was not merely the only child, but also the last child.

In contrast to his wife the doctor belonged to the class of people who at times of spiritual suffering feel a craving for movement. After standing for five minutes by his wife, he walked, raising his right foot high, from the bedroom into a little room which was half filled up by a big sofa; from there he went into the kitchen. After wandering by the stove and the cook's bed he bent down and went by a little door into the passage.

There he saw again the white scarf and the white face.

"At last," sighed Abogin, reaching towards the door-handle. "Let us go, please."

The doctor started, glanced at him, and remembered. . . .

"Why, I have told you already that I can't go!" he said, growing more animated. "How strange!"

"Doctor, I am not a stone, I fully understand your position . . . I feel for you," Abogin said in an imploring voice, laying his hand on his scarf. "But I am not asking you for myself. My wife is dying. If you had heard that cry, if you had seen her face, you would understand my pertinacity. My God, I thought you had gone to get ready! Doctor, time is precious. Let us go, I entreat you."

"I cannot go," said Kirilov emphatically and he took a step into the drawing-room.

Abogin followed him and caught hold of his sleeve.

"You are in sorrow, I understand. But I'm not asking you to a case of toothache, or to a consultation, but to save a human life!" he went on entreating like a beggar. "Life comes before any personal sorrow! Come, I ask for courage, for heroism! For the love of humanity!"

"Humanity -- that cuts both ways," Kirilov said irritably. "In the name of humanity I beg you not to take me. And how queer it is, really! I can hardly stand and you talk to me about humanity! I am fit for nothing just now. . . . Nothing will induce me to go, and I can't leave my wife alone. No, no. . ."

Kirilov waved his hands and staggered back.

"And . . . and don't ask me," he went on in a tone of alarm. "Excuse me. By No. XIII of the regulations I am obliged to go and you have the right to drag me by my collar . . . drag me if you like, but . . . I am not fit . . . I can't even speak . . . excuse me."

"There is no need to take that tone to me, doctor!" said Abogin, again taking the doctor by his sleeve. "What do I care about No. XIII! To force you against your will I have no right whatever. If you will, come; if you will not -- God forgive you; but I am not appealing to your will, but to your feelings. A young woman is dying. You were just speaking of the death of your son. Who should understand my horror if not you?"

Abogin's voice quivered with emotion; that quiver and his tone were far more persuasive than his words. Abogin was sincere, but it was remarkable that whatever he said his words sounded stilted, soulless, and inappropriately flowery, and even seemed an outrage on the atmosphere of the doctor s home and on the woman who was somewhere dying. He felt this himself, and so, afraid of not being understood, did his utmost to put softness and tenderness into his voice so that the sincerity of his tone might prevail if his words did not. As a rule, however fine and deep a phrase may be, it only affects the indifferent, and cannot fully satisfy those who are happy or unhappy; that is why dumbness is most often the highest expression of happiness or unhappiness; lovers understand each other better when they are silent, and a fervent, passionate speech delivered by the grave only touches outsiders, while to the widow and children of the dead man it seems cold and trivial.

Kirilov stood in silence. When Abogin uttered a few more phrases concerning the noble calling of a doctor, self-sacrifice, and so on, the doctor asked sullenly: "Is it far?"

"Something like eight or nine miles. I have capital horses, doctor! I give you my word of honour that I will get you there and back in an hour. Only one hour."

These words had more effect on Kirilov than the appeals to humanity or the noble calling of the doctor. He thought a moment and said with a sigh: "Very well, let us go!"

He went rapidly with a more certain step to his study, and afterwards came back in a long frock-coat. Abogin, greatly relieved, fidgeted round him and scraped with his feet as he helped him on with his overcoat, and went out of the house with him.

It was dark out of doors, though lighter than in the entry. The tall, stooping figure of the doctor, with his long, narrow beard and aquiline nose, stood out distinctly in the darkness. Abogin's big head and the little student's cap that barely covered it could be seen now as well as his pale face. The scarf showed white only in front, behind it was hidden by his long hair.

"Believe me, I know how to appreciate your generosity," Abogin muttered as he helped the doctor into the carriage. "We shall get there quickly. Drive as fast as you can, Luka, there's a good fellow! Please!"

The coachman drove rapidly. At first there was a row of indistinct buildings that stretched alongside the hospital yard; it was dark everywhere except for a bright light from a window that gleamed through the fence into the furthest part of the yard while three windows of the upper storey of the hospital looked paler than the surrounding air. Then the carriage drove into dense shadow; here there was the smell of dampness and mushrooms, and the sound of rustling trees; the crows, awakened by the noise of the wheels, stirred among the foliage and uttered prolonged plaintive cries as though they knew the doctor's son was dead and that Abogin's wife was ill. Then came glimpses of separate trees, of bushes; a pond, on which great black shadows were slumbering, gleamed with a sullen light -- and the carriage rolled over a smooth level ground. The clamour of the crows sounded dimly far away and soon ceased altogether.

Kirilov and Abogin were silent almost all the way. Only once Abogin heaved a deep sigh and muttered:

"It's an agonizing state! One never loves those who are near one so much as when one is in danger of losing them."

And when the carriage slowly drove over the river, Kirilov started all at once as though the splash of the water had frightened him, and made a movement.

"Listen -- let me go," he said miserably. "I'll come to you later. I must just send my assistant to my wife. She is alone, you know!"

Abogin did not speak. The carriage swaying from side to side and crunching over the stones drove up the sandy bank and rolled on its way. Kirilov moved restlessly and looked about him in misery. Behind them in the dim light of the stars the road could be seen and the riverside willows vanishing into the darkness. On the right lay a plain as uniform and as boundless as the sky; here and there in the distance, probably on the peat marshes, dim lights were glimmering. On the left, parallel with the road, ran a hill tufted with small bushes, and above the hill stood motionless a big, red half-moon, slightly veiled with mist and encircled by tiny clouds, which seemed to be looking round at it from all sides and watching that it did not go away.

In all nature there seemed to be a feeling of hopelessness and pain. The earth, like a ruined woman sitting alone in a dark room and trying not to think of the past, was brooding over memories of spring and summer and apathetically waiting for the inevitable winter. Wherever one looked, on all sides, nature seemed like a dark, infinitely deep, cold pit from which neither Kirilov nor Abogin nor the red half-moon could escape. . . .

The nearer the carriage got to its goal the more impatient Abogin became. He kept moving, leaping up, looking over the coachman's shoulder. And when at last the carriage stopped before the entrance, which was elegantly curtained with striped linen, and when he looked at the lighted windows of the second storey there was an audible catch in his breath.

"If anything happens . . . I shall not survive it," he said, going into the hall with the doctor, and rubbing his hands in agitation. "But there is no commotion, so everything must be going well so far," he added, listening in the stillness.

There was no sound in the hall of steps or voices and all the house seemed asleep in spite of the lighted windows. Now the doctor and Abogin, who till then had been in darkness, could see each other clearly. The doctor was tall and stooped, was untidily dressed and not good-looking. There was an unpleasantly harsh, morose, and unfriendly look about his lips, thick as a negro's, his aquiline nose, and listless, apathetic eyes. His unkempt head and sunken temples, the premature greyness of his long, narrow beard through which his chin was visible, the pale grey hue of his skin and his careless, uncouth manners -- the harshness of all this was suggestive of years of poverty, of ill fortune, of weariness with life and with men. Looking at his frigid figure one could hardly believe that this man had a wife, that he was capable of weeping over his child. Abogin presented a very different appearance. He was a thick-set, sturdy-looking, fair man with a big head and large, soft features; he was elegantly dressed in the very latest fashion. In his carriage, his closely buttoned coat, his long hair, and his face there was a suggestion of something generous, leonine; he walked with his head erect and his chest squared, he spoke in an agreeable baritone, and there was a shade of refined almost feminine elegance in the manner in which he took off his scarf and smoothed his hair. Even his paleness and the childlike terror with which he looked up at the stairs as he took off his coat did not detract from his dignity nor diminish the air of sleekness, health, and aplomb which characterized his whole figure.

"There is nobody and no sound," he said going up the stairs. "There is no commotion. God grant all is well."

He led the doctor through the hall into a big drawing-room where there was a black piano and a chandelier in a white cover; from there they both went into a very snug, pretty little drawing-room full of an agreeable, rosy twilight.

"Well, sit down here, doctor, and I . . . will be back directly. I will go and have a look and prepare them."

Kirilov was left alone. The luxury of the drawing-room, the agreeably subdued light and his own presence in the stranger's unfamiliar house, which had something of the character of an adventure, did not apparently affect him. He sat in a low chair and scrutinized his hands, which were burnt with carbolic. He only caught a passing glimpse of the bright red lamp-shade and the violoncello case, and glancing in the direction where the clock was ticking he noticed a stuffed wolf as substantial and sleek-looking as Abogin himself.

It was quiet. . . . Somewhere far away in the adjoining rooms someone uttered a loud exclamation:

"Ah!" There was a clang of a glass door, probably of a cupboard, and again all was still. After waiting five minutes Kirilov left off scrutinizing his hands and raised his eyes to the door by which Abogin had vanished.

In the doorway stood Abogin, but he was not the same as when he had gone out. The look of sleekness and refined elegance had disappeared -- his face, his hands, his attitude were contorted by a revolting expression of something between horror and agonizing physical pain. His nose, his lips, his moustache, all his features were moving and seemed trying to tear themselves from his face, his eyes looked as though they were laughing with agony. . . .

Abogin took a heavy stride into the drawing-room, bent forward, moaned, and shook his fists.

"She has deceived me," he cried, with a strong emphasis on the second syllable of the verb. "Deceived me, gone away. She fell ill and sent me for the doctor only to run away with that clown Paptchinsky! My God!"

Abogin took a heavy step towards the doctor, held out his soft white fists in his face, and shaking them went on yelling:

"Gone away! Deceived me! But why this deception? My God! My God! What need of this dirty, scoundrelly trick, this diabolical, snakish farce? What have I done to her? Gone away!"

Tears gushed from his eyes. He turned on one foot and began pacing up and down the drawing-room. Now in his short coat, his fashionable narrow trousers which made his legs look disproportionately slim, with his big head and long mane he was extremely like a lion. A gleam of curiosity came into the apathetic face of the doctor. He got up and looked at Abogin.

"Excuse me, where is the patient?" he said.

"The patient! The patient!" cried Abogin, laughing, crying, and still brandishing his fists. "She is not ill, but accursed! The baseness! The vileness! The devil himself could not have imagined anything more loathsome! She sent me off that she might run away with a buffoon, a dull-witted clown, an Alphonse! Oh God, better she had died! I cannot bear it! I cannot bear it!"

The doctor drew himself up. His eyes blinked and filled with tears, his narrow beard began moving to right and to left together with his jaw.

"Allow me to ask what's the meaning of this?" he asked, looking round him with curiosity. "My child is dead, my wife is in grief alone in the whole house. . . . I myself can scarcely stand up, I have not slept for three nights. . . . And here I am forced to play a part in some vulgar farce, to play the part of a stage property! I don't . . . don't understand it!"

Abogin unclenched one fist, flung a crumpled note on the floor, and stamped on it as though it were an insect he wanted to crush.

"And I didn't see, didn't understand," he said through his clenched teeth, brandishing one fist before his face with an expression as though some one had trodden on his corns. "I did not notice that he came every day! I did not notice that he came today in a closed carriage! What did he come in a closed carriage for? And I did not see it! Noodle!"

"I don't understand . . ." muttered the doctor. "Why, what's the meaning of it? Why, it's an outrage on personal dignity, a mockery of human suffering! It's incredible. . . . It's the first time in my life I have had such an experience!"

With the dull surprise of a man who has only just realized that he has been bitterly insulted the doctor shrugged his shoulders, flung wide his arms, and not knowing what to do or to say sank helplessly into a chair.

"If you have ceased to love me and love another -- so be it; but why this deceit, why this vulgar, treacherous trick?" Abogin said in a tearful voice. "What is the object of it? And what is there to justify it? And what have I done to you? Listen, doctor," he said hotly, going up to Kirilov. "You have been the involuntary witness of my misfortune and I am not going to conceal the truth from you. I swear that I loved the woman, loved her devotedly, like a slave! I have sacrificed everything for her; I have quarrelled with my own people, I have given up the service and music, I have forgiven her what I could not have forgiven my own mother or sister. . . I have never looked askance at her. . . . I have never gainsaid her in anything. Why this deception? I do not demand love, but why this loathsome duplicity? If she did not love me, why did she not say so openly, honestly, especially as she knows my views on the subject? . . ."

With tears in his eyes, trembling all over, Abogin opened his heart to the doctor with perfect sincerity. He spoke warmly, pressing both hands on his heart, exposing the secrets of his private life without the faintest hesitation, and even seemed to be glad that at last these secrets were no longer pent up in his breast. If he had talked in this way for an hour or two, and opened his heart, he would undoubtedly have felt better. Who knows, if the doctor had listened to him and had sympathized with him like a friend, he might perhaps, as often happens, have reconciled himself to his trouble without protest, without doing anything needless and absurd. . . . But what happened was quite different. While Abogin was speaking the outraged doctor perceptibly changed. The indifference and wonder on his face gradually gave way to an expression of bitter resentment, indignation, and anger. The features of his face became even harsher, coarser, and more unpleasant. When Abogin held out before his eyes the photograph of a young woman with a handsome face as cold and expressionless as a nun's and asked him whether, looking at that face, one could conceive that it was capable of duplicity, the doctor suddenly flew out, and with flashing eyes said, rudely rapping out each word:

"What are you telling me all this for? I have no desire to hear it! I have no desire to!" he shouted and brought his fist down on the table. "I don't want your vulgar secrets! Damnation take them! Don't dare to tell me of such vulgar doings! Do you consider that I have not been insulted enough already? That I am a flunkey whom you can insult without restraint? Is that it?"

Abogin staggered back from Kirilov and stared at him in amazement.

"Why did you bring me here?" the doctor went on, his beard quivering. "If you are so puffed up with good living that you go and get married and then act a farce like this, how do I come in? What have I to do with your love affairs? Leave me in peace! Go on squeezing money out of the poor in your gentlemanly way. Make a display of humane ideas, play (the doctor looked sideways at the violoncello case) play the bassoon and the trombone, grow as fat as capons, but don't dare to insult personal dignity! If you cannot respect it, you might at least spare it your attention!"

"Excuse me, what does all this mean?" Abogin asked, flushing red.

"It means that it's base and low to play with people like this! I am a doctor; you look upon doctors and people generally who work and don't stink of perfume and prostitution as your menials and *mauvais ton;* well, you may look upon them so, but no one has given you the right to treat a man who is suffering as a stage property!"

"How dare you say that to me!" Abogin said quietly, and his face began working again, and this time unmistakably from anger.

"No, how dared you, knowing of my sorrow, bring me here to listen to these vulgarities!" shouted the doctor, and he again banged on the table with his fist. "Who has given you the right to make a mockery of another man's sorrow?"

"You have taken leave of your senses," shouted Abogin. "It is ungenerous. I am intensely unhappy myself and . . . and . . ."

"Unhappy!" said the doctor, with a smile of contempt. "Don't utter that word, it does not concern you. The spendthrift who cannot raise a loan calls himself unhappy, too. The capon, sluggish from over-feeding, is unhappy, too. Worthless people!"

"Sir, you forget yourself," shrieked Abogin. "For saying things like that . . . people are thrashed! Do you understand?"

Abogin hurriedly felt in his side pocket, pulled out a pocket-book, and extracting two notes flung them on the table.

"Here is the fee for your visit," he said, his nostrils dilating. "You are paid."

"How dare you offer me money?" shouted the doctor and he brushed the notes off the table on to the floor. "An insult cannot be paid for in money!"

Abogin and the doctor stood face to face, and in their wrath continued flinging undeserved insults at each other. I believe that never in their lives, even in delirium, had they uttered so much that was unjust, cruel, and absurd. The egoism of the unhappy was conspicuous in both. The unhappy are egoistic, spiteful, unjust, cruel, and less capable of understanding each other than fools. Unhappiness does not bring people together but draws them apart, and even where one would fancy people should be united by the similarity of their sorrow, far more injustice and cruelty is generated than in comparatively placid surroundings.

"Kindly let me go home!" shouted the doctor, breathing hard.

Abogin rang the bell sharply. When no one came to answer the bell he rang again and angrily flung the bell on the floor; it fell on the carpet with a muffled sound, and uttered a plaintive note as though at the point of death. A footman came in.

"Where have you been hiding yourself, the devil take you?" His master flew at him, clenching his fists. "Where were you just now? Go and tell them to bring the victoria round for this gentleman, and order the closed carriage to be got ready for me. Stay," he cried as the footman turned to go out. "I won't have a single traitor in the house by tomorrow! Away with you all! I will engage fresh servants! Reptiles!"

Abogin and the doctor remained in silence waiting for the carriage. The first regained his expression of sleekness and his refined elegance. He paced up and down the room, tossed his head elegantly, and was evidently meditating on something. His anger had not cooled, but he tried to appear not to notice his enemy. . . . The doctor stood, leaning with one hand on the edge of the table, and looked at Abogin with that profound and somewhat cynical, ugly contempt only to be found in the eyes of sorrow and indigence when they are confronted with well-nourished comfort and elegance.

When a little later the doctor got into the victoria and drove off there was still a look of contempt in his eyes. It was dark, much darker than it had been an hour before. The red half-moon had sunk behind the hill and the clouds that had been guarding it lay in dark patches near the stars. The carriage with red lamps rattled along the road and soon overtook the doctor. It was Abogin driving off to protest, to do absurd things. . . .

All the way home the doctor thought not of his wife, nor of his Andrey, but of Abogin and the people in the house he had just left. His thoughts were unjust and inhumanly cruel. He condemned Abogin and his wife and Paptchinsky and all who lived in rosy, subdued light among sweet perfumes, and all the way home he hated and despised them till his head ached. And a firm conviction concerning those people took shape in his mind.

Time will pass and Kirilov's sorrow will pass, but that conviction, unjust and unworthy of the human heart, will not pass, but will remain in the doctor's mind to the grave.

DARKNESS

A young peasant, with white eyebrows and eyelashes and broad cheekbones, in a torn sheepskin and big black felt overboots, waited till the Zemstvo doctor had finished seeing his patients and came out to go home from the hospital; then he went up to him, diffidently.

"Please, your honour," he said.

"What do you want?"

The young man passed the palm of his hand up and over his nose, looked at the sky, and then answered:

"Please, your honour. . . . You've got my brother Vaska the blacksmith from Varvarino in the convict ward here, your honour. . . ."

"Yes, what then?"

"I am Vaska's brother, you see. . . . Father has the two of us: him, Vaska, and me, Kirila; besides us there are three sisters, and Vaska's a married man with a little one. . . . There are a lot of us and no one to work. . . . In the smithy it's nearly two years now since the forge has been heated. I am at the cotton factory, I can't do smith's work, and how can father work? Let alone work, he can't eat properly, he can't lift the spoon to his mouth."

"What do you want from me?"

"Be merciful! Let Vaska go!"

The doctor looked wonderingly at Kirila, and without saying a word walked on. The young peasant ran on in front and flung himself in a heap at his feet.

"Doctor, kind gentleman!" he besought him, blinking and again passing his open hand over his nose. "Show heavenly mercy; let Vaska go home! We shall remember you in our prayers for ever! Your honour, let him go! They are all starving! Mother's wailing day in, day out, Vaska's wife's wailing . . . it's worse than death! I don't care to look upon the light of day. Be merciful; let him go, kind gentleman!"

"Are you stupid or out of your senses?" asked the doctor angrily. "How can I let him go? Why, he is a convict."

Kirila began crying. "Let him go!"

"Tfoo, queer fellow! What right have I? Am I a gaoler or what? They brought him to the hospital for me to treat him, but I have as much right to let him out as I have to put you in prison, silly fellow!

"But they have shut him up for nothing! He was in prison a year before the trial, and now there is no saying what he is there for. It would have been a different thing if he had murdered someone, let us say, or stolen horses; but as it is, what is it all about?"

"Very likely, but how do I come in?"

"They shut a man up and they don't know themselves what for. He was drunk, your honour, did not know what he was doing, and even hit father on the ear and scratched his own cheek on a branch, and two of our fellows-they wanted some Turkish tobacco, you see-began telling him to go with them and break into the Armenian's shop at night for tobacco. Being drunk, he obeyed them, the fool. They broke the lock, you know, got in, and did no end of mischief; they turned everything upside down, broke the windows, and scattered the flour about. They were drunk, that is all one can say! Well, the constable turned up . . . and with one thing and another they took them off to the magistrate. They have been a whole year in prison, and a week ago, on the Wednesday, they were all three tried in the town. A soldier stood behind them with a gun . . . people were sworn in. Vaska was less to blame than any, but the gentry decided that he was the ringleader. The other two lads were sent to prison, but Vaska to a convict battalion for three years. And what for? One should judge like a Christian!"

"I have nothing to do with it, I tell you again. Go to the authorities."

"I have been already! I've been to the court; I have tried to send in a petition -- they wouldn't take a petition; I have been to the police captain, and I have been to the examining magistrate, and everyone says, 'It is not my business!' Whose business is it, then? But there is no one above you here in the hospital; you do what you like, your honour."

"You simpleton," sighed the doctor, "once the jury have found him guilty, not the governor, not even the minister, could do anything, let alone the police captain. It's no good your trying to do anything!"

"And who judged him, then?"

"The gentlemen of the jury...."

"They weren't gentlemen, they were our peasants! Andrey Guryev was one; Aloshka Huk was one."

"Well, I am cold talking to you...."

The doctor waved his hand and walked quickly to his own door. Kirila was on the point of following him, but, seeing the door slam, he stopped.

For ten minutes he stood motionless in the middle of the hospital yard, and without putting on his cap stared at the doctor's house, then he heaved a deep sigh, slowly scratched himself, and walked towards the gate.

"To whom am I to go?" he muttered as he came out on to the road. "One says it is not his business, another says it is not his business. Whose business is it, then? No, till you grease their hands you will get nothing out of them. The doctor says that, but he keeps looking all the while at my fist to see whether I am going to give him a blue note. Well, brother, I'll go, if it has to be to the governor."

Shifting from one foot to the other and continually looking round him in an objectless way, he trudged lazily along the road and was apparently wondering where to go.... It was not cold and the snow faintly crunched under his feet. Not more than half a mile in front of him the wretched little district town in which his brother had just been tried lay outstretched on the hill. On the right was the dark prison with its red roof and sentry-boxes at the corners; on the left was the big town copse, now covered with hoar-frost. It was still; only an old man, wearing a woman's short jacket and a huge cap, was walking ahead, coughing and shouting to a cow which he was driving to the town.

"Good-day, grandfather," said Kirila, overtaking him.

"Good-day. . . ."

"Are you driving it to the market?"

"No," the old man answered lazily.

"Are you a townsman?"

They got into conversation; Kirila told him what he had come to the hospital for, and what he had been talking about to the doctor.

"The doctor does not know anything about such matters, that is a sure thing," the old man said to him as they were both entering the town; "though he is a gentleman, he is only taught to cure by every means, but to give you real advice, or, let us say, write out a petition for you -- that he cannot do. There are special authorities to do that. You have been to the justice of the peace and to the police captain -- they are no good for your business either."

"Where am I to go?"

"The permanent member of the rural board is the chief person for peasants' affairs. Go to him, Mr. Sineokov."

"The one who is at Zolotovo?"

"Why, yes, at Zolotovo. He is your chief man. If it is anything that has to do with you peasants even the police captain has no authority against him."

"It's a long way to go, old man. . . . I dare say it's twelve miles and may be more."

"One who needs something will go seventy."

"That is so. . . . Should I send in a petition to him, or what?"

"You will find out there. If you should have a petition the clerk will write you one quick enough. The permanent member has a clerk."

After parting from the old man Kirila stood still in the middle of the square, thought a little, and walked back out of the town. He made up his mind to go to Zolotovo.

Five days later, as the doctor was on his way home after seeing his patients, he caught sight of Kirila again in his yard. This time the young peasant was not alone, but with a gaunt, very pale old man who nodded his head without ceasing, like a pendulum, and mumbled with his lips.

"Your honour, I have come again to ask your gracious mercy," began Kirila. "Here I have come with my father. Be merciful, let Vaska go! The permanent member would not talk to me. He said: 'Go away!' "

"Your honour," the old man hissed in his throat, raising his twitching eyebrows, "be merciful! We are poor people, we cannot repay your honour, but if you graciously please, Kiryushka or Vaska can repay you in work. Let them work."

"We will pay with work," said Kirila, and he raised his hand above his head as though he would take an oath. "Let him go! They are starving, they are crying day and night, your honour!"

The young peasant bent a rapid glance on his father, pulled him by the sleeve, and both of them, as at the word of command, fell at the doctor's feet. The latter waved his hand in despair, and, without looking round, walked quickly in at his door.

POLINKA

It is one o'clock in the afternoon. Shopping is at its height at the "Nouveauté's de Paris," a drapery establishment in one of the Arcades. There is a monotonous hum of shopmen's voices, the hum one hears at school when the teacher sets the boys to learn something by heart. This regular sound is not interrupted by the laughter of lady customers nor the slam of the glass door, nor the scurrying of the boys.

Polinka, a thin fair little person whose mother is the head of a dressmaking establishment, is standing in the middle of the shop looking about for some one. A dark-browed boy runs up to her and asks, looking at her very gravely:

"What is your pleasure, madam?"

"Nikolay Timofeitch always takes my order," answers Polinka.

Nikolay Timofeitch, a graceful dark young man, fashionably dressed, with frizzled hair and a big pin in his cravat, has already cleared a place on the counter and is craning forward, looking at Polinka with a smile.

"Morning, Pelagea Sergeevna!" he cries in a pleasant, hearty baritone voice. "What can I do for you?"

"Good-morning!" says Polinka, going up to him. "You see, I'm back again. . . . Show me some gimp, please."

"Gimp -- for what purpose?"

"For a bodice trimming -- to trim a whole dress, in fact."

"Certainly."

Nickolay Timofeitch lays several kinds of gimp before Polinka; she looks at the trimmings languidly and begins bargaining over them.

"Oh, come, a rouble's not dear," says the shopman persuasively, with a condescending smile. "It's a French trimming, pure silk. . . . We have a commoner sort, if you like, heavier. That's forty-five kopecks a yard; of course, it's nothing like the same quality."

"I want a bead corselet, too, with gimp buttons," says Polinka, bending over the gimp and sighing for some reason. "And have you any bead motifs to match?"

"Yes."

Polinka bends still lower over the counter and asks softly:

"And why did you leave us so early on Thursday, Nikolay Timofeitch?"

"Hm! It's queer you noticed it," says the shopman, with a smirk. "You were so taken up with that fine student that . . . it's queer you noticed it!"

Polinka flushes crimson and remains mute. With a nervous quiver in his fingers the shopman closes the boxes, and for no sort of object piles them one on the top of another. A moment of silence follows.

"I want some bead lace, too," says Polinka, lifting her eyes guiltily to the shopman.

"What sort? Black or coloured? Bead lace on tulle is the most fashionable trimming."

"And how much is it?"

"The black's from eighty kopecks and the coloured from two and a half roubles. I shall never come and see you again," Nikolay Timofeitch adds in an undertone.

"Why?"

"Why? It's very simple. You must understand that yourself. Why should I distress myself? It's a queer business! Do you suppose it's a pleasure to me to see that student carrying on with you? I see it all and I understand. Ever since autumn he's been hanging about you and you go for a walk with him almost every day; and when he is with you, you gaze at him as though he were an angel. You are in love with him; there's no one to beat him in your eyes. Well, all right, then, it's no good talking."

Polinka remains dumb and moves her finger on the counter in embarrassment.

"I see it all," the shopman goes on. "What inducement have I to come and see you? I've got some pride. It's not every one likes to play gooseberry. What was it you asked for?"

"Mamma told me to get a lot of things, but I've forgotten. I want some feather trimming too."

"What kind would you like?"

"The best, something fashionable."

"The most fashionable now are real bird feathers. If you want the most fashionable colour, it's heliotrope or *kanak* -- that is, claret with a yellow shade in it. We have an immense choice. And what all this affair is going to lead to, I really don't understand. Here you are in love, and how is it to end?"

Patches of red come into Nikolay Timofeitch's face round his eyes. He crushes the soft feather trimming in his hand and goes on muttering:

"Do you imagine he'll marry you -- is that it? You'd better drop any such fancies. Students are forbidden to marry. And do you suppose he comes to see you with honourable intentions? A likely idea! Why, these fine students don't look on us as human beings . . . they only go to see shopkeepers and dressmakers to laugh at their ignorance and to drink. They're ashamed to drink at home and in good houses, but with simple uneducated people like us they don't care what anyone thinks; they'd be ready to stand on their heads. Yes! Well, which feather trimming will you take? And if he hangs about and carries on with you, we know what he is after. . . . When he's a doctor or a lawyer he'll remember you: 'Ah,' he'll say, 'I used to have a pretty fair little thing! I wonder where she is now?' Even now I bet you he boasts among his friends that he's got his eye on a little dressmaker."

Polinka sits down and gazes pensively at the pile of white boxes.

"No, I won't take the feather trimming," she sighs. "Mamma had better choose it for herself; I may get the wrong one. I want six yards of fringe for an overcoat, at forty kopecks the yard. For the same coat I want cocoa-nut buttons, perforated, so they can be sown on firmly. . . ."

Nikolay Timofeitch wraps up the fringe and the buttons. She looks at him guiltily and evidently expects him to go on talking, but he remains sullenly silent while he tidies up the feather trimming.

"I mustn't forget some buttons for a dressing-gown . . ." she says after an interval of silence, wiping her pale lips with a handkerchief.

"What kind?"

"It's for a shopkeeper's wife, so give me something rather striking."

"Yes, if it's for a shopkeeper's wife, you'd better have something bright. Here are some buttons. A combination of colours -- red, blue, and the fashionable gold shade. Very glaring. The more refined prefer dull black with a bright border. But I don't understand. Can't you see for yourself? What can these . . . walks lead to?"

"I don't know," whispers Polinka, and she bends over the buttons; "I don't know myself what's come to me, Nikolay Timofeitch."

A solid shopman with whiskers forces his way behind Nikolay Timofeitch's back, squeezing him to the counter, and beaming with the choicest gallantry, shouts:

"Be so kind, madam, as to step into this department. We have three kinds of jerseys: plain, braided, and trimmed with beads! Which may I have the pleasure of showing you?"

At the same time a stout lady passes by Polinka, pronouncing in a rich, deep voice, almost a bass:

"They must be seamless, with the trade mark stamped in them, please."

"Pretend to be looking at the things," Nikolay Timofeitch whispers, bending down to Polinka with a forced smile. "Dear me, you do look pale and ill; you are quite changed. He'll throw you over, Pelagea Sergeevna! Or if he does marry you, it won't be for love but from hunger; he'll be tempted by your money. He'll furnish himself a nice home with your dowry, and then be ashamed of you. He'll keep you out of sight of his friends and visitors, because you're uneducated. He'll call you 'my dummy of a wife.' You wouldn't know how to behave in a doctor's or lawyer's circle. To them you're a dressmaker, an ignorant creature."

"Nikolay Timofeitch!" somebody shouts from the other end of the shop. "The young lady here wants three yards of ribbon with a metal stripe. Have we any?"

Nikolay Timofeitch turns in that direction, smirks and shouts:

"Yes, we have! Ribbon with a metal stripe, ottoman with a satin stripe, and satin with a moiré stripe!"

"Oh, by the way, I mustn't forget, Olga asked me to get her a pair of stays!" says Polinka.

"There are tears in your eyes," says Nikolay Timofeitch in dismay. "What's that for? Come to the corset department, I'll screen you -- it looks awkward."

With a forced smile and exaggeratedly free and easy manner, the shopman rapidly conducts Polinka to the corset department and conceals her from the public eye behind a high pyramid of boxes.

"What sort of corset may I show you?" he asks aloud, whispering immediately: "Wipe your eyes!"

"I want . . . I want . . . size forty-eight centimetres. Only she wanted one, lined . . . with real whalebone . . . I must talk to you, Nikolay Timofeitch. Come to-day!"

"Talk? What about? There's nothing to talk about."

"You are the only person who . . . cares about me, and I've no one to talk to but you."

"These are not reed or steel, but real whalebone. . . . What is there for us to talk about? It's no use talking. . . . You are going for a walk with him to-day, I suppose?"

"Yes; I . . . I am."

"Then what's the use of talking? Talk won't help. . . . You are in love, aren't you?"

"Yes . . ." Polinka whispers hesitatingly, and big tears gush from her eyes.

"What is there to say?" mutters Nikolay Timofeitch, shrugging his shoulders nervously and turning pale. "There's no need of talk. . . . Wipe your eyes, that's all. I . . . I ask for nothing."

At that moment a tall, lanky shopman comes up to the pyramid of boxes, and says to his customer:

"Let me show you some good elastic garters that do not impede the circulation, certified by medical authority . . ."

Nikolay Timofeitch screens Polinka, and, trying to conceal her emotion and his own, wrinkles his face into a smile and says aloud:

"There are two kinds of lace, madam: cotton and silk! Oriental, English, Valenciennes, crochet, torchon, are cotton. And rococo, soutache, Cambray, are silk. . . . For God's sake, wipe your eyes! They're coming this way!"

And seeing that her tears are still gushing he goes on louder than ever:

"Spanish, Rococo, soutache, Cambray . . . stockings, thread, cotton, silk . . ."

DRUNK

A manufacturer called Frolov, a handsome dark man with a round beard, and a soft, velvety expression in his eyes, and Almer, his lawyer, an elderly man with a big rough head, were drinking in one of the public rooms of a restaurant on the outskirts of the town. They had both come to the restaurant straight from a ball and so were wearing dress coats and white ties. Except them and the waiters at the door there was not a soul in the room; by Frolov's orders no one else was admitted.

They began by drinking a big wine-glass of vodka and eating oysters.

"Good!" said Almer. "It was I brought oysters into fashion for the first course, my boy. The vodka burns and stings your throat and you have a voluptuous sensation in your throat when you swallow an oyster. Don't you?"

A dignified waiter with a shaven upper lip and grey whiskers put a sauceboat on the table.

"What's that you are serving?" asked Frolov.

"Sauce Provençale for the herring, sir. . . ."

"What! is that the way to serve it?" shouted Frolov, not looking into the sauceboat. "Do you call that sauce? You don't know how to wait, you blockhead!"

Frolov's velvety eyes flashed. He twisted a corner of the table-cloth round his finger, made a slight movement, and the dishes, the candlesticks, and the bottles, all jingling and clattering, fell with a crash on the floor.

The waiters, long accustomed to pot-house catastrophes, ran up to the table and began picking up the fragments with grave and unconcerned faces, like surgeons at an operation.

"How well you know how to manage them!" said Almer, and he laughed. " But . . . move a little away from the table or you will step in the caviare."

"Call the engineer here!" cried Frolov.

This was the name given to a decrepit, doleful old man who really had once been an engineer and very well off; he had squandered all his property and towards the end of his life had got into a restaurant where he looked after the waiters and singers and carried out various commissions relating to the fair sex. Appearing at the summons, he put his head on one side respectfully.

"Listen, my good man," Frolov said, addressing him. "What's the meaning of this disorder? How queerly you fellows wait! Don't you know that I don't like it? Devil take you, I shall give up coming to you!"

"I beg you graciously to excuse it, Alexey Semyonitch!" said the engineer, laying his hand on his heart. "I will take steps immediately, and your slightest wishes shall be carried out in the best and speediest way."

"Well, that'll do, you can go. . . ."

The engineer bowed, staggered back, still doubled up, and disappeared through the doorway with a final flash of the false diamonds on his shirt-front and fingers.

The table was laid again. Almer drank red wine and ate with relish some sort of bird served with truffles, and ordered a matelote of eelpouts and a sterlet with its tail in its mouth. Frolov only drank vodka and ate nothing but bread. He rubbed his face with his open hands, scowled, and was evidently out of humour. Both were silent. There was a stillness. Two electric lights in opaque shades flickered and hissed as though they were angry. The gypsy girls passed the door, softly humming.

"One drinks and is none the merrier," said Frolov. "The more I pour into myself, the more sober I become. Other people grow festive with vodka, but I suffer from anger, disgusting thoughts, sleeplessness. Why is it, old man, that people don't invent some other pleasure besides drunkenness and debauchery? It's really horrible!"

"You had better send for the gypsy girls."

"Confound them!"

The head of an old gypsy woman appeared in the door from the passage.

"Alexey Semyonitch, the gypsies are asking for tea and brandy," said the old woman. "May we order it?"

"Yes," answered Frolov. "You know they get a percentage from the restaurant keeper for asking the visitors to treat them. Nowadays you can't even believe a man when he asks for vodka. The people are all mean, vile, spoilt. Take these waiters, for instance. They have countenances like professors, and grey heads; they get two hundred roubles a month, they live in houses of their own and send their girls to the high school, but you may swear at them and give yourself airs as much as you please. For a rouble the engineer will gulp down a whole pot of mustard and crow like a cock. On my honour, if one of them would take offence I would make him a present of a thousand roubles."

"What's the matter with you?" said Almer, looking at him with surprise. "Whence this melancholy? You are red in the face, you look like a wild animal.... What's the matter with you?"

"It's horrid. There's one thing I can't get out of my head. It seems as though it is nailed there and it won't come out."

A round little old man, buried in fat and completely bald, wearing a short reefer jacket and lilac waistcoat and carrying a guitar, walked into the room. He made an idiotic face, drew himself up, and saluted like a soldier.

"Ah, the parasite!" said Frolov, "let me introduce him, he has made his fortune by grunting like a pig. Come here!" He poured vodka, wine, and brandy into a glass, sprinkled pepper and salt into it, mixed it all up and gave it to the parasite. The latter tossed it off and smacked his lips with gusto.

"He's accustomed to drink a mess so that pure wine makes him sick," said Frolov. "Come, parasite, sit down and sing."

The old man sat down, touched the strings with his fat fingers, and began singing:

> "Neetka, neetka, Margareetka. . . ."

After drinking champagne Frolov was drunk. He thumped with his fist on the table and said:

"Yes, there's something that sticks in my head! It won't give me a minute's peace!"

"Why, what is it?"

"I can't tell you. It's a secret. It's something so private that I could only speak of it in my prayers. But if you like . . . as a sign of friendship, between ourselves . . . only mind, to no one, no, no, no, . . . I'll tell you, it will ease my heart, but for God's sake . . . listen and forget it. . . ."

Frolov bent down to Almer and for a minute breathed in his ear.

"I hate my wife!" he brought out.

The lawyer looked at him with surprise.

"Yes, yes, my wife, Marya Mihalovna," Frolov muttered, flushing red. " I hate her and that's all about it."

"What for?"

"I don't know myself! I've only been married two years. I married as you know for love, and now I hate her like a mortal enemy, like this parasite here, saving your presence. And there is no cause, no sort of cause! When she sits by me, eats, or says anything, my whole soul boils, I can scarcely restrain myself from being rude to her. It's something one can't describe. To leave her or tell her the truth is utterly impossible because it would be a scandal, and living with her is worse than hell for me. I can't stay at home! I spend my days at business and in the restaurants and spend my nights in dissipation. Come, how is one to explain this hatred? She is not an ordinary woman, but handsome, clever, quiet."

The old man stamped his foot and began singing:

"I went a walk with a captain bold, And in his ear my secrets told."

"I must own I always thought that Marya Mihalovna was not at all the right person for you," said Almer after a brief silence, and he heaved a sigh.

"Do you mean she is too well educated? . . . I took the gold medal at the commercial school myself, I have been to Paris three times. I am not cleverer than you, of course, but I am no more foolish than my wife. No, brother, education is not the sore point. Let me tell you how all the trouble began. It began with my suddenly fancying that she had married me not from love, but for the sake of my money. This idea took possession of my brain. I have done all I could think of, but the cursed thing sticks! And to make it worse my wife was overtaken with a passion for luxury. Getting into a sack of gold after poverty, she took to flinging it in all directions. She went quite off her head, and was so carried away that she used to get through twenty thousand every month. And I am a distrustful man. I don't believe in anyone, I suspect everybody. And the more friendly you are to me the greater my torment. I keep fancying I am being flattered for my money. I trust no one! I am a difficult man, my boy, very difficult!"

Frolov emptied his glass at one gulp and went on.

"But that's all nonsense," he said. "One never ought to speak of it. It's stupid. I am tipsy and I have been chattering, and now you are looking at me with lawyer's eyes -- glad you know some one else's secret. Well, well! . . . Let us drop this conversation. Let us drink! I say," he said, addressing a waiter, "is Mustafa here? Fetch him in!"

Shortly afterwards there walked into the room a little Tatar boy, aged about twelve, wearing a dress coat and white gloves.

"Come here!" Frolov said to him. "Explain to us the following fact: there was a time when you Tatars conquered us and took tribute from us, but now you serve us as waiters and sell dressing-gowns. How do you explain such a change?"

Mustafa raised his eyebrows and said in a shrill voice, with a sing-song intonation: "The mutability of destiny!"

Almer looked at his grave face and went off into peals of laughter.

"Well, give him a rouble!" said Frolov. "He is making his fortune out of the mutability of destiny. He is only kept here for the sake of those two words. Drink, Mustafa! You will make a gre-eat rascal! I mean it is awful how many of your sort are toadies hanging about rich men. The number of these peaceful bandits and robbers is beyond all reckoning! Shouldn't we send for the gypsies now? Eh? Fetch the gypsies along!"

The gypsies, who had been hanging about wearily in the corridors for a long time, burst with whoops into the room, and a wild orgy began.

"Drink!" Frolov shouted to them. "Drink! Seed of Pharaoh! Sing! A-a-ah!"

"In the winter time . . . o-o-ho! . . . the sledge was flying . . ."

The gypsies sang, whistled, danced. In the frenzy which sometimes takes possession of spoilt and very wealthy men, "broad natures," Frolov began to play the fool. He ordered supper and champagne for the gypsies, broke the shade of the electric light, shied bottles at the pictures and looking-glasses, and did it all apparently without the slightest enjoyment, scowling and shouting irritably, with contempt for the people, with an expression of hatred in his eyes and his manners. He made the engineer sing a solo, made the bass singers drink a mixture of wine, vodka, and oil.

At six o'clock they handed him the bill.

"Nine hundred and twenty-five roubles, forty kopecks," said Almer, and shrugged his shoulders. "What's it for? No, wait, we must go into it!"

"Stop!" muttered Frolov, pulling out his pocket-book. "Well! . . . let them rob me. That's what I'm rich for, to be robbed! . . . You can't get on without parasites! . . . You are my lawyer. You get six thousand a year out of me and what for? But excuse me, . . . I don't know what I am saying."

As he was returning home with Almer, Frolov murmured:

"Going home is awful to me! Yes! . . . There isn't a human being I can open my soul to. . . . They are all robbers . . . traitors. . . . Oh, why did I tell you my secret? Yes . . . why? Tell me why?"

At the entrance to his house, he craned forward towards Almer and, staggering, kissed him on the lips, having the old Moscow habit of kissing indiscriminately on every occasion.

"Good-bye . . . I am a difficult, hateful man, he said. "A horrid, drunken, shameless life. You are a well-educated, clever man, but you only laugh and drink with me . . . there's no help from any of you. . . . But if you were a friend to me, if you were an honest man, in reality you ought to have said to me: 'Ugh, you vile, hateful man! You reptile!'"

"Come, come," Almer muttered, "go to bed."

"There is no help from you; the only hope is that, when I am in the country in the summer, I may go out into the fields and a storm come on and the thunder may strike me dead on the spot. . . . Good-bye."

Frolov kissed Almer once more and muttering and dropping asleep as he walked, began mounting the stairs, supported by two footmen.

AN INADVERTENCE

Pyotr Petrovitch Strizhin, the nephew of Madame Ivanov, the colonel's widow -- the man whose new goloshes were stolen last year, -- came home from a christening party at two o'clock in the morning. To avoid waking the household he took off his things in the lobby, made his way on tiptoe to his room, holding his breath, and began getting ready for bed without lighting a candle.

Strizhin leads a sober and regular life. He has a sanctimonious expression of face, he reads nothing but religious and edifying books, but at the christening party, in his delight that Lyubov Spiridonovna had passed through her confinement successfully, he had permitted himself to drink four glasses of vodka and a glass of wine, the taste of which suggested something midway between vinegar and castor oil. Spirituous liquors are like sea-water and glory: the more you imbibe of them the greater your thirst. And now as he undressed, Strizhin was aware of an overwhelming craving for drink.

"I believe Dashenka has some vodka in the cupboard in the right-hand corner," he thought. "If I drink one wine-glassful, she won't notice it."

After some hesitation, overcoming his fears, Strizhin went to the cupboard. Cautiously opening the door he felt in the right-hand corner for a bottle and poured out a wine-glassful, put the bottle back in its place, then, making the sign of the cross, drank it off. And immediately something like a miracle took place. Strizhin was flung back from the cupboard to the chest with fearful force like a bomb. There were flashes before his eyes, he felt as though he could not breathe, and all over his body he had a sensation as though he had fallen into a marsh full of leeches. It seemed to him as though, instead of vodka, he had swallowed dynamite, which blew up his body, the house, and the whole street. . . . His head, his arms, his legs -- all seemed to be torn off and to be flying away somewhere to the devil, into space.

For some three minutes he lay on the chest, not moving and scarcely breathing, then he got up and asked himself:

"Where am I?"

The first thing of which he was clearly conscious on coming to himself was the pronounced smell of paraffin.

"Holy saints," he thought in horror, "it's paraffin I have drunk instead of vodka."

The thought that he had poisoned himself threw him into a cold shiver, then into a fever. That it was really poison that he had taken was proved not only by the smell in the room but also by the burning taste in his mouth, the flashes before his eyes, the ringing in his head, and the colicky pain in his stomach. Feeling the approach of death and not buoying himself up with false hopes, he wanted to say good-bye to those nearest to him, and made his way to Dashenka's bedroom (being a widower he had his sister-in-law called Dashenka, an old maid, living in the flat to keep house for him).

"Dashenka," he said in a tearful voice as he went into the bedroom, "dear Dashenka!"

Something grumbled in the darkness and uttered a deep sigh.

"Dashenka."

"Eh? What?" A woman's voice articulated rapidly. "Is that you, Pyotr Petrovitch? Are you back already? Well, what is it? What has the baby been christened? Who was godmother?"

"The godmother was Natalya Andreyevna Velikosvyetsky, and the godfather Pavel Ivanitch Bezsonnitsin. . . . I . . . I believe, Dashenka, I am dying. And the baby has been christened Olimpiada, in honour of their kind patroness. . . . I . . . I have just drunk paraffin, Dashenka!"

"What next! You don't say they gave you paraffin there?"

"I must own I wanted to get a drink of vodka without asking you, and . . . and the Lord chastised me: by accident in the dark I took paraffin. . . . What am I to do?"

Dashenka, hearing that the cupboard had been opened without her permission, grew more wide-awake. . . . She quickly lighted a candle, jumped out of bed, and in her nightgown, a freckled, bony figure in curl-papers, padded with bare feet to the cupboard.

"Who told you you might?" she asked sternly, as she scrutinized the inside of the cupboard. "Was the vodka put there for you?"

"I . . . I haven't drunk vodka but paraffin, Dashenka . . ." muttered Strizhin, mopping the cold sweat on his brow.

"And what did you want to touch the paraffin for? That's nothing to do with you, is it? Is it put there for you? Or do you suppose paraffin costs nothing? Eh? Do you know what paraffin is now? Do you know?"

"Dear Dashenka," moaned Strizhin, "it's a question of life and death, and you talk about money!"

"He's drunk himself tipsy and now he pokes his nose into the cupboard!" cried Dashenka, angrily slamming the cupboard door. "Oh, the monsters, the tormentors! I'm a martyr, a miserable woman, no peace day or night! Vipers, basilisks, accursed Herods, may you suffer the same in the world to come! I am going to-morrow! I am a maiden lady and I won't allow you to stand before me in your underclothes! How dare you look at me when I am not dressed!"

And she went on and on. . . . Knowing that when Dashenka was enraged there was no moving her with prayers or vows or even by firing a cannon, Strizhin waved his hand in despair, dressed, and made up his mind to go to the doctor. But a doctor is only readily found when he is not wanted. After running through three streets and ringing five times at Dr. Tchepharyants's, and seven times at Dr. Bultyhin's, Strizhin raced off to a chemist's shop, thinking possibly the chemist could help him. There, after a long interval, a little dark and curly-headed chemist came out to him in his dressing gown, with drowsy eyes, and such a wise and serious face that it was positively terrifying.

"What do you want?" he asked in a tone in which only very wise and dignified chemists of Jewish persuasion can speak.

"For God's sake . . . I entreat you . . ." said Strizhin breathlessly, "give me something. I have just accidentally drunk paraffin, I am dying!"

"I beg you not to excite yourself and to answer the questions I am about to put to you. The very fact that you are excited prevents me from understanding you. You have drunk paraffin. Yes?"

"Yes, paraffin! Please save me!"

The chemist went coolly and gravely to the desk, opened a book, became absorbed in reading it. After reading a couple of pages he shrugged one shoulder and then the other, made a contemptuous grimace and, after thinking for a minute, went into the adjoining room. The clock struck four, and when it pointed to ten minutes past the chemist came back with another book and again plunged into reading.

"H'm," he said as though puzzled, "the very fact that you feel unwell shows you ought to apply to a doctor, not a chemist."

"But I have been to the doctors already. I could not ring them up."

"H'm . . . you don't regard us chemists as human beings, and disturb our rest even at four o'clock at night, though every dog, every cat, can rest in peace. . . . You don't try to understand anything, and to your thinking we are not people and our nerves are like cords."

Strizhin listened to the chemist, heaved a sigh, and went home.

"So I am fated to die," he thought.

And in his mouth was a burning and a taste of paraffin, there were twinges in his stomach, and a sound of boom, boom, boom in his ears. Every moment it seemed to him that his end was near, that his heart was no longer beating.

Returning home he made haste to write: "Let no one be blamed for my death," then he said his prayers, lay down and pulled the bedclothes over his head. He lay awake till morning expecting death, and all the time he kept fancying how his grave would be covered with fresh green grass and how the birds would twitter over it. . . ."

And in the morning he was sitting on his bed, saying with a smile to Dashenka:

"One who leads a steady and regular life, dear sister, is unaffected by any poison. Take me, for example. I have been on the verge of death. I was dying and in agony, yet now I am all right. There is only a burning in my mouth and a soreness in my throat, but I am all right all over, thank God. . . . And why? It's because of my regular life."

"No, it's because it's inferior paraffin!" sighed Dashenka, thinking of the household expenses and gazing into space. "The man at the shop could not have given me the best quality, but that at three farthings. I am a martyr, I am a miserable woman. You monsters! May you suffer the same, in the world to come, accursed Herods. . . ."

And she went on and on. . . .

VEROTCHKA

Ivan Alexeyitch Ognev remembers how on that August evening he opened the glass door with a rattle and went out on to the verandah. He was wearing a light Inverness cape and a wide-brimmed straw hat, the very one that was lying with his top-boots in the dust under his bed. In one hand he had a big bundle of books and notebooks, in the other a thick knotted stick.

Behind the door, holding the lamp to show the way, stood the master of the house, Kuznetsov, a bald old man with a long grey beard, in a snow-white piqué jacket. The old man was smiling cordially and nodding his head.

"Good-bye, old fellow!" said Ognev.

Kuznetsov put the lamp on a little table and went out to the verandah. Two long narrow shadows moved down the steps towards the flower-beds, swayed to and fro, and leaned their heads on the trunks of the lime-trees.

"Good-bye and once more thank you, my dear fellow!" said Ivan Alexeyitch. "Thank you for your welcome, for your kindness, for your affection. . . . I shall never forget your hospitality as long as I live. You are so good, and your daughter is so good, and everyone here is so kind, so good-humoured and friendly . . . Such a splendid set of people that I don't know how to say what I feel!"

From excess of feeling and under the influence of the home-made wine he had just drunk, Ognev talked in a singing voice like a divinity student, and was so touched that he expressed his feelings not so much by words as by the blinking of his eyes and the twitching of his shoulders. Kuznetsov, who had also drunk a good deal and was touched, craned forward to the young man and kissed him.

"I've grown as fond of you as if I were your dog," Ognev went on. "I've been turning up here almost every day; I've stayed the night a dozen times. It's dreadful to think of all the home-made wine I've drunk. And thank you most of all for your co-operation and help. Without you I should have been busy here over my statistics till October. I shall put in my preface: 'I think it my duty to express my gratitude to the President of the District Zemstvo of N----, Kuznetsov, for his kind co-operation.' There is a brilliant future before statistics! My humble respects to Vera Gavrilovna, and tell the doctors, both the lawyers and your secretary, that I shall never forget their help! And now, old fellow, let us embrace one another and kiss for the last time!"

Ognev, limp with emotion, kissed the old man once more and began going down the steps. On the last step he looked round and asked: "Shall we meet again some day?"

"God knows!" said the old man. "Most likely not!"

"Yes, that's true! Nothing will tempt you to Petersburg and I am never likely to turn up in this district again. Well, good-bye!"

"You had better leave the books behind!" Kuznetsov called after him. "You don't want to drag such a weight with you. I would send them by a servant to-morrow!"

But Ognev was rapidly walking away from the house and was not listening. His heart, warmed by the wine, was brimming over with good-humour, friendliness, and sadness. He walked along thinking how frequently one met with good people, and what a pity it was that nothing was left of those meetings but memories. At times one catches a glimpse of cranes on the horizon, and a faint gust of wind brings their plaintive, ecstatic cry, and a minute later, however greedily one scans the blue distance, one cannot see a speck nor catch a sound; and like that, people with their faces and their words flit through our lives and are drowned in the past, leaving nothing except faint traces in the memory. Having been in the N---- District from the early spring, and having been almost every day at the friendly Kuznetsovs', Ivan Alexeyitch had become as much at home with the old man, his daughter, and the servants as though they were his own people; he had grown familiar with the whole house to the smallest detail, with the cosy verandah, the windings of the avenues, the silhouettes of the trees over the kitchen and the bath-house; but as soon as he was out of the gate all this would be changed to memory and would lose its meaning as reality for ever, and in a year or two all these dear images would grow as dim in his consciousness as stories he had read or things he had imagined.

"Nothing in life is so precious as people!" Ognev thought in his emotion, as he strode along the avenue to the gate. "Nothing!"

It was warm and still in the garden. There was a scent of the mignonette, of the tobacco-plants, and of the heliotrope, which were not yet over in the flower-beds. The spaces between the bushes and the tree-trunks were filled with a fine soft mist soaked through and through with moonlight, and, as Ognev long remembered, coils of mist that looked like phantoms slowly but perceptibly followed one another across the avenue. The moon stood high above the garden, and below it transparent patches of mist were floating eastward. The whole world seemed to consist of nothing but black silhouettes and wandering white shadows. Ognev, seeing the mist on a moonlight August evening almost for the first time in his life, imagined he was seeing, not nature, but a stage effect in which unskilful workmen, trying to light up the garden with white Bengal fire, hid behind the bushes and let off clouds of white smoke together with the light.

When Ognev reached the garden gate a dark shadow moved away from the low fence and came towards him.

"Vera Gavrilovna!" he said, delighted. "You here? And I have been looking everywhere for you; wanted to say good-bye. . . . Good-bye; I am going away!"

"So early? Why, it's only eleven o'clock."

"Yes, it's time I was off. I have a four-mile walk and then my packing. I must be up early to-morrow."

Before Ognev stood Kuznetsov's daughter Vera, a girl of one-and-twenty, as usual melancholy, carelessly dressed, and attractive. Girls who are dreamy and spend whole days lying down, lazily reading whatever they come across, who are bored and melancholy, are usually careless in their dress. To those of them who have been endowed by nature with taste and an instinct of beauty, the slight carelessness adds a special charm. When Ognev later on remembered her, he could not picture pretty Verotchka except in a full blouse which was crumpled in deep folds at the belt and yet did not touch her waist; without her hair done up high and a curl that had come loose from it on her forehead; without the knitted red shawl with ball fringe at the edge which hung disconsolately on Vera's shoulders in the evenings, like a flag on a windless day, and in the daytime lay about, crushed up, in the hall near the men's hats or on a box in the dining-room, where the old cat did not hesitate to sleep on it. This shawl and the folds of her blouse suggested a feeling of freedom and laziness, of good-nature and sitting at home. Perhaps because Vera attracted Ognev he saw in every frill and button something warm, naïve, cosy, something nice and poetical, just what is lacking in cold, insincere women that have no instinct for beauty.

Verotchka had a good figure, a regular profile, and beautiful curly hair. Ognev, who had seen few women in his life, thought her a beauty.

"I am going away," he said as he took leave of her at the gate. "Don't remember evil against me! Thank you for everything!"

In the same singing divinity student's voice in which he had talked to her father, with the same blinking and twitching of his shoulders, he began thanking Vera for her hospitality, kindness, and friendliness.

"I've written about you in every letter to my mother," he said. "If everyone were like you and your dad, what a jolly place the world would be! You are such a splendid set of people! All such genuine, friendly people with no nonsense about you."

"Where are you going to now?" asked Vera.

"I am going now to my mother's at Oryol; I shall be a fortnight with her, and then back to Petersburg and work."

"And then?"

"And then? I shall work all the winter and in the spring go somewhere into the provinces again to collect material. Well, be happy, live a hundred years . . . don't remember evil against me. We shall not see each other again."

Ognev stooped down and kissed Vera's hand. Then, in silent emotion, he straightened his cape, shifted his bundle of books to a more comfortable position, paused, and said:

"What a lot of mist!"

"Yes. Have you left anything behind?"

"No, I don't think so. . . ."

For some seconds Ognev stood in silence, then he moved clumsily towards the gate and went out of the garden.

"Stay; I'll see you as far as our wood," said Vera, following him out.

They walked along the road. Now the trees did not obscure the view, and one could see the sky and the distance. As though covered with a veil all nature was hidden in a transparent, colourless haze through which her beauty peeped gaily; where the mist was thicker and whiter it lay heaped unevenly about the stones, stalks, and bushes or drifted in coils over the road, clung close to the earth and seemed trying not to conceal the view. Through the haze they could see all the road as far as the wood, with dark ditches at the sides and tiny bushes which grew in the ditches and caught the straying wisps of mist. Half a mile from the gate they saw the dark patch of Kuznetsov's wood.

"Why has she come with me? I shall have to see her back," thought Ognev, but looking at her profile he gave a friendly smile and said: "One doesn't want to go away in such lovely weather. It's quite a romantic evening, with the moon, the stillness, and all the etceteras. Do you know, Vera Gavrilovna, here I have lived twenty-nine years in the world and never had a romance. No romantic episode in my whole life, so that I only know by hearsay of rendezvous, 'avenues of sighs,' and kisses. It's not normal! In town, when one sits in one's lodgings, one does not notice the blank, but here in the fresh air one feels it. . . . One resents it!"

"Why is it?"

"I don't know. I suppose I've never had time, or perhaps it was I have never met women who. . . . In fact, I have very few acquaintances and never go anywhere."

For some three hundred paces the young people walked on in silence. Ognev kept glancing at Verotchka's bare head and shawl, and days of spring and summer rose to his mind one after another. It had been a period when far from his grey Petersburg lodgings, enjoying the friendly warmth of kind people, nature, and the work he loved, he had not had time to notice how the sunsets followed the glow of dawn, and how, one after another foretelling the end of summer, first the nightingale ceased singing, then the quail, then a little later the landrail. The days slipped by unnoticed, so that life must have been happy and easy. He began calling aloud how reluctantly he, poor and unaccustomed to change of scene and society, had come at the end of April to the N---- District, where he had expected dreariness, loneliness, and indifference to statistics, which he considered was now the foremost among the sciences. When he arrived on an April morning at the little town of N---- he had put up at the inn kept by Ryabuhin, the Old Believer, where for twenty kopecks a day they had given him a light, clean room on condition that he should not smoke indoors. After resting and finding who was the president of the District Zemstvo, he had set off at once on foot to Kuznetsov. He had to walk three miles through lush meadows and young copses. Larks were hovering in the clouds, filling the air with silvery notes, and rooks flapping their wings with sedate dignity floated over the green cornland.

"Good heavens!" Ognev had thought in wonder; can it be that there's always air like this to breathe here, or is this scent only to-day, in honour of my coming?"

Expecting a cold business-like reception, he went in to Kuznetsov's diffidently, looking up from under his eyebrows and shyly pulling his beard. At first Kuznetsov wrinkled up his brows and could not understand what use the Zemstvo could be to the young man and his statistics; but when the latter explained at length what was material for statistics and how such material was collected, Kuznetsov brightened, smiled, and with childish curiosity began looking at his notebooks. On the evening of the same day Ivan Alexeyitch was already sitting at supper with the Kuznetsovs, was rapidly becoming exhilarated by their strong home-made wine, and looking at the calm faces and lazy movements of his new acquaintances, felt all over that sweet, drowsy indolence which makes one want to sleep and stretch and smile; while his new acquaintances looked at him good-naturedly and asked him whether his father and mother were living, how much he earned a month, how often he went to the theatre. . . .

Ognev recalled his expeditions about the neighbourhood, the picnics, the fishing parties, the visit of the whole party to the convent to see the Mother Superior Marfa, who had given each of the visitors a bead purse; he recalled the hot, endless typically Russian arguments in which the opponents, spluttering and banging the table with their fists, misunderstand and interrupt one another, unconsciously contradict themselves at every phrase, continually change the subject, and after arguing for two or three hours, laugh and say: "Goodness knows what we have been arguing about! Beginning with one thing and going on to another!"

"And do you remember how the doctor and you and I rode to Shestovo?" said Ivan Alexeyitch to Vera as they reached the copse. "It was there that the crazy saint met us: I gave him a five-kopeck piece, and he crossed himself three times and flung it into the rye. Good heavens! I am carrying away such a mass of memories that if I could gather them together into a whole it would make a good nugget of gold! I don't understand why clever, perceptive people crowd into Petersburg and Moscow and don't come here. Is there more truth and freedom in the Nevsky and in the big damp houses than here? Really, the idea of artists, scientific men, and journalists all living crowded together in furnished rooms has always seemed to me a mistake."

Twenty paces from the copse the road was crossed by a small narrow bridge with posts at the corners, which had always served as a resting-place for the Kuznetsovs and their guests on their evening walks. From there those who liked could mimic the forest echo, and one could see the road vanish in the dark woodland track.

"Well, here is the bridge!" said Ognev. "Here you must turn back."

Vera stopped and drew a breath.

"Let us sit down," she said, sitting down on one of the posts. "People generally sit down when they say good-bye before starting on a journey."

Ognev settled himself beside her on his bundle of books and went on talking. She was breathless from the walk, and was looking, not at Ivan Alexeyitch, but away into the distance so that he could not see her face.

"And what if we meet in ten years' time?" he said. "What shall we be like then? You will be by then the respectable mother of a family, and I shall be the author of some weighty statistical work of no use to anyone, as thick as forty thousand such works. We shall meet and think of old days. . . . Now we are conscious of the present; it absorbs and excites us, but when we meet we shall not remember the day, nor the month, nor even the year in which we saw each other for the last time on this bridge. You will be changed, perhaps. . . . Tell me, will you be different?"

Vera started and turned her face towards him.

"What?" she asked.

"I asked you just now. . . ."

"Excuse me, I did not hear what you were saying."

Only then Ognev noticed a change in Vera. She was pale, breathing fast, and the tremor in her breathing affected her hands and lips and head, and not one curl as usual, but two, came loose and fell on her forehead. . . . Evidently she avoided looking him in the face, and, trying to mask her emotion, at one moment fingered her collar, which seemed to be rasping her neck, at another pulled her red shawl from one shoulder to the other.

"I am afraid you are cold," said Ognev. "It's not at all wise to sit in the mist. Let me see you back *nach-haus*."

Vera sat mute.

"What is the matter?" asked Ognev, with a smile. "You sit silent and don't answer my questions. Are you cross, or don't you feel well?"

Vera pressed the palm of her hand to the cheek nearest to Ognev, and then abruptly jerked it away.

"An awful position!" she murmured, with a look of pain on her face. "Awful!"

"How is it awful?" asked Ognev, shrugging his shoulders and not concealing his surprise. "What's the matter?"

Still breathing hard and twitching her shoulders, Vera turned her back to him, looked at the sky for half a minute, and said:

"There is something I must say to you, Ivan Alexeyitch. . . ."

"I am listening."

"It may seem strange to you. . . . You will be surprised, but I don't care. . . ."

Ognev shrugged his shoulders once more and prepared himself to listen.

"You see . . ." Verotchka began, bowing her head and fingering a ball on the fringe of her shawl. "You see . . . this is what I wanted to tell you. . . . You'll think it strange . . . and silly, but I . . . can't bear it any longer."

Vera's words died away in an indistinct mutter and were suddenly cut short by tears. The girl hid her face in her handkerchief, bent lower than ever, and wept bitterly. Ivan Alexeyitch cleared his throat in confusion and looked about him hopelessly, at his wits' end, not knowing what to say or do. Being unused to the sight of tears, he felt his own eyes, too, beginning to smart.

"Well, what next!" he muttered helplessly. "Vera Gavrilovna, what's this for, I should like to know? My dear girl, are you . . . are you ill? Or has someone been nasty to you? Tell me, perhaps I could, so to say . . . help you. . . ."

When, trying to console her, he ventured cautiously to remove her hands from her face, she smiled at him through her tears and said:

"I . . . love you!"

These words, so simple and ordinary, were uttered in ordinary human language, but Ognev, in acute embarrassment, turned away from Vera, and got up, while his confusion was followed by terror.

The sad, warm, sentimental mood induced by leave-taking and the home-made wine suddenly vanished, and gave place to an acute and unpleasant feeling of awkwardness. He felt an inward revulsion; he looked askance at Vera, and now that by declaring her love for him she had cast off the aloofness which so adds to a woman's charm, she seemed to him, as it were, shorter, plainer, more ordinary.

"What's the meaning of it?" he thought with horror. "But I . . . do I love her or not? That's the question!"

And she breathed easily and freely now that the worst and most difficult thing was said. She, too, got up, and looking Ivan Alexeyitch straight in the face, began talking rapidly, warmly, irrepressibly.

As a man suddenly panic-stricken cannot afterwards remember the succession of sounds accompanying the catastrophe that overwhelmed him, so Ognev cannot remember Vera's words and phrases. He can only recall the meaning of what she said, and the sensation her words evoked in him. He remembers her voice, which seemed stifled and husky with emotion, and the extraordinary music and passion of her intonation. Laughing, crying with tears glistening on her eyelashes, she told him that from the first day of their acquaintance he had struck her by his originality, his intelligence, his kind intelligent eyes, by his work and objects in life; that she loved him passionately, deeply, madly; that when coming into the house from the garden in the summer she saw his cape in the hall or heard his voice in the distance, she felt a cold shudder at her heart, a foreboding of happiness; even his slightest jokes had made her laugh; in every figure in his note-books she saw something extraordinarily wise and grand; his knotted stick seemed to her more beautiful than the trees.

The copse and the wisps of mist and the black ditches at the side of the road seemed hushed listening to her, whilst something strange and unpleasant was passing in Ognev's heart. . . . Telling him of her love, Vera was enchantingly beautiful; she spoke eloquently and passionately, but he felt neither pleasure nor gladness, as he would have liked to; he felt nothing but compassion for Vera, pity and regret that a good girl should be distressed on his account. Whether he was affected by generalizations from reading or by the insuperable habit of looking at things objectively, which so often hinders people from living, but Vera's ecstasies and suffering struck him as affected, not to be taken seriously, and at the same time rebellious feeling whispered to him that all he was hearing and seeing now, from the point of view of nature and personal happiness, was more important than any statistics and books and truths. . . . And he raged and blamed himself, though he did not understand exactly where he was in fault.

To complete his embarrassment, he was absolutely at a loss what to say, and yet something he must say. To say bluntly, "I don't love you," was beyond him, and he could not bring himself to say "Yes," because however much he rummaged in his heart he could not find one spark of feeling in it. . . .

He was silent, and she meanwhile was saying that for her there was no greater happiness than to see him, to follow him wherever he liked this very moment, to be his wife and helper, and that if he went away from her she would die of misery.

"I cannot stay here!" she said, wringing her hands. "I am sick of the house and this wood and the air. I cannot bear the everlasting peace and aimless life, I can't endure our colourless, pale people, who are all as like one another as two drops of water! They are all good-natured and warm-hearted because they are all well-fed and know nothing of struggle or suffering, . . . I want to be in those big damp houses where people suffer, embittered by work and need. . ."

And this, too, seemed to Ognev affected and not to be taken seriously. When Vera had finished he still did not know what to say, but it was impossible to be silent, and he muttered:

"Vera Gavrilovna, I am very grateful to you, though I feel I've done nothing to deserve such . . . feeling . . . on your part. Besides, as an honest man I ought to tell you that . . . happiness depends on equality -- that is, when both parties are . . . equally in love. . . ."

But he was immediately ashamed of his mutterings and ceased. He felt that his face at that moment looked stupid, guilty, blank, that it was strained and affected. . . . Vera must have been able to read the truth on his countenance, for she suddenly became grave, turned pale, and bent her head.

"You must forgive me," Ognev muttered, not able to endure the silence. "I respect you so much that . . . it pains me. . . ."

Vera turned sharply and walked rapidly homewards. Ognev followed her.

"No, don't!" said Vera, with a wave of her hand. "Don't come; I can go alone."

"Oh, yes . . . I must see you home anyway."

Whatever Ognev said, it all to the last word struck him as loathsome and flat. The feeling of guilt grew greater at every step. He raged inwardly, clenched his fists, and cursed his coldness and his stupidity with women. Trying to stir his feelings, he looked at Verotchka's beautiful figure, at her hair and the traces of her little feet on the dusty road; he remembered her words and her tears, but all that only touched his heart and did not quicken his pulse.

"Ach! one can't force oneself to love," he assured himself, and at the same time he thought, "But shall I ever fall in love without? I am nearly thirty! I have never met anyone better than Vera and I never shall. . . . Oh, this premature old age! Old age at thirty!"

Vera walked on in front more and more rapidly, without looking back at him or raising her head. It seemed to him that sorrow had made her thinner and narrower in the shoulders.

"I can imagine what's going on in her heart now!" he thought, looking at her back. "She must be ready to die with shame and mortification! My God, there's so much life, poetry, and meaning in it that it would move a stone, and I . . . I am stupid and absurd!"

At the gate Vera stole a glance at him, and, shrugging and wrapping her shawl round her walked rapidly away down the avenue.

Ivan Alexeyitch was left alone. Going back to the copse, he walked slowly, continually standing still and looking round at the gate with an expression in his whole figure that suggested that he could not believe his own memory. He looked for Vera's footprints on the road, and could not believe that the girl who had so attracted him had just declared her love, and that he had so clumsily and bluntly "refused" her. For the first time in his life it was his lot to learn by experience how little that a man does depends on his own will, and to suffer in his own person the feelings of a decent kindly man who has against his will caused his neighbour cruel, undeserved anguish.

His conscience tormented him, and when Vera disappeared he felt as though he had lost something very precious, something very near and dear which he could never find again. He felt that with Vera a part of his youth had slipped away from him, and that the moments which he had passed through so fruitlessly would never be repeated.

When he reached the bridge he stopped and sank into thought. He wanted to discover the reason of his strange coldness. That it was due to something within him and not outside himself was clear to him. He frankly acknowledged to himself that it was not the intellectual coldness of which clever people so often boast, not the coldness of a conceited fool, but simply impotence of soul, incapacity for being moved by beauty, premature old age brought on by education, his casual existence, struggling for a livelihood, his homeless life in lodgings. From the bridge he walked slowly, as it were reluctantly, into the wood. Here, where in the dense black darkness glaring patches of moonlight gleamed here and there, where he felt nothing except his thoughts, he longed passionately to regain what he had lost.

And Ivan Alexeyitch remembers that he went back again. Urging himself on with his memories, forcing himself to picture Vera, he strode rapidly towards the garden. There was no mist by then along the road or in the garden, and the bright moon looked down from the sky as though it had just been washed; only the eastern sky was dark and misty. . . . Ognev remembers his cautious steps, the dark windows, the heavy scent of heliotrope and mignonette. His old friend Karo, wagging his tail amicably, came up to him and sniffed his hand. This was the one living creature who saw him walk two or three times round the house, stand near Vera's dark window, and with a deep sigh and a wave of his hand walk out of the garden.

An hour later he was in the town, and, worn out and exhausted, leaned his body and hot face against the gatepost of the inn as he knocked at the gate. Somewhere in the town a dog barked sleepily, and as though in response to his knock, someone clanged the hour on an iron plate near the church.

"You prowl about at night," grumbled his host, the Old Believer, opening the door to him, in a long nightgown like a woman's. "You had better be saying your prayers instead of prowling about."

When Ivan Alexeyitch reached his room he sank on the bed and gazed a long, long time at the light. Then he tossed his head and began packing.

SHROVE TUESDAY

"Pavel Vassilitch!" cries Pelageya Ivanovna, waking her husband. "Pavel Vassilitch! You might go and help Styopa with his lessons, he is sitting crying over his book. He can't understand something again!"

Pavel Vassilitch gets up, makes the sign of the cross over his mouth as he yawns, and says softly: "In a minute, my love!"

The cat who has been asleep beside him gets up too, straightens out its tail, arches its spine, and half-shuts its eyes. There is stillness. . . . Mice can be heard scurrying behind the wall-paper. Putting on his boots and his dressing-gown, Pavel Vassilitch, crumpled and frowning from sleepiness, comes out of his bedroom into the dining-room; on his entrance another cat, engaged in sniffing a marinade of fish in the window, jumps down to the floor, and hides behind the cupboard.

"Who asked you to sniff that!" he says angrily, covering the fish with a sheet of newspaper. "You are a pig to do that, not a cat. . . ."

From the dining-room there is a door leading into the nursery. There, at a table covered with stains and deep scratches, sits Styopa, a high-school boy in the second class, with a peevish expression of face and tear-stained eyes. With his knees raised almost to his chin, and his hands clasped round them, he is swaying to and fro like a Chinese idol and looking crossly at a sum book.

"Are you working?" asks Pavel Vassilitch, sitting down to the table and yawning. "Yes, my boy. . . . We have enjoyed ourselves, slept, and eaten pancakes, and to-morrow comes Lenten fare, repentance, and going to work. Every period of time has its limits. Why are your eyes so red? Are you sick of learning your lessons? To be sure, after pancakes, lessons are nasty to swallow. That's about it."

"What are you laughing at the child for?" Pelageya Ivanovna calls from the next room. "You had better show him instead of laughing at him. He'll get a one again to-morrow, and make me miserable."

"What is it you don't understand?" Pavel Vassilitch asks Styopa.

"Why this . . . division of fractions," the boy answers crossly. "The division of fractions by fractions. . . ."

"H'm . . . queer boy! What is there in it? There's nothing to understand in it. Learn the rules, and that's all. . . . To divide a fraction by a fraction you must multiply the numerator of the first fraction by the denominator of the second, and that will be the numerator of the quotient. . . . In this case, the numerator of the first fraction. . . ."

"I know that without your telling me," Styopa interrupts him, flicking a walnut shell off the table. "Show me the proof."

"The proof? Very well, give me a pencil. Listen. . . . Suppose we want to divide seven eighths by two fifths. Well, the point of it is, my boy, that it's required to divide these fractions by each other. . . . Have they set the samovar?"

"I don't know."

"It's time for tea. . . . It's past seven. Well, now listen. We will look at it like this. . . . Suppose we want to divide seven eighths not by two fifths but by two, that is, by the numerator only. We divide it, what do we get?

"Seven sixteenths."

"Right. Bravo! Well, the trick of it is, my boy, that if we . . . so if we have divided it by two then. . . . Wait a bit, I am getting muddled. I remember when I was at school, the teacher of arithmetic was called Sigismund Urbanitch, a Pole. He used to get into a muddle over every lesson. He would begin explaining some theory, get in a tangle, and turn crimson all over and race up and down the class-room as though someone were sticking an awl in his back, then he would blow his nose half a dozen times and begin to cry. But you know we were magnanimous to him, we pretended not to see it. 'What is it, Sigismund Urbanitch?' we used to ask him. 'Have you got toothache?' And what a set of young ruffians, regular cut-throats, we were, but yet we were magnanimous, you know! There weren't any boys like you in my day, they were all great hulking fellows, great strapping louts, one taller than another. For instance, in our third class, there was Mamahin. My goodness, he was a solid chap! You know, a regular maypole, seven feet high. When he moved, the floor shook; when he brought his great fist down on your back, he would knock the breath out of your body! Not only we boys, but even the teachers were afraid of him. So this Mamahin used to . . ."

Pelageya Ivanovna's footsteps are heard through the door. Pavel Vassilitch winks towards the door and says:

"There's mother coming. Let's get to work. Well, so you see, my boy," he says, raising his voice. "This fraction has to be multiplied by that one. Well, and to do that you have to take the numerator of the first fraction. . ."

"Come to tea!" cries Pelageya Ivanovna. Pavel Vassilitch and his son abandon arithmetic and go in to tea. Pelageya Ivanovna is already sitting at the table with an aunt who never speaks, another aunt who is deaf and dumb, and Granny Markovna, a midwife who had helped Styopa into the world. The samovar is hissing and puffing out steam which throws flickering shadows on the ceiling. The cats come in from the entry sleepy and melancholy with their tails in the air. . . .

"Have some jam with your tea, Markovna," says Pelageya Ivanovna, addressing the midwife. "To-morrow the great fast begins. Eat well to-day."

Markovna takes a heaped spoonful of jam hesitatingly as though it were a powder, raises it to her lips, and with a sidelong look at Pavel Vassilitch, eats it; at once her face is overspread with a sweet smile, as sweet as the jam itself.

"The jam is particularly good," she says. "Did you make it yourself, Pelageya Ivanovna, ma'am?"

"Yes. Who else is there to do it? I do everything myself. Styopotchka, have I given you your tea too weak? Ah, you have drunk it already. Pass your cup, my angel; let me give you some more."

"So this Mamahin, my boy, could not bear the French master," Pavel Vassilitch goes on, addressing his son. " 'I am a nobleman,' he used to shout, 'and I won't allow a Frenchman to lord it over me! We beat the French in 1812!' Well, of course they used to thrash him for it . . .

thrash him dre-ead-fully, and sometimes when he saw they were meaning to thrash him, he would jump out of window, and off he would go! Then for five or six days afterwards he would not show himself at the school. His mother would come to the head-master and beg him for God's sake: 'Be so kind, sir, as to find my Mishka, and flog him, the rascal!' And the head-master would say to her: 'Upon my word, madam, our five porters aren't a match for him!' "

"Good heavens, to think of such ruffians being born," whispers Pelageya Ivanovna, looking at her husband in horror. "What a trial for the poor mother!"

A silence follows. Styopa yawns loudly, and scrutinises the Chinaman on the tea-caddy whom he has seen a thousand times already. Markovna and the two aunts sip tea carefully out of their saucers. The air is still and stifling from the stove. . . . Faces and gestures betray the sloth and repletion that comes when the stomach is full, and yet one must go on eating. The samovar, the cups, and the table-cloth are cleared away, but still the family sits on at the table. . . . Pelageya Ivanovna is continually jumping up and, with an expression of alarm on her face, running off into the kitchen, to talk to the cook about the supper. The two aunts go on sitting in the same position immovably, with their arms folded across their bosoms and doze, staring with their pewtery little eyes at the lamp. Markovna hiccups every minute and asks:

"Why is it I have the hiccups? I don't think I have eaten anything to account for it . . . nor drunk anything either. . . . Hic!"

Pavel Vassilitch and Styopa sit side by side, with their heads touching, and, bending over the table, examine a volume of the "Neva" for 1878.

" 'The monument of Leonardo da Vinci, facing the gallery of Victor Emmanuel at Milan.' I say! . . . After the style of a triumphal arch. . . . A cavalier with his lady. . . . And there are little men in the distance. . . ."

"That little man is like a schoolfellow of mine called Niskubin," says Styopa.

"Turn over. . . . 'The proboscis of the common house-fly seen under the microscope.' So that's a proboscis! I say -- a fly. Whatever would a bug look like under a microscope, my boy? Wouldn't it be horrid!"

The old-fashioned clock in the drawing-room does not strike, but coughs ten times huskily as though it had a cold. The cook, Anna, comes into the dining-room, and plumps down at the master's feet.

"Forgive me, for Christ's sake, Pavel Vassilitch!" she says, getting up, flushed all over.

"You forgive me, too, for Christ's sake," Pavel Vassilitch responds unconcernedly.

In the same manner, Anna goes up to the other members of the family, plumps down at their feet, and begs forgiveness. She only misses out Markovna to whom, not being one of the gentry, she does not feel it necessary to bow down.

Another half-hour passes in stillness and tranquillity. The "Neva" is by now lying on the sofa, and Pavel Vassilitch, holding up his finger, repeats by heart some Latin verses he has learned in his childhood. Styopa stares at the finger with the wedding ring, listens to the unintelligible words, and dozes; he rubs his eyelids with his fists, and they shut all the tighter.

"I am going to bed . . ." he says, stretching and yawning.

"What, to bed?" says Pelageya Ivanovna. "What about supper before the fast?"

"I don't want any."

"Are you crazy?" says his mother in alarm. "How can you go without your supper before the fast? You'll have nothing but Lenten food all through the fast!"

Pavel Vassilitch is scared too.

"Yes, yes, my boy," he says. "For seven weeks mother will give you nothing but Lenten food. You can't miss the last supper before the fast."

"Oh dear, I am sleepy," says Styopa peevishly.

"Since that is how it is, lay the supper quickly," Pavel Vassilitch cries in a fluster. "Anna, why are you sitting there, silly? Make haste and lay the table."

Pelageya Ivanovna clasps her hands and runs into the kitchen with an expression as though the house were on fire.

"Make haste, make haste," is heard all over the house. "Styopotchka is sleepy. Anna! Oh dear me, what is one to do? Make haste."

Five minutes later the table is laid. Again the cats, arching their spines, and stretching themselves with their tails in the air, come into the dining-room. . . . The family begin supper. . . . No one is hungry, everyone's stomach is overfull, but yet they must eat.

A DEFENCELESS CREATURE

In spite of a violent attack of gout in the night and the nervous exhaustion left by it, Kistunov went in the morning to his office and began punctually seeing the clients of the bank and persons who had come with petitions. He looked languid and exhausted, and spoke in a faint voice hardly above a whisper, as though he were dying.

"What can I do for you?" he asked a lady in an antediluvian mantle, whose back view was extremely suggestive of a huge dung-beetle.

"You see, your Excellency," the petitioner in question began, speaking rapidly, "my husband Shtchukin, a collegiate assessor, was ill for five months, and while he, if you will excuse my saying so, was laid up at home, he was for no sort of reason dismissed, your Excellency; and when I went for his salary they deducted, if you please, your Excellency, twenty-four roubles thirty-six kopecks from his salary. 'What for?' I asked. 'He borrowed from the club fund,' they told me, 'and the other clerks had stood security for him.' How was that? How could he have borrowed it without my consent? It's impossible, your Excellency. What's the reason of it? I am a poor woman, I earn my bread by taking in lodgers. I am a weak, defenceless woman . . . I have to put up with ill-usage from everyone and never hear a kind word. . ."

The petitioner was blinking, and dived into her mantle for her handkerchief. Kistunov took her petition from her and began reading it.

"Excuse me, what's this?" he asked, shrugging his shoulders. "I can make nothing of it. Evidently you have come to the wrong place, madam. Your petition has nothing to do with us at all. You will have to apply to the department in which your husband was employed."

"Why, my dear sir, I have been to five places already, and they would not even take the petition anywhere," said Madame Shtchukin. "I'd quite lost my head, but, thank goodness -- God bless him for it -- my son-in-law, Boris Matveyitch, advised me to come to you. 'You go to Mr. Kistunov, mamma: he is an influential man, he can do anything for you. . . .' Help me, your Excellency!"

"We can do nothing for you, Madame Shtchukin. You must understand: your husband served in the Army Medical Department, and our establishment is a purely private commercial undertaking, a bank. Surely you must understand that!"

Kistunov shrugged his shoulders again and turned to a gentleman in a military uniform, with a swollen face.

"Your Excellency," piped Madame Shtchukin in a pitiful voice, " I have the doctor's certificate that my husband was ill! Here it is, if you will kindly look at it."

"Very good, I believe you," Kistunov said irritably, "but I repeat it has nothing to do with us. It's queer and positively absurd! Surely your husband must know where you are to apply?"

"He knows nothing, your Excellency. He keeps on: 'It's not your business! Get away!' -- that's all I can get out of him. . . . Whose business is it, then? It's I have to keep them all!"

Kistunov again turned to Madame Shtchukin and began explaining to her the difference between the Army Medical Department and a private bank. She listened attentively, nodded in token of assent, and said:

"Yes . . . yes . . . yes . . . I understand, sir. In that case, your Excellency, tell them to pay me fifteen roubles at least! I agree to take part on account!

"Ough!" sighed Kistunov, letting his head drop back. "There's no making you see reason. Do understand that to apply to us with such a petition is as strange as to send in a petition concerning divorce, for instance, to a chemist's or to the Assaying Board. You have not been paid your due, but what have we to do with it?"

"Your Excellency, make me remember you in my prayers for the rest of my days, have pity on a lone, lorn woman," wailed Madame Shtchukin; "I am a weak, defenceless woman. . . . I am worried to death, I've to settle with the lodgers and see to my husband's affairs and fly round looking after the house, and I am going to church every day this week, and my son-in-law is out of a job. . . . I might as well not eat or drink. . . . I can scarcely keep on my feet. . . . I haven't slept all night. . . ."

Kistunov was conscious of the palpitation of his heart. With a face of anguish, pressing his hand on his heart, he began explaining to Madame Shtchukin again, but his voice failed him.

"No, excuse me, I cannot talk to you," he said with a wave of his hand. "My head's going round. You are hindering us and wasting your time. Ough! Alexey Nikolaitch," he said, addressing one of his clerks, "please will you explain to Madame Shtchukin?"

Kistunov, passing by all the petitioners, went to his private room and signed about a dozen papers while Alexey Nikolaitch was still engaged with Madame Shtchukin. As he sat in his room Kistunov heard two voices: the monotonous, restrained bass of Alexey Nikolaitch and the shrill, wailing voice of Madame Shtchukin.

"I am a weak, defenceless woman, I am a woman in delicate health," said Madame Shtchukin. "I look strong, but if you were to overhaul me there is not one healthy fibre in me. I can scarcely keep on my feet, and my appetite is gone. . . . I drank my cup of coffee this morning without the slightest relish. . . ."

Alexey Nikolaitch explained to her the difference between the departments and the complicated system of sending in papers. He was soon exhausted, and his place was taken by the accountant.

"A wonderfully disagreeable woman!" said Kistunov, revolted, nervously cracking his fingers and continually going to the decanter of water. "She's a perfect idiot! She's worn me out and she'll exhaust them, the nasty creature! Ough! . . . my heart is throbbing."

Half an hour later he rang his bell. Alexey Nikolaitch made his appearance.

"How are things going?" Kistunov asked languidly.

"We can't make her see anything, Pyotr Alexandritch! We are simply done. We talk of one thing and she talks of something else."

"I . . . I can't stand the sound of her voice. . . . I am ill. . . . I can't bear it."

"Send for the porter, Pyotr Alexandritch, let him put her out."

"No, no," cried Kistunov in alarm. "She will set up a squeal, and there are lots of flats in this building, and goodness knows what they would think of us. . . . Do try and explain to her, my dear fellow. . . ."

A minute later the deep drone of Alexey Nikolaitch's voice was audible again. A quarter of an hour passed, and instead of his bass there was the murmur of the accountant's powerful tenor."

"Re-mark-ably nasty woman," Kistunov thought indignantly, nervously shrugging his shoulders. "No more brains than a sheep. I believe that's a twinge of the gout again. . . . My migraine is coming back. . . ."

In the next room Alexey Nikolaitch, at the end of his resources, at last tapped his finger on the table and then on his own forehead.

"The fact of the matter is you haven't a head on your shoulders," he said, "but this."

"Come, come," said the old lady, offended. "Talk to your own wife like that. . . . You screw! . . . Don't be too free with your hands."

And looking at her with fury, with exasperation, as though he would devour her, Alexey Nikolaitch said in a quiet, stifled voice:

"Clear out."

"Wha-at?" squealed Madame Shtchukin. "How dare you? I am a weak, defenceless woman; I won't endure it. My husband is a collegiate assessor. You screw! . . . I will go to Dmitri Karlitch, the lawyer, and there will be nothing left of you! I've had the law of three lodgers, and I will make you flop down at my feet for your saucy words! I'll go to your general. Your Excellency, your Excellency!"

"Be off, you pest," hissed Alexey Nikolaitch.

Kistunov opened his door and looked into the office.

"What is it?" he asked in a tearful voice.

Madame Shtchukin, as red as a crab, was standing in the middle of the room, rolling her eyes and prodding the air with her fingers. The bank clerks were standing round red in the face too, and, evidently harassed, were looking at each other distractedly.

"Your Excellency," cried Madame Shtchukin, pouncing upon Kistunov. "Here, this man, he here . . . this man . . ." (she pointed to Alexey Nikolaitch) "tapped himself on the forehead and then tapped the table. . . . You told him to go into my case, and he's jeering at me! I am a weak, defenceless woman. . . . My husband is a collegiate assessor, and I am a major's daughter myself!"

"Very good, madam," moaned Kistunov. "I will go into it . . . I will take steps. . . . Go away . . . later!"

"And when shall I get the money, your Excellency? I need it to-day!"

Kistunov passed his trembling hand over his forehead, heaved a sigh, and began explaining again.

"Madam, I have told you already this is a bank, a private commercial establishment. . . . What do you want of us? And do understand that you are hindering us."

Madame Shtchukin listened to him and sighed.

"To be sure, to be sure," she assented. "Only, your Excellency, do me the kindness, make me pray for you for the rest of my life, be a father, protect me! If a medical certificate is not enough I can produce an affidavit from the police. . . . Tell them to give me the money."

Everything began swimming before Kistunov's eyes. He breathed out all the air in his lungs in a prolonged sigh and sank helpless on a chair.

"How much do you want?" he asked in a weak voice.

"Twenty-four roubles and thirty-six kopecks."

Kistunov took his pocket-book out of his pocket, extracted a twenty-five rouble note and gave it to Madame Shtchukin.

"Take it and . . . and go away!"

Madame Shtchukin wrapped the money up in her handkerchief, put it away, and pursing up her face into a sweet, mincing, even coquettish smile, asked:

"Your Excellency, and would it be possible for my husband to get a post again?"

"I am going . . . I am ill . . ." said Kistunov in a weary voice. "I have dreadful palpitations."

When he had driven home Alexey Nikolaitch sent Nikita for some laurel drops, and, after taking twenty drops each, all the clerks set to work, while Madame Shtchukin stayed another two hours in the vestibule, talking to the porter and waiting for Kistunov to return. . . .

She came again next day.

A BAD BUSINESS

"Who goes there?"

No answer. The watchman sees nothing, but through the roar of the wind and the trees distinctly hears someone walking along the avenue ahead of him. A March night, cloudy and foggy, envelopes the earth, and it seems to the watchman that the earth, the sky, and he himself with his thoughts are all merged together into something vast and impenetrably black. He can only grope his way.

"Who goes there?" the watchman repeats, and he begins to fancy that he hears whispering and smothered laughter. "Who's there?"

"It's I, friend . . ." answers an old man's voice.

"But who are you?"

"I . . . a traveller."

"What sort of traveller?" the watchman cries angrily, trying to disguise his terror by shouting. "What the devil do you want here? You go prowling about the graveyard at night, you ruffian!"

"You don't say it's a graveyard here?"

"Why, what else? Of course it's the graveyard! Don't you see it is?"

"O-o-oh . . . Queen of Heaven!" there is a sound of an old man sighing. "I see nothing, my good soul, nothing. Oh the darkness, the darkness! You can't see your hand before your face, it is dark, friend. O-o-oh. . ."

"But who are you?"

"I am a pilgrim, friend, a wandering man."

"The devils, the nightbirds. . . . Nice sort of pilgrims! They are drunkards . . ." mutters the watchman, reassured by the tone and sighs of the stranger. "One's tempted to sin by you. They drink the day away and prowl about at night. But I fancy I heard you were not alone; it sounded like two or three of you."

"I am alone, friend, alone. Quite alone. O-o-oh our sins. . . ."

The watchman stumbles up against the man and stops.

"How did you get here?" he asks.

"I have lost my way, good man. I was walking to the Mitrievsky Mill and I lost my way."

"Whew! Is this the road to Mitrievsky Mill? You sheepshead! For the Mitrievsky Mill you must keep much more to the left, straight out of the town along the high road. You have been drinking and have gone a couple of miles out of your way. You must have had a drop in the town."

"I did, friend . . . Truly I did; I won't hide my sins. But how am I to go now?"

"Go straight on and on along this avenue till you can go no farther, and then turn at once to the left and go till you have crossed the whole graveyard right to the gate. There will be a gate there. . . . Open it and go with God's blessing. Mind you don't fall into the ditch. And when you are out of the graveyard you go all the way by the fields till you come out on the main road."

"God give you health, friend. May the Queen of Heaven save you and have mercy on you. You might take me along, good man! Be merciful! Lead me to the gate."

"As though I had the time to waste! Go by yourself!"

"Be merciful! I'll pray for you. I can't see anything; one can't see one's hand before one's face, friend. . . . It's so dark, so dark! Show me the way, sir!"

"As though I had the time to take you about; if I were to play the nurse to everyone I should never have done."

"For Christ's sake, take me! I can't see, and I am afraid to go alone through the graveyard. It's terrifying, friend, it's terrifying; I am afraid, good man."

"There's no getting rid of you," sighs the watchman. "All right then, come along."

The watchman and the traveller go on together. They walk shoulder to shoulder in silence. A damp, cutting wind blows straight into their faces and the unseen trees murmuring and rustling scatter big drops upon them. . . . The path is almost entirely covered with puddles.

"There is one thing passes my understanding," says the watchman after a prolonged silence -- "how you got here. The gate's locked. Did you climb over the wall? If you did climb over the wall, that's the last thing you would expect of an old man."

"I don't know, friend, I don't know. I can't say myself how I got here. It's a visitation. A chastisement of the Lord. Truly a visitation, the evil one confounded me. So you are a watchman here, friend?"

"Yes."

"The only one for the whole graveyard?"

There is such a violent gust of wind that both stop for a minute. Waiting till the violence of the wind abates, the watchman answers:

"There are three of us, but one is lying ill in a fever and the other's asleep. He and I take turns about."

"Ah, to be sure, friend. What a wind! The dead must hear it! It howls like a wild beast! O-o-oh."

"And where do you come from?"

"From a distance, friend. I am from Vologda, a long way off. I go from one holy place to another and pray for people. Save me and have mercy upon me, O Lord."

The watchman stops for a minute to light his pipe. He stoops down behind the traveller's back and lights several matches. The gleam of the first match lights up for one instant a bit of the avenue on the right, a white tombstone with an angel, and a dark cross; the light of the second match, flaring up brightly and extinguished by the wind, flashes like lightning on the left side, and from the darkness nothing stands out but the angle of some sort of trellis; the third match throws light to right and to left, revealing the white tombstone, the dark cross, and the trellis round a child's grave.

"The departed sleep; the dear ones sleep!" the stranger mutters, sighing loudly. "They all sleep alike, rich and poor, wise and foolish, good and wicked. They are of the same value now. And they will sleep till the last trump. The Kingdom of Heaven and peace eternal be theirs."

"Here we are walking along now, but the time will come when we shall be lying here ourselves," says the watchman.

"To be sure, to be sure, we shall all. There is no man who will not die. O-o-oh. Our doings are wicked, our thoughts are deceitful! Sins, sins! My soul accursed, ever covetous, my belly greedy and lustful! I have angered the Lord and there is no salvation for me in this world and the next. I am deep in sins like a worm in the earth."

"Yes, and you have to die."

"You are right there."

"Death is easier for a pilgrim than for fellows like us," says the watchman.

"There are pilgrims of different sorts. There are the real ones who are God-fearing men and watch over their own souls, and there are such as stray about the graveyard at night and are a delight to the devils... Ye-es! There's one who is a pilgrim could give you a crack on the pate with an axe if he liked and knock the breath out of you."

"What are you talking like that for?"

"Oh, nothing... Why, I fancy here's the gate. Yes, it is. Open it, good man.

The watchman, feeling his way, opens the gate, leads the pilgrim out by the sleeve, and says:

"Here's the end of the graveyard. Now you must keep on through the open fields till you get to the main road. Only close here there will be the boundary ditch -- don't fall in. . . . And when you come out on to the road, turn to the right, and keep on till you reach the mill. . . ."

"O-o-oh!" sighs the pilgrim after a pause, "and now I am thinking that I have no cause to go to Mitrievsky Mill. . . . Why the devil should I go there? I had better stay a bit with you here, sir. . . ."

"What do you want to stay with me for?"

"Oh . . . it's merrier with you! . . . ."

"So you've found a merry companion, have you? You, pilgrim, are fond of a joke I see. . . ."

"To be sure I am," says the stranger, with a hoarse chuckle. "Ah, my dear good man, I bet you will remember the pilgrim many a long year!"

"Why should I remember you?"

"Why I've got round you so smartly. . . . Am I a pilgrim? I am not a pilgrim at all."

"What are you then?"

"A dead man. . . . I've only just got out of my coffin. . . . Do you remember Gubaryev, the locksmith, who hanged himself in carnival week? Well, I am Gubaryev himself! . . ."

"Tell us something else!"

The watchman does not believe him, but he feels all over such a cold, oppressive terror that he starts off and begins hurriedly feeling for the gate.

"Stop, where are you off to?" says the stranger, clutching him by the arm. "Aie, aie, aie . . . what a fellow you are! How can you leave me all alone?"

"Let go!" cries the watchman, trying to pull his arm away.

"Sto-op! I bid you stop and you stop. Don't struggle, you dirty dog! If you want to stay among the living, stop and hold your tongue till I tell you. It's only that I don't care to spill blood or you would have been a dead man long ago, you scurvy rascal. . . . Stop!"

The watchman's knees give way under him. In his terror he shuts his eyes, and trembling all over huddles close to the wall. He would like to call out, but he knows his cries would not reach any living thing. The stranger stands beside him and holds him by the arm. . . . Three minutes pass in silence.

"One's in a fever, another's asleep, and the third is seeing pilgrims on their way," mutters the stranger. "Capital watchmen, they are worth their salary! Ye-es, brother, thieves have always been cleverer than watchmen! Stand still, don't stir. . . ."

Five minutes, ten minutes pass in silence. All at once the wind brings the sound of a whistle.

"Well, now you can go," says the stranger, releasing the watchman's arm. "Go and thank God you are alive!"

The stranger gives a whistle too, runs away from the gate, and the watchman hears him leap over the ditch.

With a foreboding of something very dreadful in his heart, the watchman, still trembling with terror, opens the gate irresolutely and runs back with his eyes shut.

At the turning into the main avenue he hears hurried footsteps, and someone asks him, in a hissing voice: "Is that you, Timofey? Where is Mitka?"

And after running the whole length of the main avenue he notices a little dim light in the darkness. The nearer he gets to the light the more frightened he is and the stronger his foreboding of evil.

"It looks as though the light were in the church," he thinks. "And how can it have come there? Save me and have mercy on me, Queen of Heaven! And that it is."

The watchman stands for a minute before the broken window and looks with horror towards the altar. . . . A little wax candle which the thieves had forgotten to put out flickers in the wind that bursts in at the window and throws dim red patches of light on the vestments flung about and a cupboard overturned on the floor, on numerous footprints near the high altar and the altar of offerings.

A little time passes and the howling wind sends floating over the churchyard the hurried uneven clangs of the alarm-bell. . . .

HOME

"Someone came from the Grigoryevs' to fetch a book, but I said you were not at home. The postman brought the newspaper and two letters. By the way, Yevgeny Petrovitch, I should like to ask you to speak to Seryozha. To-day, and the day before yesterday, I have noticed that he is smoking. When I began to expostulate with him, he put his fingers in his ears as usual, and sang loudly to drown my voice."

Yevgeny Petrovitch Bykovsky, the prosecutor of the circuit court, who had just come back from a session and was taking off his gloves in his study, looked at the governess as she made her report, and laughed.

"Seryozha smoking . . ." he said, shrugging his shoulders. "I can picture the little cherub with a cigarette in his mouth! Why, how old is he?"

"Seven. You think it is not important, but at his age smoking is a bad and pernicious habit, and bad habits ought to be eradicated in the beginning."

"Perfectly true. And where does he get the tobacco?"

"He takes it from the drawer in your table."

"Yes? In that case, send him to me."

When the governess had gone out, Bykovsky sat down in an arm-chair before his writing-table, shut his eyes, and fell to thinking. He pictured his Seryozha with a huge cigar, a yard long, in the midst of clouds of tobacco smoke, and this caricature made him smile; at the same time, the grave, troubled face of the governess called up memories of the long past, half-forgotten time when smoking aroused in his teachers and parents a strange, not quite intelligible horror. It really was horror. Children were mercilessly flogged and expelled from school, and their lives were made a misery on account of smoking, though not a single teacher or father knew exactly what was the harm or sinfulness of smoking. Even very intelligent people did not scruple to wage war on a vice which they did not understand. Yevgeny Petrovitch remembered the head-master of the high school, a very cultured and good-natured old man, who was so appalled when he found a high-school boy with a cigarette in his mouth that he turned pale, immediately summoned an emergency committee of the teachers, and sentenced the sinner to expulsion. This was probably a law of social life: the less an evil was understood, the more fiercely and coarsely it was attacked.

The prosecutor remembered two or three boys who had been expelled and their subsequent life, and could not help thinking that very often the punishment did a great deal more harm than the crime itself. The living organism has the power of rapidly adapting itself, growing accustomed and inured to any atmosphere whatever, otherwise man would be bound to feel at every moment what an irrational basis there often is underlying his rational activity, and how little of established truth and certainty there is even in work so responsible and so terrible in its effects as that of the teacher, of the lawyer, of the writer. . . .

And such light and discursive thoughts as visit the brain only when it is weary and resting began straying through Yevgeny Petrovitch's head; there is no telling whence and why they come, they do not remain long in the mind, but seem to glide over its surface without sinking deeply into it. For people who are forced for whole hours, and even days, to think by routine in one direction, such free private thinking affords a kind of comfort, an agreeable solace.

It was between eight and nine o'clock in the evening. Overhead, on the second storey, someone was walking up and down, and on the floor above that four hands were playing scales. The pacing of the man overhead who, to judge from his nervous step, was thinking of something harassing, or was suffering from toothache, and the monotonous scales gave the stillness of the evening a drowsiness that disposed to lazy reveries. In the nursery, two rooms away, the governess and Seryozha were talking.

"Pa-pa has come!" carolled the child. "Papa has co-ome. Pa! Pa! Pa!"

"*Votre père vous appelle, allez vite!*" cried the governess, shrill as a frightened bird. "I am speaking to you!"

"What am I to say to him, though?" Yevgeny Petrovitch wondered.

But before he had time to think of anything whatever his son Seryozha, a boy of seven, walked into the study.

He was a child whose sex could only have been guessed from his dress: weakly, white-faced, and fragile. He was limp like a hot-house plant, and everything about him seemed extraordinarily soft and tender: his movements, his curly hair, the look in his eyes, his velvet jacket.

"Good evening, papa!" he said, in a soft voice, clambering on to his father's knee and giving him a rapid kiss on his neck. "Did you send for me?"

"Excuse me, Sergey Yevgenitch," answered the prosecutor, removing him from his knee. "Before kissing we must have a talk, and a serious talk . . . I am angry with you, and don't love you any more. I tell you, my boy, I don't love you, and you are no son of mine. . . ."

Seryozha looked intently at his father, then shifted his eyes to the table, and shrugged his shoulders.

"What have I done to you?" he asked in perplexity, blinking. "I haven't been in your study all day, and I haven't touched anything."

"Natalya Semyonovna has just been complaining to me that you have been smoking. . . . Is it true? Have you been smoking?"

"Yes, I did smoke once. . . . That's true. . . ."

"Now you see you are lying as well," said the prosecutor, frowning to disguise a smile. "Natalya Semyonovna has seen you smoking twice. So you see you have been detected in three misdeeds: smoking, taking someone else's tobacco, and lying. Three faults."

"Oh yes," Seryozha recollected, and his eyes smiled. "That's true, that's true; I smoked twice: to-day and before."

"So you see it was not once, but twice. . . . I am very, very much displeased with you! You used to be a good boy, but now I see you are spoilt and have become a bad one."

Yevgeny Petrovitch smoothed down Seryozha's collar and thought:

"What more am I to say to him!"

"Yes, it's not right," he continued. "I did not expect it of you. In the first place, you ought not to take tobacco that does not belong to you. Every person has only the right to make use of his own property; if he takes anyone else's . . . he is a bad man!" ("I am not saying the right thing!" thought Yevgeny Petrovitch.) "For instance, Natalya Semyonovna has a box with her clothes in it. That's her box, and we -- that is, you and I -- dare not touch it, as it is not ours. That's right, isn't it? You've got toy horses and pictures. . . . I don't take them, do I? Perhaps I might like to take them, but . . . they are not mine, but yours!"

"Take them if you like!" said Seryozha, raising his eyebrows. "Please don't hesitate, papa, take them! That yellow dog on your table is mine, but I don't mind. . . . Let it stay."

"You don't understand me," said Bykovsky. "You have given me the dog, it is mine now and I can do what I like with it; but I didn't give you the tobacco! The tobacco is mine." ("I am not explaining properly!" thought the prosecutor. "It's wrong! Quite wrong!") "If I want to smoke someone else's tobacco, I must first of all ask his permission. . . ."

Languidly linking one phrase on to another and imitating the language of the nursery, Bykovsky tried to explain to his son the meaning of property. Seryozha gazed at his chest and listened attentively (he liked talking to his father in the evening), then he leaned his elbow on the edge of the table and began screwing up his short-sighted eyes at the papers and the inkstand. His eyes strayed over the table and rested on the gum-bottle.

"Papa, what is gum made of?" he asked suddenly, putting the bottle to his eyes.

Bykovsky took the bottle out of his hands and set it in its place and went on:

"Secondly, you smoke. . . . That's very bad. Though I smoke it does not follow that you may. I smoke and know that it is stupid, I blame myself and don't like myself for it." ("A clever teacher, I am!" he thought.) "Tobacco is very bad for the health, and anyone who smokes dies earlier than he should. It's particularly bad for boys like you to smoke.

Your chest is weak, you haven't reached your full strength yet, and smoking leads to consumption and other illness in weak people. Uncle Ignat died of consumption, you know. If he hadn't smoked, perhaps he would have lived till now."

Seryozha looked pensively at the lamp, touched the lamp-shade with his finger, and heaved a sigh.

"Uncle Ignat played the violin splendidly!" he said. "His violin is at the Grigoryevs' now."

Seryozha leaned his elbows on the edge of the table again, and sank into thought. His white face wore a fixed expression, as though he were listening or following a train of thought of his own; distress and something like fear came into his big staring eyes. He was most likely thinking now of death, which had so lately carried off his mother and Uncle Ignat. Death carries mothers and uncles off to the other world, while their children and violins remain upon the earth. The dead live somewhere in the sky beside the stars, and look down from there upon the earth. Can they endure the parting?

"What am I to say to him?" thought Yevgeny Petrovitch. "He's not listening to me. Obviously he does not regard either his misdoings or my arguments as serious. How am I to drive it home?"

The prosecutor got up and walked about the study.

"Formerly, in my time, these questions were very simply settled," he reflected. "Every urchin who was caught smoking was thrashed. The cowardly and faint-hearted did actually give up smoking, any who were somewhat more plucky and intelligent, after the thrashing took to carrying tobacco in the legs of their boots, and smoking in the barn. When they were caught in the barn and thrashed again, they would go away to smoke by the river . . . and so on, till the boy grew up. My mother used to give me money and sweets not to smoke. Now that method is looked upon as worthless and immoral. The modern teacher, taking his stand on logic, tries to make the child form good principles, not from fear, nor from desire for distinction or reward, but consciously."

While he was walking about, thinking, Seryozha climbed up with his legs on a chair sideways to the table, and began drawing. That he might not spoil official paper nor touch the ink, a heap of half-sheets, cut on purpose for him, lay on the table together with a blue pencil.

"Cook was chopping up cabbage to-day and she cut her finger," he said, drawing a little house and moving his eyebrows. "She gave such a scream that we were all frightened and ran into the kitchen. Stupid thing! Natalya Semyonovna told her to dip her finger in cold water, but she sucked it . . . And how could she put a dirty finger in her mouth! That's not proper, you know, papa!"

Then he went on to describe how, while they were having dinner, a man with a hurdy-gurdy had come into the yard with a little girl, who had danced and sung to the music.

"He has his own train of thought!" thought the prosecutor. "He has a little world of his own in his head, and he has his own ideas of what is important and unimportant. To gain possession of his attention, it's not enough to imitate his language, one must also be able to think in the way he does. He would understand me perfectly if I really were sorry for the loss of the tobacco, if I felt injured and cried. . . . That's why no one can take the place of a mother in bringing up a child, because she can feel, cry, and laugh together with the child. One can do nothing by logic and morality. What more shall I say to him? What?"

And it struck Yevgeny Petrovitch as strange and absurd that he, an experienced advocate, who spent half his life in the practice of reducing people to silence, forestalling what they had to say, and punishing them, was completely at a loss and did not know what to say to the boy.

"I say, give me your word of honour that you won't smoke again," he said.

"Word of hon-nour!" carolled Seryozha, pressing hard on the pencil and bending over the drawing. "Word of hon-nour!"

"Does he know what is meant by word of honour?" Bykovsky asked himself. "No, I am a poor teacher of morality! If some schoolmaster or one of our legal fellows could peep into my brain at this moment he would call me a poor stick, and would very likely suspect me of unnecessary subtlety. . . . But in school and in court, of course, all these wretched questions are far more simply settled than at home; here one has to do with people whom one loves beyond everything, and love is exacting and complicates the question. If this boy were not my son, but my pupil, or a prisoner on his trial, I should not be so cowardly, and my thoughts would not be racing all over the place!"

Yevgeny Petrovitch sat down to the table and pulled one of Seryozha's drawings to him. In it there was a house with a crooked roof, and smoke which came out of the chimney like a flash of lightning in zigzags up to the very edge of the paper; beside the house stood a soldier with dots for eyes and a bayonet that looked like the figure 4.

"A man can't be taller than a house," said the prosecutor.

Seryozha got on his knee, and moved about for some time to get comfortably settled there.

"No, papa!" he said, looking at his drawing. "If you were to draw the soldier small you would not see his eyes."

Ought he to argue with him? From daily observation of his son the prosecutor had become convinced that children, like savages, have their own artistic standpoints and requirements peculiar to them, beyond the grasp of grown-up people. Had he been attentively observed, Seryozha might have struck a grown-up person as abnormal. He thought it possible and reasonable to draw men taller than houses, and to represent in pencil, not only objects, but even his sensations. Thus he would depict the sounds of an orchestra in the form of smoke like spherical blurs, a whistle in the form of a spiral thread. . . . To his mind sound was closely connected with form and colour, so that when he painted letters he invariably painted the letter L yellow, M red, A black, and so on.

Abandoning his drawing, Seryozha shifted about once more, got into a comfortable attitude, and busied himself with his father's beard. First he carefully smoothed it, then he parted it and began combing it into the shape of whiskers.

"Now you are like Ivan Stepanovitch," he said, "and in a minute you will be like our porter. Papa, why is it porters stand by doors? Is it to prevent thieves getting in?"

The prosecutor felt the child's breathing on his face, he was continually touching his hair with his cheek, and there was a warm soft feeling in his soul, as soft as though not only his hands but his whole soul were lying on the velvet of Seryozha's jacket.

He looked at the boy's big dark eyes, and it seemed to him as though from those wide pupils there looked out at him his mother and his wife and everything that he had ever loved.

"To think of thrashing him . . ." he mused. "A nice task to devise a punishment for him! How can we undertake to bring up the young? In old days people were simpler and thought less, and so settled problems boldly. But we think too much, we are eaten up by logic. . . . The more developed a man is, the more he reflects and gives himself up to subtleties, the more undecided and scrupulous he becomes, and the more timidity he shows in taking action. How much courage and self-confidence it needs, when one comes to look into it closely, to undertake to teach, to judge, to write a thick book. . . ."

It struck ten.

"Come, boy, it's bedtime," said the prosecutor. "Say good-night and go."

"No, papa," said Seryozha, "I will stay a little longer. Tell me something! Tell me a story. . . ."

"Very well, only after the story you must go to bed at once."

Yevgeny Petrovitch on his free evenings was in the habit of telling Seryozha stories. Like most people engaged in practical affairs, he did not know a single poem by heart, and could not remember a single fairy tale, so he had to improvise. As a rule he began with the stereotyped: "In a certain country, in a certain kingdom," then he heaped up all kinds of innocent nonsense and had no notion as he told the beginning how the story would go on, and how it would end. Scenes, characters, and situations were taken at random, impromptu, and the plot and the moral came of itself as it were, with no plan on the part of the story-teller. Seryozha was very fond of this improvisation, and the prosecutor noticed that the simpler and the less ingenious the plot, the stronger the impression it made on the child.

"Listen," he said, raising his eyes to the ceiling. "Once upon a time, in a certain country, in a certain kingdom, there lived an old, very old emperor with a long grey beard, and . . . and with great grey moustaches like this. Well, he lived in a glass palace which sparkled and glittered in the sun, like a great piece of clear ice. The palace, my boy, stood in a huge garden, in which there grew oranges, you know . . . bergamots, cherries . . . tulips, roses, and lilies-of-the-valley were in flower in it, and birds of different colours sang there. . . . Yes. . . . On the trees there hung little glass bells, and, when the wind blew, they rang so sweetly that one was never tired of hearing them. Glass gives a softer, tenderer note than metals. . . . Well, what next? There were fountains in the garden. . . . Do you remember you saw a fountain at Auntie Sonya's summer villa? Well, there were fountains just like that in the emperor's garden, only ever so much bigger, and the jets of water reached to the top of the highest poplar."

Yevgeny Petrovitch thought a moment, and went on:

"The old emperor had an only son and heir of his kingdom -- a boy as little as you. He was a good boy. He was never naughty, he went to bed early, he never touched anything on the table, and altogether he was a sensible boy. He had only one fault, he used to smoke. . . ."

Seryozha listened attentively, and looked into his father's eyes without blinking. The prosecutor went on, thinking: "What next?" He spun out a long rigmarole, and ended like this:

"The emperor's son fell ill with consumption through smoking, and died when he was twenty. His infirm and sick old father was left without anyone to help him. There was no one to govern the kingdom and defend the palace. Enemies came, killed the old man, and destroyed the palace, and now there are neither cherries, nor birds, nor little bells in the garden. . . . That's what happened."

This ending struck Yevgeny Petrovitch as absurd and naïve, but the whole story made an intense impression on Seryozha. Again his eyes were clouded by mournfulness and something like fear; for a minute he looked pensively at the dark window, shuddered, and said, in a sinking voice:

"I am not going to smoke any more...."

When he had said good-night and gone away his father walked up and down the room and smiled to himself.

"They would tell me it was the influence of beauty, artistic form," he meditated. "It may be so, but that's no comfort. It's not the right way, all the same.... Why must morality and truth never be offered in their crude form, but only with embellishments, sweetened and gilded like pills? It's not normal.... It's falsification... deception... tricks...."

He thought of the jurymen to whom it was absolutely necessary to make a "speech," of the general public who absorb history only from legends and historical novels, and of himself and how he had gathered an understanding of life not from sermons and laws, but from fables, novels, poems.

"Medicine should be sweet, truth beautiful, and man has had this foolish habit since the days of Adam... though, indeed, perhaps it is all natural, and ought to be so.... There are many deceptions and delusions in nature that serve a purpose."

He set to work, but lazy, intimate thoughts still strayed through his mind for a good while. Overhead the scales could no longer be heard, but the inhabitant of the second storey was still pacing from one end of the room to another.

THE LOTTERY TICKET

Ivan Dmitritch, a middle-class man who lived with his family on an income of twelve hundred a year and was very well satisfied with his lot, sat down on the sofa after supper and began reading the newspaper.

"I forgot to look at the newspaper today," his wife said to him as she cleared the table. "Look and see whether the list of drawings is there."

"Yes, it is," said Ivan Dmitritch; "but hasn't your ticket lapsed?"

"No; I took the interest on Tuesday."

"What is the number?"

"Series 9,499, number 26."

"All right . . . we will look . . . 9,499 and 26."

Ivan Dmitritch had no faith in lottery luck, and would not, as a rule, have consented to look at the lists of winning numbers, but now, as he had nothing else to do and as the newspaper was before his eyes, he passed his finger downwards along the column of numbers. And immediately, as though in mockery of his scepticism, no further than the second line from the top, his eye was caught by the figure 9,499! Unable to believe his eyes, he hurriedly dropped the paper on his knees without looking to see the number of the ticket, and, just as though some one had given him a douche of cold water, he felt an agreeable chill in the pit of the stomach; tingling and terrible and sweet!

"Masha, 9,499 is there!" he said in a hollow voice.

His wife looked at his astonished and panic-stricken face, and realized that he was not joking.

"9,499?" she asked, turning pale and dropping the folded tablecloth on the table.

"Yes, yes . . . it really is there!"

"And the number of the ticket?"

"Oh, yes! There's the number of the ticket too. But stay . . . wait! No, I say! Anyway, the number of our series is there! Anyway, you understand. . . ."

Looking at his wife, Ivan Dmitritch gave a broad, senseless smile, like a baby when a bright object is shown it. His wife smiled too; it was as pleasant to her as to him that he only mentioned the series, and did not try to find out the number of the winning ticket. To torment and tantalize oneself with hopes of possible fortune is so sweet, so thrilling!

"It is our series," said Ivan Dmitritch, after a long silence. "So there is a probability that we have won. It's only a probability, but there it is!"

"Well, now look!"

"Wait a little. We have plenty of time to be disappointed. It's on the second line from the top, so the prize is seventy-five thousand. That's not money, but power, capital! And in a minute I shall look at the list, and there -- 26! Eh? I say, what if we really have won?"

The husband and wife began laughing and staring at one another in silence. The possibility of winning bewildered them; they could not have said, could not have dreamed, what they both needed that seventy-five thousand for, what they would buy, where they would go. They thought only of the figures 9,499 and 75,000 and pictured them in their imagination, while somehow they could not think of the happiness itself which was so possible.

Ivan Dmitritch, holding the paper in his hand, walked several times from corner to corner, and only when he had recovered from the first impression began dreaming a little.

"And if we have won," he said -- "why, it will be a new life, it will be a transformation! The ticket is yours, but if it were mine I should, first of all, of course, spend twenty-five thousand on real property in the shape of an estate; ten thousand on immediate expenses, new furnishing . . . travelling . . . paying debts, and so on. . . . The other forty thousand I would put in the bank and get interest on it."

"Yes, an estate, that would be nice," said his wife, sitting down and dropping her hands in her lap.

"Somewhere in the Tula or Oryol provinces. . . . In the first place we shouldn't need a summer villa, and besides, it would always bring in an income."

And pictures came crowding on his imagination, each more gracious and poetical than the last. And in all these pictures he saw himself well-fed, serene, healthy, felt warm, even hot! Here, after eating a summer soup, cold as ice, he lay on his back on the burning sand close to a stream or in the garden under a lime-tree. . . . It is hot. . . . His little boy and girl are crawling about near him, digging in the sand or catching ladybirds in the grass. He dozes sweetly, thinking of nothing, and feeling all over that he need not go to the office today, tomorrow, or the day after. Or, tired of lying still, he goes to the hayfield, or to the forest for mushrooms, or watches the peasants catching fish with a net. When the sun sets he takes a towel and soap and saunters to the bathing-shed, where he undresses at his leisure, slowly rubs his bare chest with his hands, and goes into the water. And in the water, near the opaque soapy circles, little fish flit to and fro and green water-weeds nod their heads. After bathing there is tea with cream and milk rolls. . . . In the evening a walk or *vint* with the neighbours.

"Yes, it would be nice to buy an estate," said his wife, also dreaming, and from her face it was evident that she was enchanted by her thoughts.

Ivan Dmitritch pictured to himself autumn with its rains, its cold evenings, and its St. Martin's summer. At that season he would have to take longer walks about the garden and beside the river, so as to get thoroughly chilled, and then drink a big glass of vodka and eat a salted mushroom or a soused cucumber, and then -- drink another. . . . The children would come running from the kitchen-garden, bringing a carrot and a radish smelling of fresh earth. . . . And then, he would lie stretched full length on the sofa, and in leisurely fashion turn over the pages of some illustrated magazine, or, covering his face with it and unbuttoning his waistcoat, give himself up to slumber.

The St. Martin's summer is followed by cloudy, gloomy weather. It rains day and night, the bare trees weep, the wind is damp and cold. The dogs, the horses, the fowls -- all are wet, depressed, downcast. There is nowhere to walk; one can't go out for days together; one has to pace up and down the room, looking despondently at the grey window. It is dreary!

Ivan Dmitritch stopped and looked at his wife.

"I should go abroad, you know, Masha," he said.

And he began thinking how nice it would be in late autumn to go abroad somewhere to the South of France . . . to Italy . . . . to India!

"I should certainly go abroad too," his wife said. "But look at the number of the ticket!"

"Wait, wait! . . ."

He walked about the room and went on thinking. It occurred to him: what if his wife really did go abroad? It is pleasant to travel alone, or in the society of light, careless women who live in the present, and not such as think and talk all the journey about nothing but their children, sigh, and tremble with dismay over every farthing. Ivan Dmitritch imagined his wife in the train with a multitude of parcels, baskets, and bags; she would be sighing over something, complaining that the train made her head ache, that she had spent so much money. . . . At the stations he would continually be having to run for boiling water, bread and butter. . . . She wouldn't have dinner because of its being too dear. . . .

"She would begrudge me every farthing," he thought, with a glance at his wife. "The lottery ticket is hers, not mine! Besides, what is the use of her going abroad? What does she want there? She would shut herself up in the hotel, and not let me out of her sight. . . . I know!"

And for the first time in his life his mind dwelt on the fact that his wife had grown elderly and plain, and that she was saturated through and through with the smell of cooking, while he was still young, fresh, and healthy, and might well have got married again.

"Of course, all that is silly nonsense," he thought; "but . . . why should she go abroad? What would she make of it? And yet she would go, of course. . . . I can fancy . . . In reality it is all one to her, whether it is Naples or Klin. She would only be in my way. I should be dependent upon her. I can fancy how, like a regular woman, she will lock the money up as soon as she gets it. . . . She will hide it from me. . . . She will look after her relations and grudge me every farthing."

Ivan Dmitritch thought of her relations. All those wretched brothers and sisters and aunts and uncles would come crawling about as soon as they heard of the winning ticket, would begin whining like beggars, and fawning upon them with oily, hypocritical smiles. Wretched, detestable people! If they were given anything, they would ask for more; while if they were refused, they would swear at them, slander them, and wish them every kind of misfortune.

Ivan Dmitritch remembered his own relations, and their faces, at which he had looked impartially in the past, struck him now as repulsive and hateful.

"They are such reptiles!" he thought.

And his wife's face, too, struck him as repulsive and hateful. Anger surged up in his heart against her, and he thought malignantly:

"She knows nothing about money, and so she is stingy. If she won it she would give me a hundred roubles, and put the rest away under lock and key."

And he looked at his wife, not with a smile now, but with hatred. She glanced at him too, and also with hatred and anger. She had her own daydreams, her own plans, her own reflections; she understood perfectly well what her husband's dreams were. She knew who would be the first to try and grab her winnings.

"It's very nice making daydreams at other people's expense!" is what her eyes expressed. "No, don't you dare!"

Her husband understood her look; hatred began stirring again in his breast, and in order to annoy his wife he glanced quickly, to spite her at the fourth page on the newspaper and read out triumphantly:

"Series 9,499, number 46! Not 26!"

Hatred and hope both disappeared at once, and it began immediately to seem to Ivan Dmitritch and his wife that their rooms were dark and small and low-pitched, that the supper they had been eating was not doing them good, but lying heavy on their stomachs, that the evenings were long and wearisome. . . .

"What the devil's the meaning of it?" said Ivan Dmitritch, beginning to be ill-humoured. "Wherever one steps there are bits of paper under one's feet, crumbs, husks. The rooms are never swept! One is simply forced to go out. Damnation take my soul entirely! I shall go and hang myself on the first aspen-tree!"

TOO EARLY!

The bells are ringing for service in the village of Shalmovo. The sun is already kissing the earth on the horizon; it has turned crimson and will soon disappear. In Semyon's pothouse, which has lately changed its name and become a restaurant -- a title quite out of keeping with the wretched little hut with its thatch torn off its roof, and its couple of dingy windows -- two peasant sportsmen are sitting. One of them is called Filimon Slyunka; he is an old man of sixty, formerly a house-serf, belonging to the Counts Zavalin, by trade a carpenter. He has at one time been employed in a nail factory, has been turned off for drunkenness and idleness, and now lives upon his old wife, who begs for alms. He is thin and weak, with a mangy-looking little beard, speaks with a hissing sound, and after every word twitches the right side of his face and jerkily shrugs his right shoulder. The other, Ignat Ryabov, a sturdy, broad-shouldered peasant who never does anything and is everlastingly silent, is sitting in the corner under a big string of bread rings. The door, opening inwards, throws a thick shadow upon him, so that Slyunka and Semyon the publican can see nothing but his patched knees, his long fleshy nose, and a big tuft of hair which has escaped from the thick uncombed tangle covering his head. Semyon, a sickly little man, with a pale face and a long sinewy neck, stands behind his counter, looks mournfully at the string of bread rings, and coughs meekly.

"You think it over now, if you have any sense," Slyunka says to him, twitching his cheek. "You have the thing lying by unused and get no sort of benefit from it. While we need it. A sportsman without a gun is like a sacristan without a voice. You ought to understand that, but I see you don't understand it, so you can have no real sense. . . . Hand it over!"

"You left the gun in pledge, you know!" says Semyon in a thin womanish little voice, sighing deeply, and not taking his eyes off the string of bread rings. "Hand over the rouble you borrowed, and then take your gun."

"I haven't got a rouble. I swear to you, Semyon Mitritch, as God sees me: you give me the gun and I will go to-day with Ignashka and bring it you back again. I'll bring it back, strike me dead. May I have happiness neither in this world nor the next, if I don't."

"Semyon Mitritch, do give it," Ignat Ryabov says in his bass, and his voice betrays a passionate desire to get what he asks for.

"But what do you want the gun for?" sighs Semyon, sadly shaking his head. "What sort of shooting is there now? It's still winter outside, and no game at all but crows and jackdaws."

"Winter, indeed," says Slyunka, hooing the ash out of his pipe with his finger, "it is early yet of course, but you never can tell with the snipe. The snipe's a bird that wants watching. If you are unlucky, you may sit waiting at home, and miss his flying over, and then you must wait till autumn. . . . It is a business! The snipe is not a rook. . . . Last year he was flying the week before Easter, while the year before we had to wait till the week after Easter! Come, do us a favour, Semyon Mitritch, give us the gun. Make us pray for you for ever. As ill-luck would have it, Ignashka has pledged his gun for drink too. Ah, when you drink you feel nothing, but now . . . ah, I wish I had never looked at it, the cursed vodka! Truly it is the blood of Satan! Give it us, Semyon Mitritch!"

"I won't give it you," says Semyon, clasping his yellow hands on his breast as though he were going to pray. "You must act fairly, Filimonushka. . . . A thing is not taken out of pawn just anyhow; you must pay the money. . . . Besides, what do you want to kill birds for? What's the use? It's Lent now -- you are not going to eat them."

Slyunka exchanges glances with Ryabov in embarrassment, sighs, and says: "We would only go stand-shooting."

"And what for? It's all foolishness. You are not the sort of man to spend your time in foolishness. . . . Ignashka, to be sure, is a man of no understanding, God has afflicted him, but you, thank the Lord, are an old man. It's time to prepare for your end. Here, you ought to go to the midnight service."

The allusion to his age visibly stings Slyunka. He clears his throat, wrinkles up his forehead, and remains silent for a full minute.

"I say, Semyon Mitritch," he says hotly, getting up and twitching not only in his right cheek but all over his face. "It's God's truth. . . . May the Almighty strike me dead, after Easter I shall get something from Stepan Kuzmitch for an axle, and I will pay you not one rouble but two! May the Lord chastise me! Before the holy image, I tell you, only give me the gun!"

"Gi-ive it," Ryabov says in his growling bass; they can hear him breathing hard, and it seems that he would like to say a great deal, but cannot find the words. "Gi-ive it."

"No, brothers, and don't ask," sighs Semyon, shaking his head mournfully. "Don't lead me into sin. I won't give you the gun. It's not the fashion for a thing to be taken out of pawn and no money paid. Besides -- why this indulgence? Go your way and God bless you!"

Slyunka rubs his perspiring face with his sleeve and begins hotly swearing and entreating. He crosses himself, holds out his hands to the ikon, calls his deceased father and mother to bear witness, but Semyon sighs and meekly looks as before at the string of bread rings. In the end Ignashka Ryabov, hitherto motionless, gets up impulsively and bows down to the ground before the innkeeper, but even that has no effect on him.

"May you choke with my gun, you devil," says Slyunka, with his face twitching, and his shoulders, shrugging. "May you choke, you plague, you scoundrelly soul."

Swearing and shaking his fists, he goes out of the tavern with Ryabov and stands still in the middle of the road.

"He won't give it, the damned brute," he says, in a weeping voice, looking into Ryabov's face with an injured air.

"He won't give it," booms Ryabov.

The windows of the furthest huts, the starling cote on the tavern, the tops of the poplars, and the cross on the church are all gleaming with a bright golden flame. Now they can see only half of the sun, which, as it goes to its night's rest, is winking, shedding a crimson light, and seems laughing gleefully. Slyunka and Ryabov can see the forest lying, a dark blur, to the right of the sun, a mile and a half from the village, and tiny clouds flitting over the clear sky, and they feel that the evening will be fine and still.

"Now is just the time," says Slyunka, with his face twitching. "It would be nice to stand for an hour or two. He won't give it us, the damned brute. May he. . . "

"For stand-shooting, now is the very time . . ." Ryabov articulated, as though with an effort, stammering.

After standing still for a little they walk out of the village, without saying a word to each other, and look towards the dark streak of the forest. The whole sky above the forest is studded with moving black spots, the rooks flying home to roost. The snow, lying white here and there on the dark brown plough-land, is lightly flecked with gold by the sun.

"This time last year I went stand-shooting in Zhivki," says Slyunka, after a long silence. "I brought back three snipe."

Again there follows a silence. Both stand a long time and look towards the forest, and then lazily move and walk along the muddy road from the village.

"It's most likely the snipe haven't come yet," says Slyunka, "but may be they are here."

"Kostka says they are not here yet."

"Maybe they are not, who can tell; one year is not like another. But what mud!"

"But we ought to stand."

"To be sure we ought -- why not?"

"We can stand and watch; it wouldn't be amiss to go to the forest and have a look. If they are there we will tell Kostka, or maybe get a gun ourselves and come to-morrow. What a misfortune, God forgive me. It was the devil put it in my mind to take my gun to the pothouse! I am more sorry than I can tell you, Ignashka."

Conversing thus, the sportsmen approach the forest. The sun has set and left behind it a red streak like the glow of a fire, scattered here and there with clouds; there is no catching the colours of those clouds: their edges are red, but they themselves are one minute grey, at the next lilac, at the next ashen.

In the forest, among the thick branches of fir-trees and under the birch bushes, it is dark, and only the outermost twigs on the side of the sun, with their fat buds and shining bark, stand out clearly in the air. There is a smell of thawing snow and rotting leaves. It is still; nothing stirs. From the distance comes the subsiding caw of the rooks.

"We ought to be standing in Zhivki now," whispers Slyunka, looking with awe at Ryabov; "there's good stand-shooting there."

Ryabov too looks with awe at Slyunka, with unblinking eyes and open mouth.

"A lovely time," Slyunka says in a trembling whisper. "The Lord is sending a fine spring . . . and I should think the snipe are here by now. . . . Why not? The days are warm now. . . . The cranes were flying in the morning, lots and lots of them."

Slyunka and Ryabov, splashing cautiously through the melting snow and sticking in the mud, walk two hundred paces along the edge of the forest and there halt. Their faces wear a look of alarm and expectation of something terrible and extraordinary. They stand like posts, do not speak nor stir, and their hands gradually fall into an attitude as though they were holding a gun at the cock. . . .

A big shadow creeps from the left and envelops the earth. The dusk of evening comes on. If one looks to the right, through the bushes and tree trunks, there can be seen crimson patches of the after-glow. It is still and damp. . . .

"There's no sound of them," whispers Slyunka, shrugging with the cold and sniffing with his chilly nose.

But frightened by his own whisper, he holds his finger up at some one, opens his eyes wide, and purses up his lips. There is a sound of a light snapping. The sportsmen look at each other significantly, and tell each other with their eyes that it is nothing. It is the snapping of a dry twig or a bit of bark. The shadows of evening keep growing and growing, the patches of crimson gradually grow dim, and the dampness becomes unpleasant.

The sportsmen remain standing a long time, but they see and hear nothing. Every instant they expect to see a delicate leaf float through the air, to hear a hurried call like the husky cough of a child, and the flutter of wings.

"No, not a sound," Slyunka says aloud, dropping his hands and beginning to blink. "So they have not come yet."

"It's early!"

"You are right there."

The sportsmen cannot see each other's faces, it is getting rapidly dark.

"We must wait another five days," says Slyunka, as he comes out from behind a bush with Ryabov. "It's too early!"

They go homewards, and are silent all the way.

TYPHUS

A young lieutenant called Klimov was travelling from Petersburg to Moscow in a smoking carriage of the mail train. Opposite him was sitting an elderly man with a shaven face like a sea captain's, by all appearances a well-to-do Finn or Swede. He pulled at his pipe the whole journey and kept talking about the same subject:

"Ha, you are an officer! I have a brother an officer too, only he is a naval officer. . . . He is a naval officer, and he is stationed at Kronstadt. Why are you going to Moscow?"

"I am serving there."

"Ha! And are you a family man?"

"No, I live with my sister and aunt."

"My brother's an officer, only he is a naval officer; he has a wife and three children. Ha!"

The Finn seemed continually surprised at something, and gave a broad idiotic grin when he exclaimed "Ha!" and continually puffed at his stinking pipe. Klimov, who for some reason did not feel well, and found it burdensome to answer questions, hated him with all his heart. He dreamed of how nice it would be to snatch the wheezing pipe out of his hand and fling it under the seat, and drive the Finn himself into another compartment.

"Detestable people these Finns and . . . Greeks," he thought. "Absolutely superfluous, useless, detestable people. They simply fill up space on the earthly globe. What are they for?"

And the thought of Finns and Greeks produced a feeling akin to sickness all over his body. For the sake of comparison he tried to think of the French, of the Italians, but his efforts to think of these people evoked in his mind, for some reason, nothing but images of organ-grinders, naked women, and the foreign oleographs which hung over the chest of drawers at home, at his aunt's.

Altogether the officer felt in an abnormal state. He could not arrange his arms and legs comfortably on the seat, though he had the whole seat to himself. His mouth felt dry and sticky; there was a heavy fog in his brain; his thoughts seemed to be straying, not only within his head, but outside his skull, among the seats and the people that were shrouded in the darkness of night. Through the mist in his brain, as through a dream, he heard the murmur of voices, the rumble of wheels, the slamming of doors. The sounds of the bells, the whistles, the guards, the running to and fro of passengers on the platforms, seemed more frequent than usual. The time flew by rapidly, imperceptibly, and so it seemed as though the train were stopping at stations every minute, and metallic voices crying continually:

"Is the mail ready?"

"Yes!" was repeatedly coming from outside.

It seemed as though the man in charge of the heating came in too often to look at the thermometer, that the noise of trains going in the opposite direction and the rumble of the wheels over the bridges was incessant. The noise, the whistles, the Finn, the tobacco smoke -- all this mingling with the menace and flickering of the misty images in his brain, the shape and character of which a man in health can never recall, weighed upon Klimov like an unbearable nightmare. In horrible misery he lifted his heavy head, looked at the lamp in the rays of which shadows and misty blurs seemed to be dancing. He wanted to ask for water, but his parched tongue would hardly move, and he scarcely had strength to answer the Finn's questions. He tried to lie down more comfortably and go to sleep, but he could not succeed. The Finn several times fell asleep, woke up again, lighted his pipe, addressed him with his "Ha!" and went to sleep again; and still the lieutenant's legs could not get into a comfortable position, and still the menacing images stood facing him.

At Spirovo he went out into the station for a drink of water. He saw people sitting at the table and hurriedly eating.

"And how can they eat!" he thought, trying not to sniff the air, that smelt of roast meat, and not to look at the munching mouths -- they both seemed to him sickeningly disgusting.

A good-looking lady was conversing loudly with a military man in a red cap, and showing magnificent white teeth as she smiled; and the smile, and the teeth, and the lady herself made on Klimov the same revolting impression as the ham and the rissoles. He could not understand how it was the military man in the red cap was not ill at ease, sitting beside her and looking at her healthy, smiling face.

When after drinking some water he went back to his carriage, the Finn was sitting smoking; his pipe was wheezing and squelching like a golosh with holes in it in wet weather.

"Ha!" he said, surprised; "what station is this?"

"I don't know," answered Klimov, lying down and shutting his mouth that he might not breathe the acrid tobacco smoke.

"And when shall we reach Tver?"

"I don't know. Excuse me, I . . . I can't answer. I am ill. I caught cold today."

The Finn knocked his pipe against the window-frame and began talking of his brother, the naval officer. Klimov no longer heard him; he was thinking miserably of his soft, comfortable bed, of a bottle of cold water, of his sister Katya, who was so good at making one comfortable, soothing, giving one water. He even smiled when the vision of his orderly Pavel, taking off his heavy stifling boots and putting water on the little table, flitted through his imagination. He fancied that if he could only get into his bed, have a drink of water, his nightmare would give place to sound healthy sleep.

"Is the mail ready?" a hollow voice reached him from the distance.

"Yes," answered a bass voice almost at the window.

It was already the second or third station from Spirovo.

The time was flying rapidly in leaps and bounds, and it seemed as though the bells, whistles, and stoppings would never end. In despair Klimov buried his face in the corner of the seat, clutched his head in his hands, and began again thinking of his sister Katya and his orderly Pavel, but his sister and his orderly were mixed up with the misty images in his brain, whirled round, and disappeared. His burning breath, reflected from the back of the seat, seemed to scald his face; his legs were uncomfortable; there was a draught from the window on his back; but, however wretched he was, he did not want to change his position. . . . A heavy nightmarish lethargy gradually gained possession of him and fettered his limbs.

When he brought himself to raise his head, it was already light in the carriage. The passengers were putting on their fur coats and moving about. The train was stopping. Porters in white aprons and with discs on their breasts were bustling among the passengers and snatching up their boxes. Klimov put on his great-coat, mechanically followed the other passengers out of the carriage, and it seemed to him that not he, but some one else was moving, and he felt that his fever, his thirst, and the menacing images which had not let him sleep all night, came out of the carriage with him. Mechanically he took his luggage and engaged a sledge-driver. The man asked him for a rouble and a quarter to drive to Povarsky Street, but he did not haggle, and without protest got submissively into the sledge. He still understood the difference of numbers, but money had ceased to have any value to him.

At home Klimov was met by his aunt and his sister Katya, a girl of eighteen. When Katya greeted him she had a pencil and exercise book in her hand, and he remembered that she was preparing for an examination as a teacher. Gasping with fever, he walked aimlessly through all the rooms without answering their questions or greetings, and when he reached his bed he sank down on the pillow. The Finn, the red cap, the lady with the white teeth, the smell of roast meat, the flickering blurs, filled his consciousness, and by now he did not know where he was and did not hear the agitated voices.

When he recovered consciousness he found himself in bed, undressed, saw a bottle of water and Pavel, but it was no cooler, nor softer, nor more comfortable for that. His arms and legs, as before, refused to lie comfortably; his tongue stuck to the roof of his mouth, and he heard the wheezing of the Finn's pipe. . . . A stalwart, black-bearded doctor was busy doing something beside the bed, brushing against Pavel with his broad back.

"It's all right, it's all right, young man," he muttered. "Excellent, excellent . . . goo-od, goo-od . . . !"

The doctor called Klimov "young man," said "goo-od" instead of "good" and "so-o" instead of "so."

"So-o . . . so-o . . . so-o," he murmured. "Goo-od, goo-od . . . ! Excellent, young man. You mustn't lose heart!"

The doctor's rapid, careless talk, his well-fed countenance, and condescending "young man," irritated Klimov.

"Why do you call me 'young man'?" he moaned. "What familiarity! Damn it all!"

And he was frightened by his own voice. The voice was so dried up, so weak and peevish, that he would not have known it.

"Excellent, excellent!" muttered the doctor, not in the least offended. . . . "You mustn't get angry, so-o, so-o, so-s. . . ."

And the time flew by at home with the same startling swiftness as in the railway carriage. The daylight was continually being replaced by the dusk of evening. The doctor seemed never to leave his bedside, and he heard at every moment his "so-o, so-o, so-o." A continual succession of people was incessantly crossing the bedroom. Among them were: Pavel, the Finn, Captain Yaroshevitch, Lance-Corporal Maximenko, the red cap, the lady with the white teeth, the doctor. They were all talking and waving their arms, smoking and eating. Once by daylight Klimov saw the chaplain of the regiment, Father Alexandr, who was standing before the bed, wearing a stole and with a prayer-book in his hand. He was muttering something with a grave face such as Klimov had never seen in him before. The lieutenant remembered that Father Alexandr used in a friendly way to call all the Catholic officers "Poles," and wanting to amuse him, he cried:

"Father, Yaroshevitch the Pole has climbed up a pole!"

But Father Alexandr, a light-hearted man who loved a joke, did not smile, but became graver than ever, and made the sign of the cross over Klimov. At night-time by turn two shadows came noiselessly in and out; they were his aunt and sister. His sister's shadow knelt down and prayed; she bowed down to the ikon, and her grey shadow on the wall bowed down too, so that two shadows were praying. The whole time there was a smell of roast meat and the Finn's pipe, but once Klimov smelt the strong smell of incense. He felt so sick he could not lie still, and began shouting:

"The incense! Take away the incense!"

There was no answer. He could only hear the subdued singing of the priest somewhere and some one running upstairs.

When Klimov came to himself there was not a soul in his bedroom. The morning sun was streaming in at the window through the lower blind, and a quivering sunbeam, bright and keen as the sword's edge, was flashing on the glass bottle. He heard the rattle of wheels -- so there was no snow now in the street. The lieutenant looked at the ray, at the familiar furniture, at the door, and the first thing he did was to laugh. His chest and stomach heaved with delicious, happy, tickling laughter. His whole body from head to foot was overcome by a sensation of infinite happiness and joy in life, such as the first man must have felt when he was created and first saw the world. Klimov felt a passionate desire for movement, people, talk. His body lay a motionless block; only his hands stirred, but that he hardly noticed, and his whole attention was concentrated on trifles. He rejoiced in his breathing, in his laughter, rejoiced in the existence of the water-bottle, the ceiling, the sunshine, the tape on the curtains. God's world, even in the narrow space of his bedroom, seemed beautiful, varied, grand. When the doctor made his appearance, the lieutenant was thinking what a delicious thing medicine was, how charming and pleasant the doctor was, and how nice and interesting people were in general.

"So-o, so, so. . . Excellent, excellent! . . . Now we are well again. . . . Goo-od, goo-od!" the doctor pattered.

The lieutenant listened and laughed joyously; he remembered the Finn, the lady with the white teeth, the train, and he longed to smoke, to eat.

"Doctor," he said, "tell them to give me a crust of rye bread and salt, and . . . and sardines."

The doctor refused; Pavel did not obey the order, and did not go for the bread. The lieutenant could not bear this and began crying like a naughty child.

"Baby!" laughed the doctor. "Mammy, bye-bye!"

Klimov laughed, too, and when the doctor went away he fell into a sound sleep. He woke up with the same joyfulness and sensation of happiness. His aunt was sitting near the bed.

"Well, aunt," he said joyfully. "What has been the matter?"

"Spotted typhus."

"Really. But now I am well, quite well! Where is Katya?"

"She is not at home. I suppose she has gone somewhere from her examination."

The old lady said this and looked at her stocking; her lips began quivering, she turned away, and suddenly broke into sobs. Forgetting the doctor's prohibition in her despair, she said:

"Ah, Katya, Katya! Our angel is gone! Is gone!"

She dropped her stocking and bent down to it, and as she did so her cap fell off her head. Looking at her grey head and understanding nothing, Klimov was frightened for Katya, and asked:

"Where is she, aunt?"

The old woman, who had forgotten Klimov and was thinking only of her sorrow, said:

"She caught typhus from you, and is dead. She was buried the day before yesterday."

This terrible, unexpected news was fully grasped by Klimov's consciousness; but terrible and startling as it was, it could not overcome the animal joy that filled the convalescent. He cried and laughed, and soon began scolding because they would not let him eat.

Only a week later when, leaning on Pavel, he went in his dressing-gown to the window, looked at the overcast spring sky and listened to the unpleasant clang of the old iron rails which were being carted by, his heart ached, he burst into tears, and leaned his forehead against the window-frame.

"How miserable I am!" he muttered. "My God, how miserable!"

And joy gave way to the boredom of everyday life and the feeling of his irrevocable loss.

IN PASSION WEEK

"Go along, they are ringing already; and mind, don't be naughty in church or God will punish you."

My mother thrusts a few copper coins upon me, and, instantly forgetting about me, runs into the kitchen with an iron that needs reheating. I know well that after confession I shall not be allowed to eat or drink, and so, before leaving the house, I force myself to eat a crust of white bread, and to drink two glasses of water. It is quite spring in the street. The roads are all covered with brownish slush, in which future paths are already beginning to show; the roofs and side-walks are dry; the fresh young green is piercing through the rotting grass of last year, under the fences. In the gutters there is the merry gurgling and foaming of dirty water, in which the sunbeams do not disdain to bathe. Chips, straws, the husks of sunflower seeds are carried rapidly along in the water, whirling round and sticking in the dirty foam. Where, where are those chips swimming to? It may well be that from the gutter they may pass into the river, from the river into the sea, and from the sea into the ocean. I try to imagine to myself that long terrible journey, but my fancy stops short before reaching the sea.

A cabman drives by. He clicks to his horse, tugs at the reins, and does not see that two street urchins are hanging on the back of his cab. I should like to join them, but think of confession, and the street urchins begin to seem to me great sinners.

"They will be asked on the day of judgment: 'Why did you play pranks and deceive the poor cabman?' " I think. "They will begin to defend themselves, but evil spirits will seize them, and drag them to fire everlasting. But if they obey their parents, and give the beggars a kopeck each, or a roll, God will have pity on them, and will let them into Paradise."

The church porch is dry and bathed in sunshine. There is not a soul in it. I open the door irresolutely and go into the church. Here, in the twilight which seems to me thick and gloomy as at no other time, I am overcome by the sense of sinfulness and insignificance. What strikes the eye first of all is a huge crucifix, and on one side of it the Mother of God, and on the other, St. John the Divine. The candelabra and the candlestands are draped in black mourning covers, the lamps glimmer dimly and faintly, and the sun seems intentionally to pass by the church windows. The Mother of God and the beloved disciple of Jesus Christ, depicted in profile, gaze in silence at the insufferable agony and do not observe my presence; I feel that to them I am alien, superfluous, unnoticed, that I can be no help to them by word or deed, that I am a loathsome, dishonest boy, only capable of mischief, rudeness, and tale-bearing. I think of all the people I know, and they all seem to me petty, stupid, and wicked, and incapable of bringing one drop of relief to that intolerable sorrow which I now behold.

The twilight of the church grows darker and more gloomy. And the Mother of God and St. John look lonely and forlorn to me.

Prokofy Ignatitch, a veteran soldier, the church verger's assistant, is standing behind the candle cupboard. Raising his eyebrows and stroking his beard he explains in a half-whisper to an old woman: "Matins will be in the evening to-day, directly after vespers. And they will ring for the 'hours' to-morrow between seven and eight. Do you understand? Between seven and eight."

Between the two broad columns on the right, where the chapel of Varvara the Martyr begins, those who are going to confess stand beside the screen, awaiting their turn. And Mitka is there too -- a ragged boy with his head hideously cropped, with ears that jut out, and little spiteful eyes. He is the son of Nastasya the charwoman, and is a bully and a ruffian who snatches apples from the women's baskets, and has more than once carried off myknuckle-bones. He looks at me angrily, and I fancy takes a spiteful pleasure in the fact that he, not I, will first go behind the screen. I feel boiling over with resentment, I try not to look at him, and, at the bottom of my heart, I am vexed that this wretched boy's sins will soon be forgiven.

In front of him stands a grandly dressed, beautiful lady, wearing a hat with a white feather. She is noticeably agitated, is waiting in strained suspense, and one of her cheeks is flushed red with excitement.

I wait for five minutes, for ten. . . . A well-dressed young man with a long thin neck, and rubber goloshes, comes out from behind the screen. I begin dreaming how, when I am grown up, I will buy goloshes exactly like them. I certainly will! The lady shudders and goes behind the screen. It is her turn.

In the crack, between the two panels of the screen, I can see the lady go up to the lectern and bow down to the ground, then get up, and, without looking at the priest, bow her head in anticipation. The priest stands with his back to the screen, and so I can only see his grey curly head, the chain of the cross on his chest, and his broad back. His face is not visible. Heaving a sigh, and not looking at the lady, he begins speaking rapidly, shaking his head, alternately raising and dropping his whispering voice. The lady listens meekly as though conscious of guilt, answers meekly, and looks at the floor.

"In what way can she be sinful?" I wonder, looking reverently at her gentle, beautiful face. "God forgive her sins, God send her happiness." But now the priest covers her head with the stole. "And I, unworthy priest . . ." I hear his voice, ". . . by His power given unto me, do forgive and absolve thee from all thy sins. . . ."

The lady bows down to the ground, kisses the cross, and comes back. Both her cheeks are flushed now, but her face is calm and serene and cheerful.

"She is happy now," I think to myself, looking first at her and then at the priest who had forgiven her sins. "But how happy the man must be who has the right to forgive sins!"

Now it is Mitka's turn, but a feeling of hatred for that young ruffian suddenly boils up in me. I want to go behind the screen before him, I want to be the first. Noticing my movement he hits me on the head with his candle, I respond by doing the same, and, for half a minute, there is a sound of panting, and, as it were, of someone breaking candles. . . . We are separated. My foe goes timidly up to the lectern, and bows down to the floor without bending his knees, but I do not see what happens after that; the thought that my turn is coming after Mitka's makes everything grow blurred and confused before my eyes; Mitka's protruding ears grow large, and melt into his dark head, the priest sways, the floor seems to be undulating. . . .

The priest's voice is audible: "And I, unworthy priest . . ."

Now I too move behind the screen. I do not feel the ground under my feet, it is as though I were walking on air. . . . I go up to the lectern which is taller than I am. For a minute I have a glimpse of the indifferent, exhausted face of the priest. But after that I see nothing but his sleeve with its blue lining, the cross, and the edge of the lectern. I am conscious of the close proximity of the priest, the smell of his cassock; I hear his stern voice, and my cheek turned towards him begins to burn. . . . I am so troubled that I miss a great deal that he says, but I answer his questions sincerely in an unnatural voice, not my own. I think of the forlorn figures of the Holy Mother and St. John the Divine, the crucifix, my mother, and I want to cry and beg forgiveness.

"What is your name?" the priest asks me, covering my head with the soft stole.

How light-hearted I am now, with joy in my soul!

I have no sins now, I am holy, I have the right to enter Paradise! I fancy that I already smell like the cassock. I go from behind the screen to the deacon to enter my name, and sniff at my sleeves. The dusk of the church no longer seems gloomy, and I look indifferently, without malice, at Mitka.

"What is your name?" the deacon asks.

"Fedya."

"And your name from your father?"

"I don't know."

"What is your papa's name?"

"Ivan Petrovitch."

"And your surname?"

I make no answer.

"How old are you?"

"Nearly nine."

When I get home I go to bed quickly, that I may not see them eating supper; and, shutting my eyes, dream of how fine it would be to endure martyrdom at the hands of some Herod or Dioskorus, to live in the desert, and, like St. Serafim, feed the bears, live in a cell, and eat nothing but holy bread, give my property to the poor, go on a pilgrimage to Kiev. I hear them laying the table in the dining-room -- they are going to have supper, they will eat salad, cabbage pies, fried and baked fish. How hungry I am! I would consent to endure any martyrdom, to live in the desert without my mother, to feed bears out of my own hands, if only I might first eat just one cabbage pie!

"Lord, purify me a sinner," I pray, covering my head over. "Guardian angel, save me from the unclean spirit."

The next day, Thursday, I wake up with my heart as pure and clean as a fine spring day. I go gaily and boldly into the church, feeling that I am a communicant, that I have a splendid and expensive shirt on, made out of a silk dress left by my grandmother. In the church everything has an air of joy, happiness, and spring. The faces of the Mother of God and St. John the Divine are not so sorrowful as yesterday. The faces of the communicants are radiant with hope, and it seems as though all the past is forgotten, all is forgiven. Mitka, too, has combed his hair, and is dressed in his best. I look gaily at his protruding ears, and to show that I have nothing against him, I say:

"You look nice to-day, and if your hair did not stand up so, and you weren't so poorly dressed, everybody would think that your mother was not a washerwoman but a lady. Come to me at Easter, we will play knuckle-bones."

Mitka looks at me mistrustfully, and shakes his fist at me on the sly.

And the lady I saw yesterday looks lovely. She is wearing a light blue dress, and a big sparkling brooch in the shape of a horse-shoe. I admire her, and think that, when I am grown-up, I will certainly marry a woman like that, but remembering that getting married is shameful, I leave off thinking about it, and go into the choir where the deacon is already reading the "hours."

A MYSTERY

On the evening of Easter Sunday the actual Civil Councillor, Navagin, on his return from paying calls, picked up the sheet of paper on which visitors had inscribed their names in the hall, and went with it into his study. After taking off his outer garments and drinking some seltzer water, he settled himself comfortably on a couch and began reading the signatures in the list. When his eyes reached the middle of the long list of signatures, he started, gave an ejaculation of astonishment and snapped his fingers, while his face expressed the utmost perplexity.

"Again!" he said, slapping his knee. "It's extraordinary! Again! Again there is the signature of that fellow, goodness knows who he is! Fedyukov! Again!"

Among the numerous signatures on the paper was the signature of a certain Fedyukov. Who the devil this Fedyukov was, Navagin had not a notion. He went over in his memory all his acquaintances, relations and subordinates in the service, recalled his remote past but could recollect no name like Fedyukov. What was so strange was that this *incognito*, Fedyukov, had signed his name regularly every Christmas and Easter for the last thirteen years. Neither Navagin, his wife, nor his house porter knew who he was, where he came from or what he was like.

"It's extraordinary!" Navagin thought in perplexity, as he paced about the study. "It's strange and incomprehensible! It's like sorcery!"

"Call the porter here!" he shouted.

"It's devilish queer! But I will find out who he is!"

"I say, Grigory," he said, addressing the porter as he entered, "that Fedyukov has signed his name again! Did you see him?"

"No, your Excellency."

"Upon my word, but he has signed his name! So he must have been in the hall. Has he been?"

"No, he hasn't, your Excellency."

"How could he have signed his name without being there?"

"I can't tell."

"Who is to tell, then? You sit gaping there in the hall. Try and remember, perhaps someone you didn't know came in? Think a minute!"

"No, your Excellency, there has been no one I didn't know. Our clerks have been, the baroness came to see her Excellency, the priests have been with the Cross, and there has been no one else...."

"Why, he was invisible when he signed his name, then, was he?"

"I can't say: but there has been no Fedyukov here. That I will swear before the holy image...."

"It's queer! It's incomprehensible! It's ex-traordinary!" mused Navagin. "It's positively ludicrous. A man has been signing his name here for thirteen years and you can't find out who he is. Perhaps it's a joke? Perhaps some clerk writes that name as well as his own for fun."

And Navagin began examining Fedyukov's signature.

The bold, florid signature in the old-fashioned style with twirls and flourishes was utterly unlike the handwriting of the other signatures. It was next below the signature of Shtutchkin, the provincial secretary, a scared, timorous little man who would certainly have died of fright if he had ventured upon such an impudent joke.

"The mysterious Fedyukov has signed his name again!" said Navagin, going in to see his wife. "Again I fail to find out who he is."

Madame Navagin was a spiritualist, and so for all phenomena in nature, comprehensible or incomprehensible, she had a very simple explanation.

"There's nothing extraordinary about it," she said. "You don't believe it, of course, but I have said it already and I say it again: there is a great deal in the world that is supernatural, which our feeble intellect can never grasp. I am convinced that this Fedyukov is a spirit who has a sympathy for you . . . If I were you, I would call him up and ask him what he wants."

"Nonsense, nonsense!"

Navagin was free from superstitions, but the phenomenon which interested him was so mysterious that all sorts of uncanny devilry intruded into his mind against his will. All the evening he was imagining that the incognito Fedyukov was the spirit of some long-dead clerk, who had been discharged from the service by Navagin's ancestors and was now revenging himself on their descendant; or perhaps it was the kinsman of some petty official dismissed by Navagin himself, or of a girl seduced by him. . . .

All night Navagin dreamed of a gaunt old clerk in a shabby uniform, with a face as yellow as a lemon, hair that stood up like a brush, and pewtery eyes; the clerk said something in a sepulchral voice and shook a bony finger at him. And Navagin almost had an attack of inflammation of the brain.

For a fortnight he was silent and gloomy and kept walking up and down and thinking. In the end he overcame his sceptical vanity, and going into his wife's room he said in a hollow voice:

"Zina, call up Fedyukov!"

The spiritualistic lady was delighted; she sent for a sheet of cardboard and a saucer, made her husband sit down beside her, and began upon the magic rites.

Fedyukov did not keep them waiting long. . . .

"What do you want?" asked Navagin.

"Repent," answered the saucer.

"What were you on earth?"

"A sinner. . . ."

"There, you see!" whispered his wife, "and you did not believe!"

Navagin conversed for a long time with Fedyukov, and then called up Napoleon, Hannibal, Askotchensky, his aunt Klavdya Zaharovna, and they all gave him brief but correct answers full of deep significance. He was busy with the saucer for four hours, and fell asleep soothed and happy that he had become acquainted with a mysterious world that was new to him. After that he studied spiritualism every day, and at the office, informed the clerks that there was a great deal in nature that was supernatural and marvellous to which our men of science ought to have turned their attention long ago.

Hypnotism, mediumism, bishopism, spiritualism, the fourth dimension, and other misty notions took complete possession of him, so that for whole days at a time, to the great delight of his wife, he read books on spiritualism or devoted himself to the saucer, table-turning, and discussions of supernatural phenomena. At his instigation all his clerks took up spiritualism, too, and with such ardour that the old managing clerk went out of his mind and one day sent a telegram: "Hell. Government House. I feel that I am turning into an evil spirit. What's to be done? Reply paid. Vassily Krinolinsky."

After reading several hundreds of treatises on spiritualism Navagin had a strong desire to write something himself. For five months he sat composing, and in the end had written a huge monograph, entitled: *My Opinion*. When he had finished this essay he determined to send it to a spiritualist journal.

The day on which it was intended to despatch it to the journal was a very memorable one for him. Navagin remembers that on that never-to-be-forgotten day the secretary who had made a fair copy of his article and the sacristan of the parish who had been sent for on business were in his study. Nayagin's face was beaming. He looked lovingly at his creation, felt between his fingers how thick it was, and with a happy smile said to the secretary:

"I propose, Filipp Sergeyitch, to send it registered. It will be safer. . . ." And raising his eyes to the sacristan, he said: "I have sent for you on business, my good man. I am putting my youngest son to the high school and I must have a certificate of baptism; only could you let me have it quickly?"

"Very good, your Excellency!" said the sacristan, bowing. "Very good, I understand. . . ."

"Can you let me have it by to-morrow?"

"Very well, your Excellency, set your mind at rest! To-morrow it shall be ready! Will you send someone to the church to-morrow before evening service? I shall be there. Bid him ask for Fedyukov. I am always there. . . ."

"What!" cried the general, turning pale.

"Fedyukov."

"You, . . . you are Fedyukov?" asked Navagin, looking at him with wide-open eyes.

"Just so, Fedyukov."

"You. . . . you signed your name in my hall?"

"Yes . . ." the sacristan admitted, and was overcome with confusion. "When we come with the Cross, your Excellency, to grand gentlemen's houses I always sign my name. . . . I like doing it. . . . Excuse me, but when I see the list of names in the hall I feel an impulse to sign mine. . . ."

In dumb stupefaction, understanding nothing, hearing nothing, Navagin paced about his study. He touched the curtain over the door, three times waved his hands like a *jeune premier* in a ballet when he sees *her*, gave a whistle and a meaningless smile, and pointed with his finger into space.

"So I will send off the article at once, your Excellency," said the secretary.

These words roused Navagin from his stupour. He looked blankly at the secretary and the sacristan, remembered, and stamping, his foot irritably, screamed in a high, breaking tenor:

"Leave me in peace! Lea-eave me in peace, I tell you! What you want of me I don't understand."

The secretary and the sacristan went out of the study and reached the street while he was still stamping and shouting:

"Leave me in peace! What you want of me I don't understand. Lea-eave me in peace!"

THE COSSACK

Maxim Tortchakov, a farmer in southern Russia, was driving home from church with his young wife and bringing back an Easter cake which had just been blessed. The sun had not yet risen, but the east was all tinged with red and gold and had dissipated the haze which usually, in the early morning, screens the blue of the sky from the eyes. It was quiet. . . . The birds were hardly yet awake. . . . The corncrake uttered its clear note, and far away above a little tumulus, a sleepy kite floated, heavily flapping its wings, and no other living creature could be seen all over the steppe.

Tortchakov drove on and thought that there was no better nor happier holiday than the Feast of Christ's Resurrection. He had only lately been married, and was now keeping his first Easter with his wife. Whatever he looked at, whatever he thought about, it all seemed to him bright, joyous, and happy. He thought about his farming, and thought that it was all going well, that the furnishing of his house was all the heart could desire -- there was enough of everything and all of it good; he looked at his wife, and she seemed to him lovely, kind, and gentle. He was delighted by the glow in the east, and the young grass, and his squeaking chaise, and the kite. . . . And when on the way, he ran into a tavern to light his cigarette and drank a glass, he felt happier still.

"It is said, 'Great is the day,' he chattered. "Yes, it is great! Wait a bit, Lizaveta, the sun will begin to dance. It dances every Easter. So it rejoices too!"

"It is not alive," said his wife.

"But there are people on it!" exclaimed Tortchakov, "there are really! Ivan Stepanitch told me that there are people on all the planets -- on the sun, and on the moon! Truly . . . but maybe the learned men tell lies -- the devil only knows! Stay, surely that's not a horse? Yes, it is!"

At the Crooked Ravine, which was just half-way on the journey home, Tortchakov and his wife saw a saddled horse standing motionless, and sniffing last year's dry grass. On a hillock beside the roadside a red-haired Cossack was sitting doubled up, looking at his feet.

"Christ is risen!" Maxim shouted to him. "Wo-o-o!"

"Truly He is risen," answered the Cossack, without raising his head.

"Where are you going?"

"Home on leave."

"Why are you sitting here, then?"

"Why . . . I have fallen ill . . . I haven't the strength to go on."

"What is wrong?"

"I ache all over."

"H'm. What a misfortune! People are keeping holiday, and you fall sick! But you should ride on to a village or an inn, what's the use of sitting here!"

The Cossack raised his head, and with big, exhausted eyes, scanned Maxim, his wife, and the horse.

"Have you come from church?" he asked.

"Yes."

"The holiday found me on the high road. It was not God's will for me to reach home. I'd get on my horse at once and ride off, but I haven't the strength. . . . You might, good Christians, give a wayfarer some Easter cake to break his fast!"

"Easter cake?" Tortchakov repeated, "That we can, to be sure. . . . Stay, I'll. . . ."

Maxim fumbled quickly in his pockets, glanced at his wife, and said:

"I haven't a knife, nothing to cut it with. And I don't like to break it, it would spoil the whole cake. There's a problem! You look and see if you haven't a knife?"

The Cossack got up groaning, and went to his saddle to get a knife.

"What an idea," said Tortchakov's wife angrily. "I won't let you slice up the Easter cake! What should I look like, taking it home already cut! Ride on to the peasants in the village, and break your fast there!"

The wife took the napkin with the Easter cake in it out of her husband's hands and said:

"I won't allow it! One must do things properly; it's not a loaf, but a holy Easter cake. And it's a sin to cut it just anyhow."

"Well, Cossack, don't be angry," laughed Tortchakov. "The wife forbids it! Good-bye. Good luck on your journey!"

Maxim shook the reins, clicked to his horse, and the chaise rolled on squeaking. For some time his wife went on grumbling, and declaring that to cut the Easter cake before reaching home was a sin and not the proper thing. In the east the first rays of the rising sun shone out, cutting their way through the feathery clouds, and the song of the lark was heard in the sky. Now not one but three kites were hovering over the steppe at a respectful distance from one another. Grasshoppers began churring in the young grass.

When they had driven three-quarters of a mile from the Crooked Ravine, Tortchakov looked round and stared intently into the distance.

"I can't see the Cossack," he said. "Poor, dear fellow, to take it into his head to fall ill on the road. There couldn't be a worse misfortune, to have to travel and not have the strength. . . . I shouldn't wonder if he dies by the roadside. We didn't give him any Easter cake, Lizaveta, and we ought to have given it. I'll be bound he wants to break his fast too."

The sun had risen, but whether it was dancing or not Tortchakov did not see. He remained silent all the way home, thinking and keeping his eyes fixed on the horse's black tail. For some unknown reason he felt overcome by depression, and not a trace of the holiday gladness was left in his heart. When he had arrived home and said, "Christ is risen" to his workmen, he grew cheerful again and began talking, but when he had sat down to break the fast and had taken a bite from his piece of Easter cake, he looked regretfully at his wife, and said:

"It wasn't right of us, Lizaveta, not to give that Cossack something to eat."

"You are a queer one, upon my word," said Lizaveta, shrugging her shoulders in surprise. "Where did you pick up such a fashion as giving away the holy Easter cake on the high road? Is it an ordinary loaf? Now that it is cut and lying on the table, let anyone eat it that likes -- your Cossack too! Do you suppose I grudge it?"

"That's all right, but we ought to have given the Cossack some. . . . Why, he was worse off than a beggar or an orphan. On the road, and far from home, and sick too."

Tortchakov drank half a glass of tea, and neither ate nor drank anything more. He had no appetite, the tea seemed to choke him, and he felt depressed again. After breaking their fast, his wife and he lay down to sleep. When Lizaveta woke two hours later, he was standing by the window, looking into the yard.

"Are you up already?" asked his wife.

"I somehow can't sleep. . . . Ah, Lizaveta," he sighed. "We were unkind, you and I, to that Cossack!"

"Talking about that Cossack again!" yawned his wife. "You have got him on the brain."

"He has served his Tsar, shed his blood maybe, and we treated him as though he were a pig. We ought to have brought the sick man home and fed him, and we did not even give him a morsel of bread."

"Catch me letting you spoil the Easter cake for nothing! And one that has been blessed too! You would have cut it on the road, and shouldn't I have looked a fool when I got home?"

Without saying anything to his wife, Maxim went into the kitchen, wrapped a piece of cake up in a napkin, together with half a dozen eggs, and went to the labourers in the barn.

"Kuzma, put down your concertina," he said to one of them. "Saddle the bay, or Ivantchik, and ride briskly to he Crooked Ravine. There you will see a sick Cossack with a horse, so give him this. Maybe he hasn't ridden away yet."

Maxim felt cheerful again, but after waiting for Kuzma for some hours, he could bear it no longer, so he saddled a horse and went off to meet him. He met him just at the Ravine.

"Well, have you seen the Cossack?"

"I can't find him anywhere, he must have ridden on."

"H'm . . . a queer business."

Tortchakov took the bundle from Kuzma, and galloped on farther. When he reached Shustrovo he asked the peasants:

"Friends, have you seen a sick Cossack with a horse? Didn't he ride by here? A red-headed fellow on a bay horse."

The peasants looked at one another, and said they had not seen the Cossack.

"The returning postman drove by, it's true, but as for a Cossack or anyone else, there has been no such."

Maxim got home at dinner time.

"I can't get that Cossack out of my head, do what you will!" he said to his wife. "He gives me no peace. I keep thinking: what if God meant to try us, and sent some saint or angel in the form of a Cossack? It does happen, you know. It's bad, Lizaveta; we were unkind to the man!"

"What do you keep pestering me with that Cossack for?" cried Lizaveta, losing patience at last. "You stick to it like tar!"

"You are not kind, you know . . ." said Maxim, looking into his wife's face.

And for the first time since his marriage he perceived that he wife was not kind.

"I may be unkind," cried Lizaveta, tapping angrily with her spoon, "but I am not going to give away the holy Easter cake to every drunken man in the road."

"The Cossack wasn't drunk!"

"He was drunk!"

"Well, you are a fool then!"

Maxim got up from the table and began reproaching his young wife for hard-heartedness and stupidity. She, getting angry too, answered his reproaches with reproaches, burst into tears, and went away into their bedroom, declaring she would go home to her father's. This was the first matrimonial squabble that had happened in the Tortchakov's married life. He walked about the yard till the evening, picturing his wife's face, and it seemed to him now spiteful and ugly. And as though to torment him the Cossack haunted his brain, and Maxim seemed to see now his sick eyes, now his unsteady walk.

"Ah, we were unkind to the man," he muttered.

When it got dark, he was overcome by an insufferable depression such as he had never felt before. Feeling so dreary, and being angry with his wife, he got drunk, as he had sometimes done before he was married. In his drunkenness he used bad language and shouted to his wife that she had a spiteful, ugly face, and that next day he would send her packing to her father's. On the morning of Easter Monday, he drank some more to sober himself, and got drunk again.

And with that his downfall began.

His horses, cows, sheep, and hives disappeared one by one from the yard; Maxim was more and more often drunk, debts mounted up, he felt an aversion for his wife. Maxim put down all his misfortunes to the fact that he had an unkind wife, and above all, that God was angry with him on account of the sick Cossack.

Lizaveta saw their ruin, but who was to blame for it she did not understand.

THE LETTER

The clerical superintendent of the district, his Reverence Father Fyodor Orlov, a handsome, well-nourished man of fifty, grave and important as he always was, with an habitual expression of dignity that never left his face, was walking to and fro in his little drawing-room, extremely exhausted, and thinking intensely about the same thing: "When would his visitor go?" The thought worried him and did not leave him for a minute. The visitor, Father Anastasy, the priest of one of the villages near the town, had come to him three hours before on some very unpleasant and dreary business of his own, had stayed on and on, was now sitting in the corner at a little round table with his elbow on a thick account book, and apparently had no thought of going, though it was getting on for nine o'clock in the evening.

Not everyone knows when to be silent and when to go. It not infrequently happens that even diplomatic persons of good worldly breeding fail to observe that their presence is arousing a feeling akin to hatred in their exhausted or busy host, and that this feeling is being concealed with an effort and disguised with a lie. But Father Anastasy perceived it clearly, and realized that his presence was burdensome and inappropriate, that his Reverence, who had taken an early morning service in the night and a long mass at midday, was exhausted and longing for repose; every minute he was meaning to get up and go, but he did not get up, he sat on as though he were waiting for something. He was an old man of sixty-five, prematurely aged, with a bent and bony figure, with a sunken face and the dark skin of old age, with red eyelids and a long narrow back like a fish's; he was dressed in a smart cassock of a light lilac colour, but too big for him (presented to him by the widow of a young priest lately deceased), a full cloth coat with a broad leather belt, and clumsy high boots the size and hue of which showed clearly that Father Anastasy dispensed with goloshes. In spite of his position and his venerable age, there was something pitiful, crushed and humiliated in his lustreless red eyes, in the strands of grey hair with a shade of green in it on the nape of his neck, and in the big shoulder-blades on his lean back. . . . He sat without speaking or moving, and coughed with circumspection, as though afraid that the sound of his coughing might make his presence more noticeable.

The old man had come to see his Reverence on business. Two months before he had been prohibited from officiating till further notice, and his case was being inquired into. His shortcomings were numerous. He was intemperate in his habits, fell out with the other clergy and the commune, kept the church records and accounts carelessly -- these were the formal charges against him; but besides all that, there had been rumours for a long time past that he celebrated unlawful marriages for money and sold certificates of having fasted and taken the sacrament to officials and officers who came to him from the town. These rumours were maintained the more persistently that he was poor and had nine children to keep, who were as incompetent and unsuccessful as himself. The sons were spoilt and uneducated, and stayed at home doing nothing, while the daughters were ugly and did not get married.

Not having the moral force to be open, his Reverence walked up and down the room and said nothing or spoke in hints.

"So you are not going home to-night?" he asked, stopping near the dark window and poking with his little finger into the cage where a canary was asleep with its feathers puffed out.

Father Anastasy started, coughed cautiously and said rapidly:

"Home? I don't care to, Fyodor Ilyitch. I cannot officiate, as you know, so what am I to do there? I came away on purpose that I might not have to look the people in the face. One is ashamed not to officiate, as you know. Besides, I have business here, Fyodor Ilyitch. To-morrow after breaking the fast I want to talk things over thoroughly with the Father charged with the inquiry."

"Ah! . . ." yawned his Reverence, "and where are you staying?"

"At Zyavkin's."

Father Anastasy suddenly remembered that within two hours his Reverence had to take the Easter-night service, and he felt so ashamed of his unwelcome burdensome presence that he made up his mind to go away at once and let the exhausted man rest. And the old man got up to go. But before he began saying good-bye he stood clearing his throat for a minute and looking searchingly at his Reverence's back, still with the same expression of vague expectation in his whole figure; his face was working with shame, timidity, and a pitiful forced laugh such as one sees in people who do not respect themselves. Waving his hand as it were resolutely, he said with a husky quavering laugh:

"Father Fyodor, do me one more kindness: bid them give me at leave-taking . . . one little glass of vodka."

"It's not the time to drink vodka now," said his Reverence sternly. "One must have some regard for decency."

Father Anastasy was still more overwhelmed by confusion; he laughed, and, forgetting his resolution to go away, he dropped back on his chair. His Reverence looked at his helpless, embarrassed face and his bent figure and he felt sorry for the old man.

"Please God, we will have a drink to-morrow," he said, wishing to soften his stem refusal. "Everything is good in due season."

His Reverence believed in people's reforming, but now when a feeling of pity had been kindled in him it seemed to him that this disgraced, worn-out old man, entangled in a network of sins and weaknesses, was hopelessly wrecked, that there was no power on earth that could straighten out his spine, give brightness to his eyes and restrain the unpleasant timid laugh which he laughed on purpose to smoothe over to some slight extent the repulsive impression he made on people.

The old man seemed now to Father Fyodor not guilty and not vicious, but humiliated, insulted, unfortunate; his Reverence thought of his wife, his nine children, the dirty beggarly shelter at Zyavkin's; he thought for some reason of the people who are glad to see priests drunk and persons in authority detected in crimes; and thought that the very best thing Father Anastasy could do now would be to die as soon as possible and to depart from this world for ever.

There were a sound of footsteps.

"Father Fyodor, you are not resting?" a bass voice asked from the passage.

"No, deacon; come in."

Orlov's colleague, the deacon Liubimov, an elderly man with a big bald patch on the top of his head, though his hair was still black and he was still vigorous-looking, with thick black eyebrows like a Georgian's, walked in. He bowed to Father Anastasy and sat down.

"What good news have you?" asked his Reverence.

"What good news?" answered the deacon, and after a pause he went on with a smile: "When your children are little, your trouble is small; when your children are big, your trouble is great. Such goings on, Father Fyodor, that I don't know what to think of it. It's a regular farce, that's what it is."

He paused again for a little, smiled still more broadly and said:

"Nikolay Matveyitch came back from Harkov to-day. He has been telling me about my Pyotr. He has been to see him twice, he tells me."

"What has he been telling you, then?"

"He has upset me, God bless him. He meant to please me but when I came to think it over, it seems there is not much to be pleased at. I ought to grieve rather than be pleased... 'Your Petrushka,' said he, 'lives in fine style. He is far above us now,' said he. 'Well thank God for that,' said I. 'I dined with him,' said he, 'and saw his whole manner of life. He lives like a gentleman,' he said; 'you couldn't wish to live better.' I was naturally interested and I asked, 'And what did you have for dinner?' 'First,' he said, 'a fish course something like fish soup, then tongue and peas,' and then he said, 'roast turkey.' 'Turkey in Lent? that is something to please me,' said I. 'Turkey in Lent? Eh?' "

"Nothing marvellous in that," said his Reverence, screwing up his eyes ironically. And sticking both thumbs in his belt, he drew himself up and said in the tone in which he usually delivered discourses or gave his Scripture lessons to the pupils in the district school: "People who do not keep the fasts are divided into two different categories: some do not keep them through laxity, others through infidelity. Your Pyotr does not keep them through infidelity. Yes."

The deacon looked timidly at Father Fyodor's stern face and said:

"There is worse to follow. . . . We talked and discussed one thing and another, and it turned out that my infidel of a son is living with some madame, another man's wife. She takes the place of wife and hostess in his flat, pours out the tea, receives visitors and all the rest of it, as though she were his lawful wife. For over two years he has been keeping up this dance with this viper. It's a regular farce. They have been living together for three years and no children."

"I suppose they have been living in chastity!" chuckled Father Anastasy, coughing huskily. "There are children, Father Deacon -- there are, but they don't keep them at home! They send them to the Foundling! He-he-he! . . ." Anastasy went on coughing till he choked.

"Don't interfere, Father Anastasy," said his Reverence sternly.

"Nikolay Matveyitch asked him, 'What madame is this helping the soup at your table?' " the deacon went on, gloomily scanning Anastasy's bent figure. " 'That is my wife,' said he. 'When was your wedding?' Nikolay Matveyitch asked him, and Pyotr answered, 'We were married at Kulikov's restaurant.' "

His Reverence's eyes flashed wrathfully and the colour came into his temples. Apart from his sinfulness, Pyotr was not a person he liked. Father Fyodor had, as they say, a grudge against him. He remembered him a boy at school -- he remembered him distinctly, because even then the boy had seemed to him not normal. As a schoolboy, Petrushka had been ashamed to serve at the altar, had been offended at being addressed without ceremony, had not crossed himself on entering the room, and what was still more noteworthy, was fond of talking a great deal and with heat -- and, in Father Fyodor's opinion, much talking was unseemly in children and pernicious to them; moreover Petrushka had taken up a contemptuous and critical attitude to fishing, a pursuit to which both his Reverence and the deacon were greatly addicted. As a student Pyotr had not gone to church at all, had slept till midday, had looked down on people, and had been given to raising delicate and insoluble questions with a peculiarly provoking zest.

"What would you have?" his Reverence asked, going up to the deacon and looking at him angrily. "What would you have? This was to be expected! I always knew and was convinced that nothing good would come of your Pyotr! I told you so, and I tell you so now. What you have sown, that now you must reap! Reap it!"

"But what have I sown, Father Fyodor?" the deacon asked softly, looking up at his Reverence.

"Why, who is to blame if not you? You're his father, he is your offspring! You ought to have admonished him, have instilled the fear of God into him. A child must be taught! You have brought him into the world, but you haven't trained him up in the right way. It's a sin! It's wrong! It's a shame!"

His Reverence forgot his exhaustion, paced to and fro and went on talking. Drops of perspiration came out on the deacon's bald head and forehead. He raised his eyes to his Reverence with a look of guilt, and said:

"But didn't I train him, Father Fyodor? Lord have mercy on us, haven't I been a father to my children? You know yourself I spared nothing for his good; I have prayed and done my best all my life to give him a thorough education. He went to the high school and I got him tutors, and he took his degree at the University. And as to my not being able to influence his mind, Father Fyodor, why, you can judge for yourself that I am not qualified to do so! Sometimes when he used to come here as a student, I would begin admonishing him in my way, and he wouldn't heed me. I'd say to him, 'Go to church,' and he would answer, 'What for?' I would begin explaining, and he would say, 'Why? what for?' Or he would slap me on the shoulder and say, 'Everything in this world is relative, approximate and conditional. I don't know anything, and you don't know anything either, dad.' "

Father Anastasy laughed huskily, cleared his throat and waved his fingers in the air as though preparing to say something. His Reverence glanced at him and said sternly:

"Don't interfere, Father Anastasy."

The old man laughed, beamed, and evidently listened with pleasure to the deacon as though he were glad there were other sinful persons in this world besides himself. The deacon spoke sincerely, with an aching heart. and tears actually came into his eyes. Father Fyodor felt sorry for him.

"You are to blame, deacon, you are to blame," he said, but not so sternly and heatedly as before. "If you could beget him, you ought to know how to instruct him. You ought to have trained him in his childhood; it's no good trying to correct a student."

A silence followed; the deacon clasped his hands and said with a sigh:

"But you know I shall have to answer for him!"

"To be sure you will!"

After a brief silence his Reverence yawned and sighed at the same moment and asked:

"Who is reading the 'Acts'?"

"Yevstrat. Yevstrat always reads them."

The deacon got up and, looking imploringly at his Reverence, asked:

"Father Fyodor, what am I to do now?"

"Do as you please; you are his father, not I. You ought to know best."

"I don't know anything, Father Fyodor! Tell me what to do, for goodness' sake! Would you believe it, I am sick at heart! I can't sleep now, nor keep quiet, and the holiday will be no holiday to me. Tell me what to do, Father Fyodor!"

"Write him a letter."

"What am I to write to him?"

"Write that he mustn't go on like that. Write shortly, but sternly and circumstantially, without softening or smoothing away his guilt. It is your parental duty; if you write, you will have done your duty and will be at peace."

"That's true. But what am I to write to him, to what effect? If I write to him, he will answer, 'Why? what for? Why is it a sin?' "

Father Anastasy laughed hoarsely again, and brandished his fingers.

"Why? what for? why is it a sin?" he began shrilly. "I was once confessing a gentleman, and I told him that excessive confidence in the Divine Mercy is a sin; and he asked, 'Why?' I tried to answer him, but----" Anastasy slapped himself on the forehead. "I had nothing here. He-he-he-he! . . ."

Anastasy's words, his hoarse jangling laugh at what was not laughable, had an unpleasant effect on his Reverence and on the deacon. The former was on the point of saying, "Don't interfere" again, but he did not say it, he only frowned.

"I can't write to him," sighed the deacon.

"If you can't, who can?"

"Father Fyodor!" said the deacon, putting his head on one side and pressing his hand to his heart. "I am an uneducated slow-witted man, while the Lord has vouchsafed you judgment and wisdom. You know everything and understand everything. You can master anything, while I don't know how to put my words together sensibly. Be generous. Instruct me how to write the letter. Teach me what to say and how to say it. . . ."

"What is there to teach? There is nothing to teach. Sit down and write."

"Oh, do me the favour, Father Fyodor! I beseech you! I know he will be frightened and will attend to your letter, because, you see, you are a cultivated man too. Do be so good! I'll sit down, and you'll dictate to me. It will be a sin to write to-morrow, but now would be the very time; my mind would be set at rest."

His Reverence looked at the deacon's imploring face, thought of the disagreeable Pyotr, and consented to dictate. He made the deacon sit down to his table and began.

"Well, write . . . 'Christ is risen, dear son . . .' exclamation mark. 'Rumours have reached me, your father,' then in parenthesis, 'from what source is no concern of yours . . .' close the parenthesis. . . . Have you written it? 'That you are leading a life inconsistent with the laws both of God and of man. Neither the luxurious comfort, nor the worldly splendour, nor the culture with which you seek outwardly to disguise it, can hide your heathen manner of life. In name you are a Christian, but in your real nature a heathen as pitiful and wretched as all other heathens -- more wretched, indeed, seeing that those heathens who know not Christ are lost from ignorance, while you are lost in that, possessing a treasure, you neglect it. I will not enumerate here your vices, which you know well enough; I will say that I see the cause of your ruin in your infidelity. You imagine yourself to be wise, boast of your knowledge of science, but refuse to see that science without faith, far from elevating a man, actually degrades him to the level of a lower animal, inasmuch as. . .' " The whole letter was in this strain.

When he had finished writing it the deacon read it aloud, beamed all over and jumped up.

"It's a gift, it's really a gift!" he said, clasping his hands and looking enthusiastically at his Reverence. "To think of the Lord's bestowing a gift like that! Eh? Holy Mother! I do believe I couldn't write a letter like that in a hundred years. Lord save you!"

Father Anastasy was enthusiastic too.

"One couldn't write like that without a gift," he said, getting up and wagging his fingers-- "that one couldn't! His rhetoric would trip any philosopher and shut him up. Intellect. Brilliant intellect! If you weren't married, Father Fyodor, you would have been a bishop long ago, you would really!"

Having vented his wrath in a letter, his Reverence felt relieved; his fatigue and exhaustion came back to him. The deacon was an old friend, and his Reverence did not hesitate to say to him:

"Well deacon, go, and God bless you. I'll have half an hour's nap on the sofa; I must rest."

The deacon went away and took Anastasy with him. As is always the case on Easter Eve, it was dark in the street, but the whole sky was sparkling with bright luminous stars. There was a scent of spring and holiday in the soft still air.

"How long was he dictating?" the deacon said admiringly. "Ten minutes, not more! It would have taken someone else a month to compose such a letter. Eh! What a mind! Such a mind that I don't know what to call it! It's a marvel! It's really a marvel!"

"Education!" sighed Anastasy as he crossed the muddy street; holding up his cassock to his waist. "It's not for us to compare ourselves with him. We come of the sacristan class, while he has had a learned education. Yes, he's a real man, there is no denying that."

"And you listen how he'll read the Gospel in Latin at mass to-day! He knows Latin and he knows Greek. . . . Ah Petrushka, Petrushka!" the deacon said, suddenly remembering. "Now that will make him scratch his head! That will shut his mouth, that will bring it home to him! Now he won't ask 'Why.' It is a case of one wit to outwit another! Haha-ha!"

The deacon laughed gaily and loudly. Since the letter had been written to Pyotr he had become serene and more cheerful. The consciousness of having performed his duty as a father and his faith in the power of the letter had brought back his mirthfulness and good-humour.

"Pyotr means a stone," said he, as he went into his house. "My Pyotr is not a stone, but a rag. A viper has fastened upon him and he pampers her, and hasn't the pluck to kick her out. Tfoo! To think there should be women like that, God forgive me! Eh? Has she no shame? She has fastened upon the lad, sticking to him, and keeps him tied to her apron strings. . . . Fie upon her!"

"Perhaps it's not she keeps hold of him, but he of her?"

"She is a shameless one anyway! Not that I am defending Pyotr. . . . He'll catch it. He'll read the letter and scratch his head! He'll burn with shame!"

"It's a splendid letter, only you know I wouldn't send it, Father Deacon. Let him alone."

"What?" said the deacon, disconcerted.

"Why. . . . Don't send it, deacon! What's the sense of it? Suppose you send it; he reads it, and . . . and what then? You'll only upset him. Forgive him. Let him alone!"

The deacon looked in surprise at Anastasy's dark face, at his unbuttoned cassock, which looked in the dusk like wings, and shrugged his shoulders.

"How can I forgive him like that?" he asked. "Why I shall have to answer for him to God!"

"Even so, forgive him all the same. Really! And God will forgive you for your kindness to him."

"But he is my son, isn't he? Ought I not to teach him?"

"Teach him? Of course -- why not? You can teach him, but why call him a heathen? It will hurt his feelings, you know, deacon. . . ."

The deacon was a widower, and lived in a little house with three windows. His elder sister, an old maid, looked after his house for him, though she had three years before lost the use of her legs and was confined to her bed; he was afraid of her, obeyed her, and did nothing without her advice. Father Anastasy went in with him. Seeing his table already laid with Easter cakes and red eggs, he began weeping for some reason, probably thinking of his own home, and to turn these tears into a jest, he at once laughed huskily.

"Yes, we shall soon be breaking the fast," he said. "Yes . . . it wouldn't come amiss, deacon, to have a little glass now. Can we? I'll drink it so that the old lady does not hear," he whispered, glancing sideways towards the door.

Without a word the deacon moved a decanter and wineglass towards him. He unfolded the letter and began reading it aloud. And now the letter pleased him just as much as when his Reverence had dictated it to him. He beamed with pleasure and wagged his head, as though he had been tasting something very sweet.

"A-ah, what a letter!" he said. "Petrushka has never dreamt of such a letter. It's just what he wants, something to throw him into a fever. . ."

"Do you know, deacon, don't send it!" said Anastasy, pouring himself out a second glass of vodka as though unconsciously. "Forgive him, let him alone! I am telling you . . . what I really think. If his own father can't forgive him, who will forgive him? And so he'll live without forgiveness. Think, deacon: there will be plenty to chastise him without you, but you should look out for some who will show mercy to your son! I'll . . . I'll . . . have just one more. The last, old man. . . . Just sit down and write straight off to him, 'I forgive you Pyotr!' He will understa-and! He will fe-el it! I understand it from myself, you see old man . . . deacon, I mean. When I lived like other people, I hadn't much to trouble about, but now since I lost the image and semblance, there is only one thing I care about, that good people should forgive me. And remember, too, it's not the righteous but sinners we must forgive. Why should you forgive your old woman if she is not sinful? No, you must forgive a man when he is a sad sight to look at . . . yes!"

Anastasy leaned his head on his fist and sank into thought.

"It's a terrible thing, deacon," he sighed, evidently struggling with the desire to take another glass -- "a terrible thing! In sin my mother bore me, in sin I have lived, in sin I shall die. . . . God forgive me, a sinner! I have gone astray, deacon! There is no salvation for me! And it's not as though I had gone astray in my life, but in old age -- at death's door . . . I . . ."

The old man, with a hopeless gesture, drank off another glass, then got up and moved to another seat. The deacon, still keeping the letter in his hand, was walking up and down the room. He was thinking of his son. Displeasure, distress and anxiety no longer troubled him; all that had gone into the letter. Now he was simply picturing Pyotr; he imagined his face, he thought of the past years when his son used to come to stay with him for the holidays. His thoughts were only of what was good, warm, touching, of which one might think for a whole lifetime without wearying. Longing for his son, he read the letter through once more and looked questioningly at Anastasy.

"Don't send it," said the latter, with a wave of his hand.

"No, I must send it anyway; I must . . . bring him to his senses a little, all the same. It's just as well. . . ."

The deacon took an envelope from the table, but before putting the letter into it he sat down to the table, smiled and added on his own account at the bottom of the letter:

"They have sent us a new inspector. He's much friskier than the old one. He's a great one for dancing and talking, and there's nothing he can't do, so that all the Govorovsky girls are crazy over him. Our military chief, Kostyrev, will soon get the sack too, they say. High time he did!" And very well pleased, without the faintest idea that with this postscript he had completely spoiled the stern letter, the deacon addressed the envelope and laid it in the most conspicuous place on the table.

AN ADVENTURE

(A Driver's Story)

It was in that wood yonder, behind the creek, that it happened, sir. My father, the kingdom of Heaven be his, was taking five hundred roubles to the master; in those days our fellows and the Shepelevsky peasants used to rent land from the master, so father was taking money for the half-year. He was a God-fearing man, he used to read the scriptures, and as for cheating or wronging anyone, or defrauding -- God forbid, and the peasants honoured him greatly, and when someone had to be sent to the town about taxes or such-like, or with money, they used to send him. He was a man above the ordinary, but, not that I'd speak ill of him, he had a weakness. He was fond of a drop. There was no getting him past a tavern: he would go in, drink a glass, and be completely done for! He was aware of this weakness in himself, and when he was carrying public money, that he might not fall asleep or lose it by some chance, he always took me or my sister Anyutka with him.

To tell the truth, all our family have a great taste for vodka. I can read and write, I served for six years at a tobacconist's in the town, and I can talk to any educated gentleman, and can use very fine language, but, it is perfectly true, sir, as I read in a book, that vodka is the blood of Satan. Through vodka my face has darkened. And there is nothing seemly about me, and here, as you may see, sir, I am a cab-driver like an ignorant, uneducated peasant.

And so, as I was telling you, father was taking the money to the master, Anyutka was going with him, and at that time Anyutka was seven or maybe eight -- a silly chit, not that high. He got as far as Kalantchiko successfully, he was sober, but when he reached Kalantchiko and went into Moiseika's tavern, this same weakness of his came upon him. He drank three glasses and set to bragging before people:

"I am a plain humble man," he says, "but I have five hundred roubles in my pocket; if I like," says he, "I could buy up the tavern and all the crockery and Moiseika and his Jewess and his little Jews. I can buy it all out and out," he said. That was his way of joking, to be sure, but then he began complaining: "It's a worry, good Christian people," said he, "to be a rich man, a merchant, or anything of that kind. If you have no money you have no care, if you have money you must watch over your pocket the whole time that wicked men may not rob you. It's a terror to live in the world for a man who has a lot of money."

The drunken people listened of course, took it in, and made a note of it. And in those days they were making a railway line at Kalantchiko, and there were swarms and swarms of tramps and vagabonds of all sorts like locusts. Father pulled himself up afterwards, but it was too late. A word is not a sparrow, if it flies out you can't catch it. They drove, sir, by the wood, and all at once there was someone galloping on horseback behind them. Father was not of the chicken-hearted brigade -- that I couldn't say -- but he felt uneasy; there was no regular road through the wood, nothing went that way but hay and timber, and there was no cause for anyone to be galloping there, particularly in working hours. One wouldn't be galloping after any good.

"It seems as though they are after someone," said father to Anyutka, "they are galloping so furiously. I ought to have kept quiet in the tavern, a plague on my tongue. Oy, little daughter, my heart misgives me, there is something wrong!"

He did not spend long in hesitation about his dangerous position, and he said to my sister Anyutka:

"Things don't look very bright, they really are in pursuit. Anyway, Anyutka dear, you take the money, put it away in your skirts, and go and hide behind a bush. If by ill-luck they attack me, you run back to mother, and give her the money. Let her take it to the village elder. Only mind you don't let anyone see you; keep to the wood and by the creek, that no one may see you. Run your best and call on the merciful God. Christ be with you!"

Father thrust the parcel of notes on Anyutka, and she looked out the thickest of the bushes and hid herself. Soon after, three men on horseback galloped up to father. One a stalwart, big-jawed fellow, in a crimson shirt and high boots, and the other two, ragged, shabby fellows, navvies from the line. As my father feared, so it really turned out, sir. The one in the crimson shirt, the sturdy, strong fellow, a man above the ordinary, left his horse, and all three made for my father.

"Halt you, so-and-so! Where's the money!"

"What money? Go to the devil!"

"Oh, the money you are taking the master for the rent. Hand it over, you bald devil, or we will throttle you, and you'll die in your sins."

And they began to practise their villainy on father, and, instead of beseeching them, weeping, or anything of the sort, father got angry and began to reprove them with the greatest severity.

"What are you pestering me for?" said he. "You are a dirty lot. There is no fear of God in you, plague take you! It's not money you want, but a beating, to make your backs smart for three years after. Be off, blockheads, or I shall defend myself. I have a revolver that takes six bullets, it's in my bosom!"

But his words did not deter the robbers, and they began beating him with anything they could lay their hands on.

They looked through everything in the cart, searched my father thoroughly, even taking off his boots; when they found that beating father only made him swear at them the more, they began torturing him in all sorts of ways. All the time Anyutka was sitting behind the bush, and she saw it all, poor dear. When she saw father lying on the ground and gasping, she started off and ran her hardest through the thicket and the creek towards home. She was only a little girl, with no understanding; she did not know the way, just ran on not knowing where she was going. It was some six miles to our home. Anyone else might have run there in an hour, but a little child, as we all know, takes two steps back for one forwards, and indeed it is not everyone who can run barefoot through the prickly bushes; you want to be used to it, too, and our girls used always to be crowding together on the stove or in the yard, and were afraid to run in the forest.

Towards evening Anyutka somehow reached a habitation, she looked, it was a hut. It was the forester's hut, in the Crown forest; some merchants were renting it at the time and burning charcoal. She knocked. A woman, the forester's wife, came out to her. Anyutka, first of all, burst out crying, and told her everything just as it was, and even told her about the money. The forester's wife was full of pity for her.

"My poor little dear! Poor mite, God has preserved you, poor little one! My precious! Come into the hut, and I will give you something to eat."

She began to make up to Anyutka, gave her food and drink, and even wept with her, and was so attentive to her that the girl, only think, gave her the parcel of notes.

"I will put it away, darling, and to-morrow morning I will give it you back and take you home, dearie."

The woman took the money, and put Anyutka to sleep on the stove where at the time the brooms were drying. And on the same stove, on the brooms, the forester's daughter, a girl as small as our Anyutka, was asleep. And Anyutka used to tell us afterwards that there was such a scent from the brooms, they smelt of honey! Anyutka lay down, but she could not get to sleep, she kept crying quietly; she was sorry for father, and terrified. But, sir, an hour or two passed, and she saw those very three robbers who had tortured father walk into the hut; and the one in the crimson shirt, with big jaws, their leader, went up to the woman and said:

"Well, wife, we have simply murdered a man for nothing. To-day we killed a man at dinner-time, we killed him all right, but not a farthing did we find."

So this fellow in the crimson shirt turned out to be the forester, the woman's husband.

"The man's dead for nothing," said his ragged companions. "In vain we have taken a sin on our souls."

The forester's wife looked at all three and laughed.

"What are you laughing at, silly?"

"I am laughing because I haven't murdered anyone, and I have not taken any sin on my soul, but I have found the money."

"What money? What nonsense are you talking!"

"Here, look whether I am talking nonsense."

The forester's wife untied the parcel and, wicked woman, showed them the money. Then she described how Anyutka had come, what she had said, and so on. The murderers were delighted and began to divide the money between them, they almost quarrelled, then they sat down to the table, you know, to drink. And Anyutka lay there, poor child, hearing every word and shaking like a Jew in a frying-pan. What was she to do? And from their words she learned that father was dead and lying across the road, and she fancied, in her foolishness, that the wolves and the dogs would eat father, and that our horse had gone far away into the forest, and would be eaten by wolves too, and that she, Anyutka herself, would be put in prison and beaten, because she had not taken care of the money. The robbers got drunk and sent the woman for vodka. They gave her five roubles for vodka and sweet wine. They set to singing and drinking on other people's money. They drank and drank, the dogs, and sent the woman off again that they might drink beyond all bounds.

"We will keep it up till morning," they cried. "We have plenty of money now, there is no need to spare! Drink, and don't drink away your wits."

And so at midnight, when they were all fairly fuddled, the woman ran off for vodka the third time, and the forester strode twice up and down the cottage, and he was staggering.

"Look here, lads," he said, "we must make away with the girl, too! If we leave her, she will be the first to bear witness against us."

They talked it over and discussed it, and decided that Anyutka must not be left alive, that she must be killed. Of course, to murder an innocent child's a fearful thing, even a man drunken or crazy would not take such a job on himself. They were quarrelling for maybe an hour which was to kill her, one tried to put it on the other, they almost fought again, and no one would agree to do it; then they cast lots. It fell to the forester. He drank another full glass, cleared his throat, and went to the outer room for an axe.

But Anyutka was a sharp wench. For all she was so simple, she thought of something that, I must say, not many an educated man would have thought of. Maybe the Lord had compassion on her, and gave her sense for the moment, or perhaps it was the fright sharpened her wits, anyway when it came to the test it turned out that she was cleverer than anyone. She got up stealthily, prayed to God, took the little sheepskin, the one the forester's wife had put over her, and, you understand, the forester's little daughter, a girl of the same age as herself, was lying on the stove beside her. She covered this girl with the sheepskin, and took the woman's jacket off her and threw it over herself. Disguised herself, in fact. She put it over her head, and so walked across the hut by the drunken men, and they thought it was the forester's daughter, and did not even look at her. Luckily for her the woman was not in the hut, she had gone for vodka, or maybe she would not have escaped the axe, for a woman's eyes are as far-seeing as a buzzard's. A woman's eyes are sharp.

Anyutka came out of the hut, and ran as fast as her legs could carry her. All night she was lost in the forest, but towards morning she came out to the edge and ran along the road. By the mercy of God she met the clerk Yegor Danilitch, the kingdom of Heaven be his. He was going along with his hooks to catch fish. Anyutka told him all about it. He went back quicker than he came -- thought no more of the fish -- gathered the peasants together in the village, and off they went to the forester's.

They got there, and all the murderers were lying side by side, dead drunk, each where he had fallen; the woman, too, was drunk. First thing they searched them; they took the money and then looked on the stove -- the Holy Cross be with us! The forester's child was lying on the brooms, under the sheepskin, and her head was in a pool of blood, chopped off by the axe. They roused the peasants and the woman, tied their hands behind them, and took them to the district court; the woman howled, but the forester only shook his head and asked:

"You might give me a drop, lads! My head aches!"

Afterwards they were tried in the town in due course, and punished with the utmost rigour of the law.

So that's what happened, sir, beyond the forest there, that lies behind the creek. Now you can scarcely see it, the sun is setting red behind it. I have been talking to you, and the horses have stopped, as though they were listening too. Hey there, my beauties! Move more briskly, the good gentleman will give us something extra. Hey, you darlings!

THE EXAMINING MAGISTRATE

A district doctor and an examining magistrate were driving one fine spring day to an inquest. The examining magistrate, a man of five and thirty, looked dreamily at the horses and said:

"There is a great deal that is enigmatic and obscure in nature; and even in everyday life, doctor, one must often come upon phenomena which are absolutely incapable of explanation. I know, for instance, of several strange, mysterious deaths, the cause of which only spiritualists and mystics will undertake to explain; a clear-headed man can only lift up his hands in perplexity. For example, I know of a highly cultured lady who foretold her own death and died without any apparent reason on the very day she had predicted. She said that she would die on a certain day, and she did die."

"There's no effect without a cause," said the doctor. "If there's a death there must be a cause for it. But as for predicting it there's nothing very marvellous in that. All our ladies -- all our females, in fact -- have a turn for prophecies and presentiments."

"Just so, but my lady, doctor, was quite a special case. There was nothing like the ladies' or other females' presentiments about her prediction and her death. She was a young woman, healthy and clever, with no superstitions of any sort. She had such clear, intelligent, honest eyes; an open, sensible face with a faint, typically Russian look of mockery in her eyes and on her lips. There was nothing of the fine lady or of the female about her, except -- if you like -- her beauty! She was graceful, elegant as that birch tree; she had wonderful hair. That she may be intelligible to you, I will add, too, that she was a person of the most infectious gaiety and carelessness and that intelligent, good sort of frivolity which is only found in good-natured, light-hearted people with brains. Can one talk of mysticism, spiritualism, a turn for presentiment, or anything of that sort, in this case? She used to laugh at all that."

The doctor's chaise stopped by a well. The examining magistrate and the doctor drank some water, stretched, and waited for the coachman to finish watering the horses.

"Well, what did the lady die of?" asked the doctor when the chaise was rolling along the road again.

"She died in a strange way. One fine day her husband went in to her and said that it wouldn't be amiss to sell their old coach before the spring and to buy something rather newer and lighter instead, and that it might be as well to change the left trace horse and to put Bobtchinsky (that was the name of one of her husband's horses) in the shafts.

His wife listened to him and said:

" 'Do as you think best, but it makes no difference to me now. Before the summer I shall be in the cemetery."

"Her husband, of course, shrugged his shoulders and smiled.

" 'I am not joking,' she said. 'I tell you in earnest that I shall soon be dead.'

" 'What do you mean by soon?'

" 'Directly after my confinement. I shall bear my child and die.'

"The husband attached no significance to these words. He did not believe in presentiments of any sort, and he knew that ladies in an interesting condition are apt to be fanciful and to give way to gloomy ideas generally. A day later his wife spoke to him again of dying immediately after her confinement, and then every day she spoke of it and he laughed and called her a silly woman, a fortune-teller, a crazy creature. Her approaching death became an *idée fixé* with his wife. When her husband would not listen to her she would go into the kitchen and talk of her death to the nurse and the cook.

" 'I haven't long to live now, nurse,' she would say. 'As soon as my confinement is over I shall die. I did not want to die so early, but it seems it's my fate.'

"The nurse and the cook were in tears, of course. Sometimes the priest's wife or some lady from a neighbouring estate would come and see her and she would take them aside and open her soul to them, always harping on the same subject, her approaching death. She spoke gravely with an unpleasant smile, even with an angry face which would not allow any contradiction. She had been smart and fashionable in her dress, but now in view of her approaching death she became slovenly; she did not read, she did not laugh, she did not dream aloud. What was more she drove with her aunt to the cemetery and selected a spot for her tomb. Five days before her confinement she made her will. And all this, bear in mind, was done in the best of health, without the faintest hint of illness or danger. A confinement is a difficult affair and sometimes fatal, but in the case of which I am telling you every indication was favourable, and there was absolutely nothing to be afraid of. Her husband was sick of the whole business at last. He lost his temper one day at dinner and asked her:

" 'Listen, Natasha, when is there going to be an end of this silliness?'

" 'It's not silliness, I am in earnest.'

" 'Nonsense, I advise you to give over being silly that you may not feel ashamed of it afterwards.'

"Well, the confinement came. The husband got the very best midwife from the town. It was his wife's first confinement, but it could not have gone better. When it was all over she asked to look at her baby. She looked at it and said:

" 'Well, now I can die.'

"She said good-bye, shut her eyes, and half an hour later gave up her soul to God. She was fully conscious up to the last moment. Anyway when they gave her milk instead of water she whispered softly:

" 'Why are you giving me milk instead of water?'

"So that is what happened. She died as she predicted."

The examining magistrate paused, gave a sigh and said:

"Come, explain why she died. I assure you on my honour, this is not invented, it's a fact."

The doctor looked at the sky meditatively.

"You ought to have had an inquest on her," he said.

"Why?"

"Why, to find out the cause of her death. She didn't die because she had predicted it. She poisoned herself most probably."

The examining magistrate turned quickly, facing the doctor, and screwing up his eyes, asked:

"And from what do you conclude that she poisoned herself?"

"I don't conclude it, but I assume it. Was she on good terms with her husband?"

"H'm, not altogether. There had been misunderstandings soon after their marriage. There were unfortunate circumstances. She had found her husband on one occasion with a lady. She soon forgave him however."

"And which came first, her husband's infidelity or her idea of dying?"

The examining magistrate looked attentively at the doctor as though he were trying to imagine why he put that question.

"Excuse me," he said, not quite immediately. "Let me try and remember." The examining magistrate took off his hat and rubbed his forehead. " Yes, yes . . . it was very shortly after that incident that she began talking of death. Yes, yes."

"Well, there, do you see? . . . In all probability it was at that time that she made up her mind to poison herself, but, as most likely she did not want to kill her child also, she put it off till after her confinement."

"Not likely, not likely! . . . it's impossible. She forgave him at the time."

"That she forgave it quickly means that she had something bad in her mind. Young wives do not forgive quickly."

The examining magistrate gave a forced smile, and, to conceal his too noticeable agitation, began lighting a cigarette.

"Not likely, not likely," he went on. "No notion of anything of the sort being possible ever entered into my head. . . . And besides . . . he was not so much to blame as it seems. . . . He was unfaithful to her in rather a queer way, with no desire to be; he came home at night somewhat elevated, wanted to make love to somebody, his wife was in an interesting condition . . . then he came across a lady who had come to stay for three days -- damnation take her -- an empty-headed creature, silly and not good-looking. It couldn't be reckoned as an infidelity. His wife looked at it in that way herself and soon . . . forgave it. Nothing more was said about it. . . ."

"People don't die without a reason," said the doctor.

"That is so, of course, but all the same . . . I cannot admit that she poisoned herself. But it is strange that the idea has never struck me before! And no one thought of it! Everyone was astonished that her prediction had come to pass, and the idea . . . of such a death was far from their mind. And indeed, it cannot be that she poisoned herself! No!"

The examining magistrate pondered. The thought of the woman who had died so strangely haunted him all through the inquest. As he noted down what the doctor dictated to him he moved his eyebrows gloomily and rubbed his forehead.

"And are there really poisons that kill one in a quarter of an hour, gradually, without any pain?" he asked the doctor while the latter was opening the skull.

"Yes, there are. Morphia for instance."

"H'm, strange. I remember she used to keep something of the sort. . . . But it could hardly be."

On the way back the examining magistrate looked exhausted, he kept nervously biting his moustache, and was unwilling to talk.

"Let us go a little way on foot," he said to the doctor. "I am tired of sitting."

After walking about a hundred paces, the examining magistrate seemed to the doctor to be overcome with fatigue, as though he had been climbing up a high mountain. He stopped and, looking at the doctor with a strange look in his eyes, as though he were drunk, said:

"My God, if your theory is correct, why it's. . . it was cruel, inhuman! She poisoned herself to punish some one else! Why, was the sin so great? Oh, my God! And why did you make me a present of this damnable idea, doctor!"

The examining magistrate clutched at his head in despair, and went on:

"What I have told you was about my own wife, about myself. Oh, my God! I was to blame, I wounded her, but can it have been easier to die than to forgive? That's typical feminine logic -- cruel, merciless logic. Oh, even then when she was living she was cruel! I recall it all now! It's all clear to me now!"

As the examining magistrate talked he shrugged his shoulders, then clutched at his head. He got back into the carriage, then walked again. The new idea the doctor had imparted to him seemed to have overwhelmed him, to have poisoned him; he was distracted, shattered in body and soul, and when he got back to the town he said good-bye to the doctor, declining to stay to dinner though he had promised the doctor the evening before to dine with him.

ABORIGINES

Between nine and ten in the morning. Ivan Lyashkevsky, a lieutenant of Polish origin, who has at some time or other been wounded in the head, and now lives on his pension in a town in one of the southern provinces, is sitting in his lodgings at the open window talking to Franz Stepanitch Finks, the town architect, who has come in to see him for a minute. Both have thrust their heads out of the window, and are looking in the direction of the gate near which Lyashkevsky's landlord, a plump little native with pendulous perspiring cheeks, in full, blue trousers, is sitting on a bench with his waistcoat unbuttoned. The native is plunged in deep thought, and is absent-mindedly prodding the toe of his boot with a stick.

"Extraordinary people, I tell you," grumbled Lyashkevsky, looking angrily at the native, "here he has sat down on the bench, and so he will sit, damn the fellow, with his hands folded till evening. They do absolutely nothing. The wastrels and loafers! It would be all right, you scoundrel, if you had money lying in the bank, or had a farm of your own where others would be working for you, but here you have not a penny to your name, you eat the bread of others, you are in debt all round, and you starve your family -- devil take you! You wouldn't believe me, Franz Stepanitch, sometimes it makes me so cross that I could jump out of the window and give the low fellow a good horse-whipping. Come, why don't you work? What are you sitting there for?"

The native looks indifferently at Lyashkevsky, tries to say something but cannot; sloth and the sultry heat have paralysed his conversational faculties. . . . Yawning lazily, he makes the sign of the cross over his mouth, and turns his eyes up towards the sky where pigeons fly, bathing in the hot air.

"You must not be too severe in your judgments, honoured friend," sighs Finks, mopping his big bald head with his handkerchief. "Put yourself in their place: business is slack now, there's unemployment all round, a bad harvest, stagnation in trade."

"Good gracious, how you talk!" cries Lyashkevsky in indignation, angrily wrapping his dressing gown round him. "Supposing he has no job and no trade, why doesn't he work in his own home, the devil flay him! I say! Is there no work for you at home? Just look, you brute! Your steps have come to pieces, the plankway is falling into the ditch, the fence is rotten; you had better set to and mend it all, or if you don't know how, go into the kitchen and help your wife. Your wife is running out every minute to fetch water or carry out the slops. Why shouldn't you run instead, you rascal? And then you must remember, Franz Stepanitch, that he has six acres of garden, that he has pigsties and poultry houses, but it is all wasted and no use. The flower garden is overgrown with weeds and almost baked dry, while the boys play ball in the kitchen garden. Isn't he a lazy brute? I assure you, though I have only the use of an acre and a half with my lodgings, you will always find radishes, and salad, and fennel, and onions, while that blackguard buys everything at the market."

"He is a Russian, there is no doing anything with him," said Finks with a condescending smile; "it's in the Russian blood. . . . They are a very lazy people! If all property were given to Germans or Poles, in a year's time you would not recognise the town."

The native in the blue trousers beckons a girl with a sieve, buys a kopeck's worth of sunflower seeds from her and begins cracking them.

"A race of curs!" says Lyashkevsky angrily. "That's their only occupation, they crack sunflower seeds and they talk politics! The devil take them!"

Staring wrathfully at the blue trousers, Lyashkevsky is gradually roused to fury, and gets so excited that he actually foams at the mouth. He speaks with a Polish accent, rapping out each syllable venomously, till at last the little bags under his eyes swell, and he abandons the Russian "scoundrels, blackguards, and rascals," and rolling his eyes, begins pouring out a shower of Polish oaths, coughing from his efforts. "Lazy dogs, race of curs. May the devil take them!"

The native hears this abuse distinctly, but, judging from the appearance of his crumpled little figure, it does not affect him. Apparently he has long ago grown as used to it as to the buzzing of the flies, and feels it superfluous to protest. At every visit Finks has to listen to a tirade on the subject of the lazy good-for-nothing aborigines, and every time exactly the same one.

"But . . . I must be going," he says, remembering that he has no time to spare. "Good-bye!"

"Where are you off to?"

"I only looked in on you for a minute. The wall of the cellar has cracked in the girls' high school, so they asked me to go round at once to look at it. I must go."

"H'm. . . . I have told Varvara to get the samovar," says Lyashkevsky, surprised. "Stay a little, we will have some tea; then you shall go."

Finks obediently puts down his hat on the table and remains to drink tea. Over their tea Lyashkevsky maintains that the natives are hopelessly ruined, that there is only one thing to do, to take them all indiscriminately and send them under strict escort to hard labour.

"Why, upon my word," he says, getting hot, "you may ask what does that goose sitting there live upon! He lets me lodgings in his house for seven roubles a month, and he goes to name-day parties, that's all that he has to live on, the knave, may the devil take him! He has neither earnings nor an income. They are not merely sluggards and wastrels, they are swindlers too, they are continually borrowing money from the town bank, and what do they do with it? They plunge into some scheme such as sending bulls to Moscow, or building oil presses on a new system; but to send bulls to Moscow or to press oil you want to have a head on your shoulders, and these rascals have pumpkins on theirs! Of course all their schemes end in smoke. . . . They waste their money, get into a mess, and then snap their fingers at the bank. What can you get out of them? Their houses are mortgaged over and over again, they have no other property -- it's all been drunk and eaten up long ago. Nine-tenths of them are swindlers, the scoundrels! To borrow money and not return it is their rule. Thanks to them the town bank is going smash!"

"I was at Yegorov's yesterday," Finks interrupts the Pole, anxious to change the conversation, "and only fancy, I won six roubles and a half from him at picquet."

"I believe I still owe you something at picquet," Lyashkevsky recollects, "I ought to win it back. Wouldn't you like one game?"

"Perhaps just one," Finks assents. "I must make haste to the high school, you know."

Lyashkevsky and Finks sit down at the open window and begin a game of picquet. The native in the blue trousers stretches with relish, and husks of sunflower seeds fall in showers from all over him on to the ground. At that moment from the gate opposite appears another native with a long beard, wearing a crumpled yellowish-grey cotton coat. He screws up his eyes affectionately at the blue trousers and shouts:

"Good-morning, Semyon Nikolaitch, I have the honour to congratulate you on the Thursday."

"And the same to you, Kapiton Petrovitch!"

"Come to my seat! It's cool here!"

The blue trousers, with much sighing and groaning and waddling from side to side like a duck, cross the street.

"Tierce major . . ." mutters Lyashkevsky, "from the queen. . . . Five and fifteen. . . . The rascals are talking of politics. . . . Do you hear? They have begun about England. I have six hearts."

"I have the seven spades. My point."

"Yes, it's yours. Do you hear? They are abusing Beaconsfield. They don't know, the swine, that Beaconsfield has been dead for ever so long. So I have twenty-nine. . . . Your lead."

"Eight . . . nine . . . ten . . . . Yes, amazing people, these Russians! Eleven . . . twelve. . . . The Russian inertia is unique on the terrestrial globe."

"Thirty . . . Thirty-one. . . . One ought to take a good whip, you know. Go out and give them Beaconsfield. I say, how their tongues are wagging! It's easier to babble than to work. I suppose you threw away the queen of clubs and I didn't realise it."

"Thirteen . . . Fourteen. . . . It's unbearably hot! One must be made of iron to sit in such heat on a seat in the full sun! Fifteen."

The first game is followed by a second, the second by a third.... Finks loses, and by degrees works himself up into a gambling fever and forgets all about the cracking walls of the high school cellar. As Lyashkevsky plays he keeps looking at the aborigines. He sees them, entertaining each other with conversation, go to the open gate, cross the filthy yard and sit down on a scanty patch of shade under an aspen tree. Between twelve and one o'clock the fat cook with brown legs spreads before them something like a baby's sheet with brown stains upon it, and gives them their dinner. They eat with wooden spoons, keep brushing away the flies, and go on talking.

"The devil, it is beyond everything," cries Lyashkevsky, revolted. "I am very glad I have not a gun or a revolver or I should have a shot at those cattle. I have four knaves -- fourteen.... Your point.... It really gives me a twitching in my legs. I can't see those ruffians without being upset."

"Don't excite yourself, it is bad for you."

"But upon my word, it is enough to try the patience of a stone!"

When he has finished dinner the native in blue trousers, worn out and exhausted, staggering with laziness and repletion, crosses the street to his own house and sinks feebly on to his bench. He is struggling with drowsiness and the gnats, and is looking about him as dejectedly as though he were every minute expecting his end. His helpless air drives Lyashkevsky out of all patience. The Pole pokes his head out of the window and shouts at him, spluttering:

"Been gorging? Ah, the old woman! The sweet darling. He has been stuffing himself, and now he doesn't know what to do with his tummy! Get out of my sight, you confounded fellow! Plague take you!"

The native looks sourly at him, and merely twiddles his fingers instead of answering. A school-boy of his acquaintance passes by him with his satchel on his back. Stopping him the native ponders a long time what to say to him, and asks:

"Well, what now?"

"Nothing."

"How, nothing?"

"Why, just nothing."

"H'm. . . . And which subject is the hardest?"

"That's according." The school-boy shrugs his shoulders.

"I see -- er . . . What is the Latin for tree?"

"Arbor."

"Aha. . . . And so one has to know all that," sighs the blue trousers. "You have to go into it all. . . . It's hard work, hard work. . . . Is your dear Mamma well?"

"She is all right, thank you."

"Ah. . . . Well, run along."

After losing two roubles Finks remembers the high school and is horrified.

"Holy Saints, why it's three o'clock already. How I have been staying on. Good-bye, I must run. . . ."

"Have dinner with me, and then go," says Lyashkevsky. "You have plenty of time."

Finks stays, but only on condition that dinner shall last no more than ten minutes. After dining he sits for some five minutes on the sofa and thinks of the cracked wall, then resolutely lays his head on the cushion and fills the room with a shrill whistling through his nose. While he is asleep, Lyashkevsky, who does not approve of an afternoon nap, sits at the window, stares at the dozing native, and grumbles:

"Race of curs! I wonder you don't choke with laziness. No work, no intellectual or moral interests, nothing but vegetating . . . . disgusting. Tfoo!"

At six o'clock Finks wakes up.

"It's too late to go to the high school now," he says, stretching. "I shall have to go to-morrow, and now. . . . How about my revenge? Let's have one more game. . . ."

After seeing his visitor off, between nine and ten, Lyashkevsky looks after him for some time, and says:

"Damn the fellow, staying here the whole day and doing absolutely nothing. . . . Simply get their salary and do no work; the devil take them! . . . The German pig. . . ."

He looks out of the window, but the native is no longer there. He has gone to bed. There is no one to grumble at, and for the first time in the day he keeps his mouth shut, but ten minutes passes and he cannot restrain the depression that overpowers him, and begins to grumble, shoving the old shabby armchair:

"You only take up room, rubbishy old thing! You ought to have been burnt long ago, but I keep forgetting to tell them to chop you up. It's a disgrace!"

And as he gets into bed he presses his hand on a spring of the mattress, frowns and says peevishly:

"The con--found--ed spring! It will cut my side all night. I will tell them to rip up the mattress to-morrow and get you out, you useless thing."

He falls asleep at midnight, and dreams that he is pouring boiling water over the natives, Finks, and the old armchair.

VOLODYA

At five o'clock one Sunday afternoon in summer, Volodya, a plain, shy, sickly-looking lad of seventeen, was sitting in the arbour of the Shumihins' country villa, feeling dreary. His despondent thought flowed in three directions. In the first place, he had next day, Monday, an examination in mathematics; he knew that if he did not get through the written examination on the morrow, he would be expelled, for he had already been two years in the sixth form and had two and three-quarter marks for algebra in his annual report. In the second place, his presence at the villa of the Shumihins, a wealthy family with aristocratic pretensions, was a continual source of mortification to his amour-propre. It seemed to him that Madame Shumihin looked upon him and his *maman* as poor relations and dependents, that they laughed at his *maman* and did not respect her. He had on one occasion accidently overheard Madame Shumihin, in the verandah, telling her cousin Anna Fyodorovna that his *maman* still tried to look young and got herself up, that she never paid her losses at cards, and had a partiality for other people's shoes and tobacco. Every day Volodya besought his *maman* not to go to the Shumihins', and drew a picture of the humiliating part she played with these gentlefolk. He tried to persuade her, said rude things, but she -- a frivolous, pampered woman, who had run through two fortunes, her own and her husband's, in her time, and always gravitated towards acquaintances of high rank -- did not understand him, and twice a week Volodya had to accompany her to the villa he hated.

In the third place, the youth could not for one instant get rid of a strange, unpleasant feeling which was absolutely new to him. . . . It seemed to him that he was in love with Anna Fyodorovna, the Shumihins' cousin, who was staying with them. She was a vivacious, loud-voiced, laughter-loving, healthy, and vigorous lady of thirty, with rosy cheeks, plump shoulders, a plump round chin and a continual smile on her thin lips. She was neither young nor beautiful -- Volodya knew that perfectly well; but for some reason he could not help thinking of her, looking at her while she shrugged her plump shoulders and moved her flat back as she played croquet, or after prolonged laughter and running up and down stairs, sank into a low chair, and, half closing her eyes and gasping for breath, pretended that she was stifling and could not breathe. She was married. Her husband, a staid and dignified architect, came once a week to the villa, slept soundly, and returned to town. Volodya's strange feeling had begun with his conceiving an unaccountable hatred for the architect, and feeling relieved every time he went back to town.

Now, sitting in the arbour, thinking of his examination next day, and of his *maman,* at whom they laughed, he felt an intense desire to see Nyuta (that was what the Shumihins called Anna Fyodorovna), to hear her laughter and the rustle of her dress. . . . This desire was not like the pure, poetic love of which he read in novels and about which he dreamed every night when he went to bed; it was strange, incomprehensible; he was ashamed of it, and afraid of it as of something very wrong and impure, something which it was disagreeable to confess even to himself.

"It's not love," he said to himself. "One can't fall in love with women of thirty who are married. It is only a little intrigue. . . . Yes, an intrigue. . . ."

Pondering on the "intrigue," he thought of his uncontrollable shyness, his lack of moustache, his freckles, his narrow eyes, and put himself in his imagination side by side with Nyuta, and the juxtaposition seemed to him impossible; then he made haste to imagine himself bold, handsome, witty, dressed in the latest fashion.

When his dreams were at their height, as he sat huddled together and looking at the ground in a dark corner of the arbour, he heard the sound of light footsteps. Some one was coming slowly along the avenue. Soon the steps stopped and something white gleamed in the entrance.

"Is there anyone here?" asked a woman's voice.

Volodya recognised the voice, and raised his head in a fright.

"Who is here?" asked Nyuta, going into the arbour. "Ah, it is you, Volodya? What are you doing here? Thinking? And how can you go on thinking, thinking, thinking? . . . That's the way to go out of your mind!"

Volodya got up and looked in a dazed way at Nyuta. She had only just come back from bathing. Over her shoulder there was hanging a sheet and a rough towel, and from under the white silk kerchief on her head he could see the wet hair sticking to her forehead. There was the cool damp smell of the bath-house and of almond soap still hanging about her. She was out of breath from running quickly. The top button of her blouse was undone, so that the boy saw her throat and bosom.

"Why don't you say something?" said Nyuta, looking Volodya up and down. "It's not polite to be silent when a lady talks to you. What a clumsy seal you are though, Volodya! You always sit, saying nothing, thinking like some philosopher. There's not a spark of life or fire in you! You are really horrid! . . . At your age you ought to be living, skipping, and jumping, chattering, flirting, falling in love."

Volodya looked at the sheet that was held by a plump white hand, and thought. . . .

"He's mute," said Nyuta, with wonder; "it is strange, really. . . . Listen! Be a man! Come, you might smile at least! Phew, the horrid philosopher!" she laughed. "But do you know, Volodya, why you are such a clumsy seal? Because you don't devote yourself to the ladies. Why don't you? It's true there are no girls here, but there is nothing to prevent your flirting with the married ladies! Why don't you flirt with me, for instance?"

Volodya listened and scratched his forehead in acute and painful irresolution.

"It's only very proud people who are silent and love solitude," Nyuta went on, pulling his hand away from his forehead. "You are proud, Volodya. Why do you look at me like that from under your brows? Look me straight in the face, if you please! Yes, now then, clumsy seal!"

Volodya made up his mind to speak. Wanting to smile, he twitched his lower lip, blinked, and again put his hand to his forehead.

"I . . . I love you," he said.

Nyuta raised her eyebrows in surprise, and laughed.

"What do I hear?" she sang, as prima-donnas sing at the opera when they hear something awful. "What? What did you say? Say it again, say it again...."

"I... I love you!" repeated Volodya.

And without his will's having any part in his action, without reflection or understanding, he took half a step towards Nyuta and clutched her by the arm. Everything was dark before his eyes, and tears came into them. The whole world was turned into one big, rough towel which smelt of the bathhouse.

"Bravo, bravo!" he heard a merry laugh. "Why don't you speak? I want you to speak! Well?"

Seeing that he was not prevented from holding her arm, Volodya glanced at Nyuta's laughing face, and clumsily, awkwardly, put both arms round her waist, his hands meeting behind her back. He held her round the waist with both arms, while, putting her hands up to her head, showing the dimples in her elbows, she set her hair straight under the kerchief and said in a calm voice:

"You must be tactful, polite, charming, and you can only become that under feminine influence. But what a wicked, angry face you have! You must talk, laugh.... Yes, Volodya, don't be surly; you are young and will have plenty of time for philosophising. Come, let go of me; I am going. Let go."

Without effort she released her waist, and, humming something, walked out of the arbour. Volodya was left alone. He smoothed his hair, smiled, and walked three times to and fro across the arbour, then he sat down on the bench and smiled again. He felt insufferably ashamed, so much so that he wondered that human shame could reach such a pitch of acuteness and intensity. Shame made him smile, gesticulate, and whisper some disconnected words.

He was ashamed that he had been treated like a small boy, ashamed of his shyness, and, most of all, that he had had the audacity to put his arms round the waist of a respectable married woman, though, as it seemed to him, he had neither through age nor by external quality, nor by social position any right to do so.

He jumped up, went out of the arbour, and, without looking round, walked into the recesses of the garden furthest from the house.

"Ah! only to get away from here as soon as possible," he thought, clutching his head. "My God! as soon as possible."

The train by which Volodya was to go back with his *maman* was at eight-forty. There were three hours before the train started, but he would with pleasure have gone to the station at once without waiting for his *maman*.

At eight o'clock he went to the house. His whole figure was expressive of determination: what would be, would be! He made up his mind to go in boldly, to look them straight in the face, to speak in a loud voice, regardless of everything.

He crossed the terrace, the big hall and the drawing-room, and there stopped to take breath. He could hear them in the dining-room, drinking tea. Madame Shumihin, *maman,* and Nyuta were talking and laughing about something.

Volodya listened.

"I assure you!" said Nyuta. "I could not believe my eyes! When he began declaring his passion and -- just imagine! -- put his arms round my waist, I should not have recognised him. And you know he has a way with him! When he told me he was in love with me, there was something brutal in his face, like a Circassian."

"Really!" gasped *maman,* going off into a peal of laughter. "Really! How he does remind me of his father!"

Volodya ran back and dashed out into the open air.

"How could they talk of it aloud!" he wondered in agony, clasping his hands and looking up to the sky in horror. "They talk aloud in cold blood . . . and *maman* laughed! . . . *Maman!* My God, why didst Thou give me such a mother? Why?"

But he had to go to the house, come what might. He walked three times up and down the avenue, grew a little calmer, and went into the house.

"Why didn't you come in in time for tea?" Madame Shumihin asked sternly.

"I am sorry, it's . . . it's time for me to go," he muttered, not raising his eyes. "*Maman*, it's eight o'clock!"

"You go alone, my dear," said his *maman* languidly. "I am staying the night with Lili. Goodbye, my dear. . . . Let me make the sign of the cross over you."

She made the sign of the cross over her son, and said in French, turning to Nyuta:

"He's rather like Lermontov . . . isn't he?"

Saying good-bye after a fashion, without looking anyone in the face, Volodya went out of the dining-room. Ten minutes later he was walking along the road to the station, and was glad of it. Now he felt neither frightened nor ashamed; he breathed freely and easily.

About half a mile from the station, he sat down on a stone by the side of the road, and gazed at the sun, which was half hidden behind a barrow. There were lights already here and there at the station, and one green light glimmered dimly, but the train was not yet in sight. It was pleasant to Volodya to sit still without moving, and to watch the evening coming little by little. The darkness of the arbour, the footsteps, the smell of the bath-house, the laughter, and the waist -- all these rose with amazing vividness before his imagination, and all this was no longer so terrible and important as before.

"It's of no consequence. . . . She did not pull her hand away, and laughed when I held her by the waist," he thought. "So she must have liked it. If she had disliked it she would have been angry . . . ."

And now Volodya felt sorry that he had not had more boldness there in the arbour. He felt sorry that he was so stupidly going away, and he was by now persuaded that if the same thing happened again he would be bolder and look at it more simply.

And it would not be difficult for the opportunity to occur again. They used to stroll about for a long time after supper at the Shumihins'. If

Volodya went for a walk with Nyuta in the dark garden, there would be an opportunity!

"I will go back," he thought, "and will go by the morning train to-morrow. . . . I will say I have missed the train."

And he turned back. . . . Madame Shumihin, *Maman*, Nyuta, and one of the nieces were sitting on the verandah, playing *vint*. When Volodya told them the lie that he had missed the train, they were uneasy that he might be late for the examination day, and advised him to get up early. All the while they were playing he sat on one side, greedily watching Nyuta and waiting. . . . He already had a plan prepared in his mind: he would go up to Nyuta in the dark, would take her by the hand, then would embrace her; there would be no need to say anything, as both of them would understand without words.

But after supper the ladies did not go for a walk in the garden, but went on playing cards. They played till one o'clock at night, and then broke up to go to bed.

"How stupid it all is!" Volodya thought with vexation as he got into bed. "But never mind; I'll wait till to-morrow . . . to-morrow in the arbour. It doesn't matter. . . ."

He did not attempt to go to sleep, but sat in bed, hugging his knees and thinking. All thought of the examination was hateful to him. He had already made up his mind that they would expel him, and that there was nothing terrible about his being expelled. On the contrary, it was a good thing -- a very good thing, in fact. Next day he would be as free as a bird; he would put on ordinary clothes instead of his school uniform, would smoke openly, come out here, and make love to Nyuta when he liked; and he would not be a schoolboy but "a young man." And as for the rest of it, what is called a career, a future, that was clear; Volodya would go into the army or the telegraph service, or he would go into a chemist's shop and work his way up till he was a dispenser. . . . There were lots of callings. An hour or two passed, and he was still sitting and thinking. . . .

Towards three o'clock, when it was beginning to get light, the door creaked cautiously and his *maman* came into the room.

"Aren't you asleep?" she asked, yawning. "Go to sleep; I have only come in for a minute. . . . I am only fetching the drops. . . ."

"What for?"

"Poor Lili has got spasms again. Go to sleep, my child, your examination's to-morrow. . . ."

She took a bottle of something out of the cupboard, went to the window, read the label, and went away.

"Marya Leontyevna, those are not the drops!" Volodya heard a woman's voice, a minute later. "That's convallaria, and Lili wants morphine. Is your son asleep? Ask him to look for it. . . ."

It was Nyuta's voice. Volodya turned cold. He hurriedly put on his trousers, flung his coat over his shoulders, and went to the door.

"Do you understand? Morphine," Nyuta explained in a whisper. "There must be a label in Latin. Wake Volodya; he will find it."

Maman opened the door and Volodya caught sight of Nyuta. She was wearing the same loose wrapper in which she had gone to bathe. Her hair hung loose and disordered on her shoulders, her face looked sleepy and dark in the half-light. . . .

"Why, Volodya is not asleep," she said. "Volodya, look in the cupboard for the morphine, there's a dear! What a nuisance Lili is! She has always something the matter."

Maman muttered something, yawned, and went away.

"Look for it," said Nyuta. "Why are you standing still?"

Volodya went to the cupboard, knelt down, and began looking through the bottles and boxes of medicine. His hands were trembling, and he had a feeling in his chest and stomach as though cold waves were running all over his inside. He felt suffocated and giddy from the smell of ether, carbolic acid, and various drugs, which he quite unnecessarily snatched up with his trembling fingers and spilled in so doing.

"I believe *maman* has gone," he thought. "That's a good thing . . . a good thing. . . ."

"Will you be quick?" said Nyuta, drawling.

"In a minute. . . . Here, I believe this is morphine," said Volodya, reading on one of the labels the word "morph . . ." "Here it is!"

Nyuta was standing in the doorway in such a way that one foot was in his room and one was in the passage. She was tidying her hair, which was difficult to put in order because it was so thick and long, and looked absent-mindedly at Volodya. In her loose wrap, with her sleepy face and her hair down, in the dim light that came into the white sky not yet lit by the sun, she seemed to Volodya captivating, magnificent. . . . Fascinated, trembling all over, and remembering with relish how he had held that exquisite body in his arms in the arbour, he handed her the bottle and said:

"How wonderful you are!"

"What?"

She came into the room.

"What?" she asked, smiling.

He was silent and looked at her, then, just as in the arbour, he took her hand, and she looked at him with a smile and waited for what would happen next.

"I love you," he whispered.

She left off smiling, thought a minute, and said:

"Wait a little; I think somebody is coming. Oh, these schoolboys!" she said in an undertone, going to the door and peeping out into the passage. "No, there is no one to be seen. . . ."

She came back.

Then it seemed to Volodya that the room, Nyuta, the sunrise and himself -- all melted together in one sensation of acute, extraordinary, incredible bliss, for which one might give up one's whole life and face eternal torments. . . . But half a minute passed and all that vanished. Volodya saw only a fat, plain face, distorted by an expression of repulsion, and he himself suddenly felt a loathing for what had happened.

"I must go away, though," said Nyuta, looking at Volodya with disgust. "What a wretched, ugly . . . fie, ugly duckling!"

How unseemly her long hair, her loose wrap, her steps, her voice seemed to Volodya now! . . .

" 'Ugly duckling' . . ." he thought after she had gone away. "I really am ugly . . . everything is ugly."

The sun was rising, the birds were singing loudly; he could hear the gardener walking in the garden and the creaking of his wheelbarrow . . . and soon afterwards he heard the lowing of the cows and the sounds of the shepherd's pipe. The sunlight and the sounds told him that somewhere in this world there is a pure, refined, poetical life. But where was it? Volodya had never heard a word of it from his *maman* or any of the people round about him.

When the footman came to wake him for the morning train, he pretended to be asleep. . . .

"Bother it! Damn it all!" he thought.

He got up between ten and eleven.

Combing his hair before the looking-glass, and looking at his ugly face, pale from his sleepless night, he thought:

"It's perfectly true . . . an ugly duckling!"

When *maman* saw him and was horrified that he was not at his examination, Volodya said:

"I overslept myself, *maman*. . . . But don't worry, I will get a medical certificate."

Madame Shumihin and Nyuta waked up at one o'clock. Volodya heard Madame Shumihin open her window with a bang, heard Nyuta go off into a peal of laughter in reply to her coarse voice. He saw the door open and a string of nieces and other toadies (among the latter was his *maman*) file into lunch, caught a glimpse of Nyuta's freshly washed laughing face, and, beside her, the black brows and beard of her husband the architect, who had just arrived.

Nyuta was wearing a Little Russian dress which did not suit her at all, and made her look clumsy; the architect was making dull and vulgar jokes. The rissoles served at lunch had too much onion in them -- so it seemed to Volodya. It also seemed to him that Nyuta laughed loudly on purpose, and kept glancing in his direction to give him to understand that the memory of the night did not trouble her in the least, and that she was not aware of the presence at table of the "ugly duckling."

At four o'clock Volodya drove to the station with his *maman*. Foul memories, the sleepless night, the prospect of expulsion from school, the stings of conscience -- all roused in him now an oppressive, gloomy anger. He looked at *maman*'s sharp profile, at her little nose, and at the raincoat which was a present from Nyuta, and muttered:

"Why do you powder? It's not becoming at your age! You make yourself up, don't pay your debts at cards, smoke other people's tobacco. . . . It's hateful! I don't love you . . . I don't love you!"

He was insulting her, and she moved her little eyes about in alarm, flung up her hands, and whispered in horror:

"What are you saying, my dear! Good gracious! the coachman will hear! Be quiet or the coachman will hear! He can overhear everything."

"I don't love you . . . I don't love you!" he went on breathlessly. "You've no soul and no morals. . . . Don't dare to wear that raincoat! Do you hear? Or else I will tear it into rags. . . ."

"Control yourself, my child," *maman* wept; "the coachman can hear!"

"And where is my father's fortune? Where is your money? You have wasted it all. I am not ashamed of being poor, but I am ashamed of having such a mother. . . . When my schoolfellows ask questions about you, I always blush."

In the train they had to pass two stations before they reached the town. Volodya spent all the time on the little platform between two carriages and shivered all over. He did not want to go into the compartment because there the mother he hated was sitting. He hated himself, hated the ticket collectors, the smoke from the engine, the cold to which he attributed his shivering. And the heavier the weight on his heart, the more strongly he felt that somewhere in the world, among some people, there was a pure, honourable, warm, refined life, full of love, affection, gaiety, and serenity. . . . He felt this and was so intensely miserable that one of the passengers, after looking in his face attentively, actually asked:

"You have the toothache, I suppose?"

In the town *maman* and Volodya lived with Marya Petrovna, a lady of noble rank, who had a large flat and let rooms to boarders. *maman* had two rooms, one with windows and two pictures in gold frames hanging on the walls, in which her bed stood and in which she lived, and a little dark room opening out of it in which Volodya lived. Here there was a sofa on which he slept, and, except that sofa, there was no other furniture; the rest of the room was entirely filled up with wicker baskets full of clothes, cardboard hat-boxes, and all sorts of rubbish, which *maman* preserved for some reason or other. Volodya prepared his lessons either in his mother's room or in the "general room," as the large room in which the boarders assembled at dinner-time and in the evening was called.

On reaching home he lay down on his sofa and put the quilt over him to stop his shivering. The cardboard hat-boxes, the wicker baskets, and the other rubbish, reminded him that he had not a room of his own, that he had no refuge in which he could get away from his mother, from her visitors, and from the voices that were floating up from the "general room." The satchel and the books lying about in the corners reminded him of the examination he had missed. . . . For some reason there came into his mind, quite inappropriately, Mentone, where he had lived with his father when he was seven years old; he thought of Biarritz and two little English girls with whom he ran about on the sand. . . . He tried to recall to his memory the colour of the sky, the sea, the height of the waves, and his mood at the time, but he could not succeed. The English girls flitted before his imagination as though they were living; all the rest was a medley of images that floated away in confusion. . . .

"No; it's cold here," thought Volodya. He got up, put on his overcoat, and went into the "general room."

There they were drinking tea. There were three people at the samovar: *maman;* an old lady with tortoiseshell pince-nez, who gave music lessons; and Avgustin Mihalitch, an elderly and very stout Frenchman, who was employed at a perfumery factory.

"I have had no dinner to-day," said *maman.* "I ought to send the maid to buy some bread."

"Dunyasha!" shouted the Frenchman.

It appeared that the maid had been sent out somewhere by the lady of the house.

"Oh, that's of no consequence," said the Frenchman, with a broad smile. "I will go for some bread myself at once. Oh, it's nothing."

He laid his strong, pungent cigar in a conspicuous place, put on his hat and went out. After he had gone away *maman* began telling the music teacher how she had been staying at the Shumihins', and how warmly they welcomed her.

"Lili Shumihin is a relation of mine, you know," she said. "Her late husband, General Shumihin, was a cousin of my husband. And she was a Baroness Kolb by birth. . . ."

"*Maman,* that's false!" said Volodya irritably. "Why tell lies?"

He knew perfectly well that what his mother said was true; in what she was saying about General Shumihin and about Baroness Kolb there was not a word of lying, but nevertheless he felt that she was lying. There was a suggestion of falsehood in her manner of speaking, in the expression of her face, in her eyes, in everything.

"You are lying," repeated Volodya; and he brought his fist down on the table with such force that all the crockery shook and *maman*'s tea was spilt over. "Why do you talk about generals and baronesses? It's all lies!"

The music teacher was disconcerted, and coughed into her handkerchief, affecting to sneeze, and *maman* began to cry.

"Where can I go?" thought Volodya.

He had been in the street already; he was ashamed to go to his schoolfellows. Again, quite incongruously, he remembered the two little English girls. . . . He paced up and down the "general room," and went into Avgustin Mihalitch's room. Here there was a strong smell of ethereal oils and glycerine soap. On the table, in the window, and even on the chairs, there were a number of bottles, glasses, and wineglasses containing fluids of various colours. Volodya took up from the table a newspaper, opened it and read the title *Figaro*. . . There was a strong and pleasant scent about the paper. Then he took a revolver from the table. . . .

"There, there! Don't take any notice of it." The music teacher was comforting *maman* in the next room. "He is young! Young people of his age never restrain themselves. One must resign oneself to that."

"No, Yevgenya Andreyevna; he's too spoilt," said *maman* in a singsong voice. "He has no one in authority over him, and I am weak and can do nothing. Oh, I am unhappy!"

Volodya put the muzzle of the revolver to his mouth, felt something like a trigger or spring, and pressed it with his finger. . . . Then felt something else projecting, and once more pressed it. Taking the muzzle out of his mouth, he wiped it with the lapel of his coat, looked at the lock. He had never in his life taken a weapon in his hand before. . . .

"I believe one ought to raise this . . ." he reflected. "Yes, it seems so."

Augustin Mihalitch went into the "general room," and with a laugh began telling them about something. Volodya put the muzzle in his mouth again, pressed it with his teeth, and pressed something with his fingers. There was a sound of a shot. . . . Something hit Volodya in the back of his head with terrible violence, and he fell on the table with his face downwards among the bottles and glasses. Then he saw his father, as in Mentone, in a top-hat with a wide black band on it, wearing mourning for some lady, suddenly seize him by both hands, and they fell headlong into a very deep, dark pit.

Then everything was blurred and vanished.

HAPPINESS

A flock of sheep was spending the night on the broad steppe road that is called the great highway. Two shepherds were guarding it. One, a toothless old man of eighty, with a tremulous face, was lying on his stomach at the very edge of the road, leaning his elbows on the dusty leaves of a plantain; the other, a young fellow with thick black eyebrows and no moustache, dressed in the coarse canvas of which cheap sacks are made, was lying on his back, with his arms under his head, looking upwards at the sky, where the stars were slumbering and the Milky Way lay stretched exactly above his face.

The shepherds were not alone. A couple of yards from them in the dusk that shrouded the road a horse made a patch of darkness, and, beside it, leaning against the saddle, stood a man in high boots and a short full-skirted jacket who looked like an overseer on some big estate. Judging from his upright and motionless figure, from his manners, and his behaviour to the shepherds and to his horse, he was a serious, reasonable man who knew his own value; even in the darkness signs could be detected in him of military carriage and of the majestically condescending expression gained by frequent intercourse with the gentry and their stewards.

The sheep were asleep. Against the grey background of the dawn, already beginning to cover the eastern part of the sky, the silhouettes of sheep that were not asleep could be seen here and there; they stood with drooping heads, thinking. Their thoughts, tedious and oppressive, called forth by images of nothing but the broad steppe and the sky, the days and the nights, probably weighed upon them themselves, crushing them into apathy; and, standing there as though rooted to the earth, they noticed neither the presence of a stranger nor the uneasiness of the dogs.

The drowsy, stagnant air was full of the monotonous noise inseparable from a summer night on the steppes; the grasshoppers chirruped incessantly; the quails called, and the young nightingales trilled languidly half a mile away in a ravine where a stream flowed and willows grew.

The overseer had halted to ask the shepherds for a light for his pipe. He lighted it in silence and smoked the whole pipe; then, still without uttering a word, stood with his elbow on the saddle, plunged in thought. The young shepherd took no notice of him, he still lay gazing at the sky while the old man slowly looked the overseer up and down and then asked:

"Why, aren't you Panteley from Makarov's estate?"

"That's myself," answered the overseer.

"To be sure, I see it is. I didn't know you -- that is a sign you will be rich. Where has God brought you from?"

"From the Kovylyevsky fields."

"That's a good way. Are you letting the land on the part-crop system?"

"Part of it. Some like that, and some we are letting on lease, and some for raising melons and cucumbers. I have just come from the mill."

A big shaggy old sheep-dog of a dirty white colour with woolly tufts about its nose and eyes walked three times quietly round the horse, trying to seem unconcerned in the presence of strangers, then all at once dashed suddenly from behind at the overseer with an angry aged growl; the other dogs could not refrain from leaping up too.

"Lie down, you damned brute," cried the old man, raising himself on his elbow; "blast you, you devil's creature."

When the dogs were quiet again, the old man resumed his former attitude and said quietly:

"It was at Kovyli on Ascension Day that Yefim Zhmenya died. Don't speak of it in the dark, it is a sin to mention such people. He was a wicked old man. I dare say you have heard."

"No, I haven't"

"Yefim Zhmenya, the uncle of Styopka, the blacksmith. The whole district round knew him. Aye, he was a cursed old man, he was! I knew him for sixty years, ever since Tsar Alexander who beat the French was brought from Taganrog to Moscow. We went together to meet the dead Tsar, and in those days the great highway did not run to Bahmut, but from Esaulovka to Gorodishtche, and where Kovyli is now, there were bustards' nests -- there was a bustard's nest at every step. Even then I had noticed that Yefim had given his soul to damnation, and that the Evil One was in him. I have observed that if any man of the peasant class is apt to be silent, takes up with old women's jobs, and tries to live in solitude, there is no good in it, and Yefim from his youth up was always one to hold his tongue and look at you sideways, he always seemed to be sulky and bristling like a cock before a hen. To go to church or to the tavern or to lark in the street with the lads was not his fashion, he would rather sit alone or be whispering with old women. When he was still young he took jobs to look after the bees and the market gardens. Good folks would come to his market garden sometimes and his melons were whistling. One day he caught a pike, when folks were looking on, and it laughed aloud, 'Ho-ho-ho-ho!' "

"It does happen," said Panteley.

The young shepherd turned on his side and, lifting his black eyebrows, stared intently at the old man.

"Did you hear the melons whistling?" he asked.

"Hear them I didn't, the Lord spared me," sighed the old man, "but folks told me so. It is no great wonder . . . the Evil One will begin whistling in a stone if he wants to. Before the Day of Freedom a rock was humming for three days and three nights in our parts. I heard it myself. The pike laughed because Yefim caught a devil instead of a pike."

The old man remembered something. He got up quickly on to his knees and, shrinking as though from the cold, nervously thrusting his hands into his sleeves, he muttered in a rapid womanish gabble:

"Lord save us and have mercy upon us! I was walking along the river bank one day to Novopavlovka. A storm was gathering, such a tempest it was, preserve us Holy Mother, Queen of Heaven. . . . I was hurrying on as best I could, I looked, and beside the path between the thorn bushes -- the thorn was in flower at the time -- there was a white bullock coming along. I wondered whose bullock it was, and what the devil had sent it there for. It was coming along and swinging its tail and moo-oo-oo! but would you believe it, friends, I overtake it, I come up close -- and it's not a bullock, but Yefim -- holy, holy, holy! I make the sign of the cross while he stares at me and mutters, showing the whites of his eyes; wasn't I frightened! We came alongside, I was afraid to say a word to him -- the thunder was crashing, the sky was streaked with lightning, the willows were bent right down to the water -- all at once, my friends, God strike me dead that I die impenitent, a hare ran across the path . . . it ran and stopped, and said like a man: 'Good-evening, peasants.' Lie down, you brute! " the old man cried to the shaggy dog, who was moving round the horse again. "Plague take you!"

"It does happen," said the overseer, still leaning on the saddle and not stirring; he said this in the hollow, toneless voice in which men speak when they are plunged in thought.

"It does happen," he repeated, in a tone of profundity and conviction.

"Ugh, he was a nasty old fellow," the old shepherd went on with somewhat less fervour. "Five years after the Freedom he was flogged by the commune at the office, so to show his spite he took and sent the throat illness upon all Kovyli. Folks died out of number, lots and lots of them, just as in cholera. . . ."

"How did he send the illness?" asked the young shepherd after a brief silence.

"We all know how, there is no great cleverness needed where there is a will to it. Yefim murdered people with viper's fat. That is such a poison that folks will die from the mere smell of it, let alone the fat."

"That's true," Panteley agreed.

"The lads wanted to kill him at the time, but the old people would not let them. It would never have done to kill him; he knew the place where the treasure is hidden, and not another soul did know. The treasures about here are charmed so that you may find them and not see them, but he did see them. At times he would walk along the river bank or in the forest, and under the bushes and under the rocks there would be little flames, little flames. . . little flames as though from brimstone. I have seen them myself. Everyone expected that Yefim would show people the places or dig the treasure up himself, but he -- as the saying is, like a dog in the manger -- so he died without digging it up himself or showing other people."

The overseer lit a pipe, and for an instant lighted up his big moustaches and his sharp, stern-looking, and dignified nose. Little circles of light danced from his hands to his cap, raced over the saddle along the horse's back, and vanished in its mane near its ears.

"There are lots of hidden treasures in these parts," he said.

And slowly stretching, he looked round him, resting his eyes on the whitening east and added:

"There must be treasures."

"To be sure," sighed the old man, "one can see from every sign there are treasures, only there is no one to dig them, brother. No one knows the real places; besides, nowadays, you must remember, all the treasures are under a charm. To find them and see them you must have a talisman, and without a talisman you can do nothing, lad. Yefim had talismans, but there was no getting anything out of him, the bald devil. He kept them, so that no one could get them."

The young shepherd crept two paces nearer to he old man and, propping his head on his fists, fastened his fixed stare upon him. A childish expression of terror and curiosity gleamed in his dark eyes, and seemed in the twilight to stretch and flatten out the large features of his coarse young face. He was listening intently.

"It is even written in the Scriptures that there are lots of treasures hidden here," the old man went on; "it is so for sure. . . and no mistake about it. An old soldier of Novopavlovka was shown at Ivanovka a writing, and in this writing it was printed about the place of the treasure and even how many pounds of gold was in it and the sort of vessel it was in; they would have found the treasures long ago by that writing, only the treasure is under a spell, you can't get at it."

"Why can't you get at it, grandfather?" asked the young man.

I suppose there is some reason, the soldier didn't say. It is under a spell . . . you need a talisman."

The old man spoke with warmth, as though he were pouring out his soul before the overseer. He talked through his nose and, being unaccustomed to talk much and rapidly, stuttered; and, conscious of his defects, he tried to adorn his speech with gesticulations of the hands and head and thin shoulders, and at every movement his hempen shirt crumpled into folds, slipped upwards and displayed his back, black with age and sunburn. He kept pulling it down, but it slipped up again at once. At last, as though driven out of all patience by the rebellious shirt, the old man leaped up and said bitterly:

"There is fortune, but what is the good of it if it is buried in the earth? It is just riches wasted with no profit to anyone, like chaff or sheep's dung, and yet there are riches there, lad, fortune enough for all the country round, but not a soul sees it! It will come to this, that the gentry will dig it up or the government will take it away. The gentry have begun digging the barrows. . . . They scented something! They are envious of the peasants' luck! The government, too, is looking after itself. It is written in the law that if any peasant finds the treasure he is to take it to the authorities! I dare say, wait till you get it! There is a brew but not for you!"

The old man laughed contemptuously and sat down on the ground. The overseer listened with attention and agreed, but from his silence and the expression of his figure it was evident that what the old man told him was not new to him, that he had thought it all over long ago, and knew much more than was known to the old shepherd.

"In my day, I must own, I did seek for fortune a dozen times," said the old man, scratching himself nervously. "I looked in the right places, but I must have come on treasures under a charm. My father looked for it, too, and my brother, too -- but not a thing did they find, so they died without luck. A monk revealed to my brother Ilya -- the Kingdom of Heaven be his -- that in one place in the fortress of Taganrog there was a treasure under three stones, and that that treasure was under a charm, and in those days -- it was, I remember, in the year '38 -- an Armenian used to live at Matvyeev Barrow who sold talismans. Ilya bought a talisman, took two other fellows with him, and went to Taganrog. Only when he got to the place in the fortress, brother, there was a soldier with a gun, standing at the very spot. . . ."

A sound suddenly broke on the still air, and floated in all directions over the steppe. Something in the distance gave a menacing bang, crashed against stone, and raced over the steppe, uttering, "Tah! tah! tah! tah!" When the sound had died away the old man looked inquiringly at Panteley, who stood motionless and unconcerned.

"It's a bucket broken away at the pits," said the young shepherd after a moment's thought.

It was by now getting light. The Milky Way had turned pale and gradually melted like snow, losing its outlines; the sky was becoming dull and dingy so that you could not make out whether it was clear or covered thickly with clouds, and only from the bright leaden streak in the east and from the stars that lingered here and there could one tell what was coming.

The first noiseless breeze of morning, cautiously stirring the spurges and the brown stalks of last year's grass, fluttered along the road.

The overseer roused himself from his thoughts and tossed his head. With both hands he shook the saddle, touched the girth and, as though he could not make up his mind to mount the horse, stood still again, hesitating.

"Yes," he said, "your elbow is near, but you can't bite it. There is fortune, but there is not the wit to find it."

And he turned facing the shepherds. His stern face looked sad and mocking, as though he were a disappointed man.

"Yes, so one dies without knowing what happiness is like . . ." he said emphatically, lifting his left leg into the stirrup. "A younger man may live to see it, but it is time for us to lay aside all thought of it."

Stroking his long moustaches covered with dew, he seated himself heavily on the horse and screwed up his eyes, looking into the distance, as though he had forgotten something or left something unsaid. In the bluish distance where the furthest visible hillock melted into the mist nothing was stirring; the ancient barrows, once watch-mounds and tombs, which rose here and there above the horizon and the boundless steppe had a sullen and death-like look; there was a feeling of endless time and utter indifference to man in their immobility and silence; another thousand years would pass, myriads of men would die, while they would still stand as they had stood, with no regret for the dead nor interest in the living, and no soul would ever know why they stood there, and what secret of the steppes was hidden under them.

The rooks awakening, flew one after another in silence over the earth. No meaning was to be seen in the languid flight of those long-lived birds, nor in the morning which is repeated punctually every twenty-four hours, nor in the boundless expanse of the steppe.

The overseer smiled and said:

"What space, Lord have mercy upon us! You would have a hunt to find treasure in it! Here," he went on, dropping his voice and making a serious face, "here there are two treasures buried for a certainty. The gentry don't know of them, but the old peasants, particularly the soldiers, know all about them. Here, somewhere on that ridge [the overseer pointed with his whip] robbers one time attacked a caravan of gold; the gold was being taken from Petersburg to the Emperor Peter who was building a fleet at the time at Voronezh. The robbers killed the men with the caravan and buried the gold, but did not find it again afterwards. Another treasure was buried by our Cossacks of the Don. In the year '12 they carried off lots of plunder of all sorts from the French, goods and gold and silver. When they were going homewards they heard on the way that the government wanted to take away all the gold and silver from them. Rather than give up their plunder like that to the government for nothing, the brave fellows took and buried it, so that their children, anyway, might get it; but where they buried it no one knows."

"I have heard of those treasures," the old man muttered grimly.

"Yes . . ." Panteley pondered again. "So it is. . . ."

A silence followed. The overseer looked dreamily into the distance, gave a laugh and pulled the rein, still with the same expression as though he had forgotten something or left something unsaid. The horse reluctantly started at a walking pace. After riding a hundred paces Panteley shook his head resolutely, roused himself from his thoughts and, lashing his horse, set off at a trot.

The shepherds were left alone.

"That was Panteley from Makarov's estate," said the old man. "He gets a hundred and fifty a year and provisions found, too. He is a man of education. . . ."

The sheep, waking up -- there were about three thousand of them -- began without zest to while away the time, nipping at the low, half-trampled grass. The sun had not yet risen, but by now all the barrows could be seen and, like a cloud in the distance, Saur's Grave with its peaked top. If one clambered up on that tomb one could see the plain from it, level and boundless as the sky, one could see villages, manor-houses, the settlements of the Germans and of the Molokani, and a long-sighted Kalmuck could even see the town and the railway-station. Only from there could one see that there was something else in the world besides the silent steppe and the ancient barrows, that there was another life that had nothing to do with buried treasure and the thoughts of sheep.

The old man felt beside him for his crook -- a long stick with a hook at the upper end -- and got up. He was silent and thoughtful. The young shepherd's face had not lost the look of childish terror and curiosity. He was still under the influence of what he had heard in the night, and impatiently awaiting fresh stories.

"Grandfather," he asked, getting up and taking his crook, "what did your brother Ilya do with the soldier?"

The old man did not hear the question. He looked absent-mindedly at the young man, and answered, mumbling with his lips:

"I keep thinking, Sanka, about that writing that was shown to that soldier at Ivanovka. I didn't tell Panteley -- God be with him -- but you know in that writing the place was marked out so that even a woman could find it. Do you know where it is? At Bogata Bylotchka at the spot, you know, where the ravine parts like a goose's foot into three little ravines; it is the middle one."

"Well, will you dig?"

"I will try my luck. . ."

"And, grandfather, what will you do with the treasure when you find it?"

"Do with it?" laughed the old man. "H'm! . . . If only I could find it then. . . . I would show them all. . . . H'm! . . . I should know what to do. . . ."

And the old man could not answer what he would do with the treasure if he found it. That question had presented itself to him that morning probably for the first time in his life, and judging from the expression of his face, indifferent and uncritical, it did not seem to him important and deserving of consideration. In Sanka's brain another puzzled question was stirring: why was it only old men searched for hidden treasure, and what was the use of earthly happiness to people who might die any day of old age? But Sanka could not put this perplexity into words, and the old man could scarcely have found an answer to it.

An immense crimson sun came into view surrounded by a faint haze. Broad streaks of light, still cold, bathing in the dewy grass, lengthening out with a joyous air as though to prove they were not weary of their task, began spreading over the earth. The silvery wormwood, the blue flowers of the pig's onion, the yellow mustard, the corn-flowers -- all burst into gay colours, taking the sunlight for their own smile.

The old shepherd and Sanka parted and stood at the further sides of the flock. Both stood like posts, without moving, staring at the ground and thinking. The former was haunted by thoughts of fortune, the latter was pondering on what had been said in the night; what interested him was not the fortune itself, which he did not want and could not imagine, but the fantastic, fairy-tale character of human happiness.

A hundred sheep started and, in some inexplicable panic as at a signal, dashed away from the flock; and as though the thoughts of the sheep -- tedious and oppressive -- had for a moment infected Sanka also, he, too, dashed aside in the same inexplicable animal panic, but at once he recovered himself and shouted:

"You crazy creatures! You've gone mad, plague take you!"

When the sun, promising long hours of overwhelming heat, began to bake the earth, all living things that in the night had moved and uttered sounds were sunk in drowsiness. The old shepherd and Sanka stood with their crooks on opposite sides of the flock, stood without stirring, like fakirs at their prayers, absorbed in thought. They did not heed each other; each of them was living in his own life. The sheep were pondering, too.

BAD WEATHER

Big raindrops were pattering on the dark windows. It was one of those disgusting summer holiday rains which, when they have begun, last a long time -- for weeks, till the frozen holiday maker grows used to it, and sinks into complete apathy. It was cold; there was a feeling of raw, unpleasant dampness. The mother-in-law of a lawyer, called Kvashin, and his wife, Nadyezhda Filippovna, dressed in waterproofs and shawls, were sitting over the dinner table in the dining-room. It was written on the countenance of the elder lady that she was, thank God, well-fed, well-clothed and in good health, that she had married her only daughter to a good man, and now could play her game of patience with an easy conscience; her daughter, a rather short, plump, fair young woman of twenty, with a gentle anæmic face, was reading a book with her elbows on the table; judging from her eyes she was not so much reading as thinking her own thoughts, which were not in the book. Neither of them spoke. There was the sound of the pattering rain, and from the kitchen they could hear the prolonged yawns of the cook.

Kvashin himself was not at home. On rainy days he did not come to the summer villa, but stayed in town; damp, rainy weather affected his bronchitis and prevented him from working. He was of the opinion that the sight of the grey sky and the tears of rain on the windows deprived one of energy and induced the spleen. In the town, where there was greater comfort, bad weather was scarcely noticed.

After two games of patience, the old lady shuffled the cards and took a glance at her daughter.

"I have been trying with the cards whether it will be fine to-morrow, and whether our Alexey Stepanovitch will come," she said. "It is five days since he was here. . . . The weather is a chastisement from God."

Nadyezhda Filippovna looked indifferently at her mother, got up, and began walking up and down the room.

"The barometer was rising yesterday," she said doubtfully, "but they say it is falling again to-day."

The old lady laid out the cards in three long rows and shook her head.

"Do you miss him?" she asked, glancing at her daughter.

"Of course."

"I see you do. I should think so. He hasn't been here for five days. In May the utmost was two, or at most three days, and now it is serious, five days! I am not his wife, and yet I miss him. And yesterday, when I heard the barometer was rising, I ordered them to kill a chicken and prepare a carp for Alexey Stepanovitch. He likes them. Your poor father couldn't bear fish, but he likes it. He always eats it with relish."

"My heart aches for him," said the daughter. "We are dull, but it is duller still for him, you know, mamma."

"I should think so! In the law-courts day in and day out, and in the empty flat at night alone like an owl."

"And what is so awful, mamma, he is alone there without servants; there is no one to set the samovar or bring him water. Why didn't he engage a valet for the summer months? And what use is the summer villa at all if he does not care for it? I told him there was no need to have it, but no, 'It is for the sake of your health,' he said, and what is wrong with my health? It makes me ill that he should have to put up with so much on my account."

Looking over her mother's shoulder, the daughter noticed a mistake in the patience, bent down to the table and began correcting it. A silence followed. Both looked at the cards and imagined how their Alexey Stepanovitch, utterly forlorn, was sitting now in the town in his gloomy, empty study and working, hungry, exhausted, yearning for his family. . . .

"Do you know what, mamma?" said Nadyezhda Filippovna suddenly, and her eyes began to shine. "If the weather is the same to-morrow I'll go by the first train and see him in town! Anyway, I shall find out how he is, have a look at him, and pour out his tea."

And both of them began to wonder how it was that this idea, so simple and easy to carry out, had not occurred to them before. It was only half an hour in the train to the town, and then twenty minutes in a cab.

They said a little more, and went off to bed in the same room, feeling more contented.

"Oho-ho-ho. . . . Lord, forgive us sinners!" sighed the old lady when the clock in the hall struck two. "There is no sleeping."

"You are not asleep, mamma?" the daughter asked in a whisper. "I keep thinking of Alyosha. I only hope he won't ruin his health in town. Goodness knows where he dines and lunches. In restaurants and taverns."

"I have thought of that myself," sighed the old lady. "The Heavenly Mother save and preserve him. But the rain, the rain!"

In the morning the rain was not pattering on the panes, but the sky was still grey. The trees stood looking mournful, and at every gust of wind they scattered drops. The footprints on the muddy path, the ditches and the ruts were full of water. Nadyezhda Filippovna made up her mind to go.

"Give him my love," said the old lady, wrapping her daughter up. "Tell him not to think too much about his cases. . . . And he must rest. Let him wrap his throat up when he goes out: the weather -- God help us! And take him the chicken; food from home, even if cold, is better than at a restaurant."

The daughter went away, saying that she would come back by an evening train or else next morning.

But she came back long before dinner-time, when the old lady was sitting on her trunk in her bedroom and drowsily thinking what to cook for her son-in-law's supper.

Going into the room her daughter, pale and agitated, sank on the bed without uttering a word or taking off her hat, and pressed her head into the pillow.

"But what is the matter," said the old lady in surprise, "why back so soon? Where is Alexey Stepanovitch?"

Nadyezhda Filippovna raised her head and gazed at her mother with dry, imploring eyes.

"He is deceiving us, mamma," she said.

"What are you saying? Christ be with you!" cried the old lady in alarm, and her cap slipped off her head. "Who is going to deceive us? Lord, have mercy on us!"

"He is deceiving us, mamma!" repeated her daughter, and her chin began to quiver.

"How do you know?" cried the old lady, turning pale.

"Our flat is locked up. The porter tells me that Alyosha has not been home once for these five days. He is not living at home! He is not at home, not at home!"

She waved her hands and burst into loud weeping. uttering nothing but: "Not at home! Not at home!"

She began to be hysterical.

"What's the meaning of it?" muttered the old woman in horror. "Why, he wrote the day before yesterday that he never leaves the flat! Where is he sleeping? Holy Saints!"

Nadyezhda Filippovna felt so faint that she could not take off her hat. She looked about her blankly, as though she had been drugged, and convulsively clutched at her mother's arms.

"What a person to trust: a porter!" said the old lady, fussing round her daughter and crying. "What a jealous girl you are! He is not going to deceive you, and how dare he? We are not just anybody. Though we are of the merchant class, yet he has no right, for you are his lawful wife! We can take proceedings! I gave twenty thousand roubles with you! You did not want for a dowry!"

And the old lady herself sobbed and gesticulated, and she felt faint, too, and lay down on her trunk. Neither of them noticed that patches of blue had made their appearance in the sky, that the clouds were more transparent, that the first sunbeam was cautiously gliding over the wet grass in the garden, that with renewed gaiety the sparrows were hopping about the puddles which reflected the racing clouds.

Towards evening Kvashin arrived. Before leaving town he had gone to his flat and had learned from the porter that his wife had come in his absence.

"Here I am," he said gaily, coming into his mother-in-law's room and pretending not to notice their stern and tear-stained faces. "Here I am! It's five days since we have seen each other!"

He rapidly kissed his wife's hand and his mother-in-law's, and with the air of man delighted at having finished a difficult task, he lolled in an arm-chair.

"Ough!" he said, puffing out all the air from his lungs. "Here I have been worried to death. I have scarcely sat down. For almost five days now I have been, as it were, bivouacking. I haven't been to the flat once, would you believe it? I have been busy the whole time with the meeting of Shipunov's and Ivantchikov's creditors; I had to work in Galdeyev's office at the shop. . . . I've had nothing to eat or to drink, and slept on a bench, I was chilled through. . . . I hadn't a free minute. I hadn't even time to go to the flat. That's how I came not to be at home, Nadyusha, . . And Kvashin, holding his sides as though his back were aching, glanced stealthily at his wife and mother-in-law to see the effect of his lie, or as he called it, diplomacy. The mother-in-law and wife were looking at each other in joyful astonishment, as though beyond all hope and expectation they had found something precious, which they had lost. . . . Their faces beamed, their eyes glowed. . . .

"My dear man," cried the old lady, jumping up, "why am I sitting here? Tea! Tea at once! Perhaps you are hungry?"

"Of course he is hungry," cried his wife, pulling off her head a bandage soaked in vinegar. "Mamma, bring the wine, and the savouries. Natalya, lay the table! Oh, my goodness, nothing is ready!"

And both of them, frightened, happy, and bustling, ran about the room. The old lady could not look without laughing at her daughter who had slandered an innocent man, and the daughter felt ashamed. . .

The table was soon laid. Kvashin, who smelt of madeira and liqueurs and who could scarcely breathe from repletion, complained of being hungry, forced himself to munch and kept on talking of the meeting of Shipunov's and Ivantchikov's creditors, while his wife and mother-in-law could not take their eyes off his face, and both thought:

"How clever and kind he is! How handsome!"

"All serene," thought Kvashin, as he lay down on the well-filled feather bed. "Though they are regular tradesmen's wives, though they are Philistines, yet they have a charm of their own, and one can spend a day or two of the week here with enjoyment. . . ."

He wrapped himself up, got warm, and as he dozed off, he said to himself:

"All serene!"

A PLAY

"Pavel Vassilyevitch, there's a lady here, asking for you," Luka announced. "She's been waiting a good hour. . . ."

Pavel Vassilyevitch had only just finished lunch. Hearing of the lady, he frowned and said:

"Oh, damn her! Tell her I'm busy."

"She has been here five times already, Pavel Vassilyevitch. She says she really must see you. . . . She's almost crying."

"H'm . . . very well, then, ask her into the study."

Without haste Pavel Vassilyevitch put on his coat, took a pen in one hand, and a book in the other, and trying to look as though he were very busy he went into the study. There the visitor was awaiting him -- a large stout lady with a red, beefy face, in spectacles. She looked very respectable, and her dress was more than fashionable (she had on a crinolette of four storeys and a high hat with a reddish bird in it). On seeing him she turned up her eyes and folded her hands in supplication.

"You don't remember me, of course," she began in a high masculine tenor, visibly agitated. " I . . . I have had the pleasure of meeting you at the Hrutskys. . . . I am Mme. Murashkin. . . ."

"A . . . a . . . a . . . h'm . . . Sit down! What can I do for you?"

"You . . . you see . . . I . . . I . . ." the lady went on, sitting down and becoming still more agitated. "You don't remember me. . . . I'm Mme. Murashkin. . . . You see I'm a great admirer of your talent and always read your articles with great enjoyment. . . . Don't imagine I'm flattering you -- God forbid! -- I'm only giving honour where honour is due. . . . I am always reading you . . . always! To some extent I am myself not a stranger to literature -- that is, of course . . . I will not venture to call myself an authoress, but . . . still I have added my little quota . . . I have published at different times three stories for children. . . . You have not read them, of course. . . . I have translated a good deal and . . . and my late brother used to write for *The Cause*."

"To be sure . . . er -- er -- er ---- What can I do for you?"

"You see . . . (the lady cast down her eyes and turned redder) I know your talents . . . your views, Pavel Vassilyevitch, and I have been longing to learn your opinion, or more exactly . . . to ask your advice. I must tell you I have perpetrated a play, my first-born -- *pardon pour l'expression!* -- and before sending it to the Censor I should like above all things to have your opinion on it.

Nervously, with the flutter of a captured bird, the lady fumbled in her skirt and drew out a fat manuscript.

Pavel Vassilyevitch liked no articles but his own. When threatened with the necessity of reading other people's, or listening to them, he felt as though he were facing the cannon's mouth. Seeing the manuscript he took fright and hastened to say:

"Very good, . . . leave it, . . . I'll read it."

"Pavel Vassilyevitch," the lady said languishingly, clasping her hands and raising them in supplication, "I know you're busy. . . . Your every minute is precious, and I know you're inwardly cursing me at this moment, but . . . Be kind, allow me to read you my play. . . . Do be so very sweet!"

"I should be delighted . . ." faltered Pavel Vassilyevitch; "but, Madam, I'm . . . I'm very busy . . . . I'm . . . I'm obliged to set off this minute."

"Pavel Vassilyevitch," moaned the lady and her eyes filled with tears, "I'm asking a sacrifice! I am insolent, I am intrusive, but be magnanimous. To-morrow I'm leaving for Kazan and I should like to know your opinion to-day. Grant me half an hour of your attention . . . only one half-hour . . . I implore you!

Pavel Vassilyevitch was cotton-wool at core, and could not refuse. When it seemed to him that the lady was about to burst into sobs and fall on her knees, he was overcome with confusion and muttered helplessly.

"Very well; certainly . . . I will listen . . . I will give you half an hour."

The lady uttered a shriek of joy, took off her hat and settling herself, began to read. At first she read a scene in which a footman and a house maid, tidying up a sumptuous drawing-room, talked at length about their young lady, Anna Sergyevna, who was building a school and a hospital in the village. When the footman had left the room, the maidservant pronounced a monologue to the effect that education is light and ignorance is darkness; then Mme. Murashkin brought the footman back into the drawing-room and set him uttering a long monologue concerning his master, the General, who disliked his daughter's views, intended to marry her to a rich *kammer junker,* and held that the salvation of the people lay in unadulterated ignorance. Then, when the servants had left the stage, the young lady herself appeared and informed the audience that she had not slept all night, but had been thinking of Valentin Ivanovitch, who was the son of a poor teacher and assisted his sick father gratuitously. Valentin had studied all the sciences, but had no faith in friendship nor in love; he had no object in life and longed for death, and therefore she, the young lady, must save him.

Pavel Vassilyevitch listened, and thought with yearning anguish of his sofa. He scanned the lady viciously, felt her masculine tenor thumping on his eardrums, understood nothing, and thought:

"The devil sent you . . . as though I wanted to listen to your tosh! It's not my fault you've written a play, is it? My God! what a thick manuscript! What an infliction!"

Pavel Vassilyevitch glanced at the wall where the portrait of his wife was hanging and remembered that his wife had asked him to buy and bring to their summer cottage five yards of tape, a pound of cheese, and some tooth-powder.

"I hope I've not lost the pattern of that tape," he thought, "where did I put it? I believe it's in my blue reefer jacket. . . . Those wretched flies have covered her portrait with spots already, I must tell Olga to wash the glass. . . . She's reading the twelfth scene, so we must soon be at the end of the first act. As though inspiration were possible in this heat and with such a mountain of flesh, too! Instead of writing plays she'd much better eat cold vinegar hash and sleep in a cellar. . . ."

"You don't think that monologue's a little too long?" the lady asked suddenly, raising her eyes.

Pavel Vassilyevitch had not heard the monologue, and said in a voice as guilty as though not the lady but he had written that monologue:

"No, no, not at all. It's very nice. . . ."

The lady beamed with happiness and continued reading:

ANNA: You are consumed by analysis. Too early you have ceased to live in the heart and have put your faith in the intellect.

VALENTIN: What do you mean by the heart? That is a concept of anatomy. As a conventional term for what are called the feelings, I do not admit it.

ANNA *(confused)*: And love? Surely that is not merely a product of the association of ideas? Tell me frankly, have you ever loved?

VALENTIN *(bitterly)*: Let us not touch on old wounds not yet healed. *(A pause.)* What are you thinking of?

ANNA: I believe you are unhappy.

During the sixteenth scene Pavel Vassilyevitch yawned, and accidently made with his teeth the sound dogs make when they catch a fly. He was dismayed at this unseemly sound, and to cover it assumed an expression of rapt attention.

"Scene seventeen! When will it end?" he thought. "Oh, my God! If this torture is prolonged another ten minutes I shall shout for the police. It's insufferable."

But at last the lady began reading more loudly and more rapidly, and finally raising her voice she read *"Curtain."*

Pavel Vassilyevitch uttered a faint sigh and was about to get up, but the lady promptly turned the page and went on reading.

ACT II. -- *Scene, a village street. On right, School. On left, Hospital.* Villagers, *male and female, sitting on the hospital steps.*

"Excuse me," Pavel Vassilyevitch broke in, "how many acts are there?"

"Five," answered the lady, and at once, as though fearing her audience might escape her, she went on rapidly.

VALENTIN *is looking out of the schoolhouse window. In the background* Villagers *can be seen taking their goods to the Inn.*

Like a man condemned to be executed and convinced of the impossibility of a reprieve, Pavel Vassilyevitch gave up expecting the end, abandoned all hope, and simply tried to prevent his eyes from closing, and to retain an expression of attention on his face. . . . The future when the lady would finish her play and depart seemed to him so remote that he did not even think of it.

"Trooo--too--too--too . . ." the lady's voice sounded in his ears. "Troo--too--too . . . sh--sh--sh--sh . . ."

"I forgot to take my soda," he thought. "What am I thinking about? Oh -- my soda. . . . Most likely I shall have a bilious attack. . . . It's extraordinary, Smirnovsky swills vodka all day long and yet he never has a bilious attack. . . . There's a bird settled on the window . . . a sparrow. . . ."

Pavel Vassilyevitch made an effort to unglue his strained and closing eyelids, yawned without opening his mouth, and stared at Mme. Murashkin. She grew misty and swayed before his eyes, turned into a triangle and her head pressed against the ceiling. . . .

VALENTIN No, let me depart.

ANNA *(in dismay)*: Why?

VALENTIN *(aside)*: She has turned pale! *(To her)* Do not force me to explain. Sooner would I die than you should know the reason.

ANNA *(after a pause)*: You cannot go away. . . .

The lady began to swell, swelled to an immense size, and melted into the dingy atmosphere of the study -- only her moving mouth was visible; then she suddenly dwindled to the size of a bottle, swayed from side to side, and with the table retreated to the further end of the room . . .

VALENTIN *(holding* ANNA *in his arms)*: You have given me new life! You have shown me an object to live for! You have renewed me as the Spring rain renews the awakened earth! But . . . it is too late, too late! The ill that gnaws at my heart is beyond cure. . . .

Pavel Vassilyevitch started and with dim and smarting eyes stared at the reading lady; for a minute he gazed fixedly as though understanding nothing. . . .

SCENE XI. -- *The same. The* BARON *and the* POLICE INSPECTOR *with assistants.*

VALENTIN: Take me!

ANNA: I am his! Take me too! Yes, take me too! I love him, I love him more than life!

BARON: Anna Sergyevna, you forget that you are ruining your father. . . .

The lady began swelling again. . . . Looking round him wildly Pavel Vassilyevitch got up, yelled in a deep, unnatural voice, snatched from the table a heavy paper-weight, and beside himself, brought it down with all his force on the authoress's head. . . .

* * * * * *

"Give me in charge, I've killed her!" he said to the maidservant who ran in, a minute later.

The jury acquitted him.

A TRANSGRESSION

A collegiate assessor called Miguev stopped at a telegraph-post in the course of his evening walk and heaved a deep sigh. A week before, as he was returning home from his evening walk, he had been overtaken at that very spot by his former housemaid, Agnia, who said to him viciously:

"Wait a bit! I'll cook you such a crab that'll teach you to ruin innocent girls! I'll leave the baby at your door, and I'll have the law of you, and I'll tell your wife, too. . . ."

And she demanded that he should put five thousand roubles into the bank in her name. Miguev remembered it, heaved a sigh, and once more reproached himself with heartfelt repentance for the momentary infatuation which had caused him so much worry and misery.

When he reached his bungalow, he sat down to rest on the doorstep. It was just ten o'clock, and a bit of the moon peeped out from behind the clouds. There was not a soul in the street nor near the bungalows; elderly summer visitors were already going to bed, while young ones were walking in the wood. Feeling in both his pockets for a match to light his cigarette, Miguev brought his elbow into contact with something soft. He looked idly at his right elbow, and his face was instantly contorted by a look of as much horror as though he had seen a snake beside him. On the step at the very door lay a bundle. Something oblong in shape was wrapped up in something -- judging by the feel of it, a wadded quilt. One end of the bundle was a little open, and the collegiate assessor, putting in his hand, felt something damp and warm. He leaped on to his feet in horror, and looked about him like a criminal trying to escape from his warders. . . .

"She has left it!" he muttered wrathfully through his teeth, clenching his fists. "Here it lies. . . . Here lies my transgression! O Lord!"

He was numb with terror, anger, and shame. . . What was he to do now? What would his wife say if she found out? What would his colleagues at the office say? His Excellency would be sure to dig him in the ribs, guffaw, and say: "I congratulate you! . . . He-he-he! Though your beard is gray, your heart is gay. . . . You are a rogue, Semyon Erastovitch!" The whole colony of summer visitors would know his secret now, and probably the respectable mothers of families would shut their doors to him. Such incidents always get into the papers, and the humble name of Miguev would be published all over Russia. . . .

The middle window of the bungalow was open and he could distinctly hear his wife, Anna Filippovna, laying the table for supper; in the yard close to the gate Yermolay, the porter, was plaintively strumming on the balalaika. The baby had only to wake up and begin to cry, and the secret would be discovered. Miguev was conscious of an overwhelming desire to make haste.

"Haste, haste! . . ." he muttered, "this minute, before anyone sees. I'll carry it away and lay it on somebody's doorstep. . . ."

Miguev took the bundle in one hand and quietly, with a deliberate step to avoid awakening suspicion, went down the street. . . .

"A wonderfully nasty position!" he reflected, trying to assume an air of unconcern. "A collegiate assessor walking down the street with a baby! Good heavens! if anyone sees me and understands the position, I am done for. . . . I'd better put it on this doorstep. . . . No, stay, the windows are open and perhaps someone is looking. Where shall I put it? I know! I'll take it to the merchant Myelkin's.. .. Merchants are rich people and tenderhearted; very likely they will say thank you and adopt it."

And Miguev made up his mind to take the baby to Myelkin's, although the merchant's villa was in the furthest street, close to the river.

"If only it does not begin screaming or wriggle out of the bundle," thought the collegiate assessor. "This is indeed a pleasant surprise! Here I am carrying a human being under my arm as though it were a portfolio. A human being, alive, with soul, with feelings like anyone else. . . . If by good luck the Myelkins adopt him, he may turn out somebody. . . . Maybe he will become a professor, a great general, an author. . . . Anything may happen! Now I am carrying him under my arm like a bundle of rubbish, and perhaps in thirty or forty years I may not dare to sit down in his presence. . . .

As Miguev was walking along a narrow, deserted alley, beside a long row of fences, in the thick black shade of the lime trees, it suddenly struck him that he was doing something very cruel and criminal.

"How mean it is really!" he thought. "So mean that one can't imagine anything meaner. . . . Why are we shifting this poor baby from door to door? It's not its fault that it's been born. It's done us no harm. We are scoundrels. . . . We take our pleasure, and the innocent babies have to pay the penalty. Only to think of all this wretched business! I've done wrong and the child has a cruel fate before it. If I lay it at the Myelkins' door, they'll send it to the foundling hospital, and there it will grow up among strangers, in mechanical routine, . . . no love, no petting, no spoiling. . . . And then he'll be apprenticed to a shoemaker, . . . he'll take to drink, will learn to use filthy language, will go hungry. A shoemaker! and he the son of a collegiate assessor, of good family. . . . He is my flesh and blood, . . . "

Miguev came out of the shade of the lime trees into the bright moonlight of the open road, and opening the bundle, he looked at the baby.

"Asleep!" he murmured. "You little rascal! why, you've an aquiline nose like your father's. . . . He sleeps and doesn't feel that it's his own father looking at him! . . . It's a drama, my boy. . . Well, well, you must forgive me. Forgive me, old boy. . . . It seems it's your fate. . . ."

The collegiate assessor blinked and felt a spasm running down his cheeks. . . . He wrapped up the baby, put him under his arm, and strode on. All the way to the Myelkins' villa social questions were swarming in his brain and conscience was gnawing in his bosom.

"If I were a decent, honest man, he thought, "I should damn everything, go with this baby to Anna Filippovna, fall on my knees before her, and say: 'Forgive me! I have sinned! Torture me, but we won't ruin an innocent child. We have no children; let us adopt him!" She's a good sort, she'd consent. . . . And then my child would be with me. . . . Ech!"

He reached the Myelkins' villa and stood still hesitating. He imagined himself in the parlor at home, sitting reading the paper while a little boy with an aquiline nose played with the tassels of his dressing gown. At the same time visions forced themselves on his brain of his winking colleagues, and of his Excellency digging him in the ribs and guffawing. . . . Besides the pricking of his conscience, there was something warm, sad, and tender in his heart. . . .

Cautiously the collegiate assessor laid the baby on the verandah step and waved his hand. Again he felt a spasm run over his face. . . .

"Forgive me, old fellow! I am a scoundrel, he muttered. "Don't remember evil against me."

He stepped back, but immediately cleared his throat resolutely and said:

"Oh, come what will! Damn it all! I'll take him, and let people say what they like!"

Miguev took the baby and strode rapidly back.

"Let them say what they like," he thought. "I'll go at once, fall on my knees, and say: 'Anna Filippovna!' Anna is a good sort, she'll understand. . . . And we'll bring him up. . . . If it's a boy we'll call him Vladimir, and if it's a girl we'll call her Anna! Anyway, it will be a comfort in our old age."

And he did as he determined. Weeping and almost faint with shame and terror, full of hope and vague rapture, he went into his bungalow, went up to his wife, and fell on his knees before her.

"Anna Filippovna!" he said with a sob, and he laid the baby on the floor. "Hear me before you punish. . . . I have sinned! This is my child. . . . You remember Agnia? Well, it was the devil drove me to it. . . ."

And, almost unconscious with shame and terror, he jumped up without waiting for an answer, and ran out into the open air as though he had received a thrashing. . . .

"I'll stay here outside till she calls me," he thought. "I'll give her time to recover, and to think it over. . . ."

The porter Yermolay passed him with his balalaika, glanced at him and shrugged his shoulders. A minute later he passed him again, and again he shrugged his shoulders.

"Here's a go! Did you ever!" he muttered grinning. "Aksinya, the washer-woman, was here just now, Semyon Erastovitch. The silly woman put her baby down on the steps here, and while she was indoors with me, someone took and carried off the baby. . . . Who'd have thought it!"

"What? What are you saying?" shouted Miguev at the top of his voice.

Yermolay, interpreting his master's wrath in his own fashion, scratched his head and heaved a sigh.

"I am sorry, Semyon Erastovitch," he said, "but it's the summer holidays, . . . one can't get on without . . . without a woman, I mean. . . ."

And glancing at his master's eyes glaring at him with anger and astonishment, he cleared his throat guiltily and went on:

"It's a sin, of course, but there -- what is one to do?. . . You've forbidden us to have strangers in the house, I know, but we've none of our own now. When Agnia was here I had no women to see me, for I had one at home; but now, you can see for yourself, sir, . . . one can't help having strangers. In Agnia's time, of course, there was nothing irregular, because. . ."

"Be off, you scoundrel!" Miguev shouted at him, stamping, and he went back into the room.

Anna Filippovna, amazed and wrathful, was sitting as before, her tear-stained eyes fixed on the baby. . . .

"There! there!" Miguev muttered with a pale face, twisting his lips into a smile. "It was a joke. . . . It's not my baby, . . . it's the washer-woman's! . . . I . . . I was joking. . . . Take it to the porter."

FROM THE DIARY OF A VIOLENT-TEMPERED MAN

I am a serious person and my mind is of a philosophic bent. My vocation is the study of finance. I am a student of financial law and I have chosen as the subject of my dissertation -- the Past and Future of the Dog Licence. I need hardly point out that young ladies, songs, moonlight, and all that sort of silliness are entirely out of my line.

Morning. Ten o'clock. My *maman* pours me out a cup of coffee. I drink it and go out on the little balcony to set to work on my dissertation. I take a clean sheet of paper, dip the pen into the ink, and write out the title: "The Past and Future of the Dog Licence."

After thinking a little I write: "Historical Survey. We may deduce from some allusions in Herodotus and Xenophon that the origin of the tax on dogs goes back to . . . ."

But at that point I hear footsteps that strike me as highly suspicious. I look down from the balcony and see below a young lady with a long face and a long waist. Her name, I believe, is Nadenka or Varenka, it really does not matter which. She is looking for something, pretends not to have noticed me, and is humming to herself:

"Dost thou remember that song full of tenderness?"

I read through what I have written and want to continue, but the young lady pretends to have just caught sight of me, and says in a mournful voice:

"Good morning, Nikolay Andreitch. Only fancy what a misfortune I have had! I went for a walk yesterday and lost the little ball off my bracelet!"

I read through once more the opening of my dissertation, I trim up the tail of the letter "g" and mean to go on, but the young lady persists.

"Nikolay Andreitch," she says, "won't you see me home? The Karelins have such a huge dog that I simply daren't pass it alone."

There is no getting out of it. I lay down my pen and go down to her. Nadenka (or Varenka) takes my arm and we set off in the direction of her villa.

When the duty of walking arm-in-arm with a lady falls to my lot, for some reason or other I always feel like a peg with a heavy cloak hanging on it. Nadenka (or Varenka), between ourselves, of an ardent temperament (her grandfather was an Armenian), has a peculiar art of throwing her whole weight on one's arm and clinging to one's side like a leech. And so we walk along.

As we pass the Karelins', I see a huge dog, who reminds me of the dog licence. I think with despair of the work I have begun and sigh.

"What are you sighing for?" asks Nadenka (or Varenka), and heaves a sigh herself.

Here I must digress for a moment to explain that Nadenka or Varenka (now I come to think of it, I believe I have heard her called Mashenka) imagines, I can't guess why, that I am in love with her, and therefore thinks it her duty as a humane person always to look at me with compassion and to soothe my wound with words.

"Listen," said she, stopping. "I know why you are sighing. You are in love, yes; but I beg you for the sake of our friendship to believe that the girl you love has the deepest respect for you. She cannot return your love; but is it her fault that her heart has long been another's?"

Mashenka's nose begins to swell and turn red, her eyes fill with tears: she evidently expects some answer from me, but, fortunately, at this moment we arrive. Mashenka's mamma, a good-natured woman but full of conventional ideas, is sitting on the terrace: glancing at her daughter's agitated face, she looks intently at me and sighs, as though saying to herself: "Ah, these young people! they don't even know how to keep their secrets to themselves!"

On the terrace with her are several young ladies of various colours and a retired officer who is staying in the villa next to ours. He was wounded during the last war in the left temple and the right hip. This unfortunate man is, like myself, proposing to devote the summer to literary work. He is writing the "Memoirs of a Military Man." Like me, he begins his honourable labours every morning, but before he has written more than "I was born in . . ." some Varenka or Mashenka is sure to appear under his balcony, and the wounded hero is borne off under guard.

All the party sitting on the terrace are engaged in preparing some miserable fruit for jam. I make my bows and am about to beat a retreat, but the young ladies of various colours seize my hat with a squeal and insist on my staying. I sit down. They give me a plate of fruit and a hairpin. I begin taking the seeds out.

The young ladies of various colours talk about men: they say that So-and-So is nice-looking, that So-and-So is handsome but not nice, that somebody else is nice but ugly, and that a fourth would not have been bad-looking if his nose were not like a thimble, and so on.

"And you, *Monsieur Nicolas*," says Varenka's mamma, turning to me, "are not handsome, but you are attractive. . . . There is something about your face. . . . In men, though, it's not beauty but intelligence that matters," she adds, sighing.

The young ladies sigh, too, and drop their eyes . . . they agree that the great thing in men is not beauty but intelligence. I steal a glance sideways at a looking-glass to ascertain whether I really am attractive. I see a shaggy head, a bushy beard, moustaches, eyebrows, hair on my cheeks, hair up to my eyes, a perfect thicket with a solid nose sticking up out of it like a watch-tower. Attractive! h'm!

"But it's by the qualities of your soul, after all, that you will make your way, *Nicolas*," sighs Nadenka's mamma, as though affirming some secret and original idea of her own.

And Nadenka is sympathetically distressed on my account, but the conviction that a man passionately in love with her is sitting opposite is obviously a source of the greatest enjoyment to her.

When they have done with men, the young ladies begin talking about love. After a long conversation about love, one of the young ladies gets up and goes away. Those that remain begin to pick her to pieces. Everyone agrees that she is stupid, unbearable, ugly, and that one of her shoulder-blades sticks out in a shocking way.

But at last, thank goodness! I see our maid. My *maman* has sent her to call me in to dinner. Now I can make my escape from this uncongenial company and go back to my work. I get up and make my bows.

Varenka's *maman*, Varenka herself, and the variegated young ladies surround me, and declare that I cannot possibly go, because I promised yesterday to dine with them and go to the woods to look for mushrooms. I bow and sit down again. My soul is boiling with rage, and I feel that in another moment I may not be able to answer for myself, that there may be an explosion, but gentlemanly feeling and the fear of committing a breach of good manners compels me to obey the ladies. And I obey them.

We sit down to dinner. The wounded officer, whose wound in the temple has affected the muscles of the left cheek, eats as though he had a bit in his mouth. I roll up little balls of bread, think about the dog licence, and, knowing the ungovernable violence of my temper, try to avoid speaking. Nadenka looks at me sympathetically.

Soup, tongue and peas, roast fowl, and compôte. I have no appetite, but eat from politeness.

After dinner, while I am standing alone on the terrace, smoking, Nadenka's mamma comes up to me, presses my hand, and says breathlessly:

"Don't despair, *Nicolas!* She has such a heart, . . . such a heart! . . ."

We go towards the wood to gather mushrooms. Varenka hangs on my arm and clings to my side. My sufferings are indescribable, but I bear them in patience.

We enter the wood.

Listen, *Monsieur Nicolas*," says Nadenka, sighing. "Why are you so melancholy? And why are you so silent?"

Extraordinary girl she is, really! What can I talk to her about? What have we in common?

"Oh, do say something!" she begs me.

I begin trying to think of something popular, something within the range of her understanding. After a moment's thought I say:

"The cutting down of forests has been greatly detrimental to the prosperity of Russia. . . ."

"*Nicolas,*" sighs Nadenka, and her nose begins to turn red, "Nicolas, I see you are trying to avoid being open with me. . . . You seem to wish to punish me by your silence. Your feeling is not returned, and you wish to suffer in silence, in solitude . . . it is too awful, *Nicolas!*" she cries impulsively seizing my hand, and I see her nose beginning to swell. "What would you say if the girl you love were to offer you her eternal friendship?"

I mutter something incoherent, for I really can't think what to say to her.

In the first place, I'm not in love with any girl at all; in the second, what could I possibly want her eternal friendship for? and, thirdly, I have a violent temper.

Mashenka (or Varenka) hides her face in her hands and murmurs, as though to herself:

"He will not speak; . . . it is clear that he will have me make the sacrifice! I cannot love him, if my heart is still another's . . . but . . . I will think of it. . . . Very good, I will think of it . . . I will prove the strength of my soul, and perhaps, at the cost of my own happiness, I will save this man from suffering!" . . .

I can make nothing out of all this. It seems some special sort of puzzle.

We go farther into the wood and begin picking mushrooms. We are perfectly silent the whole time. Nadenka's face shows signs of inward struggle. I hear the bark of dogs; it reminds me of my dissertation, and I sigh heavily. Between the trees I catch sight of the wounded officer limping painfully along. The poor fellow's right leg is lame from his wound, and on his left arm he has one of the variegated young ladies. His face expresses resignation to destiny.

We go back to the house to drink tea, after which we play croquet and listen to one of the variegated young ladies singing a song: "No, no, thou lovest not, no, no." At the word "no" she twists her mouth till it almost touches one ear.

"*Charmant!*" wail the other young ladies, "*Charmant!*"

The evening comes on. A detestable moon creeps up behind the bushes. There is perfect stillness in the air, and an unpleasant smell of freshly cut hay. I take up my hat and try to get away.

"I have something I must say to you!" Mashenka whispers to me significantly, "don't go away!"

I have a foreboding of evil, but politeness obliges me to remain. Mashenka takes my arm and leads me away to a garden walk. By this time her whole figure expresses conflict. She is pale and gasping for breath, and she seems absolutely set on pulling my right arm out of the socket. What can be the matter with her?

"Listen!" she mutters. "No, I cannot! No! . . ." She tries to say something, but hesitates. Now I see from her face that she has come to some decision. With gleaming eyes and swollen nose she snatches my hand, and says hurriedly, "*Nicolas,* I am yours! Love you I cannot, but I promise to be true to you!"

Then she squeezes herself to my breast, and at once springs away.

"Someone is coming," she whispers. "Farewell! . . . To-morrow at eleven o'clock I will be in the arbour. . . . Farewell!"

And she vanishes. Completely at a loss for an explanation of her conduct and suffering from a painful palpitation of the heart, I make my way home. There the "Past and Future of the Dog Licence" is awaiting me, but I am quite unable to work. I am furious. . . . I may say, my anger is terrible. Damn it all! I allow no one to treat me like a boy, I am a man of violent temper, and it is not safe to trifle with me!

When the maid comes in to call me to supper, I shout to her: "Go out of the room!" Such hastiness augurs nothing good.

Next morning. Typical holiday weather. Temperature below freezing, a cutting wind, rain, mud, and a smell of naphthaline, because my *maman* has taken all her wraps out of her trunks. A devilish morning! It is the 7th of August, 1887, the date of the solar eclipse. I may here remark that at the time of an eclipse every one of us may, without special astronomical knowledge, be of the greatest service. Thus, for example, anyone of us can (1) take the measurement of the diameters of the sun and the moon; (2) sketch the corona of the sun; (3) take the temperature; (4) take observations of plants and animals during the eclipse; (5) note down his own impressions, and so on.

It is a matter of such exceptional importance that I lay aside the "Past and Future of the Dog Licence" and make up my mind to observe the eclipse.

We all get up very early, and I divide the work as follows: I am to measure the diameter of the sun and moon; the wounded officer is to sketch the corona; and the other observations are undertaken by Mashenka and the variegated young ladies.

We all meet together and wait.

"What is the cause of the eclipse? " asks Mashenka.

I reply: "A solar eclipse occurs when the moon, moving in the plane of the ecliptic, crosses the line joining the centres of the sun and the earth."

"And what does the ecliptic mean?"

I explain. Mashenka listens attentively.

"Can one see through the smoked glass the line joining the centres of the sun and the earth?" she enquires.

I reply that this is only an imaginary line, drawn theoretically.

"If it is only an imaginary line, how can the moon cross it?" Varenka says, wondering.

I make no reply. I feel my spleen rising at this naïve question.

"It's all nonsense," says Mashenka's *maman*. "Impossible to tell what's going to happen. You've never been in the sky, so what can you know of what is to happen with the sun and moon? It's all fancy."

At that moment a black patch begins to move over the sun. General confusion follows. The sheep and horses and cows run bellowing about the fields with their tails in the air. The dogs howl. The bugs, thinking night has come on, creep out of the cracks in the walls and bite the people who are still in bed.

The deacon, who was engaged in bringing some cucumbers from the market garden, jumped out of his cart and hid under the bridge; while his horse walked off into somebody else's yard, where the pigs ate up all the cucumbers. The excise officer, who had not slept at home that night, but at a lady friend's, dashed out with nothing on but his nightshirt, and running into the crowd shouted frantically: "Save yourself, if you can!"

Numbers of the lady visitors, even young and pretty ones, run out of their villas without even putting their slippers on. Scenes occur which I hesitate to describe.

"Oh, how dreadful!" shriek the variegated young ladies. "It's really too awful!"

"Mesdames, watch!" I cry. "Time is precious!"

And I hasten to measure the diameters. I remember the corona, and look towards the wounded officer. He stands doing nothing.

"What's the matter?" I shout. "How about the corona?

He shrugs his shoulders and looks helplessly towards his arms. The poor fellow has variegated young ladies on both sides of him, clinging to him in terror and preventing him from working. I seize a pencil and note down the time to a second. That is of great importance. I note down the geographical position of the point of observation. That, too, is of importance. I am just about to measure the diameter when Mashenka seizes my hand, and says:

"Do not forget to-day, eleven o'clock."

I withdraw my hand, feeling every second precious, try to continue my observations, but Varenka clutches my arm and clings to me. Pencil, pieces of glass, drawings -- all are scattered on the grass. Hang it! It's high time the girl realized that I am a man of violent temper, and when I am roused my fury knows no bounds, I cannot answer for myself.

I try to continue, but the eclipse is over.

"Look at me!" she whispers tenderly.

Oh, that is the last straw! Trying a man's patience like that can but have a fatal ending. I am not to blame if something terrible happens. I allow no one to make a laughing stock of me, and, God knows, when I am furious, I advise nobody to come near me, damn it all! There's nothing I might not do! One of the young ladies, probably noticing from my face what a rage I am in, and anxious to propitiate me, says:

"I did exactly what you told me, Nikolay Andreitch; I watched the animals. I saw the grey dog chasing the cat just before the eclipse, and wagging his tail for a long while afterwards."

So nothing came of the eclipse after all.

I go home. Thanks to the rain, I work indoors instead of on the balcony. The wounded officer has risked it, and has again got as far as "I was born in . . ." when I see one of the variegated young ladies pounce down on him and bear him off to her villa.

I cannot work, for I am still in a fury and suffering from palpitation of the heart. I do not go to the arbour. It is impolite not to, but, after all, I can't be expected to go in the rain.

At twelve o'clock I receive a letter from Mashenka, a letter full of reproaches and entreaties to go to the arbour, addressing me as "thou." At one o'clock I get a second letter, and at two, a third. . . . I must go. . . . But before going I must consider what I am to say to her. I will behave like a gentleman.

To begin with, I will tell her that she is mistaken in supposing that I am in love with her. That's a thing one does not say to a lady as a rule, though. To tell a lady that one's not in love with her, is almost as rude as to tell an author he can't write.

The best thing will be to explain my views of marriage.

I put on my winter overcoat, take an umbrella, and walk to the arbour.

Knowing the hastiness of my temper, I am afraid I may be led into speaking too strongly; I will try to restrain myself.

I find Nadenka still waiting for me. She is pale and in tears. On seeing me she utters a cry of joy, flings herself on my neck, and says:

"At last! You are trying my patience. . . . Listen, I have not slept all night. . . . I have been thinking and thinking. . . . I believe that when I come to know you better I shall learn to love you. . . ."

I sit down, and begin to unfold my views of marriage. To begin with, to clear the ground of digressions and to be as brief as possible, I open with a short historical survey. I speak of marriage in ancient Egypt and India, then pass to more recent times, a few ideas from Schopenhauer. Mashenka listens attentively, but all of a sudden, through some strange incoherence of ideas, thinks fit to interrupt me:

"Nicolas, kiss me!" she says.

I am embarrassed and don't know what to say to her. She repeats her request. There seems no avoiding it. I get up and bend over her long face, feeling as I do so just as I did in my childhood when I was lifted up to kiss my grandmother in her coffin. Not content with the kiss, Mashenka leaps up and impulsively embraces me. At that instant, Mashenka's *maman* appears in the doorway of the arbour. . . . She makes a face as though in alarm, and saying "sh-sh" to someone with her, vanishes like Mephistopheles through the trapdoor.

Confused and enraged, I return to our villa. At home I find Varenka's *maman* embracing my *maman* with tears in her eyes. And my *maman* weeps and says:

"I always hoped for it!"

And then, if you please, Nadenka's *maman* comes up to me, embraces me, and says:

"May God bless you! . . . Mind you love her well. . . . Remember the sacrifice she is making for your sake!"

And here I am at my wedding. At the moment I write these last words, my best man is at my side, urging me to make haste. These people have no idea of my character! I have a violent temper, I cannot always answer for myself! Hang it all! God knows what will come of it! To lead a violent, desperate man to the altar is as unwise as to thrust one's hand into the cage of a ferocious tiger. We shall see, we shall see!

* * * * *

And so, I am married. Everybody congratulates me and Varenka keeps clinging to me and saying:

"Now you are mine, mine; do you understand that? Tell me that you love me!" And her nose swells as she says it.

I learn from my best man that the wounded officer has very cleverly escaped the snares of Hymen. He showed the variegated young lady a medical certificate that owing to the wound in his temple he was at times mentally deranged and incapable of contracting a valid marriage. An inspiration! I might have got a certificate too. An uncle of mine drank himself to death, another uncle was extremely absent-minded (on one occasion he put a lady's muff on his head in mistake for his hat), an aunt of mine played a great deal on the piano, and used to put out her tongue at gentlemen she did not like. And my ungovernable temper is a very suspicious symptom.

But why do these great ideas always come too late? Why?

UPROOTED

An Incident of My Travels

I was on my way back from evening service. The clock in the belfry of the Svyatogorsky Monastery pealed out its soft melodious chimes by way of prelude and then struck twelve. The great courtyard of the monastery stretched out at the foot of the Holy Mountains on the banks of the Donets, and, enclosed by the high hostel buildings as by a wall, seemed now in the night, when it was lighted up only by dim lanterns, lights in the windows, and the stars, a living hotch-potch full of movement, sound, and the most original confusion. From end to end, so far as the eye could see, it was all choked up with carts, old-fashioned coaches and chaises, vans, tilt-carts, about which stood crowds of horses, dark and white, and horned oxen, while people bustled about, and black long-skirted lay brothers threaded their way in and out in all directions. Shadows and streaks of light cast from the windows moved over the carts and the heads of men and horses, and in the dense twilight this all assumed the most monstrous capricious shapes: here the tilted shafts stretched upwards to the sky, here eyes of fire appeared in the face of a horse, there a lay brother grew a pair of black wings.... There was the noise of talk, the snorting and munching of horses, the creaking of carts, the whimpering of children. Fresh crowds kept walking in at the gate and belated carts drove up.

The pines which were piled up on the overhanging mountain, one above another, and leaned towards the roof of the hostel, gazed into the courtyard as into a deep pit, and listened in wonder; in their dark thicket the cuckoos and nightingales never ceased calling.... Looking at the confusion, listening to the uproar, one fancied that in this living hotch-potch no one understood anyone, that everyone was looking for something and would not find it, and that this multitude of carts, chaises and human beings could not ever succeed in getting off.

More than ten thousand people flocked to the Holy Mountains for the festivals of St. John the Divine and St. Nikolay the wonder-worker. Not only the hostel buildings, but even the bakehouse, the tailoring room, the carpenter's shop, the carriage house, were filled to overflowing.... Those who had arrived towards night clustered like flies in autumn, by the walls, round the wells in the yard, or in the narrow passages of the hostel, waiting to be shown a resting-place for the night. The lay brothers, young and old, were in an incessant movement, with no rest or hope of being relieved. By day or late at night they produced the same impression of men hastening somewhere and agitated by something, yet, in spite of their extreme exhaustion, their faces remained full of courage and kindly welcome, their voices friendly, their movements rapid. . . . For everyone who came they had to find a place to sleep, and to provide food and drink; to those who were deaf, slow to understand, or profuse in questions, they had to give long and wearisome explanations, to tell them why there were no empty rooms, at what o'clock the service was to be where holy bread was sold, and so on. They had to run, to carry, to talk incessantly, but more than that, they had to be polite, too, to be tactful, to try to arrange that the Greeks from Mariupol, accustomed to live more comfortably than the Little Russians, should be put with other Greeks, that some shopkeeper from Bahmut or Lisitchansk, dressed like a lady, should not be offended by being put with peasants There were continual cries of: "Father, kindly give us some kvass! Kindly give us some hay! or "Father, may I drink water after confession?" And the lay brother would have to give out kvass or hay or to answer: "Address yourself to the priest, my good woman, we have not the authority to give permission." Another question would follow, "Where is the priest then?" and the lay brother would have to explain where was the priest's cell. With all this bustling activity, he yet had to make time to go to service in the church, to serve in the part devoted to the gentry, and to give full answers to the mass of necessary and unnecessary questions which pilgrims of the educated class are fond of showering about them. Watching them during the course of twenty-four hours, I found it hard to imagine when these black moving figures sat down and when they slept.

When, coming back from the evening service, I went to the hostel in which a place had been assigned me, the monk in charge of the sleeping quarters was standing in the doorway, and beside him, on the steps, was a group of several men and women dressed like townsfolk.

"Sir," said the monk, stopping me, "will you be so good as to allow this young man to pass the night in your room? If you would do us the favour! There are so many people and no place left -- it is really dreadful!"

And he indicated a short figure in a light overcoat and a straw hat. I consented, and my chance companion followed me. Unlocking the little padlock on my door, I was always, whether I wanted to or not, obliged to look at the picture that hung on the doorpost on a level with my face. This picture with the title, "A Meditation on Death," depicted a monk on his knees, gazing at a coffin and at a skeleton laying in it. Behind the man's back stood another skeleton, somewhat more solid and carrying a scythe.

"There are no bones like that," said my companion, pointing to the place in the skeleton where there ought to have been a pelvis. "Speaking generally, you know, the spiritual fare provided for the people is not of the first quality," he added, and heaved through his nose a long and very melancholy sigh, meant to show me that I had to do with a man who really knew something about spiritual fare.

While I was looking for the matches to light a candle he sighed once more and said:

"When I was in Harkov I went several times to the anatomy theatre and saw the bones there; I have even been in the mortuary. Am I not in your way?"

My room was small and poky, with neither table nor chairs in it, but quite filled up with a chest of drawers by the window, the stove and two little wooden sofas which stood against the walls, facing one another, leaving a narrow space to walk between them. Thin rusty-looking little mattresses lay on the little sofas, as well as my belongings. There were two sofas, so this room was evidently intended for two, and I pointed out the fact to my companion. "They will soon be ringing for mass, though," he said, "and I shan't have to be in your way very

Still under the impression that he was in my way and feeling awkward, he moved with a guilty step to his little sofa, sighed guiltily and sat down. When the tallow candle with its dim, dilatory flame had left off flickering and burned up sufficiently to make us both visible, I could make out what he was like. He was a young man of two-and-twenty, with a round and pleasing face, dark childlike eyes, dressed like a townsman in grey cheap clothes, and as one could judge from his complexion and narrow shoulders, not used to manual labour. He was of a very indefinite type; one could take him neither for a student nor for a man in trade, still less for a workman. But looking at his attractive face and childlike friendly eyes, I was unwilling to believe he was one of those vagabond impostors with whom every conventual establishment where they give food and lodging is flooded, and who give themselves out as divinity students, expelled for standing up for justice, or for church singers who have lost their voice. . . . There was something characteristic, typical, very familiar in his face, but what exactly, I could not remember nor make out.

For a long time he sat silent, pondering. Probably because I had not shown appreciation of his remarks about bones and the mortuary, he thought that I was ill-humoured and displeased at his presence. Pulling a sausage out of his pocket, he turned it about before his eyes and said irresolutely:

"Excuse my troubling you, . . . have you a knife?"

I gave him a knife.

"The sausage is disgusting," he said, frowning and cutting himself off a little bit. "In the shop here they sell you rubbish and fleece you horribly. . . . I would offer you a piece, but you would scarcely care to consume it. Will you have some?"

In his language, too, there was something typical that had a very great deal in common with what was characteristic in his face, but what it was exactly I still could not decide. To inspire confidence and to show that I was not ill-humoured, I took some of the proffered sausage. It certainly was horrible; one needed the teeth of a good house-dog to deal with it. As we worked our jaws we got into conversation; we began complaining to each other of the lengthiness of the service.

"The rule here approaches that of Mount Athos," I said; "but at Athos the night services last ten hours, and on great feast-days -- fourteen! You should go there for prayers!"

"Yes," answered my companion, and he wagged his head, "I have been here for three weeks. And you know, every day services, every day services. On ordinary days at midnight they ring for matins, at five o'clock for early mass, at nine o'clock for late mass. Sleep is utterly out of the question. In the daytime there are hymns of praise, special prayers, vespers. . . . And when I was preparing for the sacrament I was simply dropping from exhaustion." He sighed and went on: "And it's awkward not to go to church. . . . The monks give one a room, feed one, and, you know, one is ashamed not to go. One wouldn't mind standing it for a day or two, perhaps, but three weeks is too much -- much too much I Are you here for long?"

"I am going to-morrow evening."

"But I am staying another fortnight."

"But I thought it was not the rule to stay for so long here?" I said.

"Yes, that's true: if anyone stays too long, sponging on the monks, he is asked to go. Judge for yourself, if the proletariat were allowed to stay on here as long as they liked there would never be a room vacant, and they would eat up the whole monastery. That's true. But the monks make an exception for me, and I hope they won't turn me out for some time. You know I am a convert."

"You mean?"

"I am a Jew baptized. . . . Only lately I have embraced orthodoxy."

Now I understood what I had before been utterly unable to understand from his face: his thick lips, and his way of twitching up the right corner of his mouth and his right eyebrow, when he was talking, and that peculiar oily brilliance of his eyes which is only found in Jews. I understood, too, his phraseology. . . . From further conversation I learned that his name was Alexandr Ivanitch, and had in the past been Isaac, that he was a native of the Mogilev province, and that he had come to the Holy Mountains from Novotcherkassk, where he had adopted the orthodox faith.

Having finished his sausage, Alexandr Ivanitch got up, and, raising his right eyebrow, said his prayer before the ikon. The eyebrow remained up when he sat down again on the little sofa and began giving me a brief account of his long biography.

"From early childhood I cherished a love for learning," he began in a tone which suggested he was not speaking of himself, but of some great man of the past. "My parents were poor Hebrews; they exist by buying and selling in a small way; they live like beggars, you know, in filth. In fact, all the people there are poor and superstitious; they don't like education, because education, very naturally, turns a man away from religion. . . . They are fearful fanatics. . . . Nothing would induce my parents to let me be educated, and they wanted me to take to trade, too, and to know nothing but the Talmud. . . . But you will agree, it is not everyone who can spend his whole life struggling for a crust of bread, wallowing in filth, and mumbling the Talmud. At times officers and country gentlemen would put up at papa's inn, and they used to talk a great deal of things which in those days I had never dreamed of; and, of course, it was alluring and moved me to envy. I used to cry and entreat them to send me to school, but they taught me to read Hebrew and nothing more. Once I found a Russian newspaper, and took it home with me to make a kite of it. I was beaten for it, though I couldn't read Russian. Of course, fanaticism is inevitable, for every people instinctively strives to preserve its nationality, but I did not know that then and was very indignant. . . ."

Having made such an intellectual observation, Isaac, as he had been, raised his right eyebrow higher than ever in his satisfaction and looked at me, as it were, sideways, like a cock at a grain of corn, with an air as though he would say: "Now at last you see for certain that I am an intellectual man, don't you?" After saying something more about fanaticism and his irresistible yearning for enlightenment, he went on:

"What could I do? I ran away to Smolensk. And there I had a cousin who relined saucepans and made tins. Of course, I was glad to work under him, as I had nothing to live upon; I was barefoot and in rags. . . . I thought I could work by day and study at night and on Saturdays. And so I did, but the police found out I had no passport and sent me back by stages to my father. . . ."

Alexandr Ivanitch shrugged one shoulder and sighed.

"What was one to do?" he went on, and the more vividly the past rose up before his mind, the more marked his Jewish accent became. "My parents punished me and handed me over to my grandfather, a fanatical old Jew, to be reformed. But I went off at night to Shklov. And when my uncle tried to catch me in Shklov, I went off to Mogilev; there I stayed two days and then I went off to Starodub with a comrade."

Later on he mentioned in his story Gonel, Kiev, Byelaya, Tserkov, Uman, Balt, Bendery and at last reached Odessa.

"In Odessa I wandered about for a whole week, out of work and hungry, till I was taken in by some Jews who went about the town buying second-hand clothes. I knew how to read and write by then, and had done arithmetic up to fractions, and I wanted to go to study somewhere, but I had not the means. What was I to do? For six months I went about Odessa buying old clothes, but the Jews paid me no wages, the rascals. I resented it and left them. Then I went by steamer to Perekop."

"What for?"

"Oh, nothing. A Greek promised me a job there. In short, till I was sixteen I wandered about like that with no definite work and no roots till I got to Poltava. There a student, a Jew, found out that I wanted to study, and gave me a letter to the Harkov students. Of course, I went to Harkov. The students consulted together and began to prepare me for the technical school. And, you know, I must say the students that I met there were such that I shall never forget them to the day of my death. To say nothing of their giving me food and lodging, they set me on the right path, they made me think, showed me the object of life. Among them were intellectual remarkable people who by now are celebrated. For instance, you have heard of Grumaher, haven't you?"

"No, I haven't."

"You haven't! He wrote very clever articles in the *Harkov Gazette,* and was preparing to be a professor. Well, I read a great deal and attended the student's societies, where you hear nothing that is commonplace. I was working up for six months, but as one has to have been through the whole high-school course of mathematics to enter the technical school, Grumaher advised me to try for the veterinary institute, where they admit high-school boys from the sixth form. Of course, I began working for it. I did not want to be a veterinary surgeon but they told me that after finishing the course at the veterinary institute I should be admitted to the faculty of medicine without examination. I learnt all Kühner; I could read Cornelius Nepos, *à livre ouvert;* and in Greek I read through almost all Curtius. But, you know, one thing and another, . . . the students leaving and the uncertainty of my position, and then I heard that my mamma had come and was looking for me all over Harkov. Then I went away. What was I to do? But luckily I learned that there was a school of mines here on the Donets line. Why should I not enter that? You know the school of mines qualifies one as a mining foreman -- a splendid berth. I know of mines where the foremen get a salary of fifteen hundred a year. Capital. . . . I entered it. . . ."

With an expression of reverent awe on his face Alexandr Ivanitch enumerated some two dozen abstruse sciences in which instruction was given at the school of mines; he described the school itself, the construction of the shafts, and the condition of the miners. . . . Then he told me a terrible story which sounded like an invention, though I could not help believing it, for his tone in telling it was too genuine and the expression of horror on his Semitic face was too evidently sincere.

"While I was doing the practical work, I had such an accident one day! " he said, raising both eyebrows. "I was at a mine here in the Donets district. You have seen, I dare say, how people are let down into the mine. You remember when they start the horse and set the gates moving one bucket on the pulley goes down into the mine, while the other comes up; when the first begins to come up, then the second goes down -- exactly like a well with two pails. Well, one day I got into the bucket, began going down, and can you fancy, all at once I heard, Trrr! The chain had broken and I flew to the devil together with the bucket and the broken bit of chain. . . . I fell from a height of twenty feet, flat on my chest and stomach, while the bucket, being heavier, reached the bottom before me, and I hit this shoulder here against its edge. I lay, you know, stunned. I thought I was killed, and all at once I saw a fresh calamity: the other bucket, which was going up, having lost the counter-balancing weight, was coming down with a crash straight upon me. . . . What was I to do? Seeing the position, I squeezed closer to the wall, crouching and waiting for the bucket to come full crush next minute on my head. I thought of papa and mamma and Mogilev and Grumaher. . . . I prayed. . . . But happily . . . it frightens me even to think of it. . . ."

Alexandr Ivanitch gave a constrained smile and rubbed his forehead with his hand.

"But happily it fell beside me and only caught this side a little. . . . It tore off coat, shirt and skin, you know, from this side. . . . The force of it was terrific. I was unconscious after it. They got me out and sent me to the hospital. I was there four months, and the doctors there said I should go into consumption. I always have a cough now and a pain in my chest. And my psychic condition is terrible. . . . When I am alone in a room I feel overcome with terror. Of course, with my health in that state, to be a mining foreman is out of the question. I had to give up the school of mines. . . ."

"And what are you doing now?" I asked.

"I have passed my examination as a village schoolmaster. Now I belong to the orthodox church, and I have a right to be a teacher. In Novotcherkassk, where I was baptized, they took a great interest in me and promised me a place in a church parish school. I am going there in a fortnight, and shall ask again."

Alexandr Ivanitch took off his overcoat and remained in a shirt with an embroidered Russian collar and a worsted belt.

"It is time for bed," he said, folding his overcoat for a pillow, and yawning." Till lately, you know, I had no knowledge of God at all. I was an atheist. When I was lying in the hospital I thought of religion, and began reflecting on that subject. In my opinion, there is only one religion possible for a thinking man, and that is the Christian religion. If you don't believe in Christ, then there is nothing else to believe in, . . . is there? Judaism has outlived its day, and is preserved only owing to the peculiarities of the Jewish race. When civilization reaches the Jews there will not be a trace of Judaism left. All young Jews are atheists now, observe. The New Testament is the natural continuation of the Old, isn't it?"

I began trying to find out the reasons which had led him to take so grave and bold a step as the change of religion, but he kept repeating the same, "The New Testament is the natural continuation of the Old" -- a formula obviously not his own, but acquired -- which did not explain the question in the least. In spite of my efforts and artifices, the reasons remained obscure. If one could believe that he had embraced Orthodoxy from conviction, as he said he had done, what was the nature and foundation of this conviction it was impossible to grasp from his words. It was equally impossible to assume that he had changed his religion from interested motives: his cheap shabby clothes, his going on living at the expense of the convent, and the uncertainty of his future, did not look like interested motives. There was nothing for it but to accept the idea that my companion had been impelled to change his religion by the same restless spirit which had flung him like a chip of wood from town to town, and which he, using the generally accepted formula, called the craving for enlightenment.

Before going to bed I went into the corridor to get a drink of water. When I came back my companion was standing in the middle of the room, and he looked at me with a scared expression. His face looked a greyish white, and there were drops of perspiration on his forehead.

"My nerves are in an awful state," he muttered with a sickly smile," awful I It's acute psychological disturbance. But that's of no consequence."

And he began reasoning again that the New Testament was a natural continuation of the Old, that Judaism has outlived its day. . . . Picking out his phrases, he seemed to be trying to put together the forces of his conviction and to smother with them the uneasiness of his soul, and to prove to himself that in giving up the religion of his fathers he had done nothing dreadful or peculiar, but had acted as a thinking man free from prejudice, and that therefore he could boldly remain in a room all alone with his conscience. He was trying to convince himself, and with his eyes besought my assistance.

Meanwhile a big clumsy wick had burned up on our tallow candle. It was by now getting light. At the gloomy little window, which was turning blue, we could distinctly see both banks of the Donets River and the oak copse beyond the river. It was time to s sleep.

"It will be very interesting here to-morrow," said my companion when I put out the candle and went o bed. After early mass, the procession will go in boats from the Monastery to the Hermitage."

Raising his right eyebrow and putting his head on one side, he prayed before the ikons, and, without undressing, lay down on his little sofa

"Yes," he said, turning over on the other side.

"Why yes?" I asked.

"When I accepted orthodoxy in Novotcherkassk my mother was looking for me in Rostov. She felt that I meant to change my religion," he sighed, and went on: "It is six years since I was there in the province of Mogilev. My sister must be married by now."

After a short silence, seeing that I was still awake, he began talking quietly of how they soon, thank God, would give him a job, and that at last he would have a home of his own, a settled position, his daily bread secure. . . . And I was thinking that this man would never have a home of his own, nor a settled position, nor his daily bread secure. He dreamed aloud of a village school as of the Promised Land; like the majority of people, he had a prejudice against a wandering life, and regarded it as something exceptional, abnormal and accidental, like an illness, and was looking for salvation in ordinary workaday life. The tone of his voice betrayed that he was conscious of his abnormal position and regretted it. He seemed as it were apologizing and justifying himself.

Not more than a yard from me lay a homeless wanderer; in the rooms of the hostels and by the carts in the courtyard among the pilgrims some hundreds of such homeless wanderers were waiting for the morning, and further away, if one could picture to oneself the whole of Russia, a vast multitude of such uprooted creatures was pacing at that moment along highroads and side-tracks, seeking something better, or were waiting for the dawn, asleep in wayside inns and little taverns, or on the grass under the open sky. . . . As I fell asleep I imagined how amazed and perhaps even overjoyed all these people would have been if reasoning and words could be found to prove to them that their life was as little in need of justification as any other. In my sleep I heard a bell ring outside as plaintively as though shedding bitter tears, and the lay brother calling out several times:

"Lord Jesus Christ, Son of God, have mercy upon us! Come to mass!"

When I woke up my companion was not in the room. It was sunny and there was a murmur of the crowds through the window. Going out, I learned that mass was over and that the procession had set off for the Hermitage some time before. The people were wandering in crowds upon the river bank and, feeling at liberty, did not know what to do with themselves: they could not eat or drink, as the late mass was not yet over at the Hermitage; the Monastery shops where pilgrims are so fond of crowding and asking prices were still shut. In spite of their exhaustion, many of them from sheer boredom were trudging to the Hermitage. The path from the Monastery to the Hermitage, towards which I directed my steps, twined like a snake along the high steep bank, going up and down and threading in and out among the oaks and pines. Below, the Donets gleamed, reflecting the sun; above, the rugged chalk cliff stood up white with bright green on the top from the young foliage of oaks and pines, which, hanging one above another, managed somehow to grow on the vertical cliff without falling. The pilgrims trailed along the path in single file, one behind another. The majority of them were Little Russians from the neighbouring districts, but there were many from a distance, too, who had come on foot from the provinces of Kursk and Orel; in the long string of varied colours there were Greek settlers, too, from Mariupol, strongly built, sedate and friendly people, utterly unlike their weakly and degenerate compatriots who fill our southern seaside towns. There were men from the Donets, too, with red stripes on their breeches, and emigrants from the Tavritchesky province. There were a good many pilgrims of a nondescript class, like my Alexandr Ivanitch; what sort of people they were and where they came from it was impossible to tell from their faces, from their clothes, or from their speech. The path ended at the little landing-stage, from which a narrow road went to the left to the Hermitage, cutting its way through the mountain. At the landing-stage stood two heavy big boats of a forbidding aspect, like the New Zealand pirogues which one may see in the works of Jules Verne. One boat with rugs on the seats was destined for the clergy and the singers, the other without rugs for the public. When the procession was returning I found myself among the elect who had succeeded in squeezing themselves into the second. There were so many of the elect that the boat scarcely moved, and one had to stand all the way without stirring and to be careful that one's hat was not crushed. The route was lovely. Both banks -- one high, steep and white, with overhanging pines and oaks, with the crowds hurrying back along the path, and the other shelving, with green meadows and an oak copse bathed in sunshine -- looked as happy and rapturous as though the May morning owed its charm only to them. The reflection of the sun in the rapidly flowing Donets quivered and raced away in all directions, and its long rays played on the chasubles, on the banners and on the drops splashed up by the oars. The singing of the Easter hymns, the ringing of the bells, the splash of the oars in the water, the calls of the birds, all mingled in the air into something tender and harmonious. The boat with the priests and the banners led the way; at its helm the black figure of a lay brother stood motionless as a statue.

When the procession was getting near the Monastery, I noticed Alexandr Ivanitch among the elect. He was standing in front of them all, and, his mouth wide open with pleasure and his right eye now? cocked up, was gazing at the procession. His face was beaming; probably at such moments, when there were so many people round him and it was so bright, he was satisfied with himself, his new religion, and his conscience.

When a little later we were sitting in our room, drinking tea, he still beamed with satisfaction; his face showed that he was satisfied both with the tea and with me, that he fully appreciated my being an intellectual," but that he would know how to play his part with credit if any intellectual topic turned up. . . .

"Tell me, what psychology ought I to read?" he began an intellectual conversation, wrinkling up his nose.

"Why, what do you want it for?"

"One cannot be a teacher without a knowledge of psychology. Before teaching a boy I ought to understand his soul."

I told him that psychology alone would not be enough to make one understand a boy's soul, and moreover psychology for a teacher who had not yet mastered the technical methods of instruction in reading, writing, and arithmetic would be a luxury as superfluous as the higher mathematics. He readily agreed with me, and began describing how hard and responsible was the task of a teacher, how hard it was to eradicate in the boy the habitual tendency to evil and superstition, to make him think honestly and independently, to instil into him true religion, the ideas of personal dignity, of freedom, and so on. In answer to this I said something to him. He agreed again. He agreed very readily, in fact. Obviously his brain had not a very firm grasp of all these "intellectual subjects."

Up to the time of my departure we strolled together about the Monastery, whiling away the long hot day. He never left my side a minute; whether he had taken a fancy to me or was afraid of solitude, God only knows! I remember we sat together under a clump of yellow acacia in one of the little gardens that are scattered on the mountain side.

"I am leaving here in a fortnight," he said; "it is high time."

"Are you going on foot?"

"From here to Slavyansk I shall walk, then by railway to Nikitovka; from Nikitovka the Donets line branches off, and along that branch line I shall walk as far as Hatsepetovka, and there a railway guard, I know, will help me on my way."

I thought of the bare, deserted steppe between Nikitovka and Hatsepetovka, and pictured to myself Alexandr Ivanitch striding along it, with his doubts, his homesickness, and his fear of solitude. . . . He read boredom in my face, and sighed.

"And my sister must be married by now," he said, thinking aloud, and at once, to shake off melancholy thoughts, pointed to the top of the rock and said:

"From that mountain one can see Izyum."

As we were walking up the mountain he had a little misfortune. I suppose he stumbled, for he slit his cotton trousers and tore the sole of his shoe.

"Tss!" he said, frowning as he took off a shoe and exposed a bare foot without a stocking. "How unpleasant! . . . That's a complication, you know, which . . . Yes!"

Turning the shoe over and over before his eyes, as though unable to believe that the sole was ruined for ever, he spent a long time frowning, sighing, and clicking with his tongue.

I had in my trunk a pair of boots, old but fashionable, with pointed toes and laces. I had brought them with me in case of need, and only wore them in wet weather. When we got back to our room I made up a phrase as diplomatic as I could and offered him these boots. He accepted them and said with dignity:

"I should thank you, but I know that you consider thanks a convention."

He was pleased as a child with the pointed toes and the laces, and even changed his plans.

"Now I shall go to Novotcherkassk in a week, and not in a fortnight," he said, thinking aloud.

In shoes like these I shall not be ashamed to show myself to my godfather. I was not going away from here just because I hadn't any decent clothes. . . ."

When the coachman was carrying out my trunk, a lay brother with a good ironical face came in to sweep out the room. Alexandr Ivanitch seemed flustered and embarrassed and asked him timidly:

"Am I to stay here or go somewhere else?"

He could not make up his mind to occupy a whole room to himself, and evidently by now was feeling ashamed of living at the expense of the Monastery. He was very reluctant to part from me; to put off being lonely as long as possible, he asked leave to see me on my way.

The road from the Monastery, which had been excavated at the cost of no little labour in the chalk mountain, moved upwards, going almost like a spiral round the mountain, over roots and under sullen overhanging pines. . . .

The Donets was the first to vanish from our sight, after it the Monastery yard with its thousands of people, and then the green roofs. . . . Since I was mounting upwards everything seemed vanishing into a pit. The cross on the church, burnished by the rays of the setting sun, gleamed brightly in the abyss and vanished. Nothing was left but the oaks, the pines, and the white road. But then our carriage came out on a level country, and that was all left below and behind us. Alexandr Ivanitch jumped out and, smiling mournfully, glanced at me for the last time with his childish eyes, and vanished from me forever. . . .

The impressions of the Holy Mountains had already become memories, and I saw something new: the level plain, the whitish-brown distance, the way side copse, and beyond it a windmill which stood without moving, and seemed bored at not being allowed to wave its sails because it was a holiday.

A FATHER

"I admit I have had a drop. . . . You must excuse me. I went into a beer shop on the way here, and as it was so hot had a couple of bottles. It's hot, my boy."

Old Musatov took a nondescript rag out of his pocket and wiped his shaven, battered face with it.

"I have come only for a minute, Borenka, my angel," he went on, not looking at his son, "about something very important. Excuse me, perhaps I am hindering you. Haven't you ten roubles, my dear, you could let me have till Tuesday? You see, I ought to have paid for my lodging yesterday, and money, you see! . . . None! Not to save my life!"

Young Musatov went out without a word, and began whispering the other side of the door with the landlady of the summer villa and his colleagues who had taken the villa with him. Three minutes later he came back, and without a word gave his father a ten-rouble note. The latter thrust it carelessly into his pocket without looking at it, and said:

"*Merci*. Well, how are you getting on? It's a long time since we met."

"Yes, a long time, not since Easter."

"Half a dozen times I have been meaning to come to you, but I've never had time. First one thing, then another. . . . It's simply awful! I am talking nonsense though. . . . All that's nonsense. Don't you believe me, Borenka. I said I would pay you back the ten roubles on Tuesday, don't believe that either. Don't believe a word I say. I have nothing to do at all, it's simply laziness, drunkenness, and I am ashamed to be seen in such clothes in the street. You must excuse me, Borenka. Here I have sent the girl to you three times for money and written you piteous letters. Thanks for the money, but don't believe the letters; I was telling fibs. I am ashamed to rob you, my angel; I know that you can scarcely make both ends meet yourself, and feed on locusts, but my impudence is too much for me. I am such a specimen of impudence -- fit for a show! . . . You must excuse me, Borenka. I tell you the truth, because I can't see your angel face without emotion."

A minute passed in silence. The old man heaved a deep sigh and said:

"You might treat me to a glass of beer perhaps."

His son went out without a word, and again there was a sound of whispering the other side of the door. When a little later the beer was brought in, the old man seemed to revive at the sight of the bottles and abruptly changed his tone.

"I was at the races the other day, my boy," he began telling him, assuming a scared expression. "We were a party of three, and we pooled three roubles on Frisky. And, thanks to that Frisky, we got thirty-two roubles each for our rouble. I can't get on without the races, my boy. It's a gentlemanly diversion. My virago always gives me a dressing over the races, but I go. I love it, and that's all about it."

Boris, a fair-haired young man with a melancholy immobile face, was walking slowly up and down, listening in silence. When the old man stopped to clear his throat, he went up to him and said:

"I bought myself a pair of boots the other day, father, which turn out to be too tight for me. Won't you take them? I'll let you have them cheap."

"If you like," said the old man with a grimace, "only for the price you gave for them, without any cheapening."

"Very well, I'll let you have them on credit."

The son groped under the bed and produced the new boots. The father took off his clumsy, rusty, evidently second-hand boots and began trying on the new ones.

"A perfect fit," he said. "Right, let me keep them. And on Tuesday, when I get my pension, I'll send you the money for them. That's not true, though," he went on, suddenly falling into the same tearful tone again. "And it was a lie about the races, too, and a lie about the pension. And you are deceiving me, Borenka.... I feel your generous tactfulness. I see through you! Your boots were too small, because your heart is too big. Ah, Borenka, Borenka! I understand it all and feel it!"

"Have you moved into new lodgings?" his son interrupted, to change the conversation.

"Yes, my boy. I move every month. My virago can't stay long in the same place with her temper."

"I went to your lodgings, I meant to ask you to stay here with me. In your state of health it would do you good to be in the fresh air."

"No," said the old man, with a wave of his hand, "the woman wouldn't let me, and I shouldn't care to myself. A hundred times you have tried to drag me out of the pit, and I have tried myself, but nothing came of it. Give it up. I must stick in my filthy hole. This minute, here I am sitting, looking at your angel face, yet something is drawing me home to my hole. Such is my fate. You can't draw a dung-beetle to a rose. But it's time I was going, my boy. It's getting dark."

"Wait a minute then, I'll come with you. I have to go to town to-day myself."

Both put on their overcoats and went out. When a little while afterwards they were driving in a cab, it was already dark, and lights began to gleam in the windows.

"I've robbed you, Borenka!" the father muttered. "Poor children, poor children! It must be a dreadful trouble to have such a father! Borenka, my angel, I cannot lie when I see your face. You must excuse me. . . . What my depravity has come to, my God. Here I have just been robbing you, and put you to shame with my drunken state; I am robbing your brothers, too, and put them to shame, and you should have seen me yesterday! I won't conceal it, Borenka. Some neighbours, a wretched crew, came to see my virago; I got drunk, too, with them, and I blackguarded you poor children for all I was worth. I abused you, and complained that you had abandoned me. I wanted, you see, to touch the drunken hussies' hearts, and pose as an unhappy father. It's my way, you know, when I want to screen my vices I throw all the blame on my innocent children. I can't tell lies and hide things from you, Borenka. I came to see you as proud as a peacock, but when I saw your gentleness and kind heart, my tongue clave to the roof of my mouth, and it upset my conscience completely."

"Hush, father, let's talk of something else."

"Mother of God, what children I have," the old man went on, not heeding his son. "What wealth God has bestowed on me. Such children ought not to have had a black sheep like me for a father, but a real man with soul and feeling! I am not worthy of you!"

The old man took off his cap with a button at the top and crossed himself several times.

"Thanks be to Thee, O Lord!" he said with a sigh, looking from side to side as though seeking for an ikon. "Remarkable, exceptional children! I have three sons, and they are all like one. Sober, steady, hard-working, and what brains! Cabman, what brains! Grigory alone has brains enough for ten. He speaks French, he speaks German, and talks better than any of your lawyers -- one is never tired of listening. My children, my children, I can't believe that you are mine! I can't believe it! You are a martyr, my Borenka, I am ruining you, and I shall go on ruining you. . . . You give to me endlessly, though you know your money is thrown away. The other day I sent you a pitiful letter, I described how ill I was, but you know I was lying, I wanted the money for rum. And you give to me because you are afraid to wound me by refusing. I know all that, and feel it. Grisha's a martyr, too. On Thursday I went to his office, drunk, filthy, ragged, reeking of vodka like a cellar . . . I went straight up, such a figure, I pestered him with nasty talk, while his colleagues and superiors and petitioners were standing round. I have disgraced him for life. And he wasn't the least confused, only turned a bit pale, but smiled and came up to me as though there were nothing the matter, even introduced me to his colleagues. Then he took me all the way home, and not a word of reproach. I rob him worse than you. Take your brother Sasha now, he's a martyr too! He married, as you know, a colonel's daughter of an aristocratic circle, and got a dowry with her. . . . You would think he would have nothing to do with me. No, brother, after his wedding he came with his young wife and paid me the first visit . . . in my hole. . . . Upon my soul!"

The old man gave a sob and then began laughing.

"And at that moment, as luck would have it, we were eating grated radish with kvass and frying fish, and there was a stink enough in the flat to make the devil sick. I was lying down -- I'd had a drop -- my virago bounced out at the young people with her face crimson, . . . It was a disgrace in fact. But Sasha rose superior to it all."

"Yes, our Sasha is a good fellow," said Boris.

"The most splendid fellow! You are all pure gold, you and Grisha and Sasha and Sonya. I worry you, torment you, disgrace you, rob you, and all my life I have not heard one word of reproach from you, you have never given me one cross look. It would be all very well if I had been a decent father to you -- but as it is! You have had nothing from me but harm. I am a bad, dissipated man. . . . Now, thank God, I am quieter and I have no strength of will, but in old days when you were little I had determination, will. Whatever I said or did I always thought it was right. Sometimes I'd come home from the club at night, drunk and ill-humoured, and scold at your poor mother for spending money. The whole night I would be railing at her, and think it the right thing too; you would get up in the morning and go to school, while I'd still be venting my temper upon her. Heavens! I did torture her, poor martyr! When you came back from school and I was asleep you didn't dare to have dinner till I got up. At dinner again there would be a flare up. I daresay you remember. I wish no one such a father; God sent me to you for a trial. Yes, for a trial! Hold out, children, to the end! Honour thy father and thy days shall be long. Perhaps for your noble conduct God will grant you long life. Cabman, stop!"

The old man jumped out of the cab and ran into a tavern. Half an hour later he came back, cleared his throat in a drunken way, and sat down beside his son.

"Where's Sonya now?" he asked. "Still at boarding-school?"

"No, she left in May, and is living now with Sasha's mother-in-law."

"There!" said the old man in surprise. "She is a jolly good girl! So she is following her brother's example. . . . Ah, Borenka, she has no mother, no one to rejoice over her! I say, Borenka, does she . . . does she know how I am living? Eh?"

Boris made no answer. Five minutes passed in profound silence. The old man gave a sob, wiped his face with a rag and said:

"I love her, Borenka! She is my only daughter, you know, and in one's old age there is no comfort like a daughter. Could I see her, Borenka?"

"Of course, when you like."

"Really? And she won't mind?"

"Of course not, she has been trying to find you so as to see you."

"Upon my soul! What children! Cabman, eh? Arrange it, Borenka darling! She is a young lady now, *delicatesse, consommé,* and all the rest of it in a refined way, and I don't want to show myself to her in such an abject state. I'll tell you how we'll contrive to work it. For three days I will keep away from spirits, to get my filthy, drunken phiz into better order. Then I'll come to you, and you shall lend me for the time some suit of yours; I'll shave and have my hair cut, then you go and bring her to your flat. Will you?"

"Very well."

"Cabman, stop!"

The old man sprang out of the cab again and ran into a tavern. While Boris was driving with him to his lodging he jumped out twice again, while his son sat silent and waited patiently for him. When, after dismissing the cab, they made their way across a long, filthy yard to the "virago's" lodging, the old man put on an utterly shamefaced and guilty air, and began timidly clearing his throat and clicking with his lips.

"Borenka," he said in an ingratiating voice, "if my virago begins saying anything, don't take any notice . . . and behave to her, you know, affably. She is ignorant and impudent, but she's a good baggage. There is a good, warm heart beating in her bosom!"

The long yard ended, and Boris found himself in a dark entry. The swing door creaked, there was a smell of cooking and a smoking samovar. There was a sound of harsh voices. Passing through the passage into the kitchen Boris could see nothing but thick smoke, a line with washing on it, and the chimney of the samovar through a crack of which golden sparks were dropping.

"And here is my cell," said the old man, stooping down and going into a little room with a low-pitched ceiling, and an atmosphere unbearably stifling from the proximity of the kitchen.

Here three women were sitting at the table regaling themselves. Seeing the visitors, they exchanged glances and left off eating.

"Well, did you get it?" one of them, apparently the "virago" herself, asked abruptly.

"Yes, yes," muttered the old man. "Well, Boris, pray sit down. Everything is plain here, young man . . . we live in a simple way."

He bustled about in an aimless way. He felt ashamed before his son, and at the same time apparently he wanted to keep up before the women his dignity as cock of the walk, and as a forsaken, unhappy father.

"Yes, young man, we live simply with no nonsense," he went on muttering. "We are simple people, young man. . . . We are not like you, we don't want to keep up a show before people. No! . . . Shall we have a drink of vodka?"

One of the women (she was ashamed to drink before a stranger) heaved a sigh and said:

"Well, I'll have another drink on account of the mushrooms. . . . They are such mushrooms, they make you drink even if you don't want to. Ivan Gerasimitch, offer the young gentleman, perhaps he will have a drink!"

The last word she pronounced in a mincing drawl.

"Have a drink, young man!" said the father, not looking at his son. "We have no wine or liqueurs, my boy, we live in a plain way."

"He doesn't like our ways," sighed the "virago." "Never mind, never mind, he'll have a drink."

Not to offend his father by refusing, Boris took a wineglass and drank in silence. When they brought in the samovar, to satisfy the old man, he drank two cups of disgusting tea in silence, with a melancholy face.

Without a word he listened to the virago dropping hints about there being in this world cruel, heartless children who abandon their parents.

"I know what you are thinking now!" said the old man, after drinking more and passing into his habitual state of drunken excitement. "You think I have let myself sink into the mire, that I am to be pitied, but to my thinking, this simple life is much more normal than your life, . . . I don't need anybody, and . . . and I don't intend to eat humble pie. . . . I can't endure a wretched boy's looking at me with compassion."

After tea he cleaned a herring and sprinkled it with onion, with such feeling, that tears of emotion stood in his eyes. He began talking again about the races and his winnings, about some Panama hat for which he had paid sixteen roubles the day before. He told lies with the same relish with which he ate herring and drank. His son sat on in silence for an hour, and began to say good-bye.

"I don't venture to keep you," the old man said, haughtily. "You must excuse me, young man, for not living as you would like!"

He ruffled up his feathers, snorted with dignity, and winked at the women.

"Good-bye, young man," he said, seeing his son into the entry. "*Attendez.*"

In the entry, where it was dark, he suddenly pressed his face against the young man's sleeve and gave a sob.

"I should like to have a look at Sonitchka," he whispered. "Arrange it, Borenka, my angel. I'll shave, I'll put on your suit . . . I'll put on a straight face . . . I'll hold my tongue while she is there. Yes, yes, I will hold my tongue! "

He looked round timidly towards the door, through which the women's voices were heard, checked his sobs, and said aloud:

"Good-bye, young man! *Attendez.*"

A HAPPY ENDING

Lyubov Grigoryevna, a substantial, buxom lady of forty who undertook matchmaking and many other matters of which it is usual to speak only in whispers, had come to see Stytchkin, the head guard, on a day when he was off duty. Stytchkin, somewhat embarrassed, but, as always, grave, practical, and severe, was walking up and down the room, smoking a cigar and saying:

"Very pleased to make your acquaintance. Semyon Ivanovitch recommended you on the ground that you may be able to assist me in a delicate and very important matter affecting the happiness of my life. I have, Lyubov Grigoryevna, reached the age of fifty-two; that is a period of life at which very many have already grown-up children. My position is a secure one. Though my fortune is not large, yet I am in a position to support a beloved being and children at my side. I may tell you between ourselves that apart from my salary I have also money in the bank which my manner of living has enabled me to save. I am a practical and sober man, I lead a sensible and consistent life, so that I may hold myself up as an example to many. But one thing I lack -- a domestic hearth of my own and a partner in life, and I live like a wandering Magyar, moving from place to place without any satisfaction. I have no one with whom to take counsel, and when I am ill no one to give me water, and so on. Apart from that, Lyubov Grigoryevna, a married man has always more weight in society than a bachelor. . . . I am a man of the educated class, with money, but if you look at me from a point of view, what am I? A man with no kith and kin, no better than some Polish priest. And therefore I should be very desirous to be united in thebonds of Hymen -- that is, to enter into matrimony with some worthy person."

"An excellent thing," said the matchmaker, with a sigh.

"I am a solitary man and in this town I know no one. Where can I go, and to whom can I apply, since all the people here are strangers to me? That is why Semyon Ivanovitch advised me to address myself to a person who is a specialist in this line, and makes the arrangement of the happiness of others her profession. And therefore I most earnestly beg you, Lyubov Grigoryevna, to assist me in ordering my future. You know all the marriageable young ladies in the town, and it is easy for you to accommodate me."

"I can. . . ."

"A glass of wine, I beg you. . . ."

With an habitual gesture the matchmaker raised her glass to her mouth and tossed it off without winking.

"I can," she repeated. "And what sort of bride would you like, Nikolay Nikolayitch?"

"Should I like? The bride fate sends me."

"Well, of course it depends on your fate, but everyone has his own taste, you know. One likes dark ladies, the other prefers fair ones."

"You see, Lyubov Grigoryevna," said Stytchkin, sighing sedately, "I am a practical man and a man of character; for me beauty and external appearance generally take a secondary place, for, as you know yourself, beauty is neither bowl nor platter, and a pretty wife involves a great deal of anxiety. The way I look at it is, what matters most in a woman is not what is external, but what lies within -- that is, that she should have soul and all the qualities. A glass of wine, I beg. . . . Of course, it would be very agreeable that one's wife should be rather plump, but for mutual happiness it is not of great consequence; what matters is the mind. Properly speaking, a woman does not need mind either, for if she has brains she will have too high an opinion of herself, and take all sorts of ideas into her head. One cannot do without education nowadays, of course, but education is of different kinds. It would be pleasing for one's wife to know French and German, to speak various languages, very pleasing; but what's the use of that if she can't sew on one's buttons, perhaps? I am a man of the educated class: I am just as much at home, I may say, with Prince Kanitelin as I am with you here now. But my habits are simple, and I want a girl who is not too much a fine lady. Above all, she must have respect for me and feel that I have made her happiness."

"To be sure."

"Well, now as regards the essential. . . . I do not want a wealthy bride; I would never condescend to anything so low as to marry for money. I desire not to be kept by my wife, but to keep her, and that she may be sensible of it. But I do not want a poor girl either. Though I am a man of means, and am marrying not from mercenary motives, but from love, yet I cannot take a poor girl, for, as you know yourself, prices have gone up so, and there will be children."

"One might find one with a dowry," said the matchmaker.

"A glass of wine, I beg. . . ."

There was a pause of five minutes.

The matchmaker heaved a sigh, took a sidelong glance at the guard, and asked:

"Well, now, my good sir . . . do you want anything in the bachelor line? I have some fine bargains. One is a French girl and one is a Greek. Well worth the money."

The guard thought a moment and said:

"No, I thank you. In view of your favourable disposition, allow me to enquire now how much you ask for your exertions in regard to a bride?"

"I don't ask much. Give me twenty-five roubles and the stuff for a dress, as is usual, and I will say thank you . . . but for the dowry, that's a different account."

Stytchkin folded his arms over his chest and fell to pondering in silence. After some thought he heaved a sigh and said:

"That's dear. . . ."

"It's not at all dear, Nikolay Nikolayitch! In old days when there were lots of weddings one did do it cheaper, but nowadays what are our earnings? If you make fifty roubles in a month that is not a fast, you may be thankful. It's not on weddings we make our money, my good sir."

Stytchkin looked at the matchmaker in amazement and shrugged his shoulders.

"H'm! . . . Do you call fifty roubles little?" he asked.

"Of course it is little! In old days we sometimes made more than a hundred."

"H'm! I should never have thought it was possible to earn such a sum by these jobs. Fifty roubles! It is not every man that earns as much! Pray drink your wine. . . ."

The matchmaker drained her glass without winking. Stytchkin looked her over from head to foot in silence, then said:

"Fifty roubles. . . . Why, that is six hundred roubles a year. . . . Please take some more. . . With such dividends, you know, Lyubov Grigoryevna, you would have no difficulty in making a match for yourself. . . ."

"For myself," laughed the matchmaker, "I am an old woman."

"Not at all. . . . You have such a figure, and your face is plump and fair, and all the rest of it."

The matchmaker was embarrassed. Stytchkin was also embarrassed and sat down beside her.

"You are still very attractive," said he; "if you met with a practical, steady, careful husband, with his salary and your earnings you might even attract him very much, and you'd get on very well together. . . ."

"Goodness knows what you are saying, Nikolay Nikolayitch."

"Well, I meant no harm. . . ."

A silence followed. Stytchkin began loudly blowing his nose, while the matchmaker turned crimson, and looking bashfully at him, asked:

"And how much do you get, Nikolay Nikolayitch?"

"I? Seventy-five roubles, besides tips. . . . Apart from that we make something out of candles and hares."

"You go hunting, then?"

"No. Passengers who travel without tickets are called hares with us."

Another minute passed in silence. Stytchkin got up and walked about the room in excitement.

"I don't want a young wife," said he. "I am a middle-aged man, and I want someone who . . . as it might be like you . . . staid and settled and a figure something like yours. . . ."

"Goodness knows what you are saying . . ." giggled the matchmaker, hiding her crimson face in her kerchief.

"There is no need to be long thinking about it. You are after my own heart, and you suit me in your qualities. I am a practical, sober man, and if you like me . . . what could be better? Allow me to make you a proposal!"

The matchmaker dropped a tear, laughed, and, in token of her consent, clinked glasses with Stytchkin.

"Well," said the happy railway guard, "now allow me to explain to you the behaviour and manner of life I desire from you. . . . I am a strict, respectable, practical man. I take a gentlemanly view of everything. And I desire that my wife should be strict also, and should understand that to her I am a benefactor and the foremost person in the world."

He sat down, and, heaving a deep sigh, began expounding to his bride-elect his views on domestic life and a wife's duties.

IN THE COACH-HOUSE

It was between nine and ten o'clock in the evening. Stepan the coachman, Mihailo the house-porter, Alyoshka the coachman's grandson, who had come up from the village to stay with his grandfather, and Nikandr, an old man of seventy, who used to come into the yard every evening to sell salt herrings, were sitting round a lantern in the big coach-house, playing "kings." Through the wide-open door could be seen the whole yard, the big house, where the master's family lived, the gates, the cellars, and the porter's lodge. It was all shrouded in the darkness of night, and only the four windows of one of the lodges which was let were brightly lit up. The shadows of the coaches and sledges with their shafts tipped upwards stretched from the walls to the doors, quivering and cutting across the shadows cast by the lantern and the players. . . . On the other side of the thin partition that divided the coach-house from the stable were the horses. There was a scent of hay, and a disagreeable smell of salt herrings coming from old Nikandr.

The porter won and was king; he assumed an attitude such as was in his opinion befitting a king, and blew his nose loudly on a red-checked handkerchief.

"Now if I like I can chop off anybody's head," he said. Alyoshka, a boy of eight with a head of flaxen hair, left long uncut, who had only missed being king by two tricks, looked angrily and with envy at the porter. He pouted and frowned.

"I shall give you the trick, grandfather," he said, pondering over his cards; "I know you have got the queen of diamonds."

"Well, well, little silly, you have thought enough!"

Alyoshka timidly played the knave of diamonds. At that moment a ring was heard from the yard.

"Oh, hang you!" muttered the porter, getting up. "Go and open the gate, O king!"

When he came back a little later, Alyoshka was already a prince, the fish-hawker a soldier, and the coachman a peasant.

"It's a nasty business," said the porter, sitting down to the cards again. "I have just let the doctors out. They have not extracted it."

"How could they? Just think, they would have to pick open the brains. If there is a bullet in the head, of what use are doctors?"

"He is lying unconscious," the porter went on. "He is bound to die. Alyoshka, don't look at the cards, you little puppy, or I will pull your ears! Yes, I let the doctors out, and the father and mother in. . . . They have only just arrived. Such crying and wailing, Lord preserve us! They say he is the only son. . . . It's a grief!"

All except Alyoshka, who was absorbed in the game, looked round at the brightly lighted windows of the lodge.

"I have orders to go to the police station tomorrow," said the porter. "There will be an inquiry . . . But what do I know about it? I saw nothing of it. He called me this morning, gave me a letter, and said: 'Put it in the letter-box for me.' And his eyes were red with crying. His wife and children were not at home. They had gone out for a walk. So when I had gone with the letter, he put a bullet into his forehead from a revolver. When I came back his cook was wailing for the whole yard to hear."

"It's a great sin," said the fish-hawker in a husky voice, and he shook his head, "a great sin!"

"From too much learning," said the porter, taking a trick; "his wits outstripped his wisdom. Sometimes he would sit writing papers all night. . . . Play, peasant! . . . But he was a nice gentleman. And so white skinned, black-haired and tall! . . . He was a good lodger."

"It seems the fair sex is at the bottom of it," said the coachman, slapping the nine of trumps on the king of diamonds. "It seems he was fond of another man's wife and disliked his own; it does happen."

"The king rebels," said the porter.

At that moment there was again a ring from the yard. The rebellious king spat with vexation and went out. Shadows like dancing couples flitted across the windows of the lodge. There was the sound of voices and hurried footsteps in the yard.

"I suppose the doctors have come again," said the coachman. "Our Mihailo is run off his legs. . . ."

A strange wailing voice rang out for a moment in the air. Alyoshka looked in alarm at his grandfather, the coachman; then at the windows, and said:

"He stroked me on the head at the gate yesterday, and said, 'What district do you come from, boy?' Grandfather, who was that howled just now?"

His grandfather trimmed the light in the lantern and made no answer.

"The man is lost," he said a little later, with a yawn. "He is lost, and his children are ruined, too. It's a disgrace for his children for the rest of their lives now."

The porter came back and sat down by the lantern.

"He is dead," he said. "They have sent to the almshouse for the old women to lay him out."

"The kingdom of heaven and eternal peace to him!" whispered the coachman, and he crossed himself.

Looking at him, Alyoshka crossed himself too.

"You can't pray for such as him," said the fish-hawker.

"Why not?"

"It's a sin."

"That's true," the porter assented. "Now his soul has gone straight to hell, to the devil. . . ."

"It's a sin," repeated the fish-hawker; "such as he have no funeral, no requiem, but are buried like carrion with no respect."

The old man put on his cap and got up.

"It was the same thing at our lady's," he said, pulling his cap on further. "We were serfs in those days; the younger son of our mistress, the General's lady, shot himself through the mouth with a pistol, from too much learning, too. It seems that by law such have to be buried outside the cemetery, without priests, without a requiem service; but to save disgrace our lady, you know, bribed the police and the doctors, and they gave her a paper to say her son had done it when delirious, not knowing what he was doing. You can do anything with money. So he had a funeral with priests and every honor, the music played, and he was buried in the church; for the deceased General had built that church with his own money, and all his family were buried there. Only this is what happened, friends. One month passed, and then another, and it was all right. In the third month they informed the General's lady that the watchmen had come from that same church. What did they want? They were brought to her, they fell at her feet. 'We can't go on serving, your excellency,' they said. 'Look out for other watchmen and graciously dismiss us.' 'What for?' 'No,' they said, 'we can't possibly; your son howls under the church all night.' "

Alyoshka shuddered, and pressed his face to the coachman's back so as not to see the windows.

"At first the General's lady would not listen," continued the old man. "'All this is your fancy, you simple folk have such notions,' she said. 'A dead man cannot howl.' Some time afterwards the watchmen came to her again, and with them the sacristan. So the sacristan, too, had heard him howling. The General's lady saw that it was a bad job; she locked herself in her bedroom with the watchmen. 'Here, my friends, here are twenty-five roubles for you, and for that go by night in secret, so that no one should hear or see you, dig up my unhappy son, and bury him,' she said, 'outside the cemetery.' And I suppose she stood them a glass . . . And the watchmen did so. The stone with the inscription on it is there to this day, but he himself, the General's son, is outside the cemetery. . . . O Lord, forgive us our transgressions!" sighed the fish-hawker. "There is only one day in the year when one may pray for such people: the Saturday before Trinity. . . . You mustn't give alms to beggars for their sake, it is a sin, but you may feed the birds for the rest of their souls. The General's lady used to go out to the crossroads every three days to feed the birds. Once at the cross-roads a black dog suddenly appeared; it ran up to the bread, and was such a . . . we all know what that dog was. The General's lady was like a half-crazy creature for five days afterwards, she neither ate nor drank. . . . All at once she fell on her knees in the garden, and prayed and prayed. . . . Well, good-by, friends, the blessing of God and the Heavenly Mother be with you. Let us go, Mihailo, you'll open the gate for me."

The fish-hawker and the porter went out. The coachman and Alyoshka went out too, so as not to be left in the coach-house.

"The man was living and is dead!" said the coachman, looking towards the windows where shadows were still flitting to and fro. "Only this morning he was walking about the yard, and now he is lying dead."

"The time will come and we shall die too," said the porter, walking away with the fish-hawker, and at once they both vanished from sight in the darkness.

The coachman, and Alyoshka after him, somewhat timidly went up to the lighted windows. A very pale lady with large tear stained eyes, and a fine-looking gray headed man were moving two card-tables into the middle of the room, probably with the intention of laying the dead man upon them, and on the green cloth of the table numbers could still be seen written in chalk. The cook who had run about the yard wailing in the morning was now standing on a chair, stretching up to try and cover the looking glass with a towel.

"Grandfather what are they doing?" asked Alyoshka in a whisper.

"They are just going to lay him on the tables," answered his grandfather. "Let us go, child, it is bedtime."

The coachman and Alyoshka went back to the coach-house. They said their prayers, and took off their boots. Stepan lay down in a corner on the floor, Alyoshka in a sledge. The doors of the coach house were shut, there was a horrible stench from the extinguished lantern. A little later Alyoshka sat up and looked about him; through the crack of the door he could still see a light from those lighted windows.

"Grandfather, I am frightened!" he said.

"Come, go to sleep, go to sleep! . . ."

"I tell you I am frightened!"

"What are you frightened of? What a baby!"

They were silent.

Alyoshka suddenly jumped out of the sledge and, loudly weeping, ran to his grandfather.

"What is it? What's the matter?" cried the coachman in a fright, getting up also.

"He's howling!"

"Who is howling?"

"I am frightened, grandfather, do you hear?"

The coachman listened.

"It's their crying," he said. "Come! there, little silly! They are sad, so they are crying."

"I want to go home, . . ." his grandson went on sobbing and trembling all over. "Grandfather, let us go back to the village, to mammy; come, grandfather dear, God will give you the heavenly kingdom for it. . . ."

"What a silly, ah! Come, be quiet, be quiet! Be quiet, I will light the lantern, . . . silly!"

The coachman fumbled for the matches and lighted the lantern. But the light did not comfort Alyoshka.

"Grandfather Stepan, let's go to the village!" he besought him, weeping. "I am frightened here; oh, oh, how frightened I am! And why did you bring me from the village, accursed man?"

"Who's an accursed man? You mustn't use such disrespectable words to your lawful grandfather. I shall whip you."

"Do whip me, grandfather, do; beat me like Sidor's goat, but only take me to mammy, for God's mercy! . . ."

"Come, come, grandson, come!" the coachman said kindly. "It's all right, don't be frightened. . . . I am frightened myself. . . . Say your prayers!"

The door creaked and the porter's head appeared. "Aren't you asleep, Stepan?" he asked. "I shan't get any sleep all night," he said, coming in. "I shall be opening and shutting the gates all night. . . . What are you crying for, Alyoshka?"

"He is frightened," the coachman answered for his grandson.

Again there was the sound of a wailing voice in the air. The porter said:

"They are crying. The mother can't believe her eyes. . . . It's dreadful how upset she is."

"And is the father there?"

"Yes. . . . The father is all right. He sits in the corner and says nothing. They have taken the children to relations. . . . Well, Stepan, shall we have a game of trumps?"

"Yes," the coachman agreed, scratching himself, "and you, Alyoshka, go to sleep. Almost big enough to be married, and blubbering, you rascal. Come, go along, grandson, go along. . . .

The presence of the porter reassured Alyoshka. He went, not very resolutely, towards the sledge and lay down. And while he was falling asleep he heard a half-whisper.

"I beat and cover," said his grandfather.

"I beat and cover," repeated the porter.

The bell rang in the yard, the door creaked and seemed also saying: "I beat and cover." When Alyoshka dreamed of the gentleman and, frightened by his eyes, jumped up and burst out crying, it was morning, his grandfather was snoring, and the coach-house no longer seemed terrible.

ZINOTCHKA

The party of sportsmen spent the night in a peasant's hut on some newly mown hay. The moon peeped in at the window; from the street came the mournful wheezing of a concertina; from the hay came a sickly sweet, faintly troubling scent. The sportsmen talked about dogs, about women, about first love, and about snipe. After all the ladies of their acquaintance had been picked to pieces, and hundreds of stories had been told, the stoutest of the sportsmen, who looked in the darkness like a haycock, and who talked in the mellow bass of a staff officer, gave a loud yawn and said:

"It is nothing much to be loved; the ladies are created for the purpose of loving us men. But, tell me, has anyone of you fellows been hated -- passionately, furiously hated? Has anyone of you watched the ecstasies of hatred? Eh?"

No answer followed.

"Has no one, gentlemen?" asked the staff officer's bass voice. "But I, now, have been hated, hated by a pretty girl, and have been able to study the symptoms of first hatred directed against myself. It was the first, because it was something exactly the converse of first love. What I am going to tell, however, happened when I knew nothing about love or hate. I was eight at the time, but that made no difference; in this case it was not *he* but *she* that mattered. Well, I beg your attention. One fine summer evening, just before sunset, I was sitting in the nursery, doing my lesson with my governess, Zinotchka, a very charming and poetical creature who had left boarding school not long before. Zinotchka looked absent-mindedly towards the window and said:

" 'Yes. We breathe in oxygen; now tell me, Petya, what do we breathe out?'

" 'Carbonic acid gas,' I answered, looking towards the same window.

" 'Right,' assented Zinotchka. 'Plants, on the contrary, breathe in carbonic acid gas, and breathe out oxygen. Carbonic acid gas is contained in seltzer water, and in the fumes from the samovar.... It is a very noxious gas. Near Naples there is the so-called Cave of Dogs, which contains carbonic acid gas; a dog dropped into it is suffocated and dies.'

"This luckless Cave of Dogs near Naples is a chemical marvel beyond which no governess ventures to go. Zinotchka always hotly maintained the usefulness of natural science, but I doubt if she knew any chemistry beyond this Cave.

"Well, she told me to repeat it. I repeated it. She asked me what was meant by the horizon. I answered. And meantime, while we were ruminating over the horizon and the Cave, in the yard below, my father was just getting ready to go shooting. The dogs yapped, the trace horses shifted from one leg to another impatiently and coquetted with the coachman, the footman packed the waggonette with parcels and all sorts of things. Beside the waggonette stood a brake in which my mother and sisters were sitting to drive to a name-day party at the Ivanetskys'. No one was left in the house but Zinotchka, me, and my eldest brother, a student, who had toothache. You can imagine my envy and my boredom.

" 'Well, what do we breathe in?' asked Zinotchka, looking at the window.

" 'Oxygen. . .'

" 'Yes. And the horizon is the name given to the place where it seems to us as though the earth meets the sky.'

"Then the waggonette drove off, and after it the brake. . . . I saw Zinotchka take a note out of her pocket, crumple it up convulsively and press it to her temple, then she flushed crimson and looked at her watch.

" 'So, remember,' she said, 'that near Naples is the so-called Cave of Dogs. . . .' She glanced at her watch again and went on: 'where the sky seems to us to meet the earth. . . .'

"The poor girl in violent agitation walked about the room, and once more glanced at her watch. There was another half-hour before the end of our lesson.

" 'Now arithmetic,' she said, breathing hard and turning over the pages of the sum-book with a trembling hand. 'Come, you work out problem 325 and I . . . will be back directly.'

"She went out. I heard her scurry down the stairs, and then I saw her dart across the yard in her blue dress and vanish through the garden gate. The rapidity of her movements, the flush on her cheeks and her excitement, aroused my curiosity. Where had she run, and what for? Being intelligent beyond my years I soon put two and two together, and understood it all: she had run into the garden, taking advantage of the absence of my stern parents, to steal in among the raspberry bushes, or to pick herself some cherries. If that were so, dash it all, I would go and have some cherries too. I threw aside the sum-book and ran into the garden. I ran to the cherry orchard, but she was not there. Passing by the raspberries, the gooseberries, and the watchman's shanty, she crossed the kitchen garden and reached the pond, pale, and starting at every sound. I stole after her, and what I saw, my friends, was this. At the edge of the pond, between the thick stumps of two old willows, stood my elder brother, Sasha; one could not see from his face that he had toothache. He looked towards Zinotchka as she approached him, and his whole figure was lighted up by an expression of happiness as though by sunshine. And Zinotchka, as though she were being driven into the Cave of Dogs, and were being forced to breathe carbonic acid gas, walked towards him, scarcely able to move one leg before the other, breathing hard, with her head thrown back. . . . To judge from appearances she was going to a rendezous for the first time in her life. But at last she reached him. . . . For half a minute they gazed at each other in silence, as though they could not believe their eyes. Thereupon some force seemed to shove Zinotchka; she laid her hands on Sasha's shoulders and let her head droop upon his waistcoat. Sasha laughed, muttered something incoherent, and with the clumsiness of a man head over ears in love, laid both hands on Zinotchka's face. And the weather, gentlemen, was exquisite. . . . The hill behind which the sun was setting, the two willows, the green bank, the sky -- all together with Sasha and Zinotchka were reflected in the pond . . . perfect stillness . . . you can imagine it. Millions of butterflies with long whiskers gleamed golden above the reeds; beyond the garden they were driving the cattle. In fact, it was a perfect picture.

"Of all I had seen the only thing I understood was that Sasha was kissing Zinotchka. That was improper. If *maman* heard of it they would both catch it. Feeling for some reason ashamed I went back to the nursery, not waiting for the end of the rendezvous. There I sat over the sum-book, pondered and reflected. A triumphant smile strayed upon my countenance. On one side it was agreeable to be the possessor of another person's secret; on the other it was also very agreeable that such authorities as Sasha and Zinotchka might at any moment be convicted by me of ignorance of the social proprieties. Now they were in my power, and their peace was entirely dependent on my magnanimity. I'd let them know.

"When I went to bed, Zinotchka came into the nursery as usual to find out whether I had dropped asleep without undressing and whether I had said my prayers. I looked at her pretty, happy face and grinned. I was bursting with my secret and itching to let it out. I had to drop a hint and enjoy the effect.

" 'I know,' I said, grinning. 'Gy--y.'

" 'What do you know?'

" 'Gy--y! I saw you near the willows kissing Sasha. I followed you and saw it all.'

"Zinotchka started, flushed all over, and overwhelmed by 'my hint' she sank down on the chair, on which stood a glass of water and a candlestick.

" 'I saw you . . . kissing . . .' I repeated, sniggering and enjoying her confusion. 'Aha! I'll tell mamma!'

"Cowardly Zinotchka gazed at me intently, and convincing herself that I really did know all about it, clutched my hand in despair and muttered in a trembling whisper:

" 'Petya, it is low. . . . I beg of you, for God's sake. . . . Be a man . . . don't tell anyone. . . . Decent people don't spy. . . . It's low. . . . I entreat you.'

"The poor girl was terribly afraid of my mother, a stern and virtuous lady -- that was one thing; and the second was that my grinning countenance could not but outrage her first love so pure and poetical, and you can imagine the state of her heart. Thanks to me, she did not sleep a wink all night, and in the morning she appeared at breakfast with blue rings round her eyes. When I met Sasha after breakfast I could not refrain from grinning and boasting:

" 'I know! I saw you yesterday kissing Mademoiselle Zina!'

"Sasha looked at me and said:

" 'You are a fool.'

"He was not so cowardly as Zinotchka, and so my effect did not come off. That provoked me to further efforts. If Sasha was not frightened it was evident that he did not believe that I had seen and knew all about it; wait a bit, I would show him.

"At our lessons before dinner Zinotchka did not look at me, and her voice faltered. Instead of trying to scare me she tried to propitiate me in every way, giving me full marks, and not complaining to my father of my naughtiness. Being intelligent beyond my years I exploited her secret: I did not learn my lessons, walked into the schoolroom on my head, and said all sorts of rude things. In fact, if I had remained in that vein till to-day I should have become a famous blackmailer. Well, a week passed. Another person's secret irritated and fretted me like a splinter in my soul. I longed at all costs to blurt it out and gloat over the effect. And one day at dinner, when we had a lot of visitors, I gave a stupid snigger, looked fiendishly at Zinotchka and said:

" 'I know. Gy--y! I saw! . . .'

" 'What do you know?' asked my mother.

"I looked still more fiendishly at Zinotchka and Sasha. You ought to have seen how the girl flushed up, and how furious Sasha's eyes were! I bit my tongue and did not go on. Zinotchka gradually turned pale, clenched her teeth, and ate no more dinner. At our evening lessons that day I noticed a striking change in Zinotchka's face. It looked sterner, colder, as it were, more like marble, while her eyes gazed strangely straight into my face, and I give you my word of honour I have never seen such terrible, annihilating eyes, even in hounds when they overtake the wolf. I understood their expression perfectly, when in the middle of a lesson she suddenly clenched her teeth and hissed through them:

" 'I hate you! Oh, you vile, loathsome creature, if you knew how I hate you, how I detest your cropped head, your vulgar, prominent ears!'

"But at once she took fright and said:

" 'I am not speaking to you, I am repeating a part out of a play. . . .'

"Then, my friends, at night I saw her come to my bedside and gaze a long time into my face. She hated me passionately, and could not exist away from me. The contemplation of my hated pug of a face had become a necessity to her. I remember a lovely summer evening . . . with the scent of hay, perfect stillness, and so on. The moon was shining. I was walking up and down the avenue, thinking of cherry jam. Suddenly Zinotchka, looking pale and lovely, came up to me, she caught hold of my hand, and breathlessly began expressing herself:

" 'Oh, how I hate you! I wish no one harm as I do you! Let me tell you that! I want you to understand that!'

"You understand, moonlight, her pale face, breathless with passion, the stillness . . . little pig as I was I actually enjoyed it. I listened to her, looked at her eyes. . . . At first I liked it, and enjoyed the novelty. Then I was suddenly seized with terror, I gave a scream, and ran into the house at breakneck speed.

"I made up my mind that the best thing to do was to complain to *maman*. And I did complain, mentioning incidentally how Sasha had kissed Zinotchka. I was stupid, and did not know what would follow, or I should have kept the secret to myself. . . . After hearing my story *maman* flushed with indignation and said:

" 'It is not your business to speak about that, you are still very young. . . . But, what an example for children.'

"My *maman* was not only virtuous but diplomatic. To avoid a scandal she did not get rid of Zinotchka at once, but set to work gradually, systematically, to pave the way for her departure, as one does with well-bred but intolerable people. I remember that when Zinotchka did leave us the last glance she cast at the house was directed at the window at which I was sitting, and I assure you, I remember that glance to this day.

"Zinotchka soon afterwards became my brother's wife. She is the Zinaida Nikolaevna whom you know. The next time I met her I was already an ensign. In spite of all her efforts she could not recognize the hated Petya in the ensign with his moustache, but still she did not treat me quite like a relation. . . . And even now, in spite of my good-humoured baldness, meek corpulence, and unassuming air, she still looks askance at me, and feels put out when I go to see my brother. Hatred it seems can no more be forgotten than love. . . .

"Tchoo! I hear the cock crowing! Good-night. Milord! Lie down!"

THE DOCTOR

It was still in the drawing-room, so still that a house-fly that had flown in from outside could be distinctly heard brushing against the ceiling. Olga Ivanovna, the lady of the villa, was standing by the window, looking out at the flower-beds and thinking. Dr. Tsvyetkov, who was her doctor as well as an old friend, and had been sent for to treat her son Misha, was sitting in an easy chair and swinging his hat, which he held in both hands, and he too was thinking. Except them, there was not a soul in the drawing-room or in the adjoining rooms. The sun had set, and the shades of evening began settling in the corners under the furniture and on the cornices.

The silence was broken by Olga Ivanovna.

"No misfortune more terrible can be imagined," she said, without turning from the window. "You know that life has no value for me whatever apart from the boy."

"Yes, I know that," said the doctor.

"No value whatever," said Olga Ivanovna, and her voice quivered. "He is everything to me. He is my joy, my happiness, my wealth. And if, as you say, I cease to be a mother, if he . . . dies, there will be nothing left of me but a shadow. I cannot survive it."

Wringing her hands, Olga Ivanovna walked from one window to the other and went on:

"When he was born, I wanted to send him away to the Foundling Hospital, you remember that, but, my God, how can that time be compared with now? Then I was vulgar, stupid, feather-headed, but now I am a mother, do you understand? I am a mother, and that's all I care to know. Between the present and the past there is an impassable gulf."

Silence followed again. The doctor shifted his seat from the chair to the sofa and impatiently playing with his hat, kept his eyes fixed upon Olga Ivanovna. From his face it could be seen that he wanted to speak, and was waiting for a fitting moment.

"You are silent, but still I do not give up hope," said the lady, turning round. "Why are you silent?"

"I should be as glad of any hope as you, Olga, but there is none," Tsvyetkov answered, "we must look the hideous truth in the face. The boy has a tumour on the brain, and we must try to prepare ourselves for his death, for such cases never recover."

"Nikolay, are you certain you are not mistaken?"

"Such questions lead to nothing. I am ready to answer as many as you like, but it will make it no better for us."

Olga Ivanovna pressed her face into the window curtains, and began weeping bitterly. The doctor got up and walked several times up and down the drawing-room, then went to the weeping woman, and lightly touched her arm. Judging from his uncertain movements, from the expression of his gloomy face, which looked dark in the dusk of the evening, he wanted to say something.

"Listen, Olga," he began. "Spare me a minute's attention; there is something I must ask you. You can't attend to me now, though. I'll come later, afterwards...." He sat down again, and sank into thought. The bitter, imploring weeping, like the weeping of a little girl, continued. Without waiting for it to end, Tsvyetkov heaved a sigh and walked out of the drawing-room. He went into the nursery to Misha. The boy was lying on his back as before, staring at one point as though he were listening. The doctor sat down on his bed and felt his pulse.

"Misha, does your head ache?" he asked.

Misha answered, not at once: "Yes. I keep dreaming."

"What do you dream?"

"All sorts of things...."

The doctor, who did not know how to talk with weeping women or with children, stroked his burning head, and muttered:

"Never mind, poor boy, never mind.... One can't go through life without illness.... Misha, who am I -- do you know me?"

Misha did not answer.

"Does your head ache very badly?"

"Ve-ery. I keep dreaming."

After examining him and putting a few questions to the maid who was looking after the sick child, the doctor went slowly back to the drawing-room. There it was by now dark, and Olga Ivanovna, standing by the window, looked like a silhouette.

"Shall I light up?" asked Tsvyetkov.

No answer followed. The house-fly was still brushing against the ceiling. Not a sound floated in from outside as though the whole world, like the doctor, were thinking, and could not bring itself to speak. Olga Ivanovna was not weeping now, but as before, staring at the flower-bed in profound silence. When Tsvyetkov went up to her, and through the twilight glanced at her pale face, exhausted with grief, her expression was such as he had seen before during her attacks of acute, stupefying, sick headache.

"Nikolay Trofimitch!" she addressed him, "and what do you think about a consultation?"

"Very good; I'll arrange it to-morrow."

From the doctor's tone it could be easily seen that he put little faith in the benefit of a consultation. Olga Ivanovna would have asked him something else, but her sobs prevented her. Again she pressed her face into the window curtain. At that moment, the strains of a band playing at the club floated in distinctly. They could hear not only the wind instruments, but even the violins and the flutes.

"If he is in pain, why is he silent?" asked Olga Ivanovna. "All day long, not a sound, he never complains, and never cries. I know God will take the poor boy from us because we have not known how to prize him. Such a treasure!"

The band finished the march, and a minute later began playing a lively waltz for the opening of the ball.

"Good God, can nothing really be done?" moaned Olga Ivanovna. "Nikolay, you are a doctor and ought to know what to do! You must understand that I can't bear the loss of him! I can't survive it."

The doctor, who did not know how to talk to weeping women, heaved a sigh, and paced slowly about the drawing-room. There followed a succession of oppressive pauses interspersed with weeping and the questions which lead to nothing. The band had already played a quadrille, a polka, and another quadrille. It got quite dark. In the adjoining room, the maid lighted the lamp; and all the while the doctor kept his hat in his hands, and seemed trying to say something. Several times Olga Ivanovna went off to her son, sat by him for half an hour, and came back again into the drawing-room; she was continually breaking into tears and lamentations. The time dragged agonisingly, and it seemed as though the evening had no end.

At midnight, when the band had played the cotillion and ceased altogether, the doctor got ready to go.

"I will come again to-morrow," he said, pressing the mother's cold hand. "You go to bed."

After putting on his greatcoat in the passage and picking up his walking-stick, he stopped, thought a minute, and went back into the drawing-room.

"I'll come to-morrow, Olga," he repeated in a quivering voice. "Do you hear?"

She did not answer, and it seemed as though grief had robbed her of all power of speech. In his greatcoat and with his stick still in his hand, the doctor sat down beside her, and began in a soft, tender half-whisper, which was utterly out of keeping with his heavy, dignified figure:

"Olga! For the sake of your sorrow which I share. . . . Now, when falsehood is criminal, I beseech you to tell me the truth. You have always declared that the boy is my son. Is that the truth?"

Olga Ivanovna was silent.

"You have been the one attachment in my life," the doctor went on, "and you cannot imagine how deeply my feeling is wounded by falsehood. . . . Come, I entreat you, Olga, for once in your life, tell me the truth. . . . At these moments one cannot lie. Tell me that Misha is not my son. I am waiting."

"He is."

Olga Ivanovna's face could not be seen, but in her voice the doctor could hear hesitation. He sighed.

"Even at such moments you can bring yourself to tell a lie," he said in his ordinary voice. "There is nothing sacred to you! Do listen, do understand me. . . . You have been the one only attachment in my life. Yes, you were depraved, vulgar, but I have loved no one else but you in my life. That trivial love, now that I am growing old, is the one solitary bright spot in my memories. Why do you darken it with deception? What is it for?"

"I don't understand you."

"Oh my God!" cried Tsvyetkov. "You are lying, you understand very well!" he cried more loudly, and he began pacing about the drawing-room, angrily waving his stick. "Or have you forgotten? Then I will remind you! A father's rights to the boy are equally shared with me by Petrov and Kurovsky the lawyer, who still make you an allowance for their son's education, just as I do! Yes, indeed! I know all that quite well! I forgive your lying in the past, what does it matter? But now when you have grown older, at this moment when the boy is dying, your lying stifles me! How sorry I am that I cannot speak, how sorry I am!"

The doctor unbuttoned his overcoat, and still pacing about, said:

"Wretched woman! Even such moments have no effect on her! Even now she lies as freely as nine years ago in the Hermitage Restaurant! She is afraid if she tells me the truth I shall leave off giving her money, she thinks that if she did not lie I should not love the boy! You are lying! It's contemptible!"

The doctor rapped the floor with his stick, and cried:

"It's loathsome. Warped, corrupted creature! I must despise you, and I ought to be ashamed of my feeling. Yes! Your lying has stuck in my throat these nine years, I have endured it, but now it's too much -- too much."

From the dark corner where Olga Ivanovna was sitting there came the sound of weeping. The doctor ceased speaking and cleared his throat. A silence followed. The doctor slowly buttoned up his over-coat, and began looking for his hat which he had dropped as he walked about.

"I lost my temper," he muttered, bending down to the floor. "I quite lost sight of the fact that you cannot attend to me now. . . . God knows what I have said. . . . Don't take any notice of it, Olga."

He found his hat and went towards the dark corner.

"I have wounded you," he said in a soft, tender half-whisper, "but once more I entreat you, tell me the truth; there should not be lying between us. . . . I blurted it out, and now you know that Petrov and Kurovsky are no secret to me. So now it is easy for you to tell me the truth."

Olga Ivanovna thought a moment, and with perceptible hesitation, said:

"Nikolay, I am not lying -- Misha is your child."

"My God," moaned the doctor, "then I will tell you something more: I have kept your letter to Petrov in which you call him Misha's father! Olga, I know the truth, but I want to hear it from you! Do you hear?"

Olga Ivanovna made no reply, but went on weeping. After waiting for an answer the doctor shrugged his shoulders and went out.

"I will come to-morrow," he called from the passage.

All the way home, as he sat in his carriage, he was shrugging his shoulders and muttering:

"What a pity that I don't know how to speak! I haven't the gift of persuading and convincing. It's evident she does not understand me since she lies! It's evident! How can I make her see? How?"

THE SHEPHERD'S PIPE

Meliton Shishkin, a bailiff from the Dementyev farm, exhausted by the sultry heat of the fir-wood and covered with spiders' webs and pine-needles, made his way with his gun to the edge of the wood. His Damka -- a mongrel between a yard dog and a setter -- an extremely thin bitch heavy with young, trailed after her master with her wet tail between her legs, doing all she could to avoid pricking her nose. It was a dull, overcast morning. Big drops dripped from the bracken and from the trees that were wrapped in a light mist; there was a pungent smell of decay from the dampness of the wood.

There were birch-trees ahead of him where the wood ended, and between their stems and branches he could see the misty distance. Beyond the birch-trees someone was playing on a shepherd's rustic pipe. The player produced no more than five or six notes, dragged them out languidly with no attempt at forming a tune, and yet there was something harsh and extremely dreary in the sound of the piping.

As the copse became sparser, and the pines were interspersed with young birch-trees, Meliton saw a herd. Hobbled horses, cows, and sheep were wandering among the bushes and, snapping the dry branches, sniffed at the herbage of the copse. A lean old shepherd, bareheaded, in a torn grey smock, stood leaning against the wet trunk of a birch-tree. He stared at the ground, pondering something, and played his pipe, it seemed, mechanically.

"Good-day, grandfather! God help you!" Meliton greeted him in a thin, husky voice which seemed incongruous with his huge stature and big, fleshy face. "How cleverly you are playing your pipe! Whose herd are you minding?"

"The Artamonovs'," the shepherd answered reluctantly, and he thrust the pipe into his bosom.

"So I suppose the wood is the Artamonovs' too?" Meliton inquired, looking about him. "Yes, it is the Artamonovs'; only fancy . . . I had completely lost myself. I got my face scratched all over in the thicket."

He sat down on the wet earth and began rolling up a bit of newspaper into a cigarette.

Like his voice, everything about the man was small and out of keeping with his height, his breadth, and his fleshy face: his smiles, his eyes, his buttons, his tiny cap, which would hardly keep on his big, closely-cropped head. When he talked and smiled there was something womanish, timid, and meek about his puffy, shaven face and his whole figure.

"What weather! God help us!" he said, and he turned his head from side to side. "Folk have not carried the oats yet, and the rain seems as though it had been taken on for good, God bless it."

The shepherd looked at the sky, from which a drizzling rain was falling, at the wood, at the bailiff's wet clothes, pondered, and said nothing.

"The whole summer has been the same," sighed Meliton. "A bad business for the peasants and no pleasure for the gentry."

The shepherd looked at the sky again, thought a moment, and said deliberately, as though chewing each word:

"It's all going the same way. . . . There is nothing good to be looked for."

"How are things with you here?" Meliton inquired, lighting his cigarette. "Haven't you seen any coveys of grouse in the Artamonovs' clearing?"

The shepherd did not answer at once. He looked again at the sky and to right and left, thought a little, blinked. . . . Apparently he attached no little significance to his words, and to increase their value tried to pronounce them with deliberation and a certain solemnity. The expression of his face had the sharpness and staidness of old age, and the fact that his nose had a saddle-shaped depression across the middle and his nostrils turned upwards gave him a sly and sarcastic look.

"No, I believe I haven't," he said. "Our huntsman Eryomka was saying that on Elijah's Day he started one covey near Pustoshye, but I dare say he was lying. There are very few birds."

"Yes, brother, very few. . . . Very few everywhere! The shooting here, if one is to look at it with common sense, is good for nothing and not worth having. There is no game at all, and what there is is not worth dirtying your hands over -- it is not full-grown. It is such poor stuff that one is ashamed to look at it."

Meliton gave a laugh and waved his hands.

"Things happen so queerly in this world that it is simply laughable and nothing else. Birds nowadays have become so unaccountable: they sit late on their eggs, and there are some, I declare, that have not hatched them by St. Peter's Day!"

"It's all going the same," said the shepherd, turning his face upwards. "There was little game last year, this year there are fewer birds still, and in another five years, mark my words, there will be none at all. As far as I can see there will soon be not only no game, but no birds at all."

Yes," Meliton assented, after a moment's thought. "That's true."

The shepherd gave a bitter smile and shook his head.

"It's a wonder," he said, "what has become of them all! I remember twenty years ago there used to be geese here, and cranes and ducks and grouse -- clouds and clouds of them! The gentry used to meet together for shooting, and one heard nothing but pouf-pouf-pouf! pouf-pouf-pouf! There was no end to the woodcocks, the snipe, and the little teals, and the water-snipe were as common as starlings, or let us say sparrows -- lots and lots of them! And what has become of them all? We don't even see the birds of prey. The eagles, the hawks, and the owls have all gone. . . . There are fewer of every sort of wild beast, too. Nowadays, brother, even the wolf and the fox have grown rare, let alone the bear or the otter. And you know in old days there were even elks! For forty years I have been observing the works of God from year to year, and it is my opinion that everything is going the same way."

"What way?"

"To the bad, young man. To ruin, we must suppose. . . The time has come for God's world to perish."

The old man put on his cap and began gazing at the sky.

"It's a pity," he sighed, after a brief silence. "O God, what a pity! Of course it is God's will; the world was not created by us, but yet it is a pity, brother. If a single tree withers away, or let us say a single cow dies, it makes one sorry, but what will it be, good man, if the whole world crumbles into dust? Such blessings, Lord Jesus! The sun, and the sky, and the forest, and the rivers, and the creatures -- all these have been created, adapted, and adjusted to one another. Each has been put to its appointed task and knows its place. And all that must perish."

A mournful smile gleamed on the shepherd's face, and his eyelids quivered.

"You say -- the world is perishing," said Meliton, pondering. "It may be that the end of the world is near at hand, but you can't judge by the birds. I don't think the birds can be taken as a sign."

"Not the birds only," said the shepherd. "It's the wild beasts, too, and the cattle, and the bees, and the fish. . . . If you don't believe me ask the old people; every old man will tell you that the fish are not at all what they used to be. In the seas, in the lakes, and in the rivers, there are fewer fish from year to year. In our Pestchanka, I remember, pike used to be caught a yard long, and there were eel-pouts, and roach, and bream, and every fish had a presentable appearance; while nowadays, if you catch a wretched little pikelet or perch six inches long you have to be thankful. There are not any gudgeon even worth talking about. Every year it is worse and worse, and in a little while there will be no fish at all. And take the rivers now . . . the rivers are drying up, for sure."

"It is true; they are drying up."

"To be sure, that's what I say. Every year they are shallower and shallower, and there are not the deep holes there used to be. And do you see the bushes yonder?" the old man asked, pointing to one side. "Beyond them is an old river-bed; it's called a backwater. In my father's time the Pestchanka flowed there, but now look; where have the evil spirits taken it to? It changes its course, and, mind you, it will go on changing till such time as it has dried up altogether. There used to be marshes and ponds beyond Kurgasovo, and where are they now? And what has become of the streams? Here in this very wood we used to have a stream flowing, and such a stream that the peasants used to set creels in it and caught pike; wild ducks used to spend the winter by it, and nowadays there is no water in it worth speaking of, even at the spring floods. Yes, brother, look where you will, things are bad everywhere. Everywhere!"

A silence followed. Meliton sank into thought, with his eyes fixed on one spot. He wanted to think of some one part of nature as yet untouched by the all-embracing ruin. Spots of light glistened on the mist and the slanting streaks of rain as though on opaque glass, and immediately died away again -- it was the rising sun trying to break through the clouds and peep at the earth.

"Yes, the forests, too . . ." Meliton muttered.

"The forests, too," the shepherd repeated. "They cut them down, and they catch fire, and they wither away, and no new ones are growing. Whatever does grow up is cut down at once; one day it shoots up and the next it has been cut down -- and so on without end till nothing's left. I have kept the herds of the commune ever since the time of Freedom, good man; before the time of Freedom I was shepherd of the master's herds. I have watched them in this very spot, and I can't remember a summer day in all my life that I have not been here. And all the time I have been observing the works of God. I have looked at them in my time till I know them, and it is my opinion that all things growing are on the decline. Whether you take the rye, or the vegetables, or flowers of any sort, they are all going the same way."

"But people have grown better," observed the bailiff.

"In what way better?"

"Cleverer."

"Cleverer, maybe, that's true, young man; but what's the use of that? What earthly good is cleverness to people on the brink of ruin? One can perish without cleverness. What's the good of cleverness to a huntsman if there is no game? What I think is that God has given men brains and taken away their strength. People have grown weak, exceedingly weak. Take me, for instance . . . I am not worth a halfpenny, I am the humblest peasant in the whole village, and yet, young man, I have strength. Mind you, I am in my seventies, and I tend my herd day in and day out, and keep the night watch, too, for twenty kopecks, and I don't sleep, and I don't feel the cold; my son is cleverer than I am, but put him in my place and he would ask for a raise next day, or would be going to the doctors. There it is. I eat nothing but bread, for 'Give us this day our daily bread,' and my father ate nothing but bread, and my grandfather; but the peasant nowadays must have tea and vodka and white loaves, and must sleep from sunset to dawn, and he goes to the doctor and pampers himself in all sorts of ways. And why is it? He has grown weak; he has not the strength to endure. If he wants to stay awake, his eyes close -- there is no doing anything."

"That's true," Meliton agreed; "the peasant is good for nothing nowadays."

"It's no good hiding what is wrong; we get worse from year to year. And if you take the gentry into consideration, they've grown feebler even more than the peasants have. The gentleman nowadays has mastered everything; he knows what he ought not to know, and what is the sense of it? It makes you feel pitiful to look at him. . . . He is a thin, puny little fellow, like some Hungarian or Frenchman; there is no dignity nor air about him; it's only in name he is a gentleman. There is no place for him, poor dear, and nothing for him to do, and there is no making out what he wants. Either he sits with a hook catching fish, or he lolls on his back reading, or trots about among the peasants saying all sorts of things to them, and those that are hungry go in for being clerks. So he spends his life in vain. And he has no notion of doing something real and useful. The gentry in old days were half of them generals, but nowadays they are -- a poor lot."

"They are badly off nowadays," said Meliton.

"They are poorer because God has taken away their strength. You can't go against God."

Meliton stared at a fixed point again. After thinking a little he heaved a sigh as staid, reasonable people do sigh, shook his head, and said:

"And all because of what? We have sinned greatly, we have forgotten God . . and it seems that the time has come for all to end. And, after all, the world can't last for ever -- it's time to know when to take leave."

The shepherd sighed and, as though wishing to cut short an unpleasant conversation, he walked away from the birch-tree and began silently reckoning over the cows.

"Hey-hey-hey!" he shouted. "Hey-hey-hey! Bother you, the plague take you! The devil has taken you into the thicket. Tu-lu-lu!"

With an angry face he went into the bushes to collect his herd. Meliton got up and sauntered slowly along the edge of the wood. He looked at the ground at his feet and pondered; he still wanted to think of something which had not yet been touched by death. Patches of light crept upon the slanting streaks of rain again; they danced on the tops of the trees and died away among the wet leaves. Damka found a hedgehog under a bush, and wanting to attract her master's attention to it, barked and howled.

"Did you have an eclipse or not?" the shepherd called from the bushes.

"Yes, we had," answered Meliton.

"Ah! Folks are complaining all about that there was one. It shows there is disorder even in the heavens! It's not for nothing. . . . Hey-hey-hey! Hey!"

Driving his herd together to the edge of the wood, the shepherd leaned against the birch-tree, looked up at the sky, without haste took his pipe from his bosom and began playing. As before, he played mechanically and took no more than five or six notes; as though the pipe had come into his hands for the first time, the sounds floated from it uncertainly, with no regularity, not blending into a tune, but to Meliton, brooding on the destruction of the world, there was a sound in it of something very depressing and revolting which he would much rather not have heard. The highest, shrillest notes, which quivered and broke, seemed to be weeping disconsolately, as though the pipe were sick and frightened, while the lowest notes for some reason reminded him of the mist, the dejected trees, the grey sky. Such music seemed in keeping with the weather, the old man and his sayings.

Meliton wanted to complain. He went up to the old man and, looking at his mournful, mocking face and at the pipe, muttered:

"And life has grown worse, grandfather. It is utterly impossible to live. Bad crops, want. . . . Cattle plague continually, diseases of all sorts. . . . We are crushed by poverty."

The bailiff's puffy face turned crimson and took a dejected, womanish expression. He twirled his fingers as though seeking words to convey his vague feeling and went on:

"Eight children, a wife . . . and my mother still living, and my whole salary ten roubles a month and to board myself. My wife has become a Satan from poverty. . . . I go off drinking myself. I am a sensible, steady man; I have education. I ought to sit at home in peace, but I stray about all day with my gun like a dog because it is more than I can stand; my home is hateful to me!"

Feeling that his tongue was uttering something quite different from what he wanted to say, the bailiff waved his hand and said bitterly:

"If the world's going to end I wish it would make haste about it. There's no need to drag it out and make folks miserable for nothing. . . ."

The old man took the pipe from his lips and, screwing up one eye, looked into its little opening. His face was sad and covered with thick drops like tears. He smiled and said:

"It's a pity, my friend! My goodness, what a pity! The earth, the forest, the sky, the beasts of all sorts -- all this has been created, you know, adapted; they all have their intelligence. It is all going to ruin. And most of all I am sorry for people."

There was the sound in the wood of heavy rain coming nearer. Meliton looked in the direction of the sound, did up all his buttons, and said:

"I am going to the village. Good-bye, grandfather. What is your name?"

"Luka the Poor."

"Well, good-bye, Luka! Thank you for your good words. Damka, ici!"

After parting from the shepherd Meliton made his way along the edge of the wood, and then down hill to a meadow which by degrees turned into a marsh. There was a squelch of water under his feet, and the rusty marsh sedge, still green and juicy, drooped down to the earth as though afraid of being trampled underfoot. Beyond the marsh, on the bank of the Pestchanka, of which the old man had spoken, stood a row of willows, and beyond the willows a barn looked dark blue in the mist. One could feel the approach of that miserable, utterly inevitable season, when the fields grow dark and the earth is muddy and cold, when the weeping willow seems still more mournful and tears trickle down its stem, and only the cranes fly away from the general misery, and even they, as though afraid of insulting dispirited nature by the expression of their happiness, fill the air with their mournful, dreary notes.

Meliton plodded along to the river, and heard the sounds of the pipe gradually dying away behind him. He still wanted to complain. He looked dejectedly about him, and he felt insufferably sorry for the sky and the earth and the sun and the woods and his Damka, and when the highest drawn-out note of the pipe floated quivering in the air, like a voice weeping, he felt extremely bitter and resentful of the impropriety in the conduct of nature.

The high note quivered, broke off, and the pipe was silent.

AN AVENGER

Shortly after finding his wife *in flagrante delicto* Fyodor Fyodorovitch Sigaev was standing in Schmuck and Co.'s, the gunsmiths, selecting a suitable revolver. His countenance expressed wrath, grief, and unalterable determination.

"I know what I must do," he was thinking. "The sanctities of the home are outraged, honour is trampled in the mud, vice is triumphant, and therefore as a citizen and a man of honour I must be their avenger. First, I will kill her and her lover and then myself."

He had not yet chosen a revolver or killed anyone, but already in imagination he saw three bloodstained corpses, broken skulls, brains oozing from them, the commotion, the crowd of gaping spectators, the post-mortem. . . . With the malignant joy of an insulted man he pictured the horror of the relations and the public, the agony of the traitress, and was mentally reading leading articles on the destruction of the traditions of the home.

The shopman, a sprightly little Frenchified figure with rounded belly and white waistcoat, displayed the revolvers, and smiling respectfully and scraping with his little feet observed:

". . . I would advise you, M'sieur, to take this superb revolver, the Smith and Wesson pattern, the last word in the science of firearms: triple-action, with ejector, kills at six hundred paces, central sight. Let me draw your attention, M'sieu, to the beauty of the finish. The most fashionable system, M'sieu. We sell a dozen every day for burglars, wolves, and lovers. Very correct and powerful action, hits at a great distance, and kills wife and lover with one bullet. As for suicide, M'sieu, I don't know a better pattern."

The shopman pulled and cocked the trigger, breathed on the barrel, took aim, and affected to be breathless with delight. Looking at his ecstatic countenance, one might have supposed that he would readily have put a bullet through his brains if he had only possessed a revolver of such a superb pattern as a Smith-Wesson.

"And what price?" asked Sigaev.

"Forty-five roubles, M'sieu."

"Mm! . . . that's too dear for me."

"In that case, M'sieu, let me offer you another make, somewhat cheaper. Here, if you'll kindly look, we have an immense choice, at all prices. . . . Here, for instance, this revolver of the Lefaucher pattern costs only eighteen roubles, but . . ." (the shopman pursed up his face contemptuously) ". . . but, M'sieu, it's an old-fashioned make. They are only bought by hysterical ladies or the mentally deficient. To commit suicide or shoot one's wife with a Lefaucher revolver is considered bad form nowadays. Smith-Wesson is the only pattern that's correct style."

"I don't want to shoot myself or to kill anyone," said Sigaev, lying sullenly. "I am buying it simply for a country cottage . . . to frighten away burglars. . . ."

"That's not our business, what object you have in buying it." The shopman smiled, dropping his eyes discreetly. "If we were to investigate the object in each case, M'sieu, we should have to close our shop. To frighten burglars Lefaucher is not a suitable pattern, M'sieu, for it goes off with a faint, muffled sound. I would suggest Mortimer's, the so-called duelling pistol. . . ."

"Shouldn't I challenge him to a duel?" flashed through Sigaev's mind. "It's doing him too much honour, though. . . . Beasts like that are killed like dogs. . . ."

The shopman, swaying gracefully and tripping to and fro on his little feet, still smiling and chattering, displayed before him a heap of revolvers. The most inviting and impressive of all was the Smith and Wesson's. Sigaev picked up a pistol of that pattern, gazed blankly at it, and sank into brooding. His imagination pictured how he would blow out their brains, how blood would flow in streams over the rug and the parquet, how the traitress's legs would twitch in her last agony. . . . But that was not enough for his indignant soul. The picture of blood, wailing, and horror did not satisfy him. He must think of something more terrible.

"I know! I'll kill myself and him," he thought, "but I'll leave her alive. Let her pine away from the stings of conscience and the contempt of all surrounding her. For a sensitive nature like hers that will be far more agonizing than death."

And he imagined his own funeral: he, the injured husband, lies in his coffin with a gentle smile on his lips, and she, pale, tortured by remorse, follows the coffin like a Niobe, not knowing where to hide herself to escape from the withering, contemptuous looks cast upon her by the indignant crowd.

"I see, M'sieu, that you like the Smith and Wesson make," the shopman broke in upon his broodings. "If you think it too dear, very well, I'll knock off five roubles. . . . But we have other makes, cheaper."

The little Frenchified figure turned gracefully and took down another dozen cases of revolvers from the shelf.

"Here, M'sieu, price thirty roubles. That's not expensive, especially as the rate of exchange has dropped terribly and the Customs duties are rising every hour. M'sieu, I vow I am a Conservative, but even I am beginning to murmur. Why, with the rate of exchange and the Customs tariff, only the rich can purchase firearms. There's nothing left for the poor but Tula weapons and phosphorus matches, and Tula weapons are a misery! You may aim at your wife with a Tula revolver and shoot yourself through the shoulder-blade."

Sigaev suddenly felt mortified and sorry that he would be dead, and would miss seeing the agonies of the traitress. Revenge is only sweet when one can see and taste its fruits, and what sense would there be in it if he were lying in his coffin, knowing nothing about it?

"Hadn't I better do this?" he pondered. "I'll kill him, then I'll go to his funeral and look on, and after the funeral I'll kill myself. They'd arrest me, though, before the funeral, and take away my pistol. . . . And so I'll kill him, she shall remain alive, and I . . . for the time, I'll not kill myself, but go and be arrested. I shall always have time to kill myself. There will be this advantage about being arrested, that at the preliminary investigation I shall have an opportunity of exposing to the authorities and to the public all the infamy of her conduct. If I kill myself she may, with her characteristic duplicity and impudence, throw all the blame on me, and society will justify her behaviour and will very likely laugh at me. . . . If I remain alive, then . . ."

A minute later he was thinking:

"Yes, if I kill myself I may be blamed and suspected of petty feeling. . . . Besides, why should I kill myself? That's one thing. And for another, to shoot oneself is cowardly. And so I'll kill him and let her live, and I'll face my trial. I shall be tried, and she will be brought into court as a witness. . . . I can imagine her confusion, her disgrace when she is examined by my counsel! The sympathies of the court, of the Press, and of the public will certainly be with me."

While he deliberated the shopman displayed his wares, and felt it incumbent upon him to entertain his customer.

"Here are English ones, a new pattern, only just received," he prattled on. " But I warn you, M'sieu, all these systems pale beside the Smith and Wesson. The other day-as I dare say you have read-an officer bought from u~ a Smith and Wesson. He shot his wife's lover, and-would you believe it?-the bullet passed through him, pierced the bronze lamp, then the piano, and ricochetted back from the piano, killing the lap-dog and bruising the wife. A magnificent record redounding to the honour of our firm! The officer is now under arrest. He will no doubt be convicted and sent to penal servitude. In the first place, our penal code is quite out of date; and, secondly, M'sieu, the sympathies of the court are always with the lover. Why is it? Very simple, M'sieu. The judges and the jury and the prosecutor and the counsel for the defence are all living with other men's wives, and it'll add to their comfort that there will be one husband the less in Russia. Society would be pleased if the Government were to send all the husbands to Sahalin. Oh, M'sieu, you don't know how it excites my indignation to see the corruption of morals nowadays. To love other men's wives is as much the regular thing to-day as to smoke other men s cigarettes and to read other men's books. Every year our trade gets worse and worse -- it doesn't mean that wives are more faithful, but that husbands resign themselves to their position and are afraid of the law and penal servitude."

The shopman looked round and whispered: "And whose fault is it, M'sieu? The Government's."

"To go to Sahalin for the sake of a pig like that -- there's no sense in that either," Sigaev pondered. "If I go to penal servitude it will only give my wife an opportunity of marrying again and deceiving a second husband. She would triumph. . . . And so I will leave *her* alive, I won't kill myself, *him* . . . I won't kill either. I must think of something more sensible and more effective. I will punish them with my contempt, and will take divorce proceedings that will make a scandal."

"Here, M'sieu, is another make," said the shopman, taking down another dozen from the shelf. "Let me call your attention to the original mechanism of the lock."

In view of his determination a revolver was now of no use to Sigaev, but the shopman, meanwhile, getting more and more enthusiastic, persisted in displaying his wares before him. The outraged husband began to feel ashamed that the shopman should be taking so much trouble on his account for nothing, that he should be smiling, wasting time, displaying enthusiasm for nothing.

Very well, in that case," he muttered, "I'll look in again later on . . . or I'll send someone."

He didn't see the expression of the shopman's face, but to smooth over the awkwardness of the position a little he felt called upon to make some purchase. But what should he buy? He looked round the walls of the shop to pick out something inexpensive, and his eyes rested on a green net hanging near the door.

"That's . . . what's that?" he asked.

"That's a net for catching quails."

"And what price is it?"

"Eight roubles, M'sieu."

"Wrap it up for me. . . ."

The outraged husband paid his eight roubles, took the net, and, feeling even more outraged, walked out of the shop.

THE POST

It was three o'clock in the night. The postman, ready to set off, in his cap and his coat, with a rusty sword in his hand, was standing near the door, waiting for the driver to finish putting the mail bags into the cart which had just been brought round with three horses. The sleepy postmaster sat at his table, which was like a counter; he was filling up a form and saying:

"My nephew, the student, wants to go to the station at once. So look here, Ignatyev, let him get into the mail cart and take him with you to the station: though it is against the regulations to take people with the mail, what's one to do? It's better for him to drive with you free than for me to hire horses for him."

"Ready!" they heard a shout from the yard.

"Well, go then, and God be with you," said the postmaster. "Which driver is going?"

"Semyon Glazov."

"Come, sign the receipt."

The postman signed the receipt and went out. At the entrance of the post-office there was the dark outline of a cart and three horses. The horses were standing still except that one of the tracehorses kept uneasily shifting from one leg to the other and tossing its head, making the bell clang from time to time. The cart with the mail bags looked like a patch of darkness. Two silhouettes were moving lazily beside it: the student with a portmanteau in his hand and a driver. The latter was smoking a short pipe; the light of the pipe moved about in the darkness, dying away and flaring up again; for an instant it lighted up a bit of a sleeve, then a shaggy moustache and big copper-red nose, then stern-looking, overhanging eyebrows. The postman pressed down the mail bags with his hands, laid his sword on them and jumped into the cart. The student clambered irresolutely in after him, and accidentally touching him with his elbow, said timidly and politely: "I beg your pardon."

The pipe went out. The postmaster came out of the post-office just as he was, in his waistcoat and slippers; shrinking from the night dampness and clearing his throat, he walked beside the cart and said:

"Well, God speed! Give my love to your mother, Mihailo. Give my love to them all. And you, Ignatyev, mind you don't forget to give the parcel to Bystretsov. . . . Off!"

The driver took the reins in one hand, blew his nose, and, arranging the seat under himself, clicked to the horses.

"Give them my love," the postmaster repeated.

The big bell clanged something to the little bells, the little bells gave it a friendly answer. The cart squeaked, moved. The big bell lamented, the little bells laughed. Standing up in his seat the driver lashed the restless tracehorse twice, and the cart rumbled with a hollow sound along the dusty road. The little town was asleep. Houses and trees stood black on each side of the broad street, and not a light was to be seen. Narrow clouds stretched here and there over the star-spangled sky, and where the dawn would soon be coming there was a narrow crescent moon; but neither the stars, of which there were many, nor the half-moon, which looked white, lighted up the night air. It was cold and damp, and there was a smell of autumn.

The student, who thought that politeness required him to talk affably to a man who had not refused to let him accompany him, began:

"In summer it would be light at this time, but now there is not even a sign of the dawn. Summer is over!"

The student looked at the sky and went on:

"Even from the sky one can see that it is autumn. Look to the right. Do you see three stars side by side in a straight line? That is the constellation of Orion, which, in our hemisphere, only becomes visible in September."

The postman, thrusting his hands into his sleeves and retreating up to his ears into his coat collar, did not stir and did not glance at the sky. Apparently the constellation of Orion did not interest him. He was accustomed to see the stars, and probably he had long grown weary of them. The student paused for a while and then said:

"It's cold! It's time for the dawn to begin. Do you know what time the sun rises?"

"What?"

"What time does the sun rise now?"

"Between five and six," said the driver.

The mail cart drove out of the town. Now nothing could be seen on either side of the road but the fences of kitchen gardens and here and there a solitary willow-tree; everything in front of them was shrouded in darkness. Here in the open country the half-moon looked bigger and the stars shone more brightly. Then came a scent of dampness; the postman shrank further into his collar, the student felt an unpleasant chill first creeping about his feet, then over the mail bags, over his hands and his face. The horses moved more slowly; the bell was mute as though it were frozen. There was the sound of the splash of water, and stars reflected in the water danced under the horses' feet and round the wheels.

But ten minutes later it became so dark that neither the stars nor the moon could be seen. The mail cart had entered the forest. Prickly pine branches were continually hitting the student on his cap and a spider's web settled on his face. Wheels and hoofs knocked against huge roots, and the mail cart swayed from side to side as though it were drunk.

"Keep to the road," said the postman angrily. "Why do you run up the edge? My face is scratched all over by the twigs! Keep more to the right!"

But at that point there was nearly an accident. The cart suddenly bounded as though in the throes of a convulsion, began trembling, and, with a creak, lurched heavily first to the right and then to the left, and at a fearful pace dashed along the forest track. The horses had taken fright at something and bolted.

"Wo! wo!" the driver cried in alarm. "Wo . . . you devils!

The student, violently shaken, bent forward and tried to find something to catch hold of so as to keep his balance and save himself from being thrown out, but the leather mail bags were slippery, and the driver, whose belt the student tried to catch at, was himself tossed up and down and seemed every moment on the point of flying out. Through the rattle of the wheels and the creaking of the cart they heard the sword fall with a clank on the ground, then a little later something fell with two heavy thuds behind the mail cart.

"Wo!" the driver cried in a piercing voice, bending backwards. "Stop!"

The student fell on his face and bruised his forehead against the driver's seat, but was at once tossed back again and knocked his spine violently against the back of the cart.

"I am falling!" was the thought that flashed through his mind, but at that instant the horses dashed out of the forest into the open, turned sharply to the right, and rumbling over a bridge of logs, suddenly stopped dead, and the suddenness of this halt flung the student forward again.

The driver and the student were both breathless. The postman was not in the cart. He had been thrown out, together with his sword, the student's portmanteau, and one of the mail bags.

"Stop, you rascal! Sto-op!" they heard him shout from the forest. "You damned blackguard!" he shouted, running up to the cart, and there was a note of pain and fury in his tearful voice. "You anathema, plague take you!" he roared, dashing up to the driver and shaking his fist at him.

"What a to-do! Lord have mercy on us!" muttered the driver in a conscience-stricken voice, setting right something in the harness at the horses' heads. "It's all that devil of a tracehorse. Cursed filly; it is only a week since she has run in harness. She goes all right, but as soon as we go down hill there is trouble! She wants a touch or two on the nose, then she wouldn't play about like this. . . Stea-eady! Damn!"

While the driver was setting the horses to rights and looking for the portmanteau, the mail bag, and the sword on the road, the postman in a plaintive voice shrill with anger ejaculated oaths. After replacing the luggage the driver for no reason whatever led the horses for a hundred paces, grumbled at the restless tracehorse, and jumped up on the box.

When his fright was over the student felt amused and good-humoured. It was the first time in his life that he had driven by night in a mail cart, and the shaking he had just been through, the postman's having been thrown out, and the pain in his own back struck him as interesting adventures. He lighted a cigarette and said with a laugh:

"Why you know, you might break your neck like that! I very nearly flew out, and I didn't even notice you had been thrown out. I can fancy what it is like driving in autumn!"

The postman did not speak.

"Have you been going with the post for long?" the student asked.

"Eleven years."

"Oho; every day?"

"Yes, every day. I take this post and drive back again at once. Why?"

Making the journey every day, he must have had a good many interesting adventures in eleven years. On bright summer and gloomy autumn nights, or in winter when a ferocious snowstorm whirled howling round the mail cart, it must have been hard to avoid feeling frightened and uncanny. No doubt more than once the horses had bolted, the mail cart had stuck in the mud, they had been attacked by highwaymen, or had lost their way in the blizzard. . . .

"I can fancy what adventures you must have had in eleven years!" said the student. "I expect it must be terrible driving?"

He said this and expected that the postman would tell him something, but the latter preserved a sullen silence and retreated into his collar. Meanwhile it began to get light. The sky changed colour imperceptibly; it still seemed dark, but by now the horses and the driver and the road could be seen. The crescent moon looked bigger and bigger, and the cloud that stretched below it, shaped like a cannon in a gun-carriage, showed a faint yellow on its lower edge. Soon the postman's face was visible. It was wet with dew, grey and rigid as the face of a corpse. An expression of dull, sullen anger was set upon it, as though the postman were still in pain and still angry with the driver.

"Thank God it is daylight!" said the student, looking at his chilled and angry face. "I am quite frozen. The nights are cold in September, but as soon as the sun rises it isn't cold. Shall we soon reach the station?"

The postman frowned and made a wry face.

"How fond you are of talking, upon my word!" he said. "Can't you keep quiet when you are travelling?"

The student was confused, and did not approach him again all the journey. The morning came on rapidly. The moon turned pale and melted away into the dull grey sky, the cloud turned yellow all over, the stars grew dim, but the east was still cold-looking and the same colour as the rest of the sky, so that one could hardly believe the sun was hidden in it.

The chill of the morning and the surliness of the postman gradually infected the student. He looked apathetically at the country around him, waited for the warmth of the sun, and thought of nothing but how dreadful and horrible it must be for the poor trees and the grass to endure the cold nights. The sun rose dim, drowsy, and cold. The tree-tops were not gilded by the rays of the rising sun, as usually described, the sunbeams did not creep over the earth and there was no sign of joy in the flight of the sleepy birds. The cold remained just the same now that the sun was up as it had been in the night.

The student looked drowsily and ill-humouredly at the curtained windows of a mansion by which the mail cart drove. Behind those windows, he thought, people were most likely enjoying their soundest morning sleep not hearing the bells, nor feeling the cold, nor seeing the postman's angry face; and if the bell did wake some young lady, she would turn over on the other side, smile in the fulness of her warmth and comfort, and, drawing up her feet and putting her hand under her cheek, would go off to sleep more soundly than ever.

The student looked at the pond which gleamed near the house and thought of the carp and the pike which find it possible to live in cold water. . . .

"It's against the regulations to take anyone with the post. . . ." the postman said unexpectedly. "It's not allowed! And since it is not allowed, people have no business . . . to get in. . . . Yes. It makes no difference to me, it's true, only I don't like it, and I don't wish it."

"Why didn't you say so before, if you don't like it?"

The postman made no answer but still had an unfriendly, angry expression. When, a little later, the horses stopped at the entrance of the station the student thanked him and got out of the cart. The mail train had not yet come in. A long goods train stood in a siding; in the tender the engine driver and his assistant, with faces wet with dew, were drinking tea from a dirty tin teapot. The carriages, the platforms, the seats were all wet and cold. Until the train came in the student stood at the buffet drinking tea while the postman, with his hands thrust up his sleeves and the same look of anger still on his face, paced up and down the platform in solitude, staring at the ground under his feet.

With whom was he angry? Was it with people, with poverty, with the autmn nights?

THE RUNAWAY

It had been a long business. At first Pashka had walked with his mother in the rain, at one time across a mown field, then by forest paths, where the yellow leaves stuck to his boots; he had walked until it was daylight. Then he had stood for two hours in the dark passage, waiting for the door to open. It was not so cold and damp in the passage as in the yard, but with the high wind spurts of rain flew in even there. When the passage gradually became packed with people Pashka, squeezed among them, leaned his face against somebody's sheepskin which smelt strongly of salt fish, and sank into a doze. But at last the bolt clicked, the door flew open, and Pashka and his mother went into the waiting-room. All the patients sat on benches without stirring or speaking. Pashka looked round at them, and he too was silent, though he was seeing a great deal that was strange and funny. Only once, when a lad came into the waiting-room hopping on one leg, Pashka longed to hop too; he nudged his mother's elbow, giggled in his sleeve, and said: "Look, mammy, a sparrow."

"Hush, child, hush!" said his mother.

A sleepy-looking hospital assistant appeared at the little window.

"Come and be registered!" he boomed out.

All of them, including the funny lad who hopped, filed up to the window. The assistant asked each one his name, and his father's name, where he lived, how long he had been ill, and so on. From his mother's answers, Pashka learned that his name was not Pashka, but Pavel Galaktionov, that he was seven years old, that he could not read or write, and that he had been ill ever since Easter.

Soon after the registration, he had to stand up for a little while; the doctor in a white apron, with a towel round his waist, walked across the waiting-room. As he passed by the boy who hopped, he shrugged his shoulders, and said in a sing-song tenor:

"Well, you are an idiot! Aren't you an idiot? I told you to come on Monday, and you come on Friday. It's nothing to me if you don't come at all, but you know, you idiot, your leg will be done for!"

The lad made a pitiful face, as though he were going to beg for alms, blinked, and said:

"Kindly do something for me, Ivan Mikolaitch!"

"It's no use saying 'Ivan Mikolaitch,' " the doctor mimicked him. "You were told to come on Monday, and you ought to obey. You are an idiot, and that is all about it."

The doctor began seeing the patients. He sat in his little room, and called up the patients in turn. Sounds were continually coming from the little room, piercing wails, a child's crying, or the doctor's angry words:

"Come, why are you bawling? Am I murdering you, or what? Sit quiet!"

Pashka's turn came.

"Pavel Galaktionov!" shouted the doctor.

His mother was aghast, as though she had not expected this summons, and taking Pashka by the hand, she led him into the room.

The doctor was sitting at the table, mechanically tapping on a thick book with a little hammer.

"What's wrong?" he asked, without looking at them.

"The little lad has an ulcer on his elbow, sir," answered his mother, and her face assumed an expression as though she really were terribly grieved at Pashka's ulcer.

"Undress him!"

Pashka, panting, unwound the kerchief from his neck, then wiped his nose on his sleeve, and began deliberately pulling off his sheepskin.

"Woman, you have not come here on a visit!" said the doctor angrily. "Why are you dawdling? You are not the only one here."

Pashka hurriedly flung the sheepskin on the floor, and with his mother's help took off his shirt. . . The doctor looked at him lazily, and patted him on his bare stomach.

"You have grown quite a respectable corporation, brother Pashka," he said, and heaved a sigh. "Come, show me your elbow."

Pashka looked sideways at the basin full of bloodstained slops, looked at the doctor's apron, and began to cry.

"May-ay!" the doctor mimicked him. "Nearly old enough to be married, spoilt boy, and here he is blubbering! For shame!"

Pashka, trying not to cry, looked at his mother, and in that look could be read the entreaty: "Don't tell them at home that I cried at the hospital."

The doctor examined his elbow, pressed it, heaved a sigh, clicked with his lips, then pressed it again.

"You ought to be beaten, woman, but there is no one to do it," he said. "Why didn't you bring him before? Why, the whole arm is done for. Look, foolish woman. You see, the joint is diseased!"

"You know best, kind sir . . ." sighed the woman.

"Kind sir. . . . She's let the boy's arm rot, and now it is 'kind sir.' What kind of workman will he be without an arm? You'll be nursing him and looking after him for ages. I bet if you had had a pimple on your nose, you'd have run to the hospital quick enough, but you have left your boy to rot for six months. You are all like that."

The doctor lighted a cigarette. While the cigarette smoked, he scolded the woman, and shook his head in time to the song he was humming inwardly, while he thought of something else. Pashka stood naked before him, listening and looking at the smoke. When the cigarette went out, the doctor started, and said in a lower tone:

"Well, listen, woman. You can do nothing with ointments and drops in this case. You must leave him in the hospital."

"If necessary, sir, why not?"

"We must operate on him. You stop with me, Pashka," said the doctor, slapping Pashka on the shoulder. "Let mother go home, and you and I will stop here, old man. It's nice with me, old boy, it's first-rate here. I'll tell you what we'll do, Pashka, we will go catching finches together. I will show you a fox! We will go visiting together! Shall we? And mother will come for you tomorrow! Eh?"

Pashka looked inquiringly at his mother.

"You stay, child!" she said.

"He'll stay, he'll stay!" cried the doctor gleefully. "And there is no need to discuss it. I'll show him a live fox! We will go to the fair together to buy candy! Marya Denisovna, take him upstairs!"

The doctor, apparently a light-hearted and friendly fellow, seemed glad to have company; Pashka wanted to oblige him, especially as he had never in his life been to a fair, and would have been glad to have a look at a live fox, but how could he do without his mother?

After a little reflection he decided to ask the doctor to let his mother stay in the hospital too, but before he had time to open his mouth the lady assistant was already taking him upstairs. He walked up and looked about him with his mouth open. The staircase, the floors, and the doorposts -- everything huge, straight, and bright-were painted a splendid yellow colour, and had a delicious smell of Lenten oil. On all sides lamps were hanging, strips of carpet stretched along the floor, copper taps stuck out on the walls. But best of all Pashka liked the bedstead upon which he was made to sit down, and the grey woollen coverlet. He touched the pillows and the coverlet with his hands, looked round the ward, and made up his mind that it was very nice at the doctor's.

The ward was not a large one, it consisted of only three beds. One bed stood empty, the second was occupied by Pashka, and on the third sat an old man with sour eyes, who kept coughing and spitting into a mug. From Pashka's bed part of another ward could be seen with two beds; on one a very pale wasted-looking man with an india-rubber bottle on his head was asleep; on the other a peasant with his head tied up, looking very like a woman, was sitting with his arms spread out.

After making Pashka sit down, the assistant went out and came back a little later with a bundle of clothes under her arm.

"These are for you," she said, "put them on."

Pashka undressed and, not without satisfaction began attiring himself in his new array. When he had put on the shirt, the drawers, and the little grey dressing-gown, he looked at himself complacently, and thought that it would not be bad to walk through the village in that costume. His imagination pictured his mother's sending him to the kitchen garden by the river to gather cabbage leaves for the little pig; he saw himself walking along, while the boys and girls surrounded him and looked with envy at his little dressing-gown.

A nurse came into the ward, bringing two tin bowls, two spoons, and two pieces of bread. One bowl she set before the old man, the other before Pashka.

"Eat!" she said.

Looking into his bowl, Pashka saw some rich cabbage soup, and in the soup a piece of meat, and thought again that it was very nice at the doctor's, and that the doctor was not nearly so cross as he had seemed at first. He spent a long time swallowing the soup, licking the spoon after each mouthful, then when there was nothing left in the bowl but the meat he stole a look at the old man, and felt envious that he was still eating the soup. With a sigh Pashka attacked the meat, trying to make it last as long as possible, but his efforts were fruitless; the meat, too, quickly vanished. There was nothing left but the piece of bread. Plain bread without anything on it was not appetising, but there was no help for it. Pashka thought a little, and ate the bread. At that moment the nurse came in with another bowl. This time there was roast meat with potatoes in the bowl.

"And where is the bread?" asked the nurse.

Instead of answering, Pashka puffed out his cheeks, and blew out the air.

"Why did you gobble it all up?" said the nurse reproachfully. "What are you going to eat your meat with?"

She went and fetched another piece of bread. Pashka had never eaten roast meat in his life, and trying it now found it very nice. It vanished quickly, and then he had a piece of bread left bigger than the first. When the old man had finished his dinner, he put away the remains of his bread in a little table. Pashka meant to do the same, but on second thoughts ate his piece.

When he had finished he went for a walk. In the next ward, besides the two he had seen from the door, there were four other people. Of these only one drew his attention. This was a tall, extremely emaciated peasant with a morose-looking, hairy face. He was sitting on the bed, nodding his head and swinging his right arm all the time like a pendulum. Pashka could not take his eyes off him for a long time. At first the man's regular pendulum-like movements seemed to him curious, and he thought they were done for the general amusement, but when he looked into the man's face he felt frightened, and realised that he was terribly ill. Going into a third ward he saw two peasants with dark red faces as though they were smeared with clay. They were sitting motionless on their beds, and with their strange faces, in which it was hard to distinguish their features, they looked like heathen idols.

"Auntie, why do they look like that?" Pashka asked the nurse.

"They have got smallpox, little lad."

Going back to his own ward, Pashka sat down on his bed and began waiting for the doctor to come and take him to catch finches, or to go to the fair. But the doctor did not come. He got a passing glimpse of a hospital assistant at the door of the next ward. He bent over the patient on whose head lay a bag of ice, and cried: "Mihailo!"

But the sleeping man did not stir. The assistant made a gesture and went away. Pashka scrutinised the old man, his next neighbour. The old man coughed without ceasing and spat into a mug. His cough had a long-drawn-out, creaking sound.

Pashka liked one peculiarity about him; when he drew the air in as he coughed, something in his chest whistled and sang on different notes.

"Grandfather, what is it whistles in you?" Pashka asked.

The old man made no answer. Pashka waited a little and asked:

"Grandfather, where is the fox?"

"What fox?"

"The live one."

"Where should it be? In the forest!"

A long time passed, but the doctor still did not appear. The nurse brought in tea, and scolded Pashka for not having saved any bread for his tea; the assistant came once more and set to work to wake Mihailo. It turned blue outside the windows, the wards were lighted up, but the doctor did not appear. It was too late now to go to the fair and catch finches; Pashka stretched himself on his bed and began thinking. He remembered the candy promised him by the doctor, the face and voice of his mother, the darkness in his hut at home, the stove, peevish granny Yegorovna . . . and he suddenly felt sad and dreary. He remembered that his mother was coming for him next day, smiled, and shut his eyes.

He was awakened by a rustling. In the next ward someone was stepping about and speaking in a whisper. Three figures were moving about Mihailo's bed in the dim light of the night-light and the ikon lamp.

"Shall we take him, bed and all, or without?" asked one of them.

"Without. You won't get through the door with the bed."

"He's died at the wrong time, the Kingdom of Heaven be his!"

One took Mihailo by his shoulders, another by his legs and lifted him up: Mihailo's arms and the skirt of his dressing-gown hung limply to the ground. A third -- it was the peasant who looked like a woman -- crossed himself, and all three tramping clumsily with their feet and stepping on Mihailo's skirts, went out of the ward.

There came the whistle and humming on different notes from the chest of the old man who was asleep. Pashka listened, peeped at the dark windows, and jumped out of bed in terror.

"Ma-a-mka!" he moaned in a deep bass.

And without waiting for an answer, he rushed into the next ward. There the darkness was dimly lighted up by a night-light and the ikon lamp; the patients, upset by the death of Mihailo, were sitting on their bedsteads: their dishevelled figures, mixed up with the shadows, looked broader, taller, and seemed to be growing bigger and bigger; on the furthest bedstead in the corner, where it was darkest, there sat the peasant moving his head and his hand.

Pashka, without noticing the doors, rushed into the smallpox ward, from there into the corridor, from the corridor he flew into a big room where monsters, with long hair and the faces of old women, were lying and sitting on the beds. Running through the women's wing he found himself again in the corridor, saw the banisters of the staircase he knew already, and ran downstairs. There he recognised the waiting-room in which he had sat that morning, and began looking for the door into the open air.

The latch creaked, there was a whiff of cold wind, and Pashka, stumbling, ran out into the yard. He had only one thought -- to run, to run! He did not know the way, but felt convinced that if he ran he would be sure to find himself at home with his mother. The sky was overcast, but there was a moon behind the clouds. Pashka ran from the steps straight forward, went round the barn and stumbled into some thick bushes; after stopping for a minute and thinking, he dashed back again to the hospital, ran round it, and stopped again undecided; behind the hospital there were white crosses.

"Ma-a-mka! " he cried, and dashed back.

Running by the dark sinister buildings, he saw one lighted window.

The bright red patch looked dreadful in the darkness, but Pashka, frantic with terror, not knowing where to run, turned towards it. Beside the window was a porch with steps, and a front door with a white board on it; Pashka ran up the steps, looked in at the window, and was at once possessed by intense overwhelming joy. Through the window he saw the merry affable doctor sitting at the table reading a book. Laughing with happiness, Pashka stretched out his hands to the person he knew and tried to call out, but some unseen force choked him and struck at his legs; he staggered and fell down on the steps unconscious.

When he came to himself it was daylight, and a voice he knew very well, that had promised him a fair, finches, and a fox, was saying beside him:

"Well, you are an idiot, Pashka! Aren't you an idiot? You ought to be beaten, but there's no one to do it."

A PROBLEM

The strictest measures were taken that the Uskovs' family secret might not leak out and become generally known. Half of the servants were sent off to the theatre or the circus; the other half were sitting in the kitchen and not allowed to leave it. Orders were given that no one was to be admitted. The wife of the Colonel, her sister, and the governess, though they had been initiated into the secret, kept up a pretence of knowing nothing; they sat in the dining-room and did not show themselves in the drawing-room or the hall.

Sasha Uskov, the young man of twenty-five who was the cause of all the commotion, had arrived some time before, and by the advice of kind-hearted Ivan Markovitch, his uncle, who was taking his part, he sat meekly in the hall by the door leading to the study, and prepared himself to make an open, candid explanation.

The other side of the door, in the study, a family council was being held. The subject under discussion was an exceedingly disagreeable and delicate one. Sasha Uskov had cashed at one of the banks a false promissory note, and it had become due for payment three days before, and now his two paternal uncles and Ivan Markovitch, the brother of his dead mother, were deciding the question whether they should pay the money and save the family honour, or wash their hands of it and leave the case to go for trial.

To outsiders who have no personal interest in the matter such questions seem simple; for those who are so unfortunate as to have to decide them in earnest they are extremely difficult. The uncles had been talking for a long time, but the problem seemed no nearer decision.

"My friends!" said the uncle who was a colonel, and there was a note of exhaustion and bitterness in his voice. "Who says that family honour is a mere convention? I don't say that at all. I am only warning you against a false view; I am pointing out the possibility of an unpardonable mistake. How can you fail to see it? I am not speaking Chinese; I am speaking Russian!"

"My dear fellow, we do understand," Ivan Markovitch protested mildly.

"How can you understand if you say that I don't believe in family honour? I repeat once more: fa-mil-y ho-nour fal-sely un-der-stood is a prejudice! Falsely understood! That's what I say: whatever may be the motives for screening a scoundrel, whoever he may be, and helping him to escape punishment, it is contrary to law and unworthy of a gentleman. It's not saving the family honour; it's civic cowardice! Take the army, for instance. . . . The honour of the army is more precious to us than any other honour, yet we don't screen our guilty members, but condemn them. And does the honour of the army suffer in consequence? Quite the opposite!"

The other paternal uncle, an official in the Treasury, a taciturn, dull-witted, and rheumatic man, sat silent, or spoke only of the fact that the Uskovs' name would get into the newspapers if the case went for trial. His opinion was that the case ought to be hushed up from the first and not become public property; but, apart from publicity in the newspapers, he advanced no other argument in support of this opinion.

The maternal uncle, kind-hearted Ivan Markovitch, spoke smoothly, softly, and with a tremor in his voice. He began with saying that youth has its rights and its peculiar temptations. Which of us has not been young, and who has not been led astray? To say nothing of ordinary mortals, even great men have not escaped errors and mistakes in their youth. Take, for instance, the biography of great writers. Did not every one of them gamble, drink, and draw down upon himself the anger of right-thinking people in his young days? If Sasha's error bordered upon crime, they must remember that Sasha had received practically no education; he had been expelled from the high school in the fifth class; he had lost his parents in early childhood, and so had been left at the tenderest age without guidance and good, benevolent influences. He was nervous, excitable, had no firm ground under his feet, and, above all, he had been unlucky. Even if he were guilty, anyway he deserved indulgence and the sympathy of all compassionate souls. He ought, of course, to be punished, but he was punished as it was by his conscience and the agonies he was enduring now while awaiting the sentence of his relations. The comparison with the army made by the Colonel was delightful, and did credit to his lofty intelligence; his appeal to their feeling of public duty spoke for the chivalry of his soul, but they must not forget that in each individual the citizen is closely linked with the Christian. . . .

"Shall we be false to civic duty," Ivan Markovitch exclaimed passionately, "if instead of punishing an erring boy we hold out to him a helping hand?"

Ivan Markovitch talked further of family honour. He had not the honour to belong to the Uskov family himself, but he knew their distinguished family went back to the thirteenth century; he did not forget for a minute, either, that his precious, beloved sister had been the wife of one of the representatives of that name. In short, the family was dear to him for many reasons, and he refused to admit the idea that, for the sake of a paltry fifteen hundred roubles, a blot should be cast on the escutcheon that was beyond all price. If all the motives he had brought forward were not sufficiently convincing, he, Ivan Markovitch, in conclusion, begged his listeners to ask themselves what was meant by crime? Crime is an immoral act founded upon ill-will. But is the will of man free? Philosophy has not yet given a positive answer to that question. Different views were held by the learned. The latest school of Lombroso, for instance, denies the freedom of the will, and considers every crime as the product of the purely anatomical peculiarities of the individual.

"Ivan Markovitch," said the Colonel, in a voice of entreaty, "we are talking seriously about an important matter, and you bring in Lombroso, you clever fellow. Think a little, what are you saying all this for? Can you imagine that all your thunderings and rhetoric will furnish an answer to the question?"

Sasha Uskov sat at the door and listened. He felt neither terror, shame, nor depression, but only weariness and inward emptiness. It seemed to him that it made absolutely no difference to him whether they forgave him or not; he had come here to hear his sentence and to explain himself simply because kind-hearted Ivan Markovitch had begged him to do so. He was not afraid of the future. It made no difference to him where he was: here in the hall, in prison, or in Siberia.

"If Siberia, then let it be Siberia, damn it all!"

He was sick of life and found it insufferably hard. He was inextricably involved in debt; he had not a farthing in his pocket; his family had become detestable to him; he would have to part from his friends and his women sooner or later, as they had begun to be too contemptuous of his sponging on them. The future looked black.

Sasha was indifferent, and was only disturbed by one circumstance; the other side of the door they were calling him a scoundrel and a criminal. Every minute he was on the point of jumping up, bursting into the study and shouting in answer to the detestable metallic voice of the Colonel:

"You are lying!"

"Criminal" is a dreadful word -- that is what murderers, thieves, robbers are; in fact, wicked and morally hopeless people. And Sasha was very far from being all that. . . . It was true he owed a great deal and did not pay his debts. But debt is not a crime, and it is unusual for a man not to be in debt. The Colonel and Ivan Markovitch were both in debt. . . .

"What have I done wrong besides?" Sasha wondered.

He had discounted a forged note. But all the young men he knew did the same. Handrikov and Von Burst always forged IOU's from their parents or friends when their allowances were not paid at the regular time, and then when they got their money from home they redeemed them before they became due. Sasha had done the same, but had not redeemed the IOU because he had not got the money which Handrikov had promised to lend him. He was not to blame; it was the fault of circumstances. It was true that the use of another person's signature was considered reprehensible; but, still, it was not a crime but a generally accepted dodge, an ugly formality which injured no one and was quite harmless, for in forging the Colonel's signature Sasha had had no intention of causing anybody damage or loss.

"No, it doesn't mean that I am a criminal . . ." thought Sasha. "And it's not in my character to bring myself to commit a crime. I am soft, emotional. . . . When I have the money I help the poor. . . ."

Sasha was musing after this fashion while they went on talking the other side of the door.

"But, my friends, this is endless," the Colonel declared, getting excited. "Suppose we were to forgive him and pay the money. You know he would not give up leading a dissipated life, squandering money, making debts, going to our tailors and ordering suits in our names! Can you guarantee that this will be his last prank? As far as I am concerned, I have no faith whatever in his reforming!"

The official of the Treasury muttered something in reply; after him Ivan Markovitch began talking blandly and suavely again. The Colonel moved his chair impatiently and drowned the other's words with his detestable metallic voice. At last the door opened and Ivan Markovitch came out of the study; there were patches of red on his lean shaven face.

"Come along," he said, taking Sasha by the hand. "Come and speak frankly from your heart. Without pride, my dear boy, humbly and from your heart."

Sasha went into the study. The official of the Treasury was sitting down; the Colonel was standing before the table with one hand in his pocket and one knee on a chair. It was smoky and stifling in the study. Sasha did not look at the official or the Colonel; he felt suddenly ashamed and uncomfortable. He looked uneasily at Ivan Markovitch and muttered:

"I'll pay it . . . I'll give it back. . . ."

"What did you expect when you discounted the IOU?" he heard a metallic voice.

"I . . . Handrikov promised to lend me the money before now."

Sasha could say no more. He went out of the study and sat down again on the chair near the door.

He would have been glad to go away altogether at once, but he was choking with hatred and he awfully wanted to remain, to tear the Colonel to pieces, to say something rude to him. He sat trying to think of something violent and effective to say to his hated uncle, and at that moment a woman's figure, shrouded in the twilight, appeared at the drawing-room door. It was the Colonel's wife. She beckoned Sasha to her, and, wringing her hands, said, weeping:

"*Alexandre,* I know you don't like me, but . . . listen to me; listen, I beg you. . . . But, my dear, how can this have happened? Why, it's awful, awful! For goodness' sake, beg them, defend yourself, entreat them."

Sasha looked at her quivering shoulders, at the big tears that were rolling down her cheeks, heard behind his back the hollow, nervous voices of worried and exhausted people, and shrugged his shoulders. He had not in the least expected that his aristocratic relations would raise such a tempest over a paltry fifteen hundred roubles! He could not understand her tears nor the quiver of their voices.

An hour later he heard that the Colonel was getting the best of it; the uncles were finally inclining to let the case go for trial.

"The matter's settled," said the Colonel, sighing. "Enough."

After this decision all the uncles, even the emphatic Colonel, became noticeably depressed. A silence followed.

"Merciful Heavens!" sighed Ivan Markovitch. "My poor sister!"

And he began saying in a subdued voice that most likely his sister, Sasha's mother, was present unseen in the study at that moment. He felt in his soul how the unhappy, saintly woman was weeping, grieving, and begging for her boy. For the sake of her peace beyond the grave, they ought to spare Sasha.

The sound of a muffled sob was heard. Ivan Markovitch was weeping and muttering something which it was impossible to catch through the door. The Colonel got up and paced from corner to corner. The long conversation began over again.

But then the clock in the drawing-room struck two. The family council was over. To avoid seeing the person who had moved him to such wrath, the Colonel went from the study, not into the hall, but into the vestibule. . . . Ivan Markovitch came out into the hall. . . . He was agitated and rubbing his hands joyfully. His tear-stained eyes looked good-humoured and his mouth was twisted into a smile.

"Capital," he said to Sasha. "Thank God! You can go home, my dear, and sleep tranquilly. We have decided to pay the sum, but on condition that you repent and come with me tomorrow into the country and set to work."

A minute later Ivan Markovitch and Sasha in their great-coats and caps were going down the stairs. The uncle was muttering something edifying. Sasha did not listen, but felt as though some uneasy weight were gradually slipping off his shoulders. They had forgiven him; he was free! A gust of joy sprang up within him and sent a sweet chill to his heart. He longed to breathe, to move swiftly, to live! Glancing at the street lamps and the black sky, he remembered that Von Burst was celebrating his name-day that evening at the "Bear," and again a rush of joy flooded his soul. . . .

"I am going!" he decided.

But then he remembered he had not a farthing, that the companions he was going to would despise him at once for his empty pockets. He must get hold of some money, come what may!

"Uncle, lend me a hundred roubles," he said to Ivan Markovitch.

His uncle, surprised, looked into his face and backed against a lamp-post.

"Give it to me," said Sasha, shifting impatiently from one foot to the other and beginning to pant. "Uncle, I entreat you, give me a hundred roubles."

His face worked; he trembled, and seemed on the point of attacking his uncle. . . .

"Won't you?" he kept asking, seeing that his uncle was still amazed and did not understand. "Listen. If you don't, I'll give myself up tomorrow! I won't let you pay the IOU! I'll present another false note tomorrow!"

Petrified, muttering something incoherent in his horror, Ivan Markovitch took a hundred-rouble note out of his pocket-book and gave it to Sasha. The young man took it and walked rapidly away from him. . . .

Taking a sledge, Sasha grew calmer, and felt a rush of joy within him again. The "rights of youth" of which kind-hearted Ivan Markovitch had spoken at the family council woke up and asserted themselves. Sasha pictured the drinking-party before him, and, among the bottles, the women, and his friends, the thought flashed through his mind:

"Now I see that I am a criminal; yes, I am a criminal."

THE OLD HOUSE

(A Story told by a Houseowner)

The old house had to be pulled down that a new one might be built in its place. I led the architect through the empty rooms, and between our business talk told him various stories. The tattered wallpapers, the dingy windows, the dark stoves, all bore the traces of recent habitation and evoked memories. On that staircase, for instance, drunken men were once carrying down a dead body when they stumbled and flew headlong downstairs together with the coffin; the living were badly bruised, while the dead man looked very serious, as though nothing had happened, and shook his head when they lifted him up from the ground and put him back in the coffin. You see those three doors in a row: in there lived young ladies who were always receiving visitors, and so were better dressed than any other lodgers, and could pay their rent regularly. The door at the end of the corridor leads to the wash-house, where by day they washed clothes and at night made an uproar and drank beer. And in that flat of three rooms everything is saturated with bacteria and bacilli. It's not nice there. Many lodgers have died there, and I can positively assert that that flat was at some time cursed by someone, and that together with its human lodgers there was always another lodger, unseen, living in it. I remember particularly the fate of one family. Picture to yourself an ordinary man, not remarkable in any way, with a wife, a mother, and four children. His name was Putohin; he was a copying clerk at a notary's, and received thirty-five roubles a month. He was a sober, religious, serious man. When he brought me his rent for the flat he always apologised for being badly dressed; apologised for being five days late, and when I gave him a receipt he would smile good-humouredly and say: "Oh yes, there's that too, I don't like those receipts." He lived poorly but decently. In that middle room, the grandmother used to be with the four children; there they used to cook, sleep, receive their visitors, and even dance. This was Putohin's own room; he had a table in it, at which he used to work doing private jobs, copying parts for the theatre, advertisements, and so on. This room on the right was let to his lodger, Yegoritch, a locksmith -- a steady fellow, but given to drink; he was always too hot, and so used to go about in his waistcoat and barefoot. Yegoritch used to mend locks, pistols, children's bicycles, would not refuse to mend cheap clocks and make skates for a quarter-rouble, but he despised that work, and looked on himself as a specialist in musical instruments. Amongst the litter of steel and iron on his table there was always to be seen a concertina with a broken key, or a trumpet with its sides bent in. He paid Putohin two and a half roubles for his room; he was always at his work-table, and only came out to thrust some piece of iron into the stove.

On the rare occasions when I went into that flat in the evening, this was always the picture I came upon: Putohin would be sitting at his little table, copying something; his mother and his wife, a thin woman with an exhausted-looking face, were sitting near the lamp, sewing; Yegoritch would be making a rasping sound with his file. And the hot, still smouldering embers in the stove filled the room with heat and fumes; the heavy air smelt of cabbage soup, swaddling-clothes, and Yegoritch. It was poor and stuffy, but the working-class faces, the children's little drawers hung up along by the stove, Yegoritch's bits of iron had yet an air of peace, friendliness, content. . . . In the corridor outside the children raced about with well-combed heads, merry and profoundly convinced that everything was satisfactory in this world, and would be so endlessly, that one had only to say one's prayers every morning and at bedtime.

Now imagine in the midst of that same room, two paces from the stove, the coffin in which Putohin's wife is lying. There is no husband whose wife will live for ever, but there was something special about this death. When, during the requiem service, I glanced at the husband's grave face, at his stern eyes, I thought: "Oho, brother!"

It seemed to me that he himself, his children, the grandmother and Yegoritch, were already marked down by that unseen being which lived with them in that flat. I am a thoroughly superstitious man, perhaps, because I am a houseowner and for forty years have had to do with lodgers. I believe if you don't win at cards from the beginning you will go on losing to the end; when fate wants to wipe you and your family off the face of the earth, it remains inexorable in its persecution, and the first misfortune is commonly only the first of a long series. . . . Misfortunes are like stones. One stone has only to drop from a high cliff for others to be set rolling after it. In short, as I came away from the requiem service at Putohin's, I believed that he and his family were in a bad way.

And, in fact, a week afterwards the notary quite unexpectedly dismissed Putohin, and engaged a young lady in his place. And would you believe it, Putohin was not so much put out at the loss of his job as at being superseded by a young lady and not by a man. Why a young lady? He so resented this that on his return home he thrashed his children, swore at his mother, and got drunk. Yegoritch got drunk, too, to keep him company.

Putohin brought me the rent, but did not apologise this time, though it was eighteen days overdue, and said nothing when he took the receipt from me. The following month the rent was brought by his mother; she only brought me half, and promised to bring the remainder a week later. The third month, I did not get a farthing, and the porter complained to me that the lodgers in No. 23 were "not behaving like gentlemen."

These were ominous symptoms.

Picture this scene. A sombre Petersburg morning looks in at the dingy windows. By the stove, the granny is pouring out the children's tea. Only the eldest, Vassya, drinks out of a glass, for the others the tea is poured out into saucers. Yegoritch is squatting on his heels before the stove, thrusting a bit of iron into the fire. His head is heavy and his eyes are lustreless from yesterday's drinking-bout; he sighs and groans, trembles and coughs.

"He has quite put me off the right way, the devil," he grumbles; "he drinks himself and leads others into sin."

Putohin sits in his room, on the bedstead from which the bedclothes and the pillows have long ago disappeared, and with his hands straying in his hair looks blankly at the floor at his feet. He is tattered, unkempt, and ill.

"Drink it up, make haste or you will be late for school," the old woman urges on Vassya, "and it's time for me, too, to go and scrub the floors for the Jews. . . ."

The old woman is the only one in the flat who does not lose heart. She thinks of old times, and goes out to hard dirty work. On Fridays she scrubs the floors for the Jews at the crockery shop, on Saturdays she goes out washing for shopkeepers, and on Sundays she is racing about the town from morning to night, trying to find ladies who will help her. Every day she has work of some sort; she washes and scrubs, and is by turns a midwife, a matchmaker, or a beggar. It is true she, too, is not disinclined to drown her sorrows, but even when she has had a drop she does not forget her duties. In Russia there are many such tough old women, and how much of its welfare rests upon them!

When he has finished his tea, Vassya packs up his books in a satchel and goes behind the stove; his greatcoat ought to be hanging there beside his granny's clothes. A minute later he comes out from behind the stove and asks:

"Where is my greatcoat?"

The grandmother and the other children look for the greatcoat together, they waste a long time in looking for it, but the greatcoat has utterly vanished. Where is it? The grandmother and Vassya are pale and frightened. Even Yegoritch is surprised. Putohin is the only one who does not move. Though he is quick to notice anything irregular or disorderly, this time he makes a pretence of hearing and seeing nothing. That is suspicious.

"He's sold it for drink," Yegoritch declares.

Putohin says nothing, so it is the truth. Vassya is overcome with horror. His greatcoat, his splendid greatcoat, made of his dead mother's cloth dress, with a splendid calico lining, gone for drink at the tavern! And with the greatcoat is gone too, of course, the blue pencil that lay in the pocket, and the note-book with "*Nota bene*" in gold letters on it! There's another pencil with india-rubber stuck into the note-book, and, besides that, there are transfer pictures lying in it.

Vassya would like to cry, but to cry is impossible. If his father, who has a headache, heard crying he would shout, stamp with his feet, and begin fighting, and after drinking he fights horribly. Granny would stand up for Vassya, and his father would strike granny too; it would end in Yegoritch getting mixed up in it too, clutching at his father and falling on the floor with him. The two would roll on the floor, struggling together and gasping with drunken animal fury, and granny would cry, the children would scream, the neighbours would send for the porter. No, better not cry.

Because he mustn't cry, or give vent to his indignation aloud, Vassya moans, wrings his hands and moves his legs convulsively, or biting his sleeve shakes it with his teeth as a dog does a hare. His eyes are frantic, and his face is distorted with despair. Looking at him, his granny all at once takes the shawl off her head, and she too makes queer movements with her arms and legs in silence, with her eyes fixed on a point in the distance. And at that moment I believe there is a definite certainty in the minds of the boy and the old woman that their life is ruined, that there is no hope. . . .

Putohin hears no crying, but he can see it all from his room. When, half an hour later, Vassya sets off to school, wrapped in his grandmother's shawl, he goes out with a face I will not undertake to describe, and walks after him. He longs to call the boy, to comfort him, to beg his forgiveness, to promise him on his word of honour, to call his dead mother to witness, but instead of words, sobs break from him. It is a grey, cold morning. When he reaches the town school Vassya untwists his granny's shawl, and goes into the school with nothing over his jacket for fear the boys should say he looks like a woman. And when he gets home Putohin sobs, mutters some incoherent words, bows down to the ground before his mother and Yegoritch, and the locksmith's table. Then, recovering himself a little, he runs to me and begs me breathlessly, for God's sake, to find him some job. I give him hopes, of course.

"At last I am myself again," he said. "It's high time, indeed, to come to my senses. I've made a beast of myself, and now it's over."

He is delighted and thanks me, while I, who have studied these gentry thoroughly during the years I have owned the house, look at him, and am tempted to say:

"It's too late, dear fellow! You are a dead man already."

From me, Putohin runs to the town school. There he paces up and down, waiting till his boy comes out.

"I say, Vassya," he says joyfully, when the boy at last comes out, "I have just been promised a job. Wait a bit, I will buy you a splendid fur-coat. . . . I'll send you to the high school! Do you understand? To the high school! I'll make a gentleman of you! And I won't drink any more. On my honour I won't."

And he has intense faith in the bright future. But the evening comes on. The old woman, coming back from the Jews with twenty kopecks, exhausted and aching all over, sets to work to wash the children's clothes. Vassya is sitting doing a sum. Yegoritch is not working. Thanks to Putohin he has got into the way of drinking, and is feeling at the moment an overwhelming desire for drink. It's hot and stuffy in the room. Steam rises in clouds from the tub where the old woman is washing.

"Are we going?" Yegoritch asks surlily.

My lodger does not answer. After his excitement he feels insufferably dreary. He struggles with the desire to drink, with acute depression and . . . and, of course, depression gets the best of it. It is a familiar story.

Towards night, Yegoritch and Putohin go out, and in the morning Vassya cannot find granny's shawl.

That is the drama that took place in that flat. After selling the shawl for drink, Putohin did not come home again. Where he disappeared to I don't know. After he disappeared, the old woman first got drunk, then took to her bed. She was taken to the hospital, the younger children were fetched by relations of some sort, and Vassya went into the wash-house here. In the day-time he handed the irons, and at night fetched the beer. When he was turned out of the wash-house he went into the service of one of the young ladies, used to run about at night on errands of some sort, and began to be spoken of as "a dangerous customer."

What has happened to him since I don't know.

And in this room here a street musician lived for ten years. When he died they found twenty thousand roubles in his feather bed.

THE CATTLE-DEALERS

The long goods train has been standing for hours in the little station. The engine is as silent as though its fire had gone out; there is not a soul near the train or in the station yard.

A pale streak of light comes from one of the vans and glides over the rails of a siding. In that van two men are sitting on an outspread cape: one is an old man with a big gray beard, wearing a sheepskin coat and a high lambskin hat, somewhat like a busby; the other a beardless youth in a threadbare cloth reefer jacket and muddy high boots. They are the owners of the goods. The old man sits, his legs stretched out before him, musing in silence; the young man half reclines and softly strums on a cheap accordion. A lantern with a tallow candle in it is hanging on the wall near them.

The van is quite full. If one glances in through the dim light of the lantern, for the first moment the eyes receive an impression of something shapeless, monstrous, and unmistakably alive, something very much like gigantic crabs which move their claws and feelers, crowd together, and noiselessly climb up the walls to the ceiling; but if one looks more closely, horns and their shadows, long lean backs, dirty hides, tails, eyes begin to stand out in the dusk. They are cattle and their shadows. There are eight of them in the van. Some turn round and stare at the men and swing their tails. Others try to stand or lie down more comfortably. They are crowded. If one lies down the others must stand and huddle closer. No manger, no halter, no litter, not a wisp of hay. . . .*

At last the old man pulls out of his pocket a silver watch and looks at the time: a quarter past two.

"We have been here nearly two hours," he says, yawning. "Better go and stir them up, or we may be here till morning. They have gone to sleep, or goodness knows what they are up to."

The old man gets up and, followed by his long shadow, cautiously gets down from the van into the darkness. He makes his way along beside the train to the engine, and after passing some two dozen vans sees a red open furnace; a human figure sits motionless facing it; its peaked cap, nose, and knees are lighted up by the crimson glow, all the rest is black and can scarcely be distinguished in the darkness.

"Are we going to stay here much longer?" asks the old man.

No answer. The motionless figure is evidently asleep. The old man clears his throat impatiently and, shrinking from the penetrating damp, walks round the engine, and as he does so the brilliant light of the two engine lamps dazzles his eyes for an instant and makes the night even blacker to him; he goes to the station.

The platform and steps of the station are wet. Here and there are white patches of freshly fallen melting snow. In the station itself it is light and as hot as a steam-bath. There is a smell of paraffin. Except for the weighing-machine and a yellow seat on which a man wearing a guard's uniform is asleep, there is no furniture in the place at all. On the left are two wide-open doors. Through one of them the telegraphic apparatus and a lamp with a green shade on it can be seen; through the other, a small room, half of it taken up by a dark cupboard. In this room the head guard and the engine-driver are sitting on the window-sill. They are both feeling a cap with their fingers and disputing.

"That's not real beaver, it's imitation," says the engine-driver. "Real beaver is not like that. Five roubles would be a high price for the whole cap, if you care to know!"

"You know a great deal about it, . . ." the head guard says, offended. "Five roubles, indeed! Here, we will ask the merchant. Mr. Malahin," he says, addressing the old man, "what do you say: is this imitation beaver or real?"

Old Malahin takes the cap into his hand, and with the air of a connoisseur pinches the fur, blows on it, sniffs at it, and a contemptuous smile lights up his angry face.

"It must be imitation!" he says gleefully. "Imitation it is."

A dispute follows. The guard maintains that the cap is real beaver, and the engine-driver and Malahin try to persuade him that it is not. In the middle of the argument the old man suddenly remembers the object of his coming.

"Beaver and cap is all very well, but the train's standing still, gentlemen!" he says. "Who is it we are waiting for? Let us start!"

"Let us," the guard agrees. "We will smoke another cigarette and go on. But there is no need to be in a hurry. . . . We shall be delayed at the next station anyway!"

"Why should we?"

"Oh, well. . . . We are too much behind time. . . . If you are late at one station you can't help being delayed at the other stations to let the trains going the opposite way pass. Whether we set off now or in the morning we shan't be number fourteen. We shall have to be number twenty-three."

"And how do you make that out?"

"Well, there it is."

Malahin looks at the guard, reflects, and mutters mechanically as though to himself:

"God be my judge, I have reckoned it and even jotted it down in a notebook; we have wasted thirty-four hours standing still on the journey. If you go on like this, either the cattle will die, or they won't pay me two roubles for the meat when I do get there. It's not traveling, but ruination."

The guard raises his eyebrows and sighs with an air that seems to say: "All that is unhappily true!" The engine-driver sits silent, dreamily looking at the cap. From their faces one can see that they have a secret thought in common, which they do not utter, not because they want to conceal it, but because such thoughts are much better expressed by signs than by words. And the old man understands. He feels in his pocket, takes out a ten-rouble note, and without preliminary words, without any change in the tone of his voice or the expression of his face, but with the confidence and directness with which probably only Russians give and take bribes, he gives the guard the note. The latter takes it, folds it in four, and without undue haste puts it in his pocket. After that all three go out of the room, and waking the sleeping guard on the way, go on to the platform.

"What weather!" grumbles the head guard, shrugging his shoulders. "You can't see your hand before your face."

"Yes, it's vile weather."

From the window they can see the flaxen head of the telegraph clerk appear beside the green lamp and the telegraphic apparatus; soon after another head, bearded and wearing a red cap, appears beside it -- no doubt that of the station-master. The station-master bends down to the table, reads something on a blue form, rapidly passing his cigarette along the lines. . . . Malahin goes to his van.

The young man, his companion, is still half reclining and hardly audibly strumming on the accordion. He is little more than a boy, with no trace of a mustache; his full white face with its broad cheek-bones is childishly dreamy; his eyes have a melancholy and tranquil look unlike that of a grown-up person, but he is broad, strong, heavy and rough like the old man; he does not stir nor shift his position, as though he is not equal to moving his big body. It seems as though any movement he made would tear his clothes and be so noisy as to frighten both him and the cattle. From under his big fat fingers that clumsily pick out the stops and keys of the accordion comes a steady flow of thin, tinkling sounds which blend into a simple, monotonous little tune; he listens to it, and is evidently much pleased with his performance.

A bell rings, but with such a muffled note that it seems to come from far away. A hurried second bell soon follows, then a third and the guard's whistle. A minute passes in profound silence; the van does not move, it stands still, but vague sounds begin to come from beneath it, like the crunch of snow under sledge-runners; the van begins to shake and the sounds cease. Silence reigns again. But now comes the clank of buffers, the violent shock makes the van start and, as it were, give a lurch forward, and all the cattle fall against one another.

"May you be served the same in the world to come," grumbles the old man, setting straight his cap, which had slipped on the back of his head from the jolt. "He'll maim all my cattle like this!"

Yasha gets up without a word and, taking one of the fallen beasts by the horns, helps it to get on to its legs. . . . The jolt is followed by a stillness again. The sounds of crunching snow come from under the van again, and it seems as though the train had moved back a little.

"There will be another jolt in a minute," says the old man. And the convulsive quiver does, in fact, run along the train, there is a crashing sound and the bullocks fall on one another again.

"It's a job!" says Yasha, listening. "The train must be heavy. It seems it won't move."

"It was not heavy before, but now it has suddenly got heavy. No, my lad, the guard has not gone shares with him, I expect. Go and take him something, or he will be jolting us till morning."

Yasha takes a three-rouble note from the old man and jumps out of the van. The dull thud of his heavy footsteps resounds outside the van and gradually dies away. Stillness.... In the next van a bullock utters a prolonged subdued "moo," as though it were singing.

Yasha comes back. A cold damp wind darts into the van.

"Shut the door, Yasha, and we will go to bed," says the old man. "Why burn a candle for nothing?"

Yasha moves the heavy door; there is a sound of a whistle, the engine and the train set off.

"It's cold," mutters the old man, stretching himself on the cape and laying his head on a bundle. "It is very different at home! It's warm and clean and soft, and there is room to say your prayers, but here we are worse off than any pigs. It's four days and nights since I have taken off my boots."

Yasha, staggering from the jolting of the train, opens the lantern and snuffs out the wick with his wet fingers. The light flares up, hisses like a frying pan and goes out.

"Yes, my lad," Malahin goes on, as he feels Yasha lie down beside him and the young man's huge back huddle against his own, "it's cold. There is a draught from every crack. If your mother or your sister were to sleep here for one night they would be dead by morning. There it is, my lad, you wouldn't study and go to the high school like your brothers, so you must take the cattle with your father. It's your own fault, you have only yourself to blame. . . . Your brothers are asleep in their beds now, they are snug under the bedclothes, but you, the careless and lazy one, are in the same box as the cattle. . . . Yes. . . . "

The old man's words are inaudible in the noise of the train, but for a long time he goes on muttering, sighing and clearing his throat. . . . The cold air in the railway van grows thicker and more stifling The pungent odor of fresh dung and smoldering candle makes it so repulsive and acrid that it irritates Yasha's throat and chest as he falls asleep. He coughs and sneezes, while the old man, being accustomed to it, breathes with his whole chest as though nothing were amiss, and merely clears his throat.

To judge from the swaying of the van and the rattle of the wheels the train is moving rapidly and unevenly. The engine breathes heavily, snorting out of time with the pulsation of the train, and altogether there is a medley of sounds. The bullocks huddle together uneasily and knock their horns against the walls.

When the old man wakes up, the deep blue sky of early morning is peeping in at the cracks and at the little uncovered window. He feels unbearably cold, especially in the back and the feet. The train is standing still; Yasha, sleepy and morose, is busy with the cattle.

The old man wakes up out of humor. Frowning and gloomy, he clears his throat angrily and looks from under his brows at Yasha who, supporting a bullock with his powerful shoulder and slightly lifting it, is trying to disentangle its leg.

"I told you last night that the cords were too long," mutters the old man; "but no, 'It's not too long, Daddy.' There's no making you do anything, you will have everything your own way. . . . Blockhead!"

He angrily moves the door open and the light rushes into the van. A passenger train is standing exactly opposite the door, and behind it a red building with a roofed-in platform -- a big station with a refreshment bar. The roofs and bridges of the trains, the earth, the sleepers, all are covered with a thin coating of fluffy, freshly fallen snow. In the spaces between the carriages of the passenger train the passengers can be seen moving to and fro, and a red-haired, red-faced gendarme walking up and down; a waiter in a frock-coat and a snow-white shirt-front, looking cold and sleepy, and probably very much dissatisfied with his fate, is running along the platform carrying a glass of tea and two rusks on a tray.

The old man gets up and begins saying his prayers towards the east. Yasha, having finished with the bullock and put down the spade in the corner, stands beside him and says his prayers also. He merely moves his lips and crosses himself; the father prays in a loud whisper and pronounces the end of each prayer aloud and distinctly.

". . . And the life of the world to come. Amen," the old man says aloud, draws in a breath, and at once whispers another prayer, rapping out clearly and firmly at the end: " . . . and lay calves upon Thy altar!"

After saying his prayers, Yasha hurriedly crosses himself and says: "Five kopecks, please."

And on being given the five-kopeck piece, he takes a red copper teapot and runs to the station for boiling water. Taking long jumps over the rails and sleepers, leaving huge tracks in the feathery snow, and pouring away yesterday's tea out of the teapot he runs to the refreshment room and jingles his five-kopeck piece against his teapot. From the van the bar-keeper can be seen pushing away the big teapot and refusing to give half of his samovar for five kopecks, but Yasha turns the tap himself and, spreading wide his elbows so as not to be interfered with fills his teapot with boiling water.

"Damned blackguard!" the bar-keeper shouts after him as he runs back to the railway van.

The scowling face of Malahin grows a little brighter over the tea.

"We know how to eat and drink, but we don't remember our work. Yesterday we could do nothing all day but eat and drink, and I'll be bound we forgot to put down what we spent. What a memory! Lord have mercy on us!"

The old man recalls aloud the expenditure of the day before, and writes down in a tattered notebook where and how much he had given to guards, engine-drivers, oilers. . . .

Meanwhile the passenger train has long ago gone off, and an engine runs backwards and forwards on the empty line, apparently without any definite object, but simply enjoying its freedom. The sun has risen and is playing on the snow; bright drops are falling from the station roof and the tops of the vans.

Having finished his tea, the old man lazily saunters from the van to the station. Here in the middle of the first-class waiting-room he sees the familiar figure of the guard standing beside the station-master, a young man with a handsome beard and in a magnificent rough woollen overcoat. The young man, probably new to his position, stands in the same place, gracefully shifting from one foot to the other like a good racehorse, looks from side to side, salutes everyone that passes by, smiles and screws up his eyes. . . . He is red-cheeked, sturdy, and good-humored; his face is full of eagerness, and is as fresh as though he had just fallen from the sky with the feathery snow. Seeing Malahin, the guard sighs guiltily and throws up his hands.

"We can't go number fourteen," he says. "We are very much behind time. Another train has gone with that number."

The station-master rapidly looks through some forms, then turns his beaming blue eyes upon Malahin, and, his face radiant with smiles and freshness, showers questions on him:

"You are Mr. Malahin? You have the cattle? Eight vanloads? What is to be done now? You are late and I let number fourteen go in the night. What are we to do now?"

The young man discreetly takes hold of the fur of Malahin's coat with two pink fingers and, shifting from one foot to the other, explains affably and convincingly that such and such numbers have gone already, and that such and such are going, and that he is ready to do for Malahin everything in his power. And from his face it is evident that he is ready to do anything to please not only Malahin, but the whole world -- he is so happy, so pleased, and so delighted! The old man listens, and though he can make absolutely nothing of the intricate system of numbering the trains, he nods his head approvingly, and he, too, puts two fingers on the soft wool of the rough coat. He enjoys seeing and hearing the polite and genial young man. To show goodwill on his side also, he takes out a ten-rouble note and, after a moment's thought, adds a couple of rouble notes to it, and gives them to the station-master. The latter takes them, puts his finger to his cap, and gracefully thrusts them into his pocket.

"Well, gentlemen, can't we arrange it like this?" he says, kindled by a new idea that has flashed on him. "The troop train is late, . . . as you see, it is not here, . . . so why shouldn't you go as the troop train?** And I will let the troop train go as twenty-eight. Eh?"

"If you like," agrees the guard.

"Excellent!" the station-master says, delighted. "In that case there is no need for you to wait here; you can set off at once. I'll dispatch you immediately. Excellent!"

He salutes Malahin and runs off to his room, reading forms as he goes. The old man is very much pleased by the conversation that has just taken place; he smiles and looks about the room as though looking for something else agreeable.

"We'll have a drink, though," he says, taking the guard's arm.

"It seems a little early for drinking."

"No, you must let me treat you to a glass in a friendly way."

They both go to the refreshment bar. After having a drink the guard spends a long time selecting something to eat.

He is a very stout, elderly man, with a puffy and discolored face. His fatness is unpleasant, flabby-looking, and he is sallow as people are who drink too much and sleep irregularly.

"And now we might have a second glass," says Malahin. "It's cold now, it's no sin to drink. Please take some. So I can rely upon you, Mr. Guard, that there will be no hindrance or unpleasantness for the rest of the journey. For you know in moving cattle every hour is precious. To-day meat is one price; and to-morrow, look you, it will be another. If you are a day or two late and don't get your price, instead of a profit you get home -- excuse my saying it -- with out your breeches. Pray take a little. . . . I rely on you, and as for standing you something or what you like, I shall be pleased to show you my respect at any time."

After having fed the guard, Malahin goes back to the van.

"I have just got hold of the troop train," he says to his son. "We shall go quickly. The guard says if we go all the way with that number we shall arrive at eight o'clock to-morrow evening. If one does not bestir oneself, my boy, one gets nothing. . . . That's so. . . . So you watch and learn. . . ."

After the first bell a man with a face black with soot, in a blouse and filthy frayed trousers hanging very slack, comes to the door of the van. This is the oiler, who had been creeping under the carriages and tapping the wheels with a hammer.

"Are these your vans of cattle?" he asks.

"Yes. Why?"

"Why, because two of the vans are not safe. They can't go on, they must stay here to be repaired."

"Oh, come, tell us another! You simply want a drink, to get something out of me. . . . You should have said so."

"As you please, only it is my duty to report it at once."

Without indignation or protest, simply, almost mechanically, the old man takes two twenty-kopeck pieces out of his pocket and gives them to the oiler. He takes them very calmly, too, and looking good-naturedly at the old man enters into conversation.

"You are going to sell your cattle, I suppose. . . . It's good business!"

Malahin sighs and, looking calmly at the oiler's black face, tells him that trading in cattle used certainly to be profitable, but now it has become a risky and losing business.

"I have a mate here," the oiler interrupts him. "You merchant gentlemen might make him a little present. . . .."

Malahin gives something to the mate too. The troop train goes quickly and the waits at the stations are comparatively short. The old man is pleased. The pleasant impression made by the young man in the rough overcoat has gone deep, the vodka he has drunk slightly clouds his brain, the weather is magnificent, and everything seems to be going well. He talks without ceasing, and at every stopping place runs to the refreshment bar. Feeling the need of a listener, he takes with him first the guard, and then the engine-driver, and does not simply drink, but makes a long business of it, with suitable remarks and clinking of glasses.

"You have your job and we have ours," he says with an affable smile. "May God prosper us and you, and not our will but His be done."

The vodka gradually excites him and he is worked up to a great pitch of energy. He wants to bestir himself, to fuss about, to make inquiries, to talk incessantly. At one minute he fumbles in his pockets and bundles and looks for some form. Then he thinks of something and cannot remember it; then takes out his pocketbook, and with no sort of object counts over his money. He bustles about, sighs and groans, clasps his hands. . . . Laying out before him the letters and telegrams from the meat salesmen in the city, bills, post office and telegraphic receipt forms, and his note book, he reflects aloud and insists on Yasha's listening.

And when he is tired of reading over forms and talking about prices, he gets out at the stopping places, runs to the vans where his cattle are, does nothing, but simply clasps his hands and exclaims in horror.

"Oh, dear! oh, dear!" he says in a complaining voice. "Holy Martyr Vlassy! Though they are bullocks, though they are beasts, yet they want to eat and drink as men do. . . . It's four days and nights since they have drunk or eaten. Oh, dear! oh, dear!"

Yasha follows him and does what he is told like an obedient son. He does not like the old man's frequent visits to the refreshment bar. Though he is afraid of his father, he cannot refrain from remarking on it.

"So you have begun already!" he says, looking sternly at the old man. "What are you rejoicing at? Is it your name-day or what?"

"Don't you dare teach your father."

"Fine goings on!"

When he has not to follow his father along the other vans Yasha sits on the cape and strums on the accordion. Occasionally he gets out and walks lazily beside the train; he stands by the engine and turns a prolonged, unmoving stare on the wheels or on the workmen tossing blocks of wood into the tender; the hot engine wheezes, the falling blocks come down with the mellow, hearty thud of fresh wood; the engine-driver and his assistant, very phlegmatic and imperturbable persons, perform incomprehensible movements and don't hurry themselves. After standing for a while by the engine, Yasha saunters lazily to the station; here he looks at the eatables in the refreshment bar, reads aloud some quite uninteresting notice, and goes back slowly to the cattle van. His face expresses neither boredom nor desire; apparently he does not care where he is, at home, in the van, or by the engine.

Towards evening the train stops near a big station. The lamps have only just been lighted along the line; against the blue background in the fresh limpid air the lights are bright and pale like stars; they are only red and glowing under the station roof, where it is already dark. All the lines are loaded up with carriages, and it seems that if another train came in there would be no place for it. Yasha runs to the station for boiling water to make the evening tea. Well-dressed ladies and high-school boys are walking on the platform. If one looks into the distance from the platform there are far-away lights twinkling in the evening dusk on both sides of the station -- that is the town. What town? Yasha does not care to know. He sees only the dim lights and wretched buildings beyond the station, hears the cabmen shouting, feels a sharp, cold wind on his face, and imagines that the town is probably disagreeable, uncomfortable, and dull.

While they are having tea, when it is quite dark and a lantern is hanging on the wall again as on the previous evening, the train quivers from a slight shock and begins moving backwards. After going a little way it stops; they hear indistinct shouts, someone sets the chains clanking near the buffers and shouts, "Ready!" The train moves and goes forward. Ten minutes later it is dragged back again.

Getting out of the van, Malahin does not recognize his train. His eight vans of bullocks are standing in the same row with some trolleys which were not a part of the train before. Two or three of these are loaded with rubble and the others are empty The guards running to and fro on the platform are strangers. They give unwilling and indistinct answers to his questions. They have no thoughts to spare for Malahin; they are in a hurry to get the train together so as to finish as soon as possible and be back in the warmth.

"What number is this?" asks Malahin

"Number eighteen."

"And where is the troop train? Why have you taken me off the troop train?"

Getting no answer, the old man goes to the station. He looks first for the familiar figure of the head guard and, not finding him, goes to the station-master. The station-master is sitting at a table in his own room, turning over a bundle of forms. He is busy, and affects not to see the newcomer. His appearance is impressive: a cropped black head, prominent ears, a long hooked nose, a swarthy face; he has a forbidding and, as it were, offended expression. Malahin begins making his complaint at great length.

"What?" queries the station-master. "How is this?" He leans against the back of his chair and goes on, growing indignant: "What is it? and why shouldn't you go by number eighteen? Speak more clearly, I don't understand! How is it? Do you want me to be everywhere at once?"

He showers questions on him, and for no apparent reason grows sterner and sterner. Malahin is already feeling in his pocket for his pocketbook, but in the end the station-master, aggrieved and indignant, for some unknown reason jumps up from his seat and runs out of the room. Malahin shrugs his shoulders, and goes out to look for someone else to speak to.

From boredom or from a desire to put the finishing stroke to a busy day, or simply that a window with the inscription "Telegraph!" on it catches his eye, he goes to the window and expresses a desire to send off a telegram. Taking up a pen, he thinks for a moment, and writes on a blue form: "Urgent. Traffic Manager. Eight vans of live stock. Delayed at every station. Kindly send an express number. Reply paid. Malahin."

Having sent off the telegram, he goes back to the station-master's room. There he finds, sitting on a sofa covered with gray cloth, a benevolent-looking gentleman in spectacles and a cap of raccoon fur; he is wearing a peculiar overcoat very much like a lady's, edged with fur, with frogs and slashed sleeves. Another gentleman, dried-up and sinewy, wearing the uniform of a railway inspector, stands facing him.

"Just think of it," says the inspector, addressing the gentleman in the queer overcoat. " I'll tell you an incident that really is A1! The Z. railway line in the coolest possible way stole three hundred trucks from the N. line. It's a fact, sir! I swear it! They carried them off, repainted them, put their letters on them, and that's all about it. The N. line sends its agents everywhere, they hunt and hunt. And then -- can you imagine it? -- the Company happen to come upon a broken-down carriage of the Z. line. They repair it at their depot, and all at once, bless my soul! see their own mark on the wheels What do you say to that? Eh? If I did it they would send me to Siberia, but the railway companies simply snap their fingers at it!"

It is pleasant to Malahin to talk to educated, cultured people. He strokes his beard and joins in the conversation with dignity.

"Take this case, gentlemen, for instance," he says. I am transporting cattle to X. Eight vanloads. Very good. . . . Now let us say they charge me for each vanload as a weight of ten tons; eight bullocks don't weigh ten tons, but much less, yet they don't take any notice of that. . . ."

At that instant Yasha walks into the room looking for his father. He listens and is about to sit down on a chair, but probably thinking of his weight goes and sits on the window-sill

"They don't take any notice of that," Malahin goes on, "and charge me and my son the third-class fare, too, forty-two roubles, for going in the van with the bullocks. This is my son Yakov. I have two more at home, but they have gone in for study. Well and apart from that it is my opinion that the railways have ruined the cattle trade. In old days when they drove them in herds it was better."

The old man's talk is lengthy and drawn out. After every sentence he looks at Yasha as though he would say: "See how I am talking to clever people."

"Upon my word!" the inspector interrupts him. "No one is indignant, no one criticizes. And why? It is very simple. An abomination strikes the eye and arouses indignation only when it is exceptional, when the established order is broken by it. Here, where, saving your presence, it constitutes the long-established program and forms and enters into the basis of the order itself, where every sleeper on the line bears the trace of it and stinks of it, one too easily grows accustomed to it! Yes, sir!"

The second bell rings, the gentlemen in the queer overcoat gets up. The inspector takes him by the arm and, still talking with heat, goes off with him to the platform. After the third bell the station-master runs into his room, and sits down at his table.

"Listen, with what number am I to go?" asks Malahin.

The station-master looks at a form and says indignantly:

"Are you Malahin, eight vanloads? You must pay a rouble a van and six roubles and twenty kopecks for stamps. You have no stamps. Total, fourteen roubles, twenty kopecks."

Receiving the money, he writes something down, dries it with sand, and, hurriedly snatching up a bundle of forms, goes quickly out of the room.

At ten o'clock in the evening Malahin gets an answer from the traffic manager: "Give precedence."

Reading the telegram through, the old man winks significantly and, very well pleased with himself, puts it in his pocket.

"Here," he says to Yasha, "look and learn."

At midnight his train goes on. The night is dark and cold like the previous one; the waits at the stations are long. Yasha sits on the cape and imperturbably strums on the accordion, while the old man is still more eager to exert himself. At one of the stations he is overtaken by a desire to lodge a complaint. At his request a gendarme sits down and writes:

"*November* 10, 188-. -- I, non-commissioned officer of the Z. section of the N. police department of railways, Ilya Tchered, in accordance with article II of the statute of May 19, 1871, have drawn up this protocol at the station of X. as herewith follows. . . . "

"What am I to write next?" asks the gendarme.

Malahin lays out before him forms, postal and telegraph receipts, accounts. . . . He does not know himself definitely what he wants of the gendarme; he wants to describe in the protocol not any separate episode but his whole journey, with all his losses and conversations with station-masters -- to describe it lengthily and vindictively.

"At the station of Z.," he says, "write that the station-master unlinked my vans from the troop train because he did not like my countenance."

And he wants the gendarme to be sure to mention his countenance. The latter listens wearily, and goes on writing without hearing him to the end. He ends his protocol thus:

"The above deposition I, non-commissioned officer Tchered, have written down in this protocol with a view to present it to the head of the Z. section, and have handed a copy thereof to Gavril Malahin."

The old man takes the copy, adds it to the papers with which his side pocket is stuffed, and, much pleased, goes back to his van.

In the morning Malahin wakes up again in a bad humor, but his wrath vents itself not on Yasha but the cattle.

"The cattle are done for!" he grumbles. "They are done for! They are at the last gasp! God be my judge! they will all die. Tfoo!"

The bullocks, who have had nothing to drink for many days, tortured by thirst, are licking the hoar frost on the walls, and when Malachin goes up to them they begin licking his cold fur jacket. From their clear, tearful eyes it can be seen that they are exhausted by thirst and the jolting of the train, that they are hungry and miserable.

"It's a nice job taking you by rail, you wretched brutes!" mutters Malahin. "I could wish you were dead to get it over! It makes me sick to look at you!"

At midday the train stops at a big station where, according to the regulations, there was drinking water provided for cattle.

Water is given to the cattle, but the bullocks will not drink it: the water is too cold. . . .

* * * * * * *

Two more days and nights pass, and at last in the distance in the murky fog the city comes into sight. The journey is over. The train comes to a standstill before reaching the town, near a goods' station. The bullocks, released from the van, stagger and stumble as though they were walking on slippery ice.

Having got through the unloading and veterinary inspection, Malahin and Yasha take up their quarters in a dirty, cheap hotel in the outskirts of the town, in the square in which the cattle-market is held. Their lodgings are filthy and their food is disgusting, unlike what they ever have at home; they sleep to the harsh strains of a wretched steam hurdy-gurdy which plays day and night in the restaurant under their lodging.

The old man spends his time from morning till night going about looking for purchasers, and Yasha sits for days in the hotel room, or goes out into the street to look at the town. He sees the filthy square heaped up with dung, the signboards of restaurants, the turreted walls of a monastery in the fog. Sometimes he runs across the street and looks into the grocer's shop, admires the jars of cakes of different colors, yawns, and lazily saunters back to his room The city does not interest him.

At last the bullocks are sold to a dealer. Malahin hires drovers. The cattle are divided into herds, ten in each, and driven to the other end of the town. The bullocks, exhausted, go with drooping heads through the noisy streets, and look indifferently at what they see for the first and last time in their lives. The tattered drovers walk after them, their heads drooping too. They are bored. . . . Now and then some drover starts out of his brooding, remembers that there are cattle in front of him intrusted to his charge, and to show that he is doing his duty brings a stick down full swing on a bullock's back. The bullock staggers with the pain, runs forward a dozen paces, and looks about him as though he were ashamed at being beaten before people.

After selling the bullocks and buying for his family presents such as they could perfectly well have bought at home, Malahin and Yasha get ready for their journey back. Three hours before the train goes the old man, who has already had a drop too much with the purchaser and so is fussy, goes down with Yasha to the restaurant and sits down to drink tea. Like all provincials, he cannot eat and drink alone: he must have company as fussy and as fond of sedate conversation as himself.

"Call the host!" he says to the waiter; "tell him I should like to entertain him."

The hotel-keeper, a well-fed man, absolutely indifferent to his lodgers, comes and sits down to the table.

"Well, we have sold our stock," Malahin says, laughing. "I have swapped my goat for a hawk. Why, when we set off the price of meat was three roubles ninety kopecks, but when we arrived it had dropped to three roubles twenty-five. They tell us we are too late, we should have been here three days earlier, for now there is not the same demand for meat, St. Philip's fast has come. . . . Eh? It's a nice how-do-you-do! It meant a loss of fourteen roubles on each bullock. Yes. But only think what it costs to bring the stock! Fifteen roubles carriage, and you must put down six roubles for each bullock, tips, bribes, drinks, and one thing and another. . . ."

The hotel-keeper listens out of politeness and reluctantly drinks tea. Malahin sighs and groans, gesticulates, jests about his ill-luck, but everything shows that the loss he has sustained does not trouble him much. He doesn't mind whether he has lost or gained as long as he has listeners, has something to make a fuss about, and is not late for his train.

An hour later Malahin and Yasha, laden with bags and boxes, go downstairs from the hotel room to the front door to get into a sledge and drive to the station. They are seen off by the hotel-keeper, the waiter, and various women. The old man is touched. He thrusts ten-kopeck pieces in all directions, and says in a sing-song voice:

"Good by, good health to you! God grant that all may be well with you. Please God if we are alive and well we shall come again in Lent. Good-by. Thank you. God bless you!"

Getting into the sledge, the old man spends a long time crossing himself in the direction in which the monastery walls make a patch of darkness in the fog. Yasha sits beside him on the very edge of the seat with his legs hanging over the side. His face as before shows no sign of emotion and expresses neither boredom nor desire. He is not glad that he is going home, nor sorry that he has not had time to see the sights of the city.

"Drive on!"

The cabman whips up the horse and, turning round, begins swearing at the heavy and cumbersome luggage.

EXPENSIVE LESSONS

For a cultivated man to be ignorant of foreign languages is a great inconvenience. Vorotov became acutely conscious of it when, after taking his degree, he began upon a piece of research work.

"It's awful," he said, breathing hard (although he was only twenty-six he was fat, heavy, and suffered from shortness of breath).

"It's awful! Without languages I'm like a bird without wings. I might just as well give up the work."

And he made up his mind at all costs to overcome his innate laziness, and to learn French and German; and began to look out for a teacher.

One winter noon, as Vorotov was sitting in his study at work, the servant told him that a young lady was inquiring for him.

"Ask her in," said Vorotov.

And a young lady elaborately dressed in the last fashion walked in. She introduced herself as a teacher of French, Alice Osipovna Enquête, and told Vorotov that she had been sent to him by one of his friends.

"Delighted! Please sit down," said Vorotov, breathing hard and putting his hand over the collar of his nightshirt (to breathe more freely he always wore a nightshirt at work instead of a stiff linen one with collar). "It was Pyotr Sergeitch sent you? Yes, yes . . . I asked him about it. Delighted!"

As he talked to Mdlle. Enquête he looked at her shyly and with curiosity. She was a genuine Frenchwoman, very elegant and still quite young. Judging from her pale, languid face, her short curly hair, and her unnaturally slim waist, she might have been eighteen; but looking at her broad, well-developed shoulders, the elegant lines of her back and her severe eyes, Vorotov thought that she was not less than three-and-twenty and might be twenty-five; but then again he began to think she was not more than eighteen. Her face looked as cold and business-like as the face of a person who has come to speak about money. She did not once smile or frown, and only once a look of perplexity flitted over her face when she learnt that she was not required to teach children, but a stout grown-up man.

"So, Alice Osipovna," said Vorotov, "we'll have a lesson every evening from seven to eight. As regards your terms -- a rouble a lesson -- I've nothing to say against that. By all means let it be a rouble. . . ."

And he asked her if she would not have some tea or coffee, whether it was a fine day, and with a good-natured smile, stroking the baize of the table, he inquired in a friendly voice who she was, where she had studied, and what she lived on.

With a cold, business-like expression, Alice Osipovna answered that she had completed her studies at a private school and had the diploma of a private teacher, that her father had died lately of scarlet fever, that her mother was alive and made artificial flowers; that she, Mdlle. Enquête, taught in a private school till dinnertime, and after dinner was busy till evening giving lessons in different good families.

She went away leaving behind her the faint fragrance of a woman's clothes. For a long time afterwards Vorotov could not settle to work, but, sitting at the table stroking its green baize surface, he meditated.

"It's very pleasant to see a girl working to earn her own living," he thought. "On the other hand, it's very unpleasant to think that poverty should not spare such elegant and pretty girls as Alice Osipovna, and that she, too, should have to struggle for existence. It's a sad thing!"

Having never seen virtuous Frenchwomen before, he reflected also that this elegantly dressed young lady with her well-developed shoulders and exaggeratedly small waist in all probability followed another calling as well as giving French lessons.

The next evening when the clock pointed to five minutes to seven, Mdlle. Enquête appeared, rosy from the frost. She opened Margot, which she had brought with her, and without introduction began:

"French grammar has twenty-six letters. The first letter is called *A*, the second *B* . . ."

"Excuse me," Vorotov interrupted, smiling. "I must warn you, mademoiselle, that you must change your method a little in my case. You see, I know Russian, Greek, and Latin well. . . . I've studied comparative philology, and I think we might omit Margot and pass straight to reading some author."

And he explained to the French girl how grown-up people learn languages.

"A friend of mine," he said, "wanting to learn modern languages, laid before him the French, German, and Latin gospels, and read them side by side, carefully analysing each word, and would you believe it, he attained his object in less than a year. Let us do the same. We'll take some author and read him."

The French girl looked at him in perplexity. Evidently the suggestion seemed to her very naïve and ridiculous. If this strange proposal had been made to her by a child, she would certainly have been angry and have scolded it, but as he was a grown-up man and very stout and she could not scold him, she only shrugged her shoulders hardly perceptibly and said:

"As you please."

Vorotov rummaged in his bookcase and picked out a dog's-eared French book.

"Will this do?"

"It's all the same," she said.

"In that case let us begin, and good luck to it! Let's begin with the title . . . 'Mémoires.' "

"Reminiscences," Mdlle. Enquête translated.

With a good-natured smile, breathing hard, he spent a quarter of an hour over the word "Mémoires," and as much over the word *de*, and this wearied the young lady. She answered his questions languidly, grew confused, and evidently did not understand her pupil well, and did not attempt to understand him. Vorotov asked her questions, and at the same time kept looking at her fair hair and thinking:

"Her hair isn't naturally curly; she curls it. It's a strange thing! She works from morning to night, and yet she has time to curl her hair."

At eight o'clock precisely she got up, and saying coldly and dryly, "Au revoir, monsieur," walked out of the study, leaving behind her the same tender, delicate, disturbing fragrance. For a long time again her pupil did nothing; he sat at the table meditating.

During the days that followed he became convinced that his teacher was a charming, conscientious, and precise young lady, but that she was very badly educated, and incapable of teaching grown-up people, and he made up his mind not to waste his time, to get rid of her, and to engage another teacher. When she came the seventh time he took out of his pocket an envelope with seven roubles in it, and holding it in his hand, became very confused and began:

"Excuse me, Alice Osipovna, but I ought to tell you . . . I'm under painful necessity . . ."

Seeing the envelope, the French girl guessed what was meant, and for the first time during their lessons her face quivered and her cold, business-like expression vanished. She coloured a little, and dropping her eyes, began nervously fingering her slender gold chain. And Vorotov, seeing her perturbation, realised how much a rouble meant to her, and how bitter it would be to her to lose what she was earning.

"I ought to tell you," he muttered, growing more and more confused, and quavering inwardly; he hurriedly stuffed the envelope into his pocket and went on: "Excuse me, I . . . I must leave you for ten minutes."

And trying to appear as though he had not in the least meant to get rid of her, but only to ask her permission to leave her for a short time, he went into the next room and sat there for ten minutes. And then he returned more embarrassed than ever: it struck him that she might have interpreted his brief absence in some way of her own, and he felt awkward.

The lessons began again. Yorotov felt no interest in them. Realising that he would gain nothing from the lessons, he gave the French girl liberty to do as she liked, asking her nothing and not interrupting her.

She translated away as she pleased ten pages during a lesson, and he did not listen, breathed hard, and having nothing better to do, gazed at her curly head, or her soft white hands or her neck and sniffed the fragrance of her clothes. He caught himself thinking very unsuitable thoughts, and felt ashamed, or he was moved to tenderness, and then he felt vexed and wounded that she was so cold and business-like with him, and treated him as a pupil, never smiling and seeming afraid that he might accidentally touch her. He kept wondering how to inspire her with confidence and get to know her better, and to help her, to make her understand how badly she taught, poor thing.

One day Mdlle. Enquête came to the lesson in a smart pink dress, slightly *décolleté*, and surrounded by such a fragrance that she seemed to be wrapped in a cloud, and, if one blew upon her, ready to fly away into the air or melt away like smoke. She apologised and said she could stay only half an hour for the lesson, as she was going straight from the lesson to a dance.

He looked at her throat and the back of her bare neck, and thought he understood why Frenchwomen had the reputation of frivolous creatures easily seduced; he was carried away by this cloud of fragrance, beauty, and bare flesh, while she, unconscious of his thoughts and probably not in the least interested in them, rapidly turned over the pages and translated at full steam:

" 'He was walking the street and meeting a gentleman his friend and saying, "Where are you striving to seeing your face so pale it makes me sad." ' "

The "Mémoires" had long been finished, and now Alice was translating some other book. One day she came an hour too early for the lesson, apologizing and saying that she wanted to leave at seven and go to the Little Theatre. Seeing her out after the lesson, Vorotov dressed and went to the theatre himself. He went, and fancied that he was going simply for change and amusement, and that he was not thinking about Alice at all. He could not admit that a serious man, preparing for a learned career, lethargic in his habits, could fling up his work and go to the theatre simply to meet there a girl he knew very little, who was unintelligent and utterly unintellectual.

Yet for some reason his heart was beating during the intervals, and without realizing what he was doing, he raced about the corridors and foyer like a boy impatiently looking for some one, and he was disappointed when the interval was over. And when he saw the familiar pink dress and the handsome shoulders under the tulle, his heart quivered as though with a foretaste of happiness; he smiled joyfully, and for the first time in his life experienced the sensation of jealousy.

Alice was walking with two unattractive-looking students and an officer. She was laughing, talking loudly, and obviously flirting. Vorotov had never seen her like that. She was evidently happy, contented, warm, sincere. What for? Why? Perhaps because these men were her friends and belonged to her own circle. And Vorotov felt there was a terrible gulf between himself and that circle. He bowed to his teacher, but she gave him a chilly nod and walked quickly by; she evidently did not care for her friends to know that she had pupils, and that she had to give lessons to earn money.

After the meeting at the theatre Vorotov realised that he was in love.... During the subsequent lessons he feasted his eyes on his elegant teacher, and without struggling with himself, gave full rein to his imaginations, pure and impure. Mdlle. Enquête's face did not cease to be cold; precisely at eight o'clock every evening she said coldly, "Au revoir, monsieur," and he felt she cared nothing about him, and never would care anything about him, and that his position was hopeless.

Sometimes in the middle of a lesson he would begin dreaming, hoping, making plans. He inwardly composed declarations of love, remembered that Frenchwomen were frivolous and easily won, but it was enough for him to glance at the face of his teacher for his ideas to be extinguished as a candle is blown out when you bring it into the wind on the verandah. Once, overcome, forgetting himself as though in delirium, he could not restrain himself, and barred her way as she was going from the study into the entry after the lesson, and, gasping for breath and stammering, began to declare his love:

"You are dear to me! I . . . I love you! Allow me to speak."

And Alice turned pale -- probably from dismay, reflecting that after this declaration she could not come here again and get a rouble a lesson. With a frightened look in her eyes she said in a loud whisper:

"Ach, you mustn't! Don't speak, I entreat you! You mustn't!"

And Vorotov did not sleep all night afterwards; he was tortured by shame; he blamed himself and thought intensely. It seemed to him that he had insulted the girl by his declaration, that she would not come to him again.

He resolved to find out her address from the address bureau in the morning, and to write her a letter of apology. But Alice came without a letter. For the first minute she felt uncomfortable, then she opened a book and began briskly and rapidly translating as usual:

" 'Oh, young gentleman, don't tear those flowers in my garden which I want to be giving to my ill daughter. . . .' "

She still comes to this day. Four books have already been translated, but Vorotov knows no French but the word "Mémoires," and when he is asked about his literary researches, he waves his hand, and without answering, turns the conversation to the weather.

THE LION AND THE SUN

In one of the towns lying on this side of the Urals a rumour was afloat that a Persian magnate, called Rahat-Helam, was staying for a few days in the town and putting up at the "Japan Hotel." This rumour made no impression whatever upon the inhabitants; a Persian had arrived, well, so be it. Only Stepan Ivanovitch Kutsyn, the mayor of the town, hearing of the arrival of the oriental gentleman from the secretary of the Town Hall, grew thoughtful and inquired:

"Where is he going?"

"To Paris or to London, I believe."

"H'm. . . . Then he is a big-wig, I suppose?"

"The devil only knows."

As he went home from the Town Hall and had his dinner, the mayor sank into thought again, and this time he went on thinking till the evening. The arrival of the distinguished Persian greatly intrigued him. It seemed to him that fate itself had sent him this Rahat-Helam, and that a favourable opportunity had come at last for realising his passionate, secretly cherished dream. Kutsyn had already two medals, and the Stanislav of the third degree, the badge of the Red Cross, and the badge of the Society of Saving from Drowning, and in addition to these he had made himself a little gold gun crossed by a guitar, and this ornament, hung from a buttonhole in his uniform, looked in the distance like something special, and delightfully resembled a badge of distinction. It is well known that the more orders and medals you have the more you want -- and the mayor had long been desirous of receiving the Persian order of The Lion and the Sun; he desired it passionately, madly. He knew very well that there was no need to fight, or to subscribe to an asylum, or to serve on committees to obtain this order; all that was needed was a favourable opportunity. And now it seemed to him that this opportunity had come.

At noon on the following day he put on his chain and all his badges of distinction and went to the 'Japan.' Destiny favoured him. When he entered the distinguished Persian's apartment the latter was alone and doing nothing. Rahat-Helam, an enormous Asiatic, with a long nose like the beak of a snipe, with prominent eyes, and with a fez on his head, was sitting on the floor rummaging in his portmanteau.

"I beg you to excuse my disturbing you," began Kutsyn, smiling. "I have the honour to introduce myself, the hereditary, honourable citizen and cavalier, Stepan Ivanovitch Kutsyn, mayor of this town. I regard it as my duty to honour, in the person of your Highness, so to say, the representative of a friendly and neighbourly state."

The Persian turned and muttered something in very bad French, that sounded like tapping a board with a piece of wood.

"The frontiers of Persia" -- Kutsyn continued the greeting he had previously learned by heart -- "are in close contact with the borders of our spacious fatherland, and therefore mutual sympathies impel me, so to speak, to express my solidarity with you."

The illustrious Persian got up and again muttered something in a wooden tongue. Kutsyn, who knew no foreign language, shook his head to show that he did not understand.

"Well, how am I to talk to him?" he thought. "It would be a good thing to send for an interpreter at once, but it is a delicate matter, I can't talk before witnesses. The interpreter would be chattering all over the town afterwards."

And Kutsyn tried to recall the foreign words he had picked up from the newspapers.

"I am the mayor of the town," he muttered. "That is the *lord mayor* . . . *municipalais* . . . Vwee? Kompreney?"

He wanted to express his social position in words or in gesture, and did not know how. A picture hanging on the wall with an inscription in large letters, "The Town of Venice," helped him out of his difficulties. He pointed with his finger at the town, then at his own head, and in that way obtained, as he imagined, the phrase: "I am the head of the town." The Persian did not understand, but he gave a smile, and said:

"Goot, monsieur . . . goot . . . . ." Half-an-hour later the mayor was slapping the Persian, first on the knee and then on the shoulder, and saying:

"Kompreney? Vwee? As *lord mayor* and *municipalais* I suggest that you should take a little *promenage* . . . *kompreney? Promenage*."

Kutsyn pointed at Venice, and with two fingers represented walking legs. Rahat-Helam who kept his eyes fixed on his medals, and was apparently guessing that this was the most important person in the town, understood the word *promenage* and grinned politely. Then they both put on their coats and went out of the room. Downstairs near the door leading to the restaurant of the 'Japan,' Kutsyn reflected that it would not be amiss to entertain the Persian. He stopped and indicating the tables, said:

"By Russian custom it wouldn't be amiss . . . *puree, entrekot*, champagne and so on, kompreney."

The illustrious visitor understood, and a little later they were both sitting in the very best room of the restaurant, eating, and drinking champagne.

"Let us drink to the prosperity of Persia!" said Kutsyn. "We Russians love the Persians. Though we are of another faith, yet there are common interests, mutual, so to say, sympathies . . . progress . . . Asiatic markets. . . . The campaigns of peace so to say. . . ."

The illustrious Persian ate and drank with an excellent appetite, he stuck his fork into a slice of smoked sturgeon, and wagging his head, enthusiastically said: "*Goot, bien.*"

"You like it?" said the mayor delighted. "*Bien*, that's capital." And turning to the waiter he said: "Luka, my lad, see that two pieces of smoked sturgeon, the best you have, are sent up to his Highness's room!"

Then the mayor and the Persian magnate went to look at the menagerie. The townspeople saw their Stepan Ivanovitch, flushed with champagne, gay and very well pleased, leading the Persian about the principal streets and the bazaar, showing him the points of interest of the town, and even taking him to the fire tower.

Among other things the townspeople saw him stop near some stone gates with lions on it, and point out to the Persian first the lion, then the sun overhead, and then his own breast; then again he pointed to the lion and to the sun while the Persian nodded his head as though in sign of assent, and smiling showed his white teeth. In the evening they were sitting in the London Hotel listening to the harp-players, and where they spent the night is not known.

Next day the mayor was at the Town Hall in the morning; the officials there apparently already knew something and were making their conjectures, for the secretary went up to him and said with an ironical smile:

"It is the custom of the Persians when an illustrious visitor comes to visit you, you must slaughter a sheep with your own hands."

And a little later an envelope that had come by post was handed to him. The mayor tore it open and saw a caricature in it. It was a drawing of Rahat-Helam with the mayor on his knees before him, stretching out his hands and saying:

> "To prove our Russian friendship
> For Persia's mighty realm,
> And show respect for you, her envoy,
> Myself I'd slaughter like a lamb,
> But, pardon me, for I'm a -- donkey!"

The mayor was conscious of an unpleasant feeling like a gnawing in the pit of the stomach, but not for long. By midday he was again with the illustrious Persian, again he was regaling him and showing him the points of interest in the town. Again he led him to the stone gates, and again pointed to the lion, to the sun and to his own breast. They dined at the 'Japan'; after dinner, with cigars in their teeth, both, flushed and blissful, again mounted the fire tower, and the mayor, evidently wishing to entertain the visitor with an unusual spectacle, shouted from the top to a sentry walking below:

"Sound the alarm!"

But the alarm was not sounded as the firemen were at the baths at the moment.

They supped at the 'London' and, after supper, the Persian departed. When he saw him off, Stepan Ivanovitch kissed him three times after the Russian fashion, and even grew tearful. And when the train started, he shouted:

"Give our greeting to Persia! Tell her that we love her!"

A year and four months had passed. There was a bitter frost, thirty-five degrees, and a piercing wind was blowing. Stepan Ivanovitch was walking along the street with his fur coat thrown open over his chest, and he was annoyed that he met no one to see the Lion and the Sun upon his breast. He walked about like this till evening with his fur coat open, was chilled to the bone, and at night tossed from side to side and could not get to sleep.

He felt heavy at heart.

There was a burning sensation inside him, and his heart throbbed uneasily; he had a longing now to get a Serbian order. It was a painful, passionate longing.

IN TROUBLE

Pyotr Semyonitch, the bank manager, together with the book-keeper, his assistant, and two members of the board, were taken in the night to prison. The day after the upheaval the merchant Avdeyev, who was one of the committee of auditors, was sitting with his friends in the shop saying:

"So it is God's will, it seems. There is no escaping your fate. Here to-day we are eating caviare and to-morrow, for aught we know, it will be prison, beggary, or maybe death. Anything may happen. Take Pyotr Semyonitch, for instance. . . ."

He spoke, screwing up his drunken eyes, while his friends went on drinking, eating caviare, and listening. Having described the disgrace and helplessness of Pyotr Semyonitch, who only the day before had been powerful and respected by all, Avdeyev went on with a sigh:

"The tears of the mouse come back to the cat. Serve them right, the scoundrels! They could steal, the rooks, so let them answer for it!"

"You'd better look out, Ivan Danilitch, that you don't catch it too!" one of his friends observed.

"What has it to do with me?"

"Why, they were stealing, and what were you auditors thinking about? I'll be bound, you signed the audit."

"It's all very well to talk!" laughed Avdeyev: "Signed it, indeed! They used to bring the accounts to my shop and I signed them. As though I understood! Give me anything you like, I'll scrawl my name to it. If you were to write that I murdered someone I'd sign my name to it. I haven't time to go into it; besides, I can't see without my spectacles."

After discussing the failure of the bank and the fate of Pyotr Semyonitch, Avdeyev and his friends went to eat pie at the house of a friend whose wife was celebrating her name-day. At the name-day party everyone was discussing the bank failure. Avdeyev was more excited than anyone, and declared that he had long foreseen the crash and knew two years before that things were not quite right at the bank.

While they were eating pie he described a dozen illegal operations which had come to his knowledge.

"If you knew, why did you not give information?" asked an officer who was present.

"I wasn't the only one: the whole town knew of it," laughed Avdeyev. "Besides, I haven't the time to hang about the law courts, damn them!"

He had a nap after the pie and then had dinner, then had another nap, then went to the evening service at the church of which he was a warden; after the service he went back to the name-day party and played preference till midnight. Everything seemed satisfactory.

But when Avdeyev hurried home after midnight the cook, who opened the door to him, looked pale, and was trembling so violently that she could not utter a word. His wife, Elizaveta Trofimovna, a flabby, overfed woman, with her grey hair hanging loose, was sitting on the sofa in the drawing-room quivering all over, and vacantly rolling her eyes as though she were drunk. Her elder son, Vassily, a high-school boy, pale too, and extremely agitated, was fussing round her with a glass of water.

"What's the matter?" asked Avdeyev, and looked angrily sideways at the stove (his family was constantly being upset by the fumes from it).

"The examining magistrate has just been with the police," answered Vassily; "they've made a search."

Avdeyev looked round him. The cupboards, the chests, the tables -- everything bore traces of the recent search. For a minute Avdeyev stood motionless as though petrified, unable to understand; then his whole inside quivered and seemed to grow heavy, his left leg went numb, and, unable to endure his trembling, he lay down flat on the sofa. He felt his inside heaving and his rebellious left leg tapping against the back of the sofa.

In the course of two or three minutes he recalled the whole of his past, but could not remember any crime deserving of the attention of the police.

"It's all nonsense," he said, getting up. "They must have slandered me. To-morrow I must lodge a complaint of their having dared to do such a thing."

Next morning after a sleepless night Avdeyev, as usual, went to his shop. His customers brought him the news that during the night the public prosecutor had sent the deputy manager and the head-clerk to prison as well. This news did not disturb Avdeyev. He was convinced that he had been slandered, and that if he were to lodge a complaint to-day the examining magistrate would get into trouble for the search of the night before.

Between nine and ten o'clock he hurried to the town hall to see the secretary, who was the only educated man in the town council.

"Vladimir Stepanitch, what's this new fashion?" he said, bending down to the secretary's ear. "People have been stealing, but how do I come in? What has it to do with me? My dear fellow," he whispered, "there has been a search at my house last night! Upon my word! Have they gone crazy? Why touch me?"

"Because one shouldn't be a sheep," the secretary answered calmly. "Before you sign you ought to look."

"Look at what? But if I were to look at those accounts for a thousand years I could not make head or tail of them! It's all Greek to me! I am no book-keeper. They used to bring them to me and I signed them."

"Excuse me. Apart from that you and your committee are seriously compromised. You borrowed nineteen thousand from the bank, giving no security."

"Lord have mercy upon us!" cried Avdeyev in amazement. "I am not the only one in debt to the bank! The whole town owes it money. I pay the interest and I shall repay the debt. What next! And besides, to tell the honest truth, it wasn't I myself borrowed the money. Pyotr Semyonitch forced it upon me. 'Take it,' he said, 'take it. If you don't take it,' he said, 'it means that you don't trust us and fight shy of us. You take it,' he said, 'and build your father a mill.' So I took it."

"Well, you see, none but children or sheep can reason like that. In any case, *signor,* you need not be anxious. You can't escape trial, of course, but you are sure to be acquitted."

The secretary's indifference and calm tone restored Avdeyev's composure. Going back to his shop and finding friends there, he again began drinking, eating caviare, and airing his views. He almost forgot the police search, and he was only troubled by one circumstance which he could not help noticing: his left leg was strangely numb, and his stomach for some reason refused to do its work.

That evening destiny dealt another overwhelming blow at Avdeyev: at an extraordinary meeting of the town council all members who were on the staff of the bank, Avdeyev among them, were asked to resign, on the ground that they were charged with a criminal offence. In the morning he received a request to give up immediately his duties as churchwarden.

After that Avdeyev lost count of the blows dealt him by fate, and strange, unprecedented days flitted rapidly by, one after another, and every day brought some new, unexpected surprise. Among other things, the examining magistrate sent him a summons, and he returned home after the interview, insulted and red in the face.

"He gave me no peace, pestering me to tell him why I had signed. I signed, that's all about it. I didn't do it on purpose. They brought the papers to the shop and I signed them. I am no great hand at reading writing."

Young men with unconcerned faces arrived, sealed up the shop, and made an inventory of all the furniture of the house. Suspecting some intrigue behind this, and, as before, unconscious of any wrongdoing, Avdeyev in his mortification ran from one Government office to another lodging complaints. He spent hours together in waiting-rooms, composed long petitions, shed tears, swore. To his complaints the public prosecutor and the examining magistrate made the indifferent and rational reply: "Come to us when you are summoned: we have not time to attend to you now." While others answered: "It is not our business."

The secretary, an educated man, who, Avdeyev thought, might have helped him, merely shrugged his shoulders and said:

"It's your own fault. You shouldn't have been a sheep."

The old man exerted himself to the utmost, but his left leg was still numb, and his digestion was getting worse and worse. When he was weary of doing nothing and was getting poorer and poorer, he made up his mind to go to his father's mill, or to his brother, and begin dealing in corn. His family went to his father's and he was left alone. The days flitted by, one after another. Without a family, without a shop, and without money, the former churchwarden, an honoured and respected man, spent whole days going the round of his friends' shops, drinking, eating, and listening to advice. In the mornings and in the evenings, to while away the time, he went to church. Looking for hours together at the ikons, he did not pray, but pondered. His conscience was clear, and he ascribed his position to mistake and misunderstanding; to his mind, it was all due to the fact that the officials and the examining magistrates were young men and inexperienced. It seemed to him that if he were to talk it over in detail and open his heart to some elderly judge, everything would go right again. He did not understand his judges, and he fancied they did not understand him.

The days raced by, and at last, after protracted, harassing delays, the day of the trial came. Avdeyev borrowed fifty roubles, and providing himself with spirit to rub on his leg and a decoction of herbs for his digestion, set off for the town where the circuit court was being held.

The trial lasted for ten days. Throughout the trial Avdeyev sat among his companions in misfortune with the stolid composure and dignity befitting a respectable and innocent man who is suffering for no fault of his own: he listened and did not understand a word. He was in an antagonistic mood. He was angry at being detained so long in the court, at being unable to get Lenten food anywhere, at his defending counsel's not understanding him, and, as he thought, saying the wrong thing. He thought that the judges did not understand their business. They took scarcely any notice of Avdeyev, they only addressed him once in three days, and the questions they put to him were of such a character that Avdeyev raised a laugh in the audience each time he answered them. When he tried to speak of the expenses he had incurred, of his losses, and of his meaning to claim his costs from the court, his counsel turned round and made an incomprehensible grimace, the public laughed, and the judge announced sternly that that had nothing to do with the case. The last words that he was allowed to say were not what his counsel had instructed him to say, but something quite different, which raised a laugh again.

During the terrible hour when the jury were consulting in their room he sat angrily in the refreshment bar, not thinking about the jury at all. He did not understand why they were so long deliberating when everything was so clear, and what they wanted of him.

Getting hungry, he asked the waiter to give him some cheap Lenten dish. For forty kopecks they gave him some cold fish and carrots. He ate it and felt at once as though the fish were heaving in a chilly lump in his stomach; it was followed by flatulence, heartburn, and pain.

Afterwards, as he listened to the foreman of the jury reading out the questions point by point, there was a regular revolution taking place in his inside, his whole body was bathed in a cold sweat, his left leg was numb; he did not follow, understood nothing, and suffered unbearably at not being able to sit or lie down while the foreman was reading. At last, when he and his companions were allowed to sit down, the public prosecutor got up and said something unintelligible, and all at once, as though they had sprung out of the earth, some police officers appeared on the scene with drawn swords and surrounded all the prisoners. Avdeyev was told to get up and go.

Now he understood that he was found guilty and in charge of the police, but he was not frightened nor amazed; such a turmoil was going on in his stomach that he could not think about his guards.

"So they won't let us go back to the hotel?" he asked one of his companions. "But I have three roubles and an untouched quarter of a pound of tea in my room there."

He spent the night at the police station; all night he was aware of a loathing for fish, and was thinking about the three roubles and the quarter of a pound of tea. Early in the morning, when the sky was beginning to turn blue, he was told to dress and set off. Two soldiers with bayonets took him to prison. Never before had the streets of the town seemed to him so long and endless. He walked not on the pavement but in the middle of the road in the muddy, thawing snow. His inside was still at war with the fish, his left leg was numb; he had forgotten his goloshes either in the court or in the police station, and his feet felt frozen.

Five days later all the prisoners were brought before the court again to hear their sentence. Avdeyev learnt that he was sentenced to exile in the province of Tobolsk. And that did not frighten nor amaze him either. He fancied for some reason that the trial was not yet over, that there were more adjournments to come, and that the final decision had not been reached yet. . . . He went on in the prison expecting this final decision every day.

Only six months later, when his wife and his son Vassily came to say good-bye to him, and when in the wasted, wretchedly dressed old woman he scarcely recognized his once fat and dignified Elizaveta Trofimovna, and when he saw his son wearing a short, shabby reefer-jacket and cotton trousers instead of the high-school uniform, he realized that his fate was decided, and that whatever new "decision" there might be, his past would never come back to him. And for the first time since the trial and his imprisonment the angry expression left his face, and he wept bitterly.

THE KISS

At eight o'clock on the evening of the twentieth of May all the six batteries of the N---- Reserve Artillery Brigade halted for the night in the village of Myestetchki on their way to camp. When the general commotion was at its height, while some officers were busily occupied around the guns, while others, gathered together in the square near the church enclosure, were listening to the quartermasters, a man in civilian dress, riding a strange horse, came into sight round the church. The little dun-coloured horse with a good neck and a short tail came, moving not straight forward, but as it were sideways, with a sort of dance step, as though it were being lashed about the legs. When he reached the officers the man on the horse took off his hat and said:

"His Excellency Lieutenant-General von Rabbek invites the gentlemen to drink tea with him this minute...."

The horse turned, danced, and retired sideways; the messenger raised his hat once more, and in an instant disappeared with his strange horse behind the church.

"What the devil does it mean?" grumbled some of the officers, dispersing to their quarters. "One is sleepy, and here this Von Rabbek with his tea! We know what tea means."

The officers of all the six batteries remembered vividly an incident of the previous year, when during manoeuvres they, together with the officers of a Cossack regiment, were in the same way invited to tea by a count who had an estate in the neighbourhood and was a retired army officer: the hospitable and genial count made much of them, fed them, and gave them drink, refused to let them go to their quarters in the village and made them stay the night. All that, of course, was very nice -- nothing better could be desired, but the worst of it was, the old army officer was so carried away by the pleasure of the young men's company that till sunrise he was telling the officers anecdotes of his glorious past, taking them over the house, showing them expensive pictures, old engravings, rare guns, reading them autograph letters from great people, while the weary and exhausted officers looked and listened, longing for their beds and yawning in their sleeves; when at last their host let them go, it was too late for sleep.

Might not this Von Rabbek be just such another? Whether he were or not, there was no help for it. The officers changed their uniforms, brushed themselves, and went all together in search of the gentleman's house. In the square by the church they were told they could get to His Excellency's by the lower path -- going down behind the church to the river, going along the bank to the garden, and there an avenue would taken them to the house; or by the upper way -- straight from the church by the road which, half a mile from the village, led right up to His Excellency's granaries. The officers decided to go by the upper way.

"What Von Rabbek is it?" they wondered on the way. "Surely not the one who was in command of the N---- cavalry division at Plevna?"

"No, that was not Von Rabbek, but simply Rabbe and no 'von.' "

"What lovely weather!"

At the first of the granaries the road divided in two: one branch went straight on and vanished in the evening darkness, the other led to the owner's house on the right. The officers turned to the right and began to speak more softly. . . . On both sides of the road stretched stone granaries with red roofs, heavy and sullen-looking, very much like barracks of a district town. Ahead of them gleamed the windows of the manor-house.

"A good omen, gentlemen," said one of the officers. "Our setter is the foremost of all; no doubt he scents game ahead of us! . . ."

Lieutenant Lobytko, who was walking in front, a tall and stalwart fellow, though entirely without moustache (he was over five-and-twenty, yet for some reason there was no sign of hair on his round, well-fed face), renowned in the brigade for his peculiar faculty for divining the presence of women at a distance, turned round and said:

"Yes, there must be women here; I feel that by instinct."

On the threshold the officers were met by Von Rabbek himself, a comely-looking man of sixty in civilian dress. Shaking hands with his guests, he said that he was very glad and happy to see them, but begged them earnestly for God's sake to excuse him for not asking them to stay the night; two sisters with their children, some brothers, and some neighbours, had come on a visit to him, so that he had not one spare room left.

The General shook hands with every one, made his apologies, and smiled, but it was evident by his face that he was by no means so delighted as their last year's count, and that he had invited the officers simply because, in his opinion, it was a social obligation to do so. And the officers themselves, as they walked up the softly carpeted stairs, as they listened to him, felt that they had been invited to this house simply because it would have been awkward not to invite them; and at the sight of the footmen, who hastened to light the lamps in the entrance below and in the anteroom above, they began to feel as though they had brought uneasiness and discomfort into the house with them. In a house in which two sisters and their children, brothers, and neighbours were gathered together, probably on account of some family festivity, or event, how could the presence of nineteen unknown officers possibly be welcome?

At the entrance to the drawing-room the officers were met by a tall, graceful old lady with black eyebrows and a long face, very much like the Empress Eugénie. Smiling graciously and majestically, she said she was glad and happy to see her guests, and apologized that her husband and she were on this occasion unable to invite *messieurs les officiers* to stay the night. From her beautiful majestic smile, which instantly vanished from her face every time she turned away from her guests, it was evident that she had seen numbers of officers in her day, that she was in no humour for them now, and if she invited them to her house and apologized for not doing more, it was only because her breeding and position in society required it of her.

When the officers went into the big dining-room, there were about a dozen people, men and ladies, young and old, sitting at tea at the end of a long table. A group of men was dimly visible behind their chairs, wrapped in a haze of cigar smoke; and in the midst of them stood a lanky young man with red whiskers, talking loudly, with a lisp, in English. Through a door beyond the group could be seen a light room with pale blue furniture.

"Gentlemen, there are so many of you that it is impossible to introduce you all!" said the General in a loud voice, trying to sound very cheerful. "Make each other's acquaintance, gentlemen, without any ceremony!"

The officers -- some with very serious and even stern faces, others with forced smiles, and all feeling extremely awkward -- somehow made their bows and sat down to tea.

The most ill at ease of them all was Ryabovitch -- a little officer in spectacles, with sloping shoulders, and whiskers like a lynx's. While some of his comrades assumed a serious expression, while others wore forced smiles, his face, his lynx-like whiskers, and spectacles seemed to say: "I am the shyest, most modest, and most undistinguished officer in the whole brigade!" At first, on going into the room and sitting down to the table, he could not fix his attention on anyone face or object. The faces, the dresses, the cut-glass decanters of brandy, the steam from the glasses, the moulded cornices -- all blended in one general impression that inspired in Ryabovitch alarm and a desire to hide his head. Like a lecturer making his first appearance before the public, he saw everything that was before his eyes, but apparently only had a dim understanding of it (among physiologists this condition, when the subject sees but does not understand, is called psychical blindness). After a little while, growing accustomed to his surroundings, Ryabovitch saw clearly and began to observe. As a shy man, unused to society, what struck him first was that in which he had always been deficient -- namely, the extraordinary boldness of his new acquaintances. Von Rabbek, his wife, two elderly ladies, a young lady in a lilac dress, and the young man with the red whiskers, who was, it appeared, a younger son of Von Rabbek, very cleverly, as though they had rehearsed it beforehand, took seats between the officers, and at once got up a heated discussion in which the visitors could not help taking part. The lilac young lady hotly asserted that the artillery had a much better time than the cavalry and the infantry, while Von Rabbek and the elderly ladies maintained the opposite. A brisk interchange of talk followed. Ryabovitch watched the lilac young lady who argued so hotly about what was unfamiliar and utterly uninteresting to her, and watched artificial smiles come and go on her face.

Von Rabbek and his family skilfully drew the officers into the discussion, and meanwhile kept a sharp lookout over their glasses and mouths, to see whether all of them were drinking, whether all had enough sugar, why some one was not eating cakes or not drinking brandy. And the longer Ryabovitch watched and listened, the more he was attracted by this insincere but splendidly disciplined family.

After tea the officers went into the drawing-room. Lieutenant Lobytko's instinct had not deceived him. There were a great number of girls and young married ladies. The "setter" lieutenant was soon standing by a very young, fair girl in a black dress, and, bending down to her jauntily, as though leaning on an unseen sword, smiled and shrugged his shoulders coquettishly. He probably talked very interesting nonsense, for the fair girl looked at his well-fed face condescendingly and asked indifferently, "Really?" And from that uninterested "Really?" the setter, had he been intelligent, might have concluded that she would never call him to heel.

The piano struck up; the melancholy strains of a valse floated out of the wide open windows, and every one, for some reason, remembered that it was spring, a May evening. Every one was conscious of the fragrance of roses, of lilac, and of the young leaves of the poplar. Ryabovitch, in whom the brandy he had drunk made itself felt, under the influence of the music stole a glance towards the window, smiled, and began watching the movements of the women, and it seemed to him that the smell of roses, of poplars, and lilac came not from the garden, but from the ladies' faces and dresses.

Von Rabbek's son invited a scraggy-looking young lady to dance, and waltzed round the room twice with her. Lobytko, gliding over the parquet floor, flew up to the lilac young lady and whirled her away. Dancing began.... Ryabovitch stood near the door among those who were not dancing and looked on. He had never once danced in his whole life, and he had never once in his life put his arm round the waist of a respectable woman. He was highly delighted that a man should in the sight of all take a girl he did not know round the waist and offer her his shoulder to put her hand on, but he could not imagine himself in the position of such a man. There were times when he envied the boldness and swagger of his companions and was inwardly wretched; the consciousness that he was timid, that he was round-shouldered and uninteresting, that he had a long waist and lynx-like whiskers, had deeply mortified him, but with years he had grown used to this feeling, and now, looking at his comrades dancing or loudly talking, he no longer envied them, but only felt touched and mournful.

When the quadrille began, young Von Rabbek came up to those who were not dancing and invited two officers to have a game at billiards. The officers accepted and went with him out of the drawing-room. Ryabovitch, having nothing to do and wishing to take part in the general movement, slouched after them. From the big drawing-room they went into the little drawing-room, then into a narrow corridor with a glass roof, and thence into a room in which on their entrance three sleepy-looking footmen jumped up quickly from the sofa. At last, after passing through a long succession of rooms, young Von Rabbek and the officers came into a small room where there was a billiard-table. They began to play.

Ryabovitch, who had never played any game but cards, stood near the billiard-table and looked indifferently at the players, while they in unbuttoned coats, with cues in their hands, stepped about, made puns, and kept shouting out unintelligible words.

The players took no notice of him, and only now and then one of them, shoving him with his elbow or accidentally touching him with the end of his cue, would turn round and say "Pardon!" Before the first game was over he was weary of it, and began to feel he was not wanted and in the way. . . . He felt disposed to return to the drawing-room, and he went out.

On his way back he met with a little adventure. When he had gone half-way he noticed he had taken a wrong turning. He distinctly remembered that he ought to meet three sleepy footmen on his way, but he had passed five or six rooms, and those sleepy figures seemed to have vanished into the earth. Noticing his mistake, he walked back a little way and turned to the right; he found himself in a little dark room which he had not seen on his way to the billiard-room. After standing there a little while, he resolutely opened the first door that met his eyes and walked into an absolutely dark room. Straight in front could be seen the crack in the doorway through which there was a gleam of vivid light; from the other side of the door came the muffled sound of a melancholy mazurka. Here, too, as in the drawing-room, the windows were wide open and there was a smell of poplars, lilac and roses. . . .

Ryabovitch stood still in hesitation. . . . At that moment, to his surprise, he heard hurried footsteps and the rustling of a dress, a breathless feminine voice whispered "At last!" And two soft, fragrant, unmistakably feminine arms were clasped about his neck; a warm cheek was pressed to his cheek, and simultaneously there was the sound of a kiss. But at once the bestower of the kiss uttered a faint shriek and skipped back from him, as it seemed to Ryabovitch, with aversion. He, too, almost shrieked and rushed towards the gleam of light at the door. . . .

When he went back into the drawing-room his heart was beating and his hands were trembling so noticeably that he made haste to hide them behind his back. At first he was tormented by shame and dread that the whole drawing-room knew that he had just been kissed and embraced by a woman. He shrank into himself and looked uneasily about him, but as he became convinced that people were dancing and talking as calmly as ever, he gave himself up entirely to the new sensation which he had never experienced before in his life. Something strange was happening to him. . . . His neck, round which soft, fragrant arms had so lately been clasped, seemed to him to be anointed with oil; on his left cheek near his moustache where the unknown had kissed him there was a faint chilly tingling sensation as from peppermint drops, and the more he rubbed the place the more distinct was the chilly sensation; all over, from head to foot, he was full of a strange new feeling which grew stronger and stronger. . . . He wanted to dance, to talk, to run into the garden, to laugh aloud. . . . He quite forgot that he was round-shouldered and uninteresting, that he had lynx-like whiskers and an "undistinguished appearance" (that was how his appearance had been described by some ladies whose conversation he had accidentally overheard). When Von Rabbek's wife happened to pass by him, he gave her such a broad and friendly smile that she stood still and looked at him inquiringly.

"I like your house immensely!" he said, setting his spectacles straight.

The General's wife smiled and said that the house had belonged to her father; then she asked whether his parents were living, whether he had long been in the army, why he was so thin, and so on. . . . After receiving answers to her questions, she went on, and after his conversation with her his smiles were more friendly than ever, and he thought he was surrounded by splendid people. . . .

At supper Ryabovitch ate mechanically everything offered him, drank, and without listening to anything, tried to understand what had just happened to him. . . . The adventure was of a mysterious and romantic character, but it was not difficult to explain it. No doubt some girl or young married lady had arranged a tryst with some one in the dark room; had waited a long time, and being nervous and excited had taken Ryabovitch for her hero; this was the more probable as Ryabovitch had stood still hesitating in the dark room, so that he, too, had seemed like a person expecting something. . . . This was how Ryabovitch explained to himself the kiss he had received.

"And who is she?" he wondered, looking round at the women's faces. "She must be young, for elderly ladies don't give rendezvous. That she was a lady, one could tell by the rustle of her dress, her perfume, her voice. . . ."

His eyes rested on the lilac young lady, and he thought her very attractive; she had beautiful shoulders and arms, a clever face, and a delightful voice. Ryabovitch, looking at her, hoped that she and no one else was his unknown. . . . But she laughed somehow artificially and wrinkled up her long nose, which seemed to him to make her look old. Then he turned his eyes upon the fair girl in a black dress. She was younger, simpler, and more genuine, had a charming brow, and drank very daintily out of her wineglass. Ryabovitch now hoped that it was she. But soon he began to think her face flat, and fixed his eyes upon the one next her.

"It's difficult to guess," he thought, musing. "If one takes the shoulders and arms of the lilac one only, adds the brow of the fair one and the eyes of the one on the left of Lobytko, then . . ."

He made a combination of these things in his mind and so formed the image of the girl who had kissed him, the image that he wanted her to have, but could not find at the table. . . .

After supper, replete and exhilarated, the officers began to take leave and say thank you. Von Rabbek and his wife began again apologizing that they could not ask them to stay the night.

"Very, very glad to have met you, gentlemen," said Von Rabbek, and this time sincerely (probably because people are far more sincere and good-humoured at speeding their parting guests than on meeting them). "Delighted. I hope you will come on your way back! Don't stand on ceremony! Where are you going? Do you want to go by the upper way? No, go across the garden; it's nearer here by the lower way."

The officers went out into the garden. After the bright light and the noise the garden seemed very dark and quiet. They walked in silence all the way to the gate. They were a little drunk, pleased, and in good spirits, but the darkness and silence made them thoughtful for a minute. Probably the same idea occurred to each one of them as to Ryabovitch: would there ever come a time for them when, like Von Rabbek, they would have a large house, a family, a garden -- when they, too, would be able to welcome people, even though insincerely, feed them, make them drunk and contented?

Going out of the garden gate, they all began talking at once and laughing loudly about nothing. They were walking now along the little path that led down to the river, and then ran along the water's edge, winding round the bushes on the bank, the pools, and the willows that overhung the water. The bank and the path were scarcely visible, and the other bank was entirely plunged in darkness. Stars were reflected here and there on the dark water; they quivered and were broken up on the surface -- and from that alone it could be seen that the river was flowing rapidly. It was still. Drowsy curlews cried plaintively on the further bank, and in one of the bushes on the nearest side a nightingale was trilling loudly, taking no notice of the crowd of officers. The officers stood round the bush, touched it, but the nightingale went on singing.

"What a fellow!" they exclaimed approvingly. "We stand beside him and he takes not a bit of notice! What a rascal!"

At the end of the way the path went uphill, and, skirting the church enclosure, turned into the road. Here the officers, tired with walking uphill, sat down and lighted their cigarettes. On the other side of the river a murky red fire came into sight, and having nothing better to do, they spent a long time in discussing whether it was a camp fire or a light in a window, or something else. . . . Ryabovitch, too, looked at the light, and he fancied that the light looked and winked at him, as though it knew about the kiss.

On reaching his quarters, Ryabovitch undressed as quickly as possible and got into bed. Lobytko and Lieutenant Merzlyakov -- a peaceable, silent fellow, who was considered in his own circle a highly educated officer, and was always, whenever it was possible, reading the "Vyestnik Evropi," which he carried about with him everywhere -- were quartered in the same hut with Ryabovitch. Lobytko undressed, walked up and down the room for a long while with the air of a man who has not been satisfied, and sent his orderly for beer. Merzlyakov got into bed, put a candle by his pillow and plunged into reading the "Vyestnik Evropi."

"Who was she?" Ryabovitch wondered, looking at the smoky ceiling.

His neck still felt as though he had been anointed with oil, and there was still the chilly sensation near his mouth as though from peppermint drops. The shoulders and arms of the young lady in lilac, the brow and the truthful eyes of the fair girl in black, waists, dresses, and brooches, floated through his imagination. He tried to fix his attention on these images, but they danced about, broke up and flickered. When these images vanished altogether from the broad dark background which every man sees when he closes his eyes, he began to hear hurried footsteps, the rustle of skirts, the sound of a kiss and -- an intense groundless joy took possession of him. . . . Abandoning himself to this joy, he heard the orderly return and announce that there was no beer. Lobytko was terribly indignant, and began pacing up and down again.

"Well, isn't he an idiot?" he kept saying, stopping first before Ryabovitch and then before Merzlyakov. "What a fool and a dummy a man must be not to get hold of any beer! Eh? Isn't he a scoundrel?"

"Of course you can't get beer here," said Merzlyakov, not removing his eyes from the "Vyestnik Evropi."

"Oh! Is that your opinion?" Lobytko persisted. "Lord have mercy upon us, if you dropped me on the moon I'd find you beer and women directly! I'll go and find some at once. . . . You may call me an impostor if I don't!"

He spent a long time in dressing and pulling on his high boots, then finished smoking his cigarette in silence and went out.

"Rabbek, Grabbek, Labbek," he muttered, stopping in the outer room. "I don't care to go alone, damn it all! Ryabovitch, wouldn't you like to go for a walk? Eh?"

Receiving no answer, he returned, slowly undressed and got into bed. Merzlyakov sighed, put the "Vyestnik Evropi" away, and put out the light.

"H'm! . . ." muttered Lobytko, lighting a cigarette in the dark.

Ryabovitch pulled the bed-clothes over his head, curled himself up in bed, and tried to gather together the floating images in his mind and to combine them into one whole. But nothing came of it. He soon fell asleep, and his last thought was that some one had caressed him and made him happy -- that something extraordinary, foolish, but joyful and delightful, had come into his life. The thought did not leave him even in his sleep.

When he woke up the sensations of oil on his neck and the chill of peppermint about his lips had gone, but joy flooded his heart just as the day before. He looked enthusiastically at the window-frames, gilded by the light of the rising sun, and listened to the movement of the passers-by in the street. People were talking loudly close to the window. Lebedetsky, the commander of Ryabovitch's battery, who had only just overtaken the brigade, was talking to his sergeant at the top of his voice, being always accustomed to shout.

"What else?" shouted the commander.

"When they were shoeing yesterday, your high nobility, they drove a nail into Pigeon's hoof. The vet. put on clay and vinegar; they are leading him apart now. And also, your honour, Artemyev got drunk yesterday, and the lieutenant ordered him to be put in the limber of a spare gun-carriage."

The sergeant reported that Karpov had forgotten the new cords for the trumpets and the rings for the tents, and that their honours, the officers, had spent the previous evening visiting General Von Rabbek. In the middle of this conversation the red-bearded face of Lebedetsky appeared in the window. He screwed up his short-sighted eyes, looking at the sleepy faces of the officers, and said good-morning to them.

"Is everything all right?" he asked.

"One of the horses has a sore neck from the new collar," answered Lobytko, yawning.

The commander sighed, thought a moment, and said in a loud voice:

"I am thinking of going to see Alexandra Yevgrafovna. I must call on her. Well, good-bye. I shall catch you up in the evening."

A quarter of an hour later the brigade set off on its way. When it was moving along the road by the granaries, Ryabovitch looked at the house on the right. The blinds were down in all the windows. Evidently the household was still asleep. The one who had kissed Ryabovitch the day before was asleep, too. He tried to imagine her asleep. The wide-open windows of the bedroom, the green branches peeping in, the morning freshness, the scent of the poplars, lilac, and roses, the bed, a chair, and on it the skirts that had rustled the day before, the little slippers, the little watch on the table -- all this he pictured to himself clearly and distinctly, but the features of the face, the sweet sleepy smile, just what was characteristic and important, slipped through his imagination like quicksilver through the fingers. When he had ridden on half a mile, he looked back: the yellow church, the house, and the river, were all bathed in light; the river with its bright green banks, with the blue sky reflected in it and glints of silver in the sunshine here and there, was very beautiful. Ryabovitch gazed for the last time at Myestetchki, and he felt as sad as though he were parting with something very near and dear to him.

And before him on the road lay nothing but long familiar, uninteresting pictures. . . . To right and to left, fields of young rye and buckwheat with rooks hopping about in them. If one looked ahead, one saw dust and the backs of men's heads; if one looked back, one saw the same dust and faces. . . . Foremost of all marched four men with sabres -- this was the vanguard. Next, behind, the crowd of singers, and behind them the trumpeters on horseback. The vanguard and the chorus of singers, like torch-bearers in a funeral procession, often forgot to keep the regulation distance and pushed a long way ahead. . . . Ryabovitch was with the first cannon of the fifth battery. He could see all the four batteries moving in front of him. For anyone not a military man this long tedious procession of a moving brigade seems an intricate and unintelligible muddle; one cannot understand why there are so many people round one cannon, and why it is drawn by so many horses in such a strange network of harness, as though it really were so terrible and heavy. To Ryabovitch it was all perfectly comprehensible and therefore uninteresting. He had known for ever so long why at the head of each battery there rode a stalwart bombardier, and why he was called a bombardier; immediately behind this bombardier could be seen the horsemen of the first and then of the middle units. Ryabovitch knew that the horses on which they rode, those on the left, were called one name, while those on the right were called another -- it was extremely uninteresting. Behind the horsemen came two shaft-horses. On one of them sat a rider with the dust of yesterday on his back and a clumsy and funny-looking piece of wood on his leg. Ryabovitch knew the object of this piece of wood, and did not think it funny. All the riders waved their whips mechanically and shouted from time to time. The cannon itself was ugly. On the fore part lay sacks of oats covered with canvas, and the cannon itself was hung all over with kettles, soldiers' knapsacks, bags, and looked like some small harmless animal surrounded for some unknown reason by men and horses. To the leeward of it marched six men, the gunners, swinging their arms. After the cannon there came again more bombardiers, riders, shaft-horses, and behind them another cannon, as ugly and unimpressive as the first. After the second followed a third, a fourth; near the fourth an officer, and so on. There were six batteries in all in the brigade, and four cannons in each battery. The procession covered half a mile; it ended in a string of wagons near which an extremely attractive creature -- the ass, Magar, brought by a battery commander from Turkey -- paced pensively with his long-eared head drooping.

Ryabovitch looked indifferently before and behind, at the backs of heads and at faces; at any other time he would have been half asleep, but now he was entirely absorbed in his new agreeable thoughts. At first when the brigade was setting off on the march he tried to persuade himself that the incident of the kiss could only be interesting as a mysterious little adventure, that it was in reality trivial, and to think of it seriously, to say the least of it, was stupid; but now he bade farewell to logic and gave himself up to dreams. . . . At one moment he imagined himself in Von Rabbek's drawing-room beside a girl who was like the young lady in lilac and the fair girl in black; then he would close his eyes and see himself with another, entirely unknown girl, whose features were very vague. In his imagination he talked, caressed her, leaned on her shoulder, pictured war, separation, then meeting again, supper with his wife, children. . . .

"Brakes on!" the word of command rang out every time they went downhill.

He, too, shouted "Brakes on!" and was afraid this shout would disturb his reverie and bring him back to reality. . . .

As they passed by some landowner's estate Ryabovitch looked over the fence into the garden. A long avenue, straight as a ruler, strewn with yellow sand and bordered with young birch-trees, met his eyes. . . . With the eagerness of a man given up to dreaming, he pictured to himself little feminine feet tripping along yellow sand, and quite unexpectedly had a clear vision in his imagination of the girl who had kissed him and whom he had succeeded in picturing to himself the evening before at supper. This image remained in his brain and did not desert him again.

At midday there was a shout in the rear near the string of wagons:

"Easy! Eyes to the left! Officers!"

The general of the brigade drove by in a carriage with a pair of white horses. He stopped near the second battery, and shouted something which no one understood. Several officers, among them Ryabovitch, galloped up to them.

"Well?" asked the general, blinking his red eyes. "Are there any sick?"

Receiving an answer, the general, a little skinny man, chewed, thought for a moment and said, addressing one of the officers:

"One of your drivers of the third cannon has taken off his leg-guard and hung it on the fore part of the cannon, the rascal. Reprimand him."

He raised his eyes to Ryabovitch and went on:

"It seems to me your front strap is too long."

Making a few other tedious remarks, the general looked at Lobytko and grinned.

"You look very melancholy today, Lieutenant Lobytko," he said. "Are you pining for Madame Lopuhov? Eh? Gentlemen, he is pining for Madame Lopuhov."

The lady in question was a very stout and tall person who had long passed her fortieth year. The general, who had a predilection for solid ladies, whatever their ages, suspected a similar taste in his officers. The officers smiled respectfully. The general, delighted at having said something very amusing and biting, laughed loudly, touched his coachman's back, and saluted. The carriage rolled on. . . .

"All I am dreaming about now which seems to me so impossible and unearthly is really quite an ordinary thing," thought Ryabovitch, looking at the clouds of dust racing after the general's carriage. "It's all very ordinary, and every one goes through it. . . . That general, for instance, has once been in love; now he is married and has children. Captain Vahter, too, is married and beloved, though the nape of his neck is very red and ugly and he has no waist. . . . Salrnanov is coarse and very Tatar, but he has had a love affair that has ended in marriage. . . . I am the same as every one else, and I, too, shall have the same experience as every one else, sooner or later. . . ."

And the thought that he was an ordinary person, and that his life was ordinary, delighted him and gave him courage. He pictured her and his happiness as he pleased, and put no rein on his imagination.

When the brigade reached their halting-place in the evening, and the officers were resting in their tents, Ryabovitch, Merzlyakov, and Lobytko were sitting round a box having supper. Merzlyakov ate without haste, and, as he munched deliberately, read the "Vyestnik Evropi," which he held on his knees. Lobytko talked incessantly and kept filling up his glass with beer, and Ryabovitch, whose head was confused from dreaming all day long, drank and said nothing. After three glasses he got a little drunk, felt weak, and had an irresistible desire to impart his new sensations to his comrades.

"A strange thing happened to me at those Von Rabbeks'," he began, trying to put an indifferent and ironical tone into his voice. "You know I went into the billiard-room. . . ."

He began describing very minutely the incident of the kiss, and a moment later relapsed into silence. . . . In the course of that moment he had told everything, and it surprised him dreadfully to find how short a time it took him to tell it. He had imagined that he could have been telling the story of the kiss till next morning. Listening to him, Lobytko, who was a great liar and consequently believed no one, looked at him sceptically and laughed. Merzlyakov twitched his eyebrows and, without removing his eyes from the "Vyestnik Evropi," said:

"That's an odd thing! How strange! . . . throws herself on a man's neck, without addressing him by name. .. . She must be some sort of hysterical neurotic."

"Yes, she must," Ryabovitch agreed.

"A similar thing once happened to me," said Lobytko, assuming a scared expression. "I was going last year to Kovno. . . . I took a second-class ticket. The train was crammed, and it was impossible to sleep. I gave the guard half a rouble; he took my luggage and led me to another compartment. . . . I lay down and covered myself with a rug. . . . It was dark, you understand. Suddenly I felt some one touch me on the shoulder and breathe in my face. I made a movement with my hand

and felt somebody's elbow. . . . I opened my eyes and only imagine -- a woman. Black eyes, lips red as a prime salmon, nostrils breathing passionately -- a bosom like a buffer. . . ."

"Excuse me," Merzlyakov interrupted calmly, "I understand about the bosom, but how could you see the lips if it was dark?"

Lobytko began trying to put himself right and laughing at Merzlyakov's unimaginativeness. It made Ryabovitch wince. He walked away from the box, got into bed, and vowed never to confide again.

Camp life began. . . . The days flowed by, one very much like another. All those days Ryabovitch felt, thought, and behaved as though he were in love. Every morning when his orderly handed him water to wash with, and he sluiced his head with cold water, he thought there was something warm and delightful in his life.

In the evenings when his comrades began talking of love and women, he would listen, and draw up closer; and he wore the expression of a soldier when he hears the description of a battle in which he has taken part. And on the evenings when the officers, out on the spree with the setter -- Lobytko -- at their head, made Don Juan excursions to the "suburb," and Ryabovitch took part in such excursions, he always was sad, felt profoundly guilty, and inwardly begged *her* forgiveness. . . . In hours of leisure or on sleepless nights, when he felt moved to recall his childhood, his father and mother -- everything near and dear, in fact, he invariably thought of Myestetchki, the strange horse, Von Rabbek, his wife who was like the Empress Eugénie, the dark room, the crack of light at the door. . . .

On the thirty-first of August he went back from the camp, not with the whole brigade, but with only two batteries of it. He was dreaming and excited all the way, as though he were going back to his native place. He had an intense longing to see again the strange horse, the church, the insincere family of the Von Rabbeks, the dark room. The "inner voice," which so often deceives lovers, whispered to him for some reason that he would be sure to see her . . . and he was tortured by the questions, How he should meet her? What he would talk to her about? Whether she had forgotten the kiss? If the worst came to the worst, he thought, even if he did not meet her, it would be a pleasure to him merely to go through the dark room and recall the past....

Towards evening there appeared on the horizon the familiar church and white granaries. Ryabovitch's heart beat.... He did not hear the officer who was riding beside him and saying something to him, he forgot everything, and looked eagerly at the river shining in the distance, at the roof of the house, at the dovecote round which the pigeons were circling in the light of the setting sun.

When they reached the church and were listening to the billeting orders, he expected every second that a man on horseback would come round the church enclosure and invite the officers to tea, but ... the billeting orders were read, the officers were in haste to go on to the village, and the man on horseback did not appear.

"Von Rabbek will hear at once from the peasants that we have come and will send for us," thought Ryabovitch, as he went into the hut, unable to understand why a comrade was lighting a candle and why the orderlies were hurriedly setting samovars....

A painful uneasiness took possession of him. He lay down, then got up and looked out of the window to see whether the messenger were coming. But there was no sign of him.

He lay down again, but half an hour later he got up, and, unable to restrain his uneasiness, went into the street and strode towards the church. It was dark and deserted in the square near the church.... Three soldiers were standing silent in a row where the road began to go downhill. Seeing Ryabovitch, they roused themselves and saluted. He returned the salute and began to go down the familiar path.

On the further side of the river the whole sky was flooded with crimson: the moon was rising; two peasant women, talking loudly, were picking cabbage in the kitchen garden; behind the kitchen garden there were some dark huts.... And everything on the near side of the river was just as it had been in May: the path, the bushes, the willows overhanging the water ... but there was no sound of the brave nightingale, and no scent of poplar and fresh grass.

Reaching the garden, Ryabovitch looked in at the gate. The garden was dark and still. . . . He could see nothing but the white stems of the nearest birch-trees and a little bit of the avenue; all the rest melted together into a dark blur. Ryabovitch looked and listened eagerly, but after waiting for a quarter of an hour without hearing a sound or catching a glimpse of a light, he trudged back. . . .

He went down to the river. The General's bath-house and the bath-sheets on the rail of the little bridge showed white before him. . . . He went on to the bridge, stood a little, and, quite unnecessarily, touched the sheets. They felt rough and cold. He looked down at the water. . . . The river ran rapidly and with a faintly audible gurgle round the piles of the bath-house. The red moon was reflected near the left bank; little ripples ran over the reflection, stretching it out, breaking it into bits, and seemed trying to carry it away.

"How stupid, how stupid!" thought Ryabovitch, looking at the running water. "How unintelligent it all is!"

Now that he expected nothing, the incident of the kiss, his impatience, his vague hopes and disappointment, presented themselves in a clear light. It no longer seemed to him strange that he had not seen the General's messenger, and that he would never see the girl who had accidentally kissed him instead of some one else; on the contrary, it would have been strange if he had seen her. . . .

The water was running, he knew not where or why, just as it did in May. In May it had flowed into the great river, from the great river into the sea; then it had risen in vapour, turned into rain, and perhaps the very same water was running now before Ryabovitch's eyes again. . . . What for? Why?

And the whole world, the whole of life, seemed to Ryabovitch an unintelligible, aimless jest. . . . And turning his eyes from the water and looking at the sky, he remembered again how fate in the person of an unknown woman had by chance caressed him, he remembered his summer dreams and fancies, and his life struck him as extraordinarily meagre, poverty-stricken, and colourless. . . .

When he went back to his hut he did not find one of his comrades. The orderly informed him that they had all gone to "General von Rabbck's, who had sent a messenger on horseback to invite them...."

For an instant there was a flash of joy in Ryabovitch's heart, but he quenched it at once, got into bed, and in his wrath with his fate, as though to spite it, did not go to the General's.

BOYS

"Volodya's come!" someone shouted in the yard.

"Master Volodya's here!" bawled Natalya the cook, running into the dining-room. "Oh, my goodness!"

The whole Korolyov family, who had been expecting their Volodya from hour to hour, rushed to the windows. At the front door stood a wide sledge, with three white horses in a cloud of steam. The sledge was empty, for Volodya was already in the hall, untying his hood with red and chilly fingers. His school overcoat, his cap, his snowboots, and the hair on his temples were all white with frost, and his whole figure from head to foot diffused such a pleasant, fresh smell of the snow that the very sight of him made one want to shiver and say "brrr!"

His mother and aunt ran to kiss and hug him. Natalya plumped down at his feet and began pulling off his snowboots, his sisters shrieked with delight, the doors creaked and banged, and Volodya's father, in his waistcoat and shirt-sleeves, ran out into the hall with scissors in his hand, and cried out in alarm:

"We were expecting you all yesterday? Did you come all right? Had a good journey? Mercy on us! you might let him say 'how do you do' to his father! I am his father after all!"

"Bow-wow!" barked the huge black dog, Milord, in a deep bass, tapping with his tail on the walls and furniture.

For two minutes there was nothing but a general hubbub of joy. After the first outburst of delight was over the Korolyovs noticed that there was, besides their Volodya, another small person in the hall, wrapped up in scarves and shawls and white with frost. He was standing perfectly still in a corner, in the shadow of a big fox-lined overcoat.

"Volodya darling, who is it?" asked his mother, in a whisper.

"Oh!" cried Volodya." This is -- let me introduce my friend Lentilov, a schoolfellow in the second class. . . . I have brought him to stay with us."

"Delighted to hear it! You are very welcome," the father said cordially. "Excuse me, I've been at work without my coat. . . . Please come in! Natalya, help Mr. Lentilov off with his things. Mercy on us, do turn that dog out! He is unendurable!"

A few minutes later, Volodya and his friend Lentilov, somewhat dazed by their noisy welcome, and still red from the outside cold, were sitting down to tea. The winter sun, making its way through the snow and the frozen tracery on the window-panes, gleamed on the samovar, and plunged its pure rays in the tea-basin. The room was warm, and the boys felt as though the warmth and the frost were struggling together with a tingling sensation in their bodies.

"Well, Christmas will soon be here," the father said in a pleasant sing-song voice, rolling a cigarette of dark reddish tobacco. "It doesn't seem long since the summer, when mamma was crying at your going . . . and here you are back again. . . . Time flies, my boy. Before you have time to cry out, old age is upon you. Mr. Lentilov, take some more, please help yourself! We don't stand on ceremony!"

Volodya's three sisters, Katya, Sonya, and Masha (the eldest was eleven), sat at the table and never took their eyes off the newcomer.

Lentilov was of the same height and age as Volodya, but not as round-faced and fair-skinned. He was thin, dark, and freckled; his hair stood up like a brush, his eyes were small, and his lips were thick. He was, in fact, distinctly ugly, and if he had not been wearing the school uniform, he might have been taken for the son of a cook. He seemed morose, did not speak, and never once smiled. The little girls, staring at him, immediately came to the conclusion that he must be a very clever and learned person. He seemed to be thinking about something all the time, and was so absorbed in his own thoughts, that, whenever he was spoken to, he started, threw his head back, and asked to have the question repeated.

The little girls noticed that Volodya, who had always been so merry and talkative, also said very little, did not smile at all, and hardly seemed to be glad to be home. All the time they were at tea he only once addressed his sisters, and then he said something so strange. He pointed to the samovar and said:

"In California they don't drink tea, but gin."

He, too, seemed absorbed in his own thoughts, and, to judge by the looks that passed between him and his friend Lentilov, their thoughts were the same.

After tea, they all went into the nursery. The girls and their father took up the work that had been interrupted by the arrival of the boys. They were making flowers and frills for the Christmas tree out of paper of different colours. It was an attractive and noisy occupation. Every fresh flower was greeted by the little girls with shrieks of delight, even of awe, as though the flower had dropped straight from heaven; their father was in ecstasies too, and every now and then he threw the scissors on the floor, in vexation at their bluntness. Their mother kept running into the nursery with an anxious face, asking:

"Who has taken my scissors? Ivan Nikolaitch, have you taken my scissors again?"

"Mercy on us! I'm not even allowed a pair of scissors!" their father would respond in a lachrymose voice, and, flinging himself back in his chair, he would pretend to be a deeply injured man; but a minute later, he would be in ecstasies again.

On his former holidays Volodya, too, had taken part in the preparations for the Christmas tree, or had been running in the yard to look at the snow mountain that the watchman and the shepherd were building. But this time Volodya and Lentilov took no notice whatever of the coloured paper, and did not once go into the stable. They sat in the window and began whispering to one another; then they opened an atlas and looked carefully at a map.

First to Perm . . . " Lentilov said, in an undertone, "from there to Tiumen, then Tomsk . . . then . . . then . . . Kamchatka. There the Samoyedes take one over Behring's Straits in boats . . . . And then we are in America. . . . There are lots of furry animals there. . . ."

"And California?" asked Volodya.

"California is lower down.... We've only to get to America and California is not far off.... And one can get a living by hunting and plunder."

All day long Lentilov avoided the little girls, and seemed to look at them with suspicion. In the evening he happened to be left alone with them for five minutes or so. It was awkward to be silent.

He cleared his throat morosely, rubbed his left hand against his right, looked sullenly at Katya and asked:

"Have you read Mayne Reid?"

"No, I haven't.... I say, can you skate?"

Absorbed in his own reflections, Lentilov made no reply to this question; he simply puffed out his cheeks, and gave a long sigh as though he were very hot. He looked up at Katya once more and said:

"When a herd of bisons stampedes across the prairie the earth trembles, and the frightened mustangs kick and neigh."

He smiled impressively and added:

"And the Indians attack the trains, too. But worst of all are the mosquitoes and the termites."

"Why, what's that?"

"They're something like ants, but with wings. They bite fearfully. Do you know who I am?"

"Mr. Lentilov."

"No, I am Montehomo, the Hawk's Claw, Chief of the Ever Victorious."

Masha, the youngest, looked at him, then into the darkness out of window and said, wondering:

"And we had lentils for supper yesterday."

Lentilov's incomprehensible utterances, and the way he was always whispering with Volodya, and the way Volodya seemed now to be always thinking about something instead of playing . . . all this was strange and mysterious. And the two elder girls, Katya and Sonya, began to keep a sharp look-out on the boys. At night, when the boys had gone to bed, the girls crept to their bedroom door, and listened to what they were saying. Ah, what they discovered! The boys were planning to run away to America to dig for gold: they had everything ready for the journey, a pistol, two knives, biscuits, a burning glass to serve instead of matches, a compass, and four roubles in cash. They learned that the boys would have to walk some thousands of miles, and would have to fight tigers and savages on the road: then they would get gold and ivory, slay their enemies, become pirates, drink gin, and finally marry beautiful maidens, and make a plantation.

The boys interrupted each other in their excitement. Throughout the conversation, Lentilov called himself "Montehomo, the Hawk's Claw," and Volodya was "my pale-face brother!"

"Mind you don't tell mamma," said Katya, as they went back to bed. "Volodya will bring us gold and ivory from America, but if you tell mamma he won't be allowed to go."

The day before Christmas Eve, Lentilov spent the whole day poring over the map of Asia and making notes, while Volodya, with a languid and swollen face that looked as though it had been stung by a bee, walked about the rooms and ate nothing. And once he stood still before the holy image in the nursery, crossed himself, and said:

"Lord, forgive me a sinner; Lord, have pity on my poor unhappy mamma!"

In the evening he burst out crying. On saying good-night he gave his father a long hug, and then hugged his mother and sisters. Katya and Sonya knew what was the matter, but little Masha was puzzled, completely puzzled. Every time she looked at Lentilov she grew thoughtful and said with a sigh:

"When Lent comes, nurse says we shall have to eat peas and lentils."

Early in the morning of Christmas Eve, Katya and Sonya slipped quietly out of bed, and went to find out how the boys meant to run away to America. They crept to their door.

"Then you don't mean to go?" Lentilov was saying angrily. "Speak out: aren't you going?"

"Oh dear," Volodya wept softly. "How can I go? I feel so unhappy about mamma."

"My pale-face brother, I pray you, let us set off. You declared you were going, you egged me on, and now the time comes, you funk it!"

"I . . . I . . . I'm not funking it, but I . . . I . . . I'm sorry for mamma."

"Say once and for all, are you going or are you not?"

"I am going, only . . . wait a little . . . I want to be at home a little."

"In that case I will go by myself," Lentilov declared. "I can get on without you. And you wanted to hunt tigers and fight! Since that's how it is, give me back my cartridges!"

At this Volodya cried so bitterly that his sisters could not help crying too. Silence followed.

"So you are not coming?" Lentilov began again.

"I . . . I . . . I am coming!"

"Well, put on your things, then."

And Lentilov tried to cheer Volodya up by singing the praises of America, growling like a tiger, pretending to be a steamer, scolding him, and promising to give him all the ivory and lions' and tigers' skins.

And this thin, dark boy, with his freckles and his bristling shock of hair, impressed the little girls as an extraordinary remarkable person. He was a hero, a determined character, who knew no fear, and he growled so ferociously, that, standing at the door, they really might imagine there was a tiger or lion inside. When the little girls went back to their room and dressed, Katya's eyes were full of tears, and she said:

"Oh, I feel so frightened!"

Everything was as usual till two o'clock, when they sat down to dinner. Then it appeared that the boys were not in the house. They sent to the servants' quarters, to the stables, to the bailiff's cottage. They were not to be found. They sent into the village -- they were not there.

At tea, too, the boys were still absent, and by supper-time Volodya's mother was dreadfully uneasy, and even shed tears.

Late in the evening they sent again to the village, they searched everywhere, and walked along the river bank with lanterns. Heavens! what a fuss there was!

Next day the police officer came, and a paper of some sort was written out in the dining-room. Their mother cried. . . .

All of a sudden a sledge stopped at the door, with three white horses in a cloud of steam.

"Volodya's come," someone shouted in the yard.

"Master Volodya's here!" bawled Natalya, running into the dining-room. And Milord barked his deep bass, "bow-wow."

It seemed that the boys had been stopped in the Arcade, where they had gone from shop to shop asking where they could get gunpowder.

Volodya burst into sobs as soon as he came into the hall, and flung himself on his mother's neck. The little girls, trembling, wondered with terror what would happen next. They saw their father take Volodya and Lentilov into his study, and there he talked to them a long while.

"Is this a proper thing to do?" their father said to them. "I only pray they won't hear of it at school, you would both be expelled. You ought to be ashamed, Mr. Lentilov, really. It's not at all the thing to do! You began it, and I hope you will be punished by your parents. How could you? Where did you spend the night?"

"At the station," Lentilov answered proudly.

Then Volodya went to bed, and had a compress, steeped in vinegar, on his forehead.

A telegram was sent off, and next day a lady, Lentilov's mother, made her appearance and bore off her son.

Lentilov looked morose and haughty to the end, and he did not utter a single word at taking leave of the little girls. But he took Katya's book and wrote in it as a souvenir: "Montehomo, the Hawk's Claw, Chief of the Ever Victorious."

KASHTANKA

I

Misbehaviour

A young dog, a reddish mongrel, between a dachshund and a "yard-dog," very like a fox in face, was running up and down the pavement looking uneasily from side to side. From time to time she stopped and, whining and lifting first one chilled paw and then another, tried to make up her mind how it could have happened that she was lost.

She remembered very well how she had passed the day, and how, in the end, she had found herself on this unfamiliar pavement.

The day had begun by her master Luka Alexandritch's putting on his hat, taking something wooden under his arm wrapped up in a red handkerchief, and calling: "Kashtanka, come along!"

Hearing her name the mongrel had come out from under the work-table, where she slept on the shavings, stretched herself voluptuously and run after her master. The people Luka Alexandritch worked for lived a very long way off, so that, before he could get to anyone of them, the carpenter had several times to step into a tavern to fortify himself. Kashtanka remembered that on the way she had behaved extremely improperly. In her delight that she was being taken for a walk she jumped about, dashed barking after the trains, ran into yards, and chased other dogs. The carpenter was continually losing sight of her, stopping, and angrily shouting at her. Once he had even, with an expression of fury in his face, taken her fox-like ear in his fist, smacked her, and said emphatically: "Pla-a-ague take you, you pest!"

After having left the work where it had been bespoken, Luka Alexandritch went into his sister's and there had something to eat and drink; from his sister's he had gone to see a bookbinder he knew; from the bookbinder's to a tavern, from the tavern to another crony's, and so on. In short, by the time Kashtanka found herself on the unfamiliar pavement, it was getting dusk, and the carpenter was as drunk as a cobbler. He was waving his arms and, breathing heavily, muttered:

"In sin my mother bore me! Ah, sins, sins! Here now we are walking along the street and looking at the street lamps, but when we die, we shall burn in a fiery Gehenna. . . ."

Or he fell into a good-natured tone, called Kashtanka to him, and said to her: "You, Kashtanka, are an insect of a creature, and nothing else. Beside a man, you are much the same as a joiner beside a cabinet-maker. . . ."

While he talked to her in that way, there was suddenly a burst of music. Kashtanka looked round and saw that a regiment of soldiers was coming straight towards her. Unable to endure the music, which unhinged her nerves, she turned round and round and wailed. To her great surprise, the carpenter, instead of being frightened, whining and barking, gave a broad grin, drew himself up to attention, and saluted with all his five fingers. Seeing that her master did not protest, Kashtanka whined louder than ever, and dashed across the road to the opposite pavement.

When she recovered herself, the band was not playing and the regiment was no longer there. She ran across the road to the spot where she had left her master, but alas, the carpenter was no longer there. She dashed forward, then back again and ran across the road once more, but the carpenter seemed to have vanished into the earth. Kashtanka began sniffing the pavement, hoping to find her master by the scent of his tracks, but some wretch had been that way just before in new rubber goloshes, and now all delicate scents were mixed with an acute stench of india-rubber, so that it was impossible to make out anything.

Kashtanka ran up and down and did not find her master, and meanwhile it had got dark. The street lamps were lighted on both sides of the road, and lights appeared in the windows. Big, fluffy snowflakes were falling and painting white the pavement, the horses' backs and the cabmen's caps, and the darker the evening grew the whiter were all these objects. Unknown customers kept walking incessantly to and fro, obstructing her field of vision and shoving against her with their feet. (All mankind Kashtanka divided into two uneven parts: masters and customers; between them there was an essential difference: the first had the right to beat her, and the second she had the right to nip by the calves of their legs.) These customers were hurrying off somewhere and paid no attention to her.

When it got quite dark, Kashtanka was overcome by despair and horror. She huddled up in an entrance and began whining piteously. The long day's journeying with Luka Alexandritch had exhausted her, her ears and her paws were freezing, and, what was more, she was terribly hungry. Only twice in the whole day had she tasted a morsel: she had eaten a little paste at the bookbinder's, and in one of the taverns she had found a sausage skin on the floor, near the counter -- that was all. If she had been a human being she would have certainly thought: "No, it is impossible to live like this! I must shoot myself!"

II

A Mysterious Stranger

But she thought of nothing, she simply whined. When her head and back were entirely plastered over with the soft feathery snow, and she had sunk into a painful doze of exhaustion, all at once the door of the entrance clicked, creaked, and struck her on the side. She jumped up. A man belonging to the class of customers came out. As Kashtanka whined and got under his feet, he could not help noticing her. He bent down to her and asked:

"Doggy, where do you come from? Have I hurt you? O, poor thing, poor thing. . . . Come, don't be cross, don't be cross. . . . I am sorry."

Kashtanka looked at the stranger through the snow-flakes that hung on her eyelashes, and saw before her a short, fat little man, with a plump, shaven face wearing a top hat and a fur coat that swung open.

"What are you whining for?" he went on, knocking the snow off her back with his fingers. "Where is your master? I suppose you are lost? Ah, poor doggy! What are we going to do now?"

Catching in the stranger's voice a warm, cordial note, Kashtanka licked his hand, and whined still more pitifully.

"Oh, you nice funny thing!" said the stranger. "A regular fox! Well, there's nothing for it, you must come along with me! Perhaps you will be of use for something. . . . Well!"

He clicked with his lips, and made a sign to Kashtanka with his hand, which could only mean one thing: "Come along!" Kashtanka went.

Not more than half an hour later she was sitting on the floor in a big, light room, and, leaning her head against her side, was looking with tenderness and curiosity at the stranger who was sitting at the table, dining. He ate and threw pieces to her. . . . At first he gave her bread and the green rind of cheese, then a piece of meat, half a pie and chicken bones, while through hunger she ate so quickly that she had not time to distinguish the taste, and the more she ate the more acute was the feeling of hunger.

"Your masters don't feed you properly," said the stranger, seeing with what ferocious greediness she swallowed the morsels without munching them. "And how thin you are! Nothing but skin and bones. . . ."

Kashtanka ate a great deal and yet did not satisfy her hunger, but was simply stupefied with eating. After dinner she lay down in the middle of the room, stretched her legs and, conscious of an agreeable weariness all over her body, wagged her tail. While her new master, lounging in an easy-chair, smoked a cigar, she wagged her tail and considered the question, whether it was better at the stranger's or at the carpenter's. The stranger's surroundings were poor and ugly; besides the easy-chairs, the sofa, the lamps and the rugs, there was nothing, and the room seemed empty. At the carpenter's the whole place was stuffed full of things: he had a table, a bench, a heap of shavings, planes, chisels, saws, a cage with a goldfinch, a basin. . . . The stranger's room smelt of nothing, while there was always a thick fog in the carpenter's room, and a glorious smell of glue, varnish, and shavings. On the other hand, the stranger had one great superiority -- he gave her a great deal to eat and, to do him full justice, when Kashtanka sat facing the table and looking wistfully at him, he did not once hit or kick her, and did not once shout: "Go away, damned brute!"

When he had finished his cigar her new master went out, and a minute later came back holding a little mattress in his hands.

"Hey, you dog, come here!" he said, laying the mattress in the corner near the dog. "Lie down here, go to sleep!"

Then he put out the lamp and went away. Kashtanka lay down on the mattress and shut her eyes; the sound of a bark rose from the street, and she would have liked to answer it, but all at once she was overcome with unexpected melancholy. She thought of Luka Alexandritch, of his son Fedyushka, and her snug little place under the bench. . . . She remembered on the long winter evenings, when the carpenter was planing or reading the paper aloud, Fedyushka usually played with her. . . . He used to pull her from under the bench by her hind legs, and play such tricks with her, that she saw green before her eyes, and ached in every joint. He would make her walk on her hind legs, use her as a bell, that is, shake her violently by the tail so that she squealed and barked, and give her tobacco to sniff. . . . The following trick was particularly agonising: Fedyushka would tie a piece of meat to a thread and give it to Kashtanka, and then, when she had swallowed it he would, with a loud laugh, pull it back again from her stomach, and the more lurid were her memories the more loudly and miserably Kashtanka whined.

But soon exhaustion and warmth prevailed over melancholy. She began to fall asleep. Dogs ran by in her imagination: among them a shaggy old poodle, whom she had seen that day in the street with a white patch on his eye and tufts of wool by his nose. Fedyushka ran after the poodle with a chisel in his hand, then all at once he too was covered with shaggy wool, and began merrily barking beside Kashtanka. Kashtanka and he goodnaturedly sniffed each other's noses and merrily ran down the street. . . .

III

New and Very Agreeable Acquaintances

When Kashtanka woke up it was already light, and a sound rose from the street, such as only comes in the day-time. There was not a soul in the room. Kashtanka stretched, yawned and, cross and ill-humoured, walked about the room. She sniffed the corners and the furniture, looked into the passage and found nothing of interest there. Besides the door that led into the passage there was another door. After thinking a little Kashtanka scratched on it with both paws, opened it, and went into the adjoining room. Here on the bed, covered with a rug, a customer, in whom she recognised the stranger of yesterday, lay asleep.

"Rrrrr . . . " she growled, but recollecting yesterday's dinner, wagged her tail, and began sniffing.

She sniffed the stranger's clothes and boots and thought they smelt of horses. In the bedroom was another door, also closed. Kashtanka scratched at the door, leaned her chest against it, opened it, and was instantly aware of a strange and very suspicious smell. Foreseeing an unpleasant encounter, growling and looking about her, Kashtanka walked into a little room with a dirty wall-paper and drew back in alarm. She saw something surprising and terrible. A grey gander came straight towards her, hissing, with its neck bowed down to the floor and its wings outspread. Not far from him, on a little mattress, lay a white tom-cat; seeing Kashtanka, he jumped up, arched his back, wagged his tail with his hair standing on end and he, too, hissed at her. The dog was frightened in earnest, but not caring to betray her alarm, began barking loudly and dashed at the cat. . . . The cat arched his back more than ever, mewed and gave Kashtanka a smack on the head with his paw. Kashtanka jumped back, squatted on all four paws, and craning her nose towards the cat, went off into loud, shrill barks; meanwhile the gander came up behind and gave her a painful peck in the back. Kashtanka leapt up and dashed at the gander.

"What's this?" They heard a loud angry voice, and the stranger came into the room in his dressing-gown, with a cigar between his teeth. "What's the meaning of this? To your places!"

He went up to the cat, flicked him on his arched back, and said:

"Fyodor Timofeyitch, what's the meaning of this? Have you got up a fight? Ah, you old rascal! Lie down!"

And turning to the gander he shouted: "Ivan Ivanitch, go home!"

The cat obediently lay down on his mattress and closed his eyes. Judging from the expression of his face and whiskers, he was displeased with himself for having lost his temper and got into a fight.

Kashtanka began whining resentfully, while the gander craned his neck and began saying something rapidly, excitedly, distinctly, but quite unintelligibly.

"All right, all right," said his master, yawning. "You must live in peace and friendship." He stroked Kashtanka and went on: "And you, redhair, don't be frightened. . . . They are capital company, they won't annoy you. Stay, what are we to call you? You can't go on without a name, my dear."

The stranger thought a moment and said: "I tell you what . . . you shall be Auntie. . . . Do you understand? Auntie!"

And repeating the word "Auntie" several times he went out. Kashtanka sat down and began watching. The cat sat motionless on his little mattress, and pretended to be asleep. The gander, craning his neck and stamping, went on talking rapidly and excitedly about something. Apparently it was a very clever gander; after every long tirade, he always stepped back with an air of wonder and made a show of being highly delighted with his own speech. . . . Listening to him and answering "R-r-r-r," Kashtanka fell to sniffing the corners. In one of the corners she found a little trough in which she saw some soaked peas and a sop of rye crusts. She tried the peas; they were not nice; she tried the sopped bread and began eating it. The gander was not at all offended that the strange dog was eating his food, but, on the contrary, talked even more excitedly, and to show his confidence went to the trough and ate a few peas himself.

IV

Marvels on a Hurdle

A little while afterwards the stranger came in again, and brought a strange thing with him like a hurdle, or like the figure II. On the crosspiece on the top of this roughly made wooden frame hung a bell, and a pistol was also tied to it; there were strings from the tongue of the bell, and the trigger of the pistol. The stranger put the frame in the middle of the room, spent a long time tying and untying something, then looked at the gander and said: "Ivan Ivanitch, if you please!"

The gander went up to him and stood in an expectant attitude.

"Now then," said the stranger, "let us begin at the very beginning. First of all, bow and make a curtsey! Look sharp!"

Ivan Ivanitch craned his neck, nodded in all directions, and scraped with his foot.

"Right. Bravo. . . . Now die!"

The gander lay on his back and stuck his legs in the air. After performing a few more similar, unimportant tricks, the stranger suddenly clutched at his head, and assuming an expression of horror, shouted: "Help! Fire! We are burning!"

Ivan Ivanitch ran to the frame, took the string in his beak, and set the bell ringing.

The stranger was very much pleased. He stroked the gander's neck and said:

"Bravo, Ivan Ivanitch! Now pretend that you are a jeweller selling gold and diamonds. Imagine now that you go to your shop and find thieves there. What would you do in that case?"

The gander took the other string in his beak and pulled it, and at once a deafening report was heard. Kashtanka was highly delighted with the bell ringing, and the shot threw her into so much ecstasy that she ran round the frame barking.

"Auntie, lie down!" cried the stranger; "be quiet!"

Ivan Ivanitch's task was not ended with the shooting. For a whole hour afterwards the stranger drove the gander round him on a cord, cracking a whip, and the gander had to jump over barriers and through hoops; he had to rear, that is, sit on his tail and wave his legs in the air. Kashtanka could not take her eyes off Ivan Ivanitch, wriggled with delight, and several times fell to running after him with shrill barks. After exhausting the gander and himself, the stranger wiped the sweat from his brow and cried:

"Marya, fetch Havronya Ivanovna here!"

A minute later there was the sound of grunting. Kashtanka growled, assumed a very valiant air, and to be on the safe side, went nearer to the stranger. The door opened, an old woman looked in, and, saying something, led in a black and very ugly sow. Paying no attention to

Kashtanka's growls, the sow lifted up her little hoof and grunted good-humouredly. Apparently it was very agreeable to her to see her master, the cat, and Ivan Ivanitch. When she went up to the cat and gave him a light tap on the stomach with her hoof, and then made some remark to the gander, a great deal of good-nature was expressed in her movements, and the quivering of her tail. Kashtanka realised at once that to growl and bark at such a character was useless.

The master took away the frame and cried. "Fyodor Timofeyitch, if you please!"

The cat stretched lazily, and reluctantly, as though performing a duty, went up to the sow.

"Come, let us begin with the Egyptian pyramid," began the master.

He spent a long time explaining something, then gave the word of command, "One . . . two . . . three!" At the word "three" Ivan Ivanitch flapped his wings and jumped on to the sow's back. . . . When, balancing himself with his wings and his neck, he got a firm foothold on the bristly back, Fyodor Timofeyitch listlessly and lazily, with manifest disdain, and with an air of scorning his art and not caring a pin for it, climbed on to the sow's back, then reluctantly mounted on to the gander, and stood on his hind legs. The result was what the stranger called the Egyptian pyramid. Kashtanka yapped with delight, but at that moment the old cat yawned and, losing his balance, rolled off the gander. Ivan Ivanitch lurched and fell off too. The stranger shouted, waved his hands, and began explaining something again. After spending an hour over the pyramid their indefatigable master proceeded to teach Ivan Ivanitch to ride on the cat, then began to teach the cat to smoke, and so on.

The lesson ended in the stranger's wiping the sweat off his brow and going away. Fyodor Timofeyitch gave a disdainful sniff, lay down on his mattress, and closed his eyes; Ivan Ivanitch went to the trough, and the pig was taken away by the old woman. Thanks to the number of her new impressions, Kashranka hardly noticed how the day passed, and in the evening she was installed with her mattress in the room with the dirty wall-paper, and spent the night in the society of Fyodor Timofeyitch and the gander.

V
Talent! Talent!

A month passed.

Kashtanka had grown used to having a nice dinner every evening, and being called Auntie. She had grown used to the stranger too, and to her new companions. Life was comfortable and easy.

Every day began in the same way. As a rule, Ivan Ivanitch was the first to wake up, and at once went up to Auntie or to the cat, twisting his neck, and beginning to talk excitedly and persuasively, but, as before, unintelligibly. Sometimes he would crane up his head in the air and utter a long monologue. At first Kashtanka thought he talked so much because he was very clever, but after a little time had passed, she lost all her respect for him; when he went up to her with his long speeches she no longer wagged her tail, but treated him as a tiresome chatterbox, who would not let anyone sleep and, without the slightest ceremony, answered him with "R-r-r-r!"

Fyodor Timofeyitch was a gentleman of a very different sort. When he woke he did not utter a sound, did not stir, and did not even open his eyes. He would have been glad not to wake, for, as was evident, he was not greatly in love with life. Nothing interested him, he showed an apathetic and nonchalant attitude to everything, he disdained everything and, even while eating his delicious dinner, sniffed contemptuously.

When she woke Kashtanka began walking about the room and sniffing the corners. She and the cat were the only ones allowed to go all over the flat; the gander had not the right to cross the threshold of the room with the dirty wall-paper, and Hayronya Ivanovna lived somewhere in a little outhouse in the yard and made her appearance only during the lessons. Their master got up late, and immediately after drinking his tea began teaching them their tricks. Every day the frame, the whip, and the hoop were brought in, and every day almost the same performance took place. The lesson lasted three or four hours, so that sometimes Fyodor Timofeyitch was so tired that he staggered about like a drunken man, and Ivan Ivanitch opened his beak and breathed heavily, while their master became red in the face and could not mop the sweat from his brow fast enough.

The lesson and the dinner made the day very interesting, but the evenings were tedious. As a rule, their master went off somewhere in the evening and took the cat and the gander with him. Left alone, Auntie lay down on her little mattress and began to feel sad.

Melancholy crept on her imperceptibly and took possession of her by degrees, as darkness does of a room. It began with the dog's losing every inclination to bark, to eat, to run about the rooms, and even to look at things; then vague figures, half dogs, half human beings, with countenances attractive, pleasant, but incomprehensible, would appear in her imagination; when they came Auntie wagged her tail, and it seemed to her that she had somewhere, at some time, seen them and loved them. And as she dropped asleep, she always felt that those figures smelt of glue, shavings, and varnish.

When she had grown quite used to her new life, and from a thin, long mongrel, had changed into a sleek, well-groomed dog, her master looked at her one day before the lesson and said:

"It's high time, Auntie, to get to business. You have kicked up your heels in idleness long enough. I want to make an artiste of you. . . . Do you want to be an artiste?"

And he began teaching her various accomplishments. At the first lesson he taught her to stand and walk on her hind legs, which she liked extremely. At the second lesson she had to jump on her hind legs and catch some sugar, which her teacher held high above her head. After that, in the following lessons she danced, ran tied to a cord, howled to music, rang the bell, and fired the pistol, and in a month could successfully replace Fyodor Timofeyitch in the "Egyptian Pyramid." She learned very eagerly and was pleased with her own success; running with her tongue out on the cord, leaping through the hoop, and riding on old Fyodor Timofeyitch, gave her the greatest enjoyment. She accompanied every successful trick with a shrill, delighted bark, while her teacher wondered, was also delighted, and rubbed his hands.

"It's talent! It's talent!" he said. "Unquestionable talent! You will certainly be successful!"

And Auntie grew so used to the word talent, that every time her master pronounced it, she jumped up as if it had been her name.

VI

An Uneasy Night

Auntie had a doggy dream that a porter ran after her with a broom, and she woke up in a fright.

It was quite dark and very stuffy in the room. The fleas were biting. Auntie had never been afraid of darkness before, but now, for some reason, she felt frightened and inclined to bark.

Her master heaved a loud sigh in the next room, then soon afterwards the sow grunted in her sty, and then all was still again. When one thinks about eating one's heart grows lighter, and Auntie began thinking how that day she had stolen the leg of a chicken from Fyodor Timofeyitch, and had hidden it in the drawing-room, between the cupboard and the wall, where there were a great many spiders' webs and a great deal of dust. Would it not be as well to go now and look whether the chicken leg were still there or not? It was very possible that her master had found it and eaten it. But she must not go out of the room before morning, that was the rule. Auntie shut her eyes to go to sleep as quickly as possible, for she knew by experience that the sooner you go to sleep the sooner the morning comes. But all at once there was a strange scream not far from her which made her start and jump up on all four legs. It was Ivan Ivanitch, and his cry was not babbling and persuasive as usual, but a wild, shrill, unnatural scream like the squeak of a door opening. Unable to distinguish anything in the darkness, and not understanding what was wrong, Auntie felt still more frightened and growled: "R-r-r-r. . . ."

Some time passed, as long as it takes to eat a good bone; the scream was not repeated. Little by little Auntie's uneasiness passed off and she began to doze. She dreamed of two big black dogs with tufts of last year's coat left on their haunches and sides; they were eating out of a big basin some swill, from which there came a white steam and a most appetising smell; from time to time they looked round at Auntie, showed their teeth and growled: "We are not going to give you any!" But a peasant in a fur-coat ran out of the house and drove them away with a whip; then Auntie went up to the basin and began eating, but as soon as the peasant went out of the gate, the two black dogs rushed at her growling, and all at once there was again a shrill scream.

"K-gee! K-gee-gee!" cried Ivan Ivanitch.

Auntie woke, jumped up and, without leaving her mattress, went off into a yelping bark. It seemed to her that it was not Ivan Ivanitch that was screaming but someone else, and for some reason the sow again grunted in her sty.

Then there was the sound of shuffling slippers, and the master came into the room in his dressing-gown with a candle in his hand. The flickering light danced over the dirty wall-paper and the ceiling, and chased away the darkness. Auntie saw that there was no stranger in the room. Ivan Ivanitch was sitting on the floor and was not asleep. His wings were spread out and his beak was open, and altogether he looked as though he were very tired and thirsty. Old Fyodor Timofeyitch was not asleep either. He, too, must have been awakened by the scream.

"Ivan Ivanitch, what's the matter with you?" the master asked the gander. "Why are you screaming? Are you ill?"

The gander did not answer. The master touched him on the neck, stroked his back, and said: "You are a queer chap. You don't sleep yourself, and you don't let other people. . . ."

When the master went out, carrying the candle with him, there was darkness again. Auntie felt frightened. The gander did not scream, but again she fancied that there was some stranger in the room. What was most dreadful was that this stranger could not be bitten, as he was unseen and had no shape. And for some reason she thought that something very bad would certainly happen that night. Fyodor Timofeyitch was uneasy too.

Auntie could hear him shifting on his mattress, yawning and shaking his head.

Somewhere in the street there was a knocking at a gate and the sow grunted in her sty. Auntie began to whine, stretched out her front-paws and laid her head down upon them. She fancied that in the knocking at the gate, in the grunting of the sow, who was for some reason awake, in the darkness and the stillness, there was something as miserable and dreadful as in Ivan Ivanitch's scream. Everything was in agitation and anxiety, but why? Who was the stranger who could not be seen? Then two dim flashes of green gleamed for a minute near Auntie. It was Fyodor Timofeyitch, for the first time of their whole acquaintance coming up to her. What did he want? Auntie licked his paw, and not asking why he had come, howled softly and on various notes.

"K-gee!" cried Ivan Ivanitch, "K-g-ee!"

The door opened again and the master came in with a candle.

The gander was sitting in the same attitude as before, with his beak open, and his wings spread out, his eyes were closed.

"Ivan Ivanitch!" his master called him.

The gander did not stir. His master sat down before him on the floor, looked at him in silence for a minute, and said:

"Ivan Ivanitch, what is it? Are you dying? Oh, I remember now, I remember!" he cried out, and clutched at his head. "I know why it is! It's because the horse stepped on you to-day! My God! My God!"

Auntie did not understand what her master was saying, but she saw from his face that he, too, was expecting something dreadful. She stretched out her head towards the dark window, where it seemed to her some stranger was looking in, and howled.

"He is dying, Auntie!" said her master, and wrung his hands. "Yes, yes, he is dying! Death has come into your room. What are we to do?"

Pale and agitated, the master went back into his room, sighing and shaking his head. Auntie was afraid to remain in the darkness, and followed her master into his bedroom. He sat down on the bed and repeated several times: "My God, what's to be done?"

Auntie walked about round his feet, and not understanding why she was wretched and why they were all so uneasy, and trying to understand, watched every movement he made. Fyodor Timofeyitch, who rarely left his little mattress, came into the master's bedroom too, and began rubbing himself against his feet. He shook his head as though he wanted to shake painful thoughts out of it, and kept peeping suspiciously under the bed.

The master took a saucer, poured some water from his wash-stand into it, and went to the gander again.

"Drink, Ivan Ivanitch!" he said tenderly, setting the saucer before him; "drink, darling."

But Ivan Ivanitch did not stir and did not open his eyes. His master bent his head down to the saucer and dipped his beak into the water, but the gander did not drink, he spread his wings wider than ever, and his head remained lying in the saucer.

"No, there's nothing to be done now," sighed his master. "It's all over. Ivan Ivanitch is gone!"

And shining drops, such as one sees on the window-pane when it rains, trickled down his cheeks. Not understanding what was the matter, Auntie and Fyodor Timofeyitch snuggled up to him and looked with horror at the gander.

"Poor Ivan Ivanitch!" said the master, sighing mournfully. "And I was dreaming I would take you in the spring into the country, and would walk with you on the green grass. Dear creature, my good comrade, you are no more! How shall I do without you now?"

It seemed to Auntie that the same thing would happen to her, that is, that she too, there was no knowing why, would close her eyes, stretch out her paws, open her mouth, and everyone would look at her with horror. Apparently the same reflections were passing through the brain of Fyodor Timofeyitch. Never before had the old cat been so morose and gloomy.

It began to get light, and the unseen stranger who had so frightened Auntie was no longer in the room. When it was quite daylight, the porter came in, took the gander, and carried him away. And soon afterwards the old woman came in and took away the trough.

Auntie went into the drawing-room and looked behind the cupboard: her master had not eaten the chicken bone, it was lying in its place among the dust and spiders' webs. But Auntie felt sad and dreary and wanted to cry. She did not even sniff at the bone, but went under the sofa, sat down there, and began softly whining in a thin voice.

VII

An Unsuccessful Début

One fine evening the master came into the room with the dirty wall-paper, and, rubbing his hands, said:

"Well. . . ."

He meant to say something more, but went away without saying it. Auntie, who during her lessons had thoroughly studied his face and intonations, divined that he was agitated, anxious and, she fancied, angry. Soon afterwards he came back and said:

"To-day I shall take with me Auntie and F'yodor Timofeyitch. To-day, Auntie, you will take the place of poor Ivan Ivanitch in the 'Egyptian Pyramid.' Goodness knows how it will be! Nothing is ready, nothing has been thoroughly studied, there have been few rehearsals! We shall be disgraced, we shall come to grief!"

Then he went out again, and a minute later, came back in his fur-coat and top hat. Going up to the cat he took him by the fore-paws and put him inside the front of his coat, while Fyodor Timofeyitch appeared completely unconcerned, and did not even trouble to open his eyes. To him it was apparently a matter of absolute indifference whether he remained lying down, or were lifted up by his paws, whether he rested on his mattress or under his master's fur-coat.

"Come along, Auntie," said her master.

Wagging her tail, and understanding nothing, Auntie followed him. A minute later she was sitting in a sledge by her master's feet and heard him, shrinking with cold and anxiety, mutter to himself:

"We shall be disgraced! We shall come to grief!"

The sledge stopped at a big strange-looking house, like a soup-ladle turned upside down. The long entrance to this house, with its three glass doors, was lighted up with a dozen brilliant lamps. The doors opened with a resounding noise and, like jaws, swallowed up the people who were moving to and fro at the entrance. There were a great many people, horses, too, often ran up to the entrance, but no dogs were to be seen.

The master took Auntie in his arms and thrust her in his coat, where Fyodor Timofeyirch already was. It was dark and stuffy there, but warm. For an instant two green sparks flashed at her; it was the cat, who opened his eyes on being disturbed by his neighbour's cold rough paws. Auntie licked his ear, and, trying to settle herself as comfortably as possible, moved uneasily, crushed him under her cold paws, and casually poked her head out from under the coat, but at once growled angrily, and tucked it in again. It seemed to her that she had seen a huge, badly lighted room, full of monsters; from behind screens and gratings, which stretched on both sides of the room, horrible faces looked out: faces of horses with horns, with long ears, and one fat, huge countenance with a tail instead of a nose, and two long gnawed bones sticking out of his mouth.

The cat mewed huskily under Auntie's paws, but at that moment the coat was flung open, the master said, "Hop!" and Fyodor Timofeyitch and Auntie jumped to the floor. They were now in a little room with grey plank walls; there was no other furniture in it but a little table with a looking-glass on it, a stool, and some rags hung about the corners, and instead of a lamp or candles, there was a bright fan-shaped light attached to a little pipe fixed in the wall. Fyodor Timofeyitch licked his coat which had been ruffled by Auntie, went under the stool, and lay down. Their master, still agitated and rubbing his hands, began undressing. . . . He undressed as he usually did at home when he was preparing to get under the rug, that is, took off everything but his underlinen, then he sat down on the stool, and, looking in the looking-glass, began playing the most surprising tricks with himself. . . . First of all he put on his head a wig, with a parting and with two tufts of hair standing up like horns, then he smeared his face thickly with something white, and over the white colour painted his eyebrows, his moustaches, and red on his cheeks. His antics did not end with that. After smearing his face and neck, he began putting himself into an extraordinary and incongruous costume, such as Auntie had never seen before, either in houses or in the street. Imagine very full trousers, made of chintz covered with big flowers, such as is used in working-class houses for curtains and covering furniture, trousers which buttoned up just under his armpits. One trouser leg was made of brown chintz, the other of bright yellow. Almost lost in these, he then put on a short chintz jacket, with a big scalloped collar, and a gold star on the back, stockings of different colours, and green slippers.

Everything seemed going round before Auntie's eyes and in her soul. The white-faced, sack-like figure smelt like her master, its voice, too, was the familiar master's voice, but there were moments when Auntie was tortured by doubts, and then she was ready to run away from the parti-coloured figure and to bark. The new place, the fan-shaped light, the smell, the transformation that had taken place in her master -- all this aroused in her a vague dread and a foreboding that she would certainly meet with some horror such as the big face with the tail instead of a nose. And then, somewhere through the wall, some hateful band was playing, and from time to time she heard an incomprehensible roar. Only one thing reassured her -- that was the imperturbability of Fyodor Timofeyitch. He dozed with the utmost tranquillity under the stool, and did not open his eyes even when it was moved.

A man in a dress coat and a white waistcoat peeped into the little room and said:

"Miss Arabella has just gone on. After her -- you."

Their master made no answer. He drew a small box from under the table, sat down, and waited. From his lips and his hands it could be seen that he was agitated, and Auntie could hear how his breathing came in gasps.

"Monsieur George, come on!" someone shouted behind the door. Their master got up and crossed himself three times, then took the cat from under the stool and put him in the box.

"Come, Auntie," he said softly.

Auntie, who could make nothing out of it, went up to his hands, he kissed her on the head, and put her beside Fyodor Timofeyitch. Then followed darkness.... Auntie trampled on the cat, scratched at the walls of the box, and was so frightened that she could not utter a sound, while the box swayed and quivered, as though it were on the waves....

"Here we are again!" her master shouted aloud: "here we are again!"

Auntie felt that after that shout the box struck against something hard and left off swaying. There was a loud deep roar, someone was being slapped, and that someone, probably the monster with the tail instead of a nose, roared and laughed so loud that the locks of the box trembled. In response to the roar, there came a shrill, squeaky laugh from her master, such as he never laughed at home.

"Ha!" he shouted, trying to shout above the roar. "Honoured friends! I have only just come from the station! My granny's kicked the bucket and left me a fortune! There is something very heavy in the box, it must be gold, ha! ha! I bet there's a million here! We'll open it and look. . . ."

The lock of the box clicked. The bright light dazzled Auntie's eyes, she jumped out of the box, and, deafened by the roar, ran quickly round her master, and broke into a shrill bark.

"Ha!" exclaimed her master. "Uncle Fyodor Timofeyitch! Beloved Aunt, dear relations! The devil take you!"

He fell on his stomach on the sand, seized the cat and Auntie, and fell to embracing them. While he held Auntie tight in his arms, she glanced round into the world into which fate had brought her and, impressed by its immensity, was for a minute dumbfounded with amazement and delight, then jumped out of her master's arms, and to express the intensity of her emotions, whirled round and round on one spot like a top. This new world was big and full of bright light; wherever she looked, on all sides, from floor to ceiling there were faces, faces, faces, and nothing else.

"Auntie, I beg you to sit down!" shouted her master. Remembering what that meant, Auntie jumped on to a chair, and sat down. She looked at her master. His eyes looked at her gravely and kindly as always, but his face, especially his mouth and teeth, were made grotesque by a broad immovable grin. He laughed, skipped about, twitched his shoulders, and made a show of being very merry in the presence of the thousands of faces. Auntie believed in his merriment, all at once felt all over her that those thousands of faces were looking at her, lifted up her fox-like head, and howled joyously.

"You sit there, Auntie," her master said to her., "while Uncle and I will dance the Kamarinsky."

Fyodor Timofeyitch stood looking about him indifferently, waiting to be made to do something silly. He danced listlessly, carelessly, sullenly, and one could see from his movements, his tail and his ears, that he had a profound contempt for the crowd, the bright light, his master and himself. When he had performed his allotted task, he gave a yawn and sat down.

"Now, Auntie!" said her master, "we'll have first a song, and then a dance, shall we?"

He took a pipe out of his pocket, and began playing. Auntie, who could not endure music, began moving uneasily in her chair and howled. A roar of applause rose from all sides. Her master bowed, and when all was still again, went on playing. . . . Just as he took one very high note, someone high up among the audience uttered a loud exclamation:

"Auntie!" cried a child's voice, "why it's Kashtanka!"

"Kashtanka it is!" declared a cracked drunken tenor. "Kashtanka! Strike me dead, Fedyushka, it is Kashtanka. Kashtanka! here!"

Someone in the gallery gave a whistle, and two voices, one a boy's and one a man's, called loudly: "Kashtanka! Kashtanka!"

Auntie started, and looked where the shouting came from. Two faces, one hairy, drunken and grinning, the other chubby, rosy-cheeked and frightened-looking, dazed her eyes as the bright light had dazed them before. . . . She remembered, fell off the chair, struggled on the sand, then jumped up, and with a delighted yap dashed towards those faces.

There was a deafening roar, interspersed with whistles and a shrill childish shout: "Kashtanka! Kashtanka!"

Auntie leaped over the barrier, then across someone's shoulders. She found herself in a box: to get into the next tier she had to leap over a high wall. Auntie jumped, but did not jump high enough, and slipped back down the wall. Then she was passed from hand to hand, licked hands and faces, kept mounting higher and higher, and at last got into the gallery. . . .

Half an hour afterwards, Kashtanka was in the street, following the people who smelt of glue and varnish. Luka Alexandritch staggered and instinctively, taught by experience, tried to keep as far from the gutter as possible.

"In sin my mother bore me," he muttered. "And you, Kashtanka, are a thing of little understanding. Beside a man, you are like a joiner beside a cabinetmaker."

Fedyushka walked beside him, wearing his father's cap. Kashtanka looked at their backs, and it seemed to her that she had been following them for ages, and was glad that there had not been a break for a minute in her life.

She remembered the little room with dirty wall-paper, the gander, Fyodor Timofeyitch, the delicious dinners, the lessons, the circus, but all that seemed to her now like a long, tangled, oppressive dream.

A LADY'S STORY

Nine years ago Pyotr Sergeyitch, the deputy prosecutor, and I were riding towards evening in hay-making time to fetch the letters from the station. The weather was magnificent, but on our way back we heard a peal of thunder, and saw an angry black storm-cloud which was coming straight towards us. The storm-cloud was approaching us and we were approaching it. Against the background of it our house and church looked white and the tall poplars shone like silver. There was a scent of rain and mown hay. My companion was in high spirits. He kept laughing and talking all sorts of nonsense. He said it would be nice if we could suddenly come upon a medieval castle with turreted towers, with moss on it and owls, in which we could take shelter from the rain and in the end be killed by a thunderbolt....

Then the first wave raced through the rye and a field of oats, there was a gust of wind, and the dust flew round and round in the air. Pyotr Sergeyitch laughed and spurred on his horse.

"It's fine!" he cried, "it's splendid!"

Infected by his gaiety, I too began laughing at the thought that in a minute I should be drenched to the skin and might be struck by lightning. Riding swiftly in a hurricane when one is breathless with the wind, and feels like a bird, thrills one and puts one's heart in a flutter. By the time we rode into our courtyard the wind had gone down, and big drops of rain were pattering on the grass and on the roofs. There was not a soul near the stable. Pyotr Sergeyitch himself took the bridles off, and led the horses to their stalls. I stood in the doorway waiting for him to finish, and watching the slanting streaks of rain; the sweetish, exciting scent of hay was even stronger here than in the fields; the storm-clouds and the rain made it almost twilight.

"What a crash!" said Pyotr Sergeyitch, coming up to me after a very loud rolling peal of thunder when it seemed as though the sky were split in two. "What do you say to that?" He stood beside me in the doorway and, still breathless from his rapid ride, looked at me. I could see that he was admiring me.

"Natalya Vladimirovna," he said, "I would give anything only to stay here a little longer and look at you. You are lovely to-day."

His eyes looked at me with delight and supplication, his face was pale. On his beard and mustache were glittering raindrops, and they, too, seemed to be looking at me with love. "I love you," he said. "I love you, and I am happy at seeing you. I know you cannot be my wife, but I want nothing, I ask nothing; only know that I love you. Be silent, do not answer me, take no notice of it, but only know that you are dear to me and let me look at you."

His rapture affected me too; I looked at his enthusiastic face, listened to his voice which mingled with the patter of the rain, and stood as though spellbound, unable to stir. I longed to go on endlessly looking at his shining eyes and listening.

"You say nothing, and that is splendid," said Pyotr Sergeyitch. "Go on being silent."

I felt happy. I laughed with delight and ran through the drenching rain to the house; he laughed too, and, leaping as he went, ran after me. Both drenched, panting, noisily clattering up the stairs like children, we dashed into the room. My father and brother, who were not used to seeing me laughing and light-hearted, looked at me in surprise and began laughing too.

The storm-clouds had passed over and the thunder had ceased, but the raindrops still glittered on Pyotr Sergeyitch's beard. The whole evening till supper-time he was singing, whistling, playing noisily with the dog and racing about the room after it, so that he nearly upset the servant with the samovar. And at supper he ate a great deal, talked nonsense, and maintained that when one eats fresh cucumbers in winter there is the fragrance of spring in one's mouth.

When I went to bed I lighted a candle and threw my window wide open, and an undefined feeling took possession of my soul. I remembered that I was free and healthy, that I had rank and wealth, that I was beloved; above all, that I had rank and wealth, rank and wealth, my God! how nice that was!... Then, huddling up in bed at a touch of cold which reached me from the garden with the dew, I tried to discover whether I loved Pyotr Sergeyitch or not,... and fell asleep unable to reach any conclusion.

And when in the morning I saw quivering patches of sunlight and the shadows of the lime trees on my bed, what had happened yesterday rose vividly in my memory. Life seemed to me rich, varied, full of charm. Humming, I dressed quickly and went out into the garden....

And what happened afterwards? Why -- nothing. In the winter when we lived in town Pyotr Sergeyitch came to see us from time to time. Country acquaintances are charming only in the country and in summer; in the town and in winter they lose their charm. When you pour out tea for them in the town it seems as though they are wearing other people's coats, and as though they stirred their tea too long. In the town, too, Pyotr Sergeyitch spoke sometimes of love, but the effect was not at all the same as in the country. In the town we were more vividly conscious of the wall that stood between us. I had rank and wealth, while he was poor, and he was not even a nobleman, but only the son of a deacon and a deputy public prosecutor; we both of us -- I through my youth and he for some unknown reason -- thought of that wall as very high and thick, and when he was with us in the town he would criticize aristocratic society with a forced smile, and maintain a sullen silence when there was anyone else in the drawing-room. There is no wall that cannot be broken through, but the heroes of the modern romance, so far as I know them, are too timid, spiritless, lazy, and oversensitive, and are too ready to resign themselves to the thought that they are doomed to failure, that personal life has disappointed them; instead of struggling they merely criticize, calling the world vulgar and forgetting that their criticism passes little by little into vulgarity.

I was loved, happiness was not far away, and seemed to be almost touching me; I went on living in careless ease without trying to understand myself, not knowing what I expected or what I wanted from life, and time went on and on.... People passed by me with their love, bright days and warm nights flashed by, the nightingales sang, the hay smelt fragrant, and all this, sweet and overwhelming in remembrance, passed with me as with everyone rapidly, leaving no trace, was not prized, and vanished like mist.... Where is it all?

My father is dead, I have grown older; everything that delighted me, caressed me, gave me hope -- the patter of the rain, the rolling of the thunder, thoughts of happiness, talk of love -- all that has become nothing but a memory, and I see before me a flat desert distance; on the plain not one living soul, and out there on the horizon it is dark and terrible....

A ring at the bell.... It is Pyotr Sergeyitch. When in the winter I see the trees and remember how green they were for me in the summer I whisper:

"Oh, my darlings!"

And when I see people with whom I spent my spring-time, I feel sorrowful and warm and whisper the same thing.

He has long ago by my father's good offices been transferred to town. He looks a little older, a little fallen away. He has long given up declaring his love, has left off talking nonsense, dislikes his official work, is ill in some way and disillusioned; he has given up trying to get anything out of life, and takes no interest in living. Now he has sat down by the hearth and looks in silence at the fire....

Not knowing what to say I ask him:

"Well, what have you to tell me?"

"Nothing," he answers.

And silence again. The red glow of the fire plays about his melancholy face.

I thought of the past, and all at once my shoulders began quivering, my head dropped, and I began weeping bitterly. I felt unbearably sorry for myself and for this man, and passionately longed for what had passed away and what life refused us now. And now I did not think about rank and wealth.

I broke into loud sobs, pressing my temples, and muttered:

"My God! my God! my life is wasted!"

And he sat and was silent, and did not say to me: "Don't weep." He understood that I must weep, and that the time for this had come.

I saw from his eyes that he was sorry for me; and I was sorry for him, too, and vexed with this timid, unsuccessful man who could not make a life for me, nor for himself.

When I saw him to the door, he was, I fancied, purposely a long while putting on his coat. Twice he kissed my hand without a word, and looked a long while into my tear-stained face. I believe at that moment he recalled the storm, the streaks of rain, our laughter, my face that day; he longed to say something to me, and he would have been glad to say it; but he said nothing, he merely shook his head and pressed my hand. God help him!

After seeing him out, I went back to my study and again sat on the carpet before the fireplace; the red embers were covered with ash and began to grow dim. The frost tapped still more angrily at the windows, and the wind droned in the chimney. The maid came in and, thinking I was asleep, called my name.

Printed in Great Britain
by Amazon.co.uk, Ltd.,
Marston Gate.